A
Kazan
Reader
ELIA
KAZAN

A
Kazan
Reader
ELIA
KAZAN

𝔰𝔡

STEIN AND DAY/*Publishers*/New York

First published in 1977

Printed in the United States of America
Stein and Day/*Publishers*/Scarborough House,
Briarcliff Manor, N.Y. 10510

"What a Film Director Needs to Know" was first published as "On What Makes a Director" in *Action*, the magazine of the Directors Guild of America.

Library of Congress Cataloging in Publication Data

Kazan, Elia.
  A Kazan reader.

  CONTENTS: America, America.—3 chapters from The arrangement.—scenes from The assassins. [etc.]
  I. Title.
PS3561.A93A6   1977   813'.5'4   76-54440
ISBN 0-8128-2193-9
ISBN 0-8128-2194-7 deluxe lim. ed.
ISBN 0-8128-2195-5 pbk.

Envoi

Fifteen years ago a remarkably versatile American artist began to find his own voice.

In 1962, Elia Kazan was known throughout the world as a stage and film director who had guided the words of Arthur Miller, Tennessee Williams, Thornton Wilder, Budd Schulberg, Archibald MacLeish, Robert Anderson, and others in the performances of their work. But for *America America* Kazan decided to write his own screenplay. It turned out to be the best piece of imaginative writing about the only indigenous American theme: immigration. The book was called "a minor literary miracle" * and has since become a permanent part of American literature. It was, fortuitously, the first book published by the new firm of Stein and Day.

The success of *America America* caused Kazan, for the first time, to pay attention to himself as an initiator of writing rather than an interpreter of other people's writing. He began his first work intended for the reading public. He, who had always worked surrounded by crews and actors, relished the solitude of the man alone with his typewriter. The result was a novel called *The Arrangement*. More than halfway through the months-long process of revision, a contract was drawn up, as if it were a second thought and of little consequence. *The Arrangement,* when published in early 1967, shot to the top of the bestseller lists and remained there, number one for a period of thirty-seven weeks. It was said that that summer, on the beaches of America, only one book could be seen. In all, it sold that year nearly one million hardcover copies in its book club and bookstore editions. It came as a surprise that *The Arrangement* coined a meaning for the language; all over America people began talking about their own "arrangements."

* Orville Prescott in *The New York Times*

The extraordinary success of *The Arrangement* is attributable, at least in part, to the fact that the story was in substantial measure yanked by Kazan out of his own experience, and his experience coincided with much that was suddenly recognized as symptomatic of marriage at the time. For his next work, Kazan picked a story from the outside, as it were. From a brief newspaper story about a killing, he led himself to the Southwest of the United States and fed on the material that he was to shape into *The Assassins.*

In *The Understudy,* Kazan turned to the theater as a background, with a theme that is pervasive in human experience: how we use our mentors to become ourselves.

I am pleased to be bringing together in one volume Kazan as writer, the whole of *America America,* some scenes from *The Arrangement* and *The Assassins,* and the center section of *The Understudy,* a brilliant portrait of the animals we see and are.

Sol Stein

Scarborough, New York
March 17, 1977

Contents

And they heard the soldiers shouting
"Thalatta! Thalatta!"
　　　　　　　　　　—XENOPHON

America America

1

The Beginning

1896
*Turkey in Asia,
the land known as Anatolia.*

Mount Aergius is seen from a great distance, beautifully shaped, perfectly proportioned, its peak and sides covered with snow. We hear a song, the voices of two men. We do not get the words, for they are in another tongue.

High on the cool side of the mountain is an ice field. A wagon and an old horse are standing at its edge. Two men are cutting ice into manageable pieces.

The work is heavy, but they are young and strong. They labor in the rhythm of men who are working for themselves. Their voices, though untrained, blend pleasantly. Here is the rapport of close friends.

Stavros Topouzoglou is a boy of twenty. There is something at once delicate and passionate about his face. It is full of inarticulated yearning. His brown eyes shine like moist olives.

Working next to him is Vartan Damadian. He is twenty-eight. His face has a wild, swarthy cast. An enormous nose, bent but defiant, a low forehead, hair of electric vitality, full sensuous lips. These features and his bearlike heft make him a formidable figure.

The two men are small figures against the icefield. Behind them is a vast panorama. We hear the ominous sound of the wind that inhabits this plateau.

Once long ago, Anatolia was a part of the Byzantine Empire, inhabited by the Greek and Armenian people of that time. In 1381 this land was conquered by the Turks, and since that day the Greeks and the Armenians have lived here as minorities, subject to their Mohammedan conquerors.

In the foreground a single telegraph wire is strung on a series of primitive poles which recede into the distance, emphasizing the effect of space.

Far back is Mount Aergius. Nearby a community of houses can be seen, built partly on the sides of two facing cliffs, partly in the narrow level between. This town is named Germeer. We notice a minaret or two.

This is the day of the holiday known as "Bayram," when every Turk, who can afford it, slaughters a lamb and offers part of the meat to the poor. A herd of sheep is being driven through a crowded street. The shepherd stops to sell one of his animals to a householder. Behind him his family is dressed in their holiday best. Drinks are being poured.

A tethered lamb bleats. He knows what's in store for him. As the drinks are passed among other members of the family, the father is sharpening a kitchen knife. He is clearly very familiar with it both as a utensil and as a weapon.

The entire family is here. The women are in the doorway, their faces partly covered. They are all watching the head of the family dress a newly slaughtered animal. A little girl brings her father a drink on a small tray. He takes it, then kisses his child passionately.

Some well-dressed men gallop down the street on horseback. Women pull children to safety. Behind the riders, a brace of horses race, the driver crying a wild command. The horses veer away, the carriage following. At the front of the Municipal Building, men are arriving, some in carriages, some on horseback, some on foot, all dressed for the holiday. There is something threatening in the air.

Inside the Municipal Building, the Wali or governor of the province has summoned his council to an emergency meeting.

The door to the Wali's inner office is suddenly thrown open. Two soldiers, powerful men, come through, stamping their feet in a style taught them by the German military who trained the Turkish army. They set the stage for the entrance of a formidable man. Instead, through the door comes a worried little bureaucrat—the Wali.

The council members leap to their feet. The Wali hurries to his desk.

The Wali, querulously: "Be seated . . . please . . ."

The council members sit. The soldiers stand at fixed attention.

The Wali, complaining: "Where are my . . .?"

An aide jumps as though his life depended upon it, and brings him his glasses.

The Wali unfolds a telegram: "This came on the wire from the Capital an hour ago." He reads, " 'Your excellency! On this day, the eve of our holy feast of Bayram, Armenian fanatics have dared to set fire to the National Turkish Bank in Constantinople.' "

The Wali looks up. Among the members of the council there is some sort of reaction, but not a clear one. Anger? Impatience? Some men simply sigh.

The Wali continues with the telegram: " 'We have reason to believe it is the wish of our Sultan, Abdulhammid the Resplendent, the Shadow of God on earth, that the Armenian subject people throughout his empire be taught once and for all that acts of terrorism will not be tolerated. Our Sultan has the patience of the prophet, but he has now given signs that he would be pleased if this lesson were impressed once and for all upon this disorderly and dangerous minority. How this is to be effected will be left to their Excellencies, the Governors of each Province, and to the Army Commander in each Capital.' "

Behind the Wali, the soldiers are at attention, listening.

At the office of the Commander of the Army post, the Pasha, or General, a dark, bulky man, is finishing reading the same telegram to his staff. An attendant brings him a water pipe. The Pasha puts the telegram down and sighs deeply. No army man likes to receive orders of this kind.

The Pasha, with sudden vehemence: "I will not send soldiers to do this!"

An officer: "There was writing again . . . insults . . . on the wall of the Mosque, your Excellency!"

A crowd has gathered in front of a small mosque. On the walls, some crude scrawls can be seen. A *hodja,* or holy man, comes out, with pail and brush to wash the markings off. The crowd mutters and curses. Elsewhere in the town, angry men are gathering. The entire Turkish community is furious.

Back on the cool, clean side of Mount Aergius, Stavros and Vartan have finished loading their wagon with ice, and now, weary, stand for a moment, looking up at Aergius. It is restful to look up at this fine mountain.

Stavros: "You say in America they have mountains bigger than that one?"

Vartan: "In America everything is bigger."

Stavros: "What else?"

Vartan: "What else what?"

Stavros: "What else in America? What else will we do when we get there?"

Vartan: "We'll stop talking about it for one thing. Let's go there, with the help of Jesus! Why do we let the days pass?" Then, seductively, "Come on you! Let's go you!"

Stavros looks at him with abject hero worship. He idolizes this man.

Vartan, brusquely: "Better sell this ice before it melts."

They finish covering their load with old scraps of rugs and cloths, leap on the wagon, and are off. The horse, since it is going downhill, manages a trot. Stavros notices something ahead. He points.

On the slope of the mountain below, a small encampment of soldiers sits at ease around campfires. An officer is walking out onto the road to intercept the wagon.

Vartan looks around for some escape. There is none.

Vartan: "A day's work for nothing!"

Stavros, under his breath: "Allah!" It is his favorite expression.

The officer, now in the middle of the road, holds up his hand, commanding the wagon to stop. The wagon stops. The officer walks around it.

Vartan, his head down: "Help yourself, sir. Help yourself."

There is just the least sarcasm in his tone. Vartan's game is to see how close he can come to saying what he thinks without endangering his life. He doesn't come very close, but this subtle game does save a little of his dignity.

The officer, at the back of the wagon, ignores or does not notice the effrontery. He turns and bellows toward the encampment.

Officer: "Chelal!!"

A soldier-cook runs out of the mess tent with some brass pots. Within seconds, a dozen soldiers are helping themselves to bits of ice from the wagon.

Vartan sits with his head still bowed, apparently uninterested in what's happening in the wagon behind him. Stavros looks at his hero anxiously. Then he decides to play Vartan's game, nudges him as if to say, "Watch!"

Stavros has turned in his seat in the direction of the officer.

Stavros: "Sir! Your honor!"

Vartan looks straight down his horse's back, waiting the incident out.

Stavros, a little bolder, speaks to the officer again: "Your honor!!"

The officer finally looks at him. Stavros quickly retreats behind a smile. This smile, the most characteristic thing about the boy, has a strong element of anxiety. It is so often the unhappy brand of the minority person—whether Negro, Jew, or yellow man—the only way he had found to face his oppressor, a mask to conceal the hostility he dares not show, and at the same time an escape for the shame he feels as he violates his true feelings.

Stavros: "Sir, help yourself, help yourself!"

Vartan, mumbling so that only Stavros can hear him: "That's what he needs. Encouragement!"

Stavros, flattering but insolent, to the officer: "But your honor . . ."

Officer: "What do you want?"

Stavros: "It is not I, your honor, it is the ice. Its nature is to melt. It does not consider that we have to go all the way to the market place to sell it."

Stavros smiles nervously. The officer is a vigorous and impulsive man. He is quick to anger, dangerous when aroused.

Officer: "In plain language, you want me to hurry?"

Stavros turns and looks at Vartan. But Vartan offers no help. All Stavros can do is smile!

The officer suddenly leaps on the wagon, begins to throw off big pieces of ice. In no time the wagon is half empty. Vartan barely takes notice. Stavros still holds his smile, but now we see how strained and anxious it is.

The officer leaps off the wagon. His men are convulsed with laughter. He responds to their laughter by moving toward the front of the wagon in a slow strut.

Officer: "You had too much of a load for this dear old horse. Now he'll get you to the market more quickly. Agree? Eh?"

Stavros looks at Vartan to see what he'll say. Vartan says nothing. Stavros is frightened. The officer demands an answer.

Stavros: "Yes, sir."

Officer: "What are you, Armenians?"

Stavros: "Greek, sir, a poor Greek."

Officer, to Vartan: "And you?"

Stavros looks at Vartan. Vartan does not raise his head.

Vartan: "I'm an Armenian."

Officer: "Oh, Armenian? Did you have anything to do with the burning of the State Bank yesterday in Constantinople?"

Vartan does not answer. Stavros is still holding the bag.

Officer, to Stavros: "Why do you smile?"

Stavros: "You're joking, your honor."

Officer: "Oh?"

Stavros: "Forgive me, but how could he have been in Constantinople yesterday? It's a two weeks' journey."

Officer: "Even with this horse?"

His men all laugh, appreciating his sadistic game. Stavros seems to join in. Suddenly Vartan leaps out of the wagon and walks toward the officer. Despite himself, the officer is startled and puts his hand to his sidearm.

Vartan, to the officer: "Captain Mehmet. You don't recognize me? We served together—eight years ago. That is, I served you, and you served the Sultan. I was your orderly, so naturally you have forgotten me. Remember, I stole chickens for you."

The officer looks Vartan straight in the face and for the first time sees him.

Officer: "Vartan? You?"

Vartan: "Yes, Vartan. The same."

The officer throws his arms around Vartan. A warm embrace. Stavros stares at Vartan with the purest hero worship!

Officer: "Vartan, my little lamb, what's happened to you?"

Vartan: "As you see—I'm trying to make a few coppers with this dear dying stud."

Officer, shouting: "Enver! Chelal! Put the ice back. Quickly! Come, jump! Before it melts."

The men begin to reload the wagon frantically. The officer draws Vartan to one side. Stavros steals up to hear their conversation.

Officer: "Your people burn our building and you expect us to thank you! No. Today no Armenian will be forgiven for being an Armenian. You better stay up here with me."

Stavros interrupts them: "He has his mother and his father down there. And his little brother."

The officer pauses: "Then it's in the hands of God."

In the town, people in terror are entering the Armenian Church. The front door is guarded from the inside and opened cautiously to admit the late arrivals. Hysterically frightened men and women crowd through the door as it is pulled shut. We get a glimpse of the panic within. After an instant the door is reopened just enough so that a boy of eleven can slip out of the sanctuary. He is Vartan's younger brother, Dikran. The door is immediately pulled to again and bolted.

On the road in the outskirts of town, Dikran, breathless from running, waves down Vartan's wagon. The boy leaps up on the driver's seat. There begins a frantic consultation in whispers.

Dirkan: "But Vartan, father says come now!"

Vartan: "I have this ice to sell *now.*"

Dikran: "You want me to say that to him?"

Vartan: "Yes. And get off the streets! Go back in the church. Dikran, go!"

When next seen the wagon is parked near a central square of the city. By now most of the ice has been sold. Stavros is dealing with an old Turkish woman. Vartan stands on the driver's seat, singing out.

Vartan: "Ice!! Little pieces of the mountain!! Mount Aergius ice!!"

The old woman pays Stavros, meantime speaking to him in a confidential tone.

Old Woman: "There's an old well under our house. He could hide there."

Stavros: "Vartan wouldn't do that."

Old Woman: "That's the way those Armenians are. You see! Well, he'll be dead soon."

She goes. Stavros looks up at Vartan. The ice is about gone. Vartan jumps down off the wagon seat.

Vartan: "You'd better go home now!"

Stavros: "And you?"

Vartan: "I'm going to the Guitars."

Stavros: "What for!"

Vartan: "I will drink with my murderers."

Stavros: "What for !!!???"

Vartan: "For my satisfaction!"

Stavros: "Allah!"

Then as he starts to protest again, Vartan points.

Vartan: "Your mother's coming!"

A woman about forty-five, her face covered in the traditional manner, is hurrying toward the wagon. She is Vasso Topouzoglou, Stavros' mother, and she is furious.

She goes up to Stavros, seizes him by the lobe of one ear, and starts dragging him off. People take notice.

Vartan laughs. Vasso suddenly releases Stavros and turns to his companion.

Vasso: "Vartan, stay away from my son. Play games with your own life."

Then she goes back to Stavros and begins to drive him off before her.

Vasso: "What did you father tell you? Stay away from that man? Did he tell you that? Do you listen? Can you hear?"

Vasso, still in a fury, drives her son before her all the way to their house.

Inside it is almost dark. Around a single oil lamp huddle a dozen men, the leaders of the Greek community. Among them are Stavros' father, Isaac Topouzoglou, and a bearded Orthodox Priest. Vasso and Stavros enter.

Vasso. "Here he is, Isaac. Your eldest!"

Some men fall away and reveal Isaac. In his own home he sits like a king. He waits.

Vasso: "He was with the Armenian again."

Isaac doesn't answer. Stavros says nothing.

Vasso, to the boy: "You have given your father a day of terrible worry. Go kiss his hand and ask his forgiveness."

The boy starts toward his father.

Vasso: "He's too easy with you." Then to her husband: "You're too easy with him, Isaac. If you'll forgive me to say so, it's not my place to say so, but ..."

The boy has reached his father and stands in front of him. The father suddenly whacks the boy across the face.

Vasso: "Good."

The father now extends this same hand to be kissed. Stavros kisses it.

Vasso: *"Good!"*

Then Isaac kisses the boy. Vasso nods her approval of this too. Thus the ceremony is completed.

Isaac, to Stavros: "Have you had dinner?"

Stavros: "I'm not hungry."

Vasso: "You will eat something."

She leaves for the kitchen.

The group huddles around the lamp.

A Man: "Who is this Armenian?"

Isaac: "Damadian's son, Vartan."

Men (a murmur of bees): "No good, he's no good, no good, no good ... no good at all ..."

A Man: "He doesn't know his place!"

Stavros has been listening intently. What is being said infuriates him. Now he gets up and starts for the stairs.

Isaac: "Well—it's not our affair. They're Armenians. We're Greeks. Their necks are not our necks."

Stavros, on the stairs, as he goes up, has to speak.

Stavros: "True. They're saving our necks for their next holiday."

He's up and out of sight.

Everyone is astonished at this remark, not only because of the sentiment expressed, but because of the sudden liberty Stavros has taken in the council of his elders.

One of the Men: "What! What did he say?"

The Orthodox Priest: "We all heard what he said."

A moment of bewilderment. Then all start talking at the same time, vehemently.

Isaac: "Shhhh!"

Instant silence. The men look toward the windows, anxiously, afraid they might be overheard by strangers. The discussion continues, now in a sort of whisper.

Stavros enters his bedroom, closes the door, goes to the window, opens it, and drops out into the night.

The Guitars is a combination raki house, coffee house, and cabaret. The floor is of compacted dirt. The place is Turkish-owned, Turkish-operated. The partrons—at the moment overflowing the place—are *lumpen,* many drunk, all filthy. They are vagabonds, hamals (porters), camel drivers, criminals, soldiers out of uniform, servants after hours. The lone woman present is a singer. And she is almost male. She is seated between a couple of guitarists, a match for them in any contest. She pushes a deep contralto voice through an "Aman" song. A couple of hamals are dancing on a small wooden floor in front of the musicians.

Stavros is looking for Vartan, and finds him in a corner, drinking alone at a table. Stavros sits.

Vartan drinks, then indicates the crowd: "The jails are empty!"

The music stops. The dancers leave the floor. Vartan gets up and starts toward the door. Stavros follows. Vartan goes to the musicians and, as is the custom, throws some coins at their feet. They begin to play. Stavros comes up and he and Vartan begin to dance, each solo but in the same rhythm, with the same feeling. There is great beauty in their slow, circular movements. And despite the fact that they are not looking at each other, we feel that they are dancing together.

Suddenly, as what seems to be a peak in their slow, somehow orgiastic turning, Stavros whispers.

Stavros: "America America!"

He says this as if it were one word and with the deepest yearning.

Vartan: "Are you ready?"

Stavros nods slowly.

Vartan: "Come on you!! Let's go you! If we don't go tomorrow ..."

A couple of men have come up and have been talking to the musicians. All are looking at Vartan and Stavros. The music stops. Then the lead guitar player kicks the coins which Vartan has thrown at his feet off the platform. Everyone in the room stares at the two boys. A resounding silence. A pause. Then the sound of a commotion in the distance. Finally, a huge shout. A man runs in with news. There is much milling around.

Man, shouting: "It's beginning!"

Back at the Armenian Church, where the people have taken refuge, brush, old timber, and scraps of wood are being piled against the side of the building. Coarse shouts are heard. A fence is ripped up and added to the pile. A great shout. It is a sadists' holiday. Some soldiers—half out of uniform—are supervising.

Vartan and Stavros come up. Some boys, among them Dikran, gather around Vartan, awed, frightened. Dikran takes Vartan's hand. Vartan puts his arm around his little brother. Shouts, laughter, cheers are heard.

In front of the Church, an army veteran, wearing the coat of his uniform, holds an old Armenian by the beard. His other hand brandishes a curved sword. The old man has his arms thrown out in a gesture of self-immolation.

Officer: "We don't want you, father. We want the ones who still carry the seed. Now go back in there and tell them to come out and beg for mercy."

He releases the old man, who glances at a window of the church. His wife is watching him. The old man picks himself up and chooses what will be the last act of his life.

He spits in the face of the officer.

This is the excuse that the Turkish officer has been waiting for. He shouts, "Aaahhtesh! AAHtesh!" (Fire! Fire!)

In the church window, the old woman watches her husband's quick death. Her eyes fill with horror as the officer's sword comes whacking down!

Soldiers immediately set fire to the piles of brush and timber around the Church. The fires at the side of the Church burn hungrily.

Inside, the Church begins to fill with smoke. The Armenians, about fifty or sixty in number, are huddled around the altar praying. As the place begins to fill with smoke, they panic, children cry, men shout.

Outside, Stavros backs off a little, thoroughly frightened. Dikran and some other young boys are as close to the front door of the church as they can be, considering the fire and smoke.

Inside the church, as the building itself begins to burn, there is pandemonium.

Vartan has a desperate plan for this emergency. Suddenly he screams "Dikran!" and throws himself on the Turkish officer, pulls a dagger out of the officer's belt, and stabs him. Then he wrestles free the man's pistol and starts holding off the men who come at him from all sides.

The front door of the church is left temporarily unguarded by Vartan's tactic. Dikran and some of the other little boys run and throw it open. People run out.

Murderous men cover Vartan. A pack of dogs on a fox. Stavros doesn't know what to do. Suddenly it is not possible to save Vartan. It is impossible.

People are rushing out of the front door of the Church in all directions—men, women, and children. The Turks take out after the Armenians, killing those they catch regardless of age or sex. A Turk shouts at the top of his lungs.

Turk: "The men! The men! Leave the women! The men! Get the men . . ."

It is a gray morning. Women in black have come to the burned out church for the bodies of their men. Vartan's body is covered with a piece of burned carpet. Stavros sits there, crying in chokes. In his hand, he holds Vartan's fez.

Stavros carries the body of his friend home. The Armenian section is ringed by Turkish soldiers "preserving order." The street is strewn with discarded household furnishings. Pillaging is still going on.

Stavros is exhausted. Vartan is very heavy. Stavros walks a few steps, stops, then a few more, leans against a tree, then on for a few more steps. Vartan's fez is still clutched in his hand.

Two Turkish guards see Stavros. One of them moves forward and trips the boy. The body falls and rolls heavily. Stavros get up and starts to pick it up. But the two soldiers are on him. As they arrest Stavros, some women in black rush in, lift up the body of Vartan, and carry it off.

At a large outdoor compound, which is part of the city prison, about fifty men, Armenians in all conditions of desperation, cover the ground. The place is filthy. Stavros sits holding Vartan's fez in his hands. A boot nudges him.

Voice: "Up!"

Stavros' father, Isaac, sits in the Wali's office in the attitude of a suppliant. In various corners of the office, members of the council discuss in whispers the events of the night before.

The conversation between the Wali and Isaac is private. The Wali passes Isaac some cologne to refresh his hands and face.

Wali: "Once these horrors start they must run their course. The patient man waits. As the Prophet said: hatred exhausts itself. It's no comfort for me that the Armenians started this. I believe that some day, with Allah's help, all races will live together in peace. Even the Armenians."

Isaac: "That's the hope of mankind."

Isaac can't help but look anxiously toward the door. The Wali notices this, laughs gently.

Wali: "They're bringing him, my friend. They're bringing him. Sit back in your chair! That's it. A smile? Eh?"

Isaac, smiling: "Yes, yes. I'm so grateful to you."

Wali: "So! It's not only that I like you. I like all the Greek subject people."

Isaac: "We all know that."

Wali: "I am here only for the good I can do. I make nothing here. You realize that."

Out of long habit, Isaac reaches into his pocket.

Wali: "And I do good. I *do* help. Don't you think?"

Isaac: "Oh, yes. We're all very grateful."

Wali: "I was referring particularly to you. You have a good business here. The Turkish people like you and you have a good business."

Isaac: "We make a living."

Wali: "I happen to know you do very well. And that makes me happy."

The door to the office is slowly opened. An attendant is standing there. He does not permit the door to open more than halfway. A soldier puts his head in and whispers to the attendant. Behind him Stavros can be seen. The attendant rushes halfway to the Wali, stops short. He speaks softly.

Attendant: "You honor. Forgive me ... but ..."

Wali: "Hold him there a moment!!!"

Then he turns and looks at Isaac. Isaac's hand now comes out of his pocket. Holding money! He stands. The Wali stands. An ancient ritual. Isaac bends over and kisses the Wali's hand. Simultaneously he presses money into the hand of the Turk.

Stavros, at the door of the office, takes in the incident. He's ashamed for his father. He watches as a servant with a tray of refreshments serves the members of the council. At a signal from the Wali, the servant offers a drink to Isaac. Isaac takes it. The members of the council, drinks in hand, move in towards their Governor. Isaac is surrounded. A toast is offered. They all drink except Isaac. Then one of the coucil members notices that Isaac is not drinking. He indicates with insistent conviviality that he must or else offend his hosts.

Stavros, in the doorway, watches to see what his father will do. Isaac, surrounded by the council members, drinks. What else could he possibly do? Laughter!

Isaac and Stavros walk down the front steps of the Municipal Building. Stavros is looking at his father—with a new awareness. Suddenly Isaac jerks his head up and looks at the boy. Stavros drops his eyes.

Isaac: "Stavros? What?"

The boy drops his eyes, keeps walking. Isaac falls behind, trying to puzzle out his son.

Stavros has come to a narrow side street. Abruptly, without explanation, he turns and disappears down this alley. Isaac runs to the head of the alley, calls.

Isaac: "Stavros! Stavros!"

Stavros now begins to run down the alley with demonic speed. In a second or two he is gone. Isaac turns and walks away. He is very troubled.

From very far away we see a great cliff. Long ago, the people who lived in this area built their homes into the sides of this cliff for safety from their enemies and from the roaming bandits who terrorized the plain. In time, many of these homes were abandoned and collapsed, but people still live in the ruins. At this moment the only thing that moves is a tiny figure, far below. It is Stavros, looking up and calling out.

Stavros: "Yaya! Yaya!" (Grandmother!)

In the rubble and among the scattered boulders of the ruins can be seen a decaying wooden structure. There is some sort of movement. A human figure appears in a doorway at the head of a cellar dwelling.

She is an old woman, seventy or more, but in full vigor. Her face is dehydrated meat. We hear Stavros yell "Yaya!" again. The old woman watches the approaching boy without a sign of welcome. The air above is full of pigeons.

As Stavros approaches, he waves. His grandmother makes no sign, merely stares at the boy. Stavros comes up, smiling.

Grandmother: "What do you want?"

Stavros: "I came to see you, Yaya."

Grandmother: "What for? You don't look well. How's the good Greek, your father? You know why the fox loves the rabbit? Because it's got no teeth. How's your father? Your grandfather was a man! I've been expecting you. He told me you were coming."

Stavros: "Who?"

Grandmother: "Your grandfather. He came to see me last night. I think he found a new wife in the land of the dead. Well, what can you do?! But he still comes to see me. What's the matter?"

Stavros: "Nothing. Why?"

Grandmother: "You're moving around like a criminal. What do you want?"

Stavros: "I just came to see you."

Grandmother: "You're lying. My God, I hope you're not going to be like your father. You already have his smile. Well! What can you do?!

All the men in our family lie now. The Turk spits in their face and they say it's raining. Well? Say! What have you come for? And don't lie again because your grandfather told me what you wanted."

Stavros: "What did he tell you I wanted?"

Grandmother: "Money. True? Say!"

Stavros: "True."

Grandmother: "Why should I give you money?"

Stavros: "What do you need it for? You're an old woman!"

She picks up a stick and begins to hit him with all her might.

Grandmother: "Go on, go on, get out, get out!"

Stavros take the stick from her and breaks it.

Stavros: "Now you're going to listen to me. I'm going away."

Grandmother: "Good!"

Stavros: "Far away."

Grandmother: "The farther the better."

Stavros: "To America. I'm going to America."

Grandmother: "You!"

Stavros: "You're not going to see me again!"

Grandmother: "You! You'll stay at your father's side. You're a good boy."

Stavros: "Only give me enough to get to Constantinople. There I'll work and make the rest. Hear me! You are my only hope. Don't turn your back on me!!"

Suddenly the old woman turns and goes into her cellar dwelling. Stavros follows.

The cellar is very small and packed with everything she has ever had and valued. When Stavros enters she is down on her knees, searching in the back of an old chest.

Grandmother: "I remember you as a baby, soft and round, made of butter. And I remember you in that little blue sailor suit your mother made you. A saint with a blessed pale face, your eyes shining with God's own light."

Stavros' face does indeed have innocence and purity.

She pulls out an object wrapped in some cloths.

Grandmother: "Oh, I thought, Oh if only the world were like that!!"

She has unwrapped the cloth and now holds up a murderous curved dagger. Her voice is hard now.

Grandmother: "Here! It was your grandfather's."

Stavros: "Oh God, I don't need this! I need money."

Grandmother: "You need this more. Take it. It will remind you no sheep ever saved his neck by bleating."

Stavros snatches the dagger from her: "All right! I'll walk into the city and I'll put this into the first soldier I meet and . . ."

Grandmother: "Stavros, you can't frighten me."

Suddenly the frantic boy begins to rip up the planks, the pieces of metal, the old rags and bits of rug which cover the floor. His grandmother watches sardonically for a moment.

Grandmother: "It's here ... under my clothing."

She indicates her middle, stands there, stooped, bent, challenging. Stavros, dagger in hand, stares at her. For a moment it appears he might rip her open. He walks slowly towards where she stands. Then the moment passes.

Grandmother: "You're not going to America. You're your father's son. Go home. Be what you are."

She turns her back on him and slowly begins to stuff back into the chest the articles she took out. A cry breaks from the boy—frustration, grief, fury at himself. Then still holding the dagger, he leaves.

Stavros walks, taking the road back to the city. The sun is setting. Coming up behind him and about to overtake him is a young man, gaunt as a board: Hohanness Gardashian. He is pitched in perpetual motion forward. His clothes, all tatters and patches, are saturated in dust. A small pack is tied to his back. His face is alight with the most perfect hope.

Hohanness goes past Stavros. Then he stops, taken with a fit of coughing of such intensity that he crouches at the side of the road to "ride it out." It subsides as Stavros comes up to him, and Hohanness turns, extends one hand, smiles ...

Hohanness: "Anything! Anything!"

Stavros, not in the mood to think of anyone else, shakes his head, almost viciously, and goes on.

Hohanness, from behind him: "Hear me ... I'll remember you. From America, I'll pray for you."

Stavros stops short and turns. Hohanness is still crouched at the side of the road ... smiling.

Hohanness, extending a hand: "Anything, anything ..."

Stavros, going back to him: "You go to America ... you!"

Hohanness: "With the help of Jesus."

Stavros: "On foot?!"

Hohanness: "However."

Stavros: "And with nothing?!"

Hohanness: "Each day. Part of the distance."

Stavros glares at him. He is bitterly jealous.

Stavros: "How are you going to get there with those?? Eh??"

He indicates Hohanness's shoes, which are flapping out their last days. Hohanness looks at his shoes, ashamed, smiles.

Stavros: "Here!"

He pulls off his own shoes and throws them at the boy's feet. Then, without another word, he turns and takes off. After a few steps, he stops and turns over his shoulder.

Stavros: "Where do you come from?"

Hohanness is frantically pulling on Stavros's shoes, fearful that he might change his mind.

Hohanness: "From far behind there. Behind those clouds are mountains, the mountains of Armenia. I won't ever see them again."

He jumps up, heartened by the gift. He tries out the shoes.

Hohanness: "Thank you. I'll remember you."

He turns west and walks directly into the setting sun.

In the Topouzoglou home, Stavros' family is at dinner. Seated on the floor around a low table are his four brothers and his three sisters, all younger than Stavros, two maiden aunts, and an old uncle. They pay no attention to anything except the food. Vasso is preparing a plate for Isaac, who is not in his place at the head of the table. She fills the plate and goes back and enters their bedroom. The family eats. They hear Vasso's voice.

Vasso: "Isaac, I have brought you some food."

All stop eating for a moment and listen. They hear no answer from Isaac. They shake their heads and cluck. Then they resume eating.

Vasso's voice: "Isaac! Now I want you to eat something."

Old Uncle: "He did this once before. Stayed in there for nine days."

Again, all stop eating and consider the gravity of the situation, making tststststtttssst sounds. Then back to their food.

In the parents' bedroom Isaac is sitting in a dark corner, his back to the door and to the room. Vasso makes a last effort.

Vasso: "Isaac!"

Isaac, finally, gravely: "Vasso, you are forgetting who you are and who I am. If I want food I will call you." Then sternly, but gently: "I don't want to see you now. I want to see my son."

Vasso exits without another word.

She somes to the table and puts down the plate of food. The boys immediately divide it among themselves.

Vasso: "He has something in his mind . . . something deep."

The door to the outside opens. They all turn.

Vasso: "So . . . at last . . ."

In the bedroom, Isaac has also heard the door open.

Isaac, a sudden cry: "Stavros!!"

He waits. After an instant, the boy comes in, followed by a demonic Vasso.

Isaac: "I've been waiting for you."

Vasso, a fury: "Where are your shoes. What did you do with your shoes???"

Isaac: "Vasso!"

Vasso: "Well? Well? What? Where?"

Isaac: "Vasso! Leave ... now!"

Vasso, after a moment: "Yes, Isaac." Then, quietly to Stavros: "Remember! You're speaking to your father!"

She leaves. Father and son are alone.

Isaac: "Come here, boy. Sit here, close to me. When I don't see you for a day, you look changed. Will you have a coffee?"

Stavros: "No thank you, father."

Vasso comes back, carrying a pair of bedroom slippers. She kneels at Stavros' feet and puts them on him.

Isaac: "You'll have a coffee with me."

Vasso: "Tststtttssstttsst ..."

Isaac: "Vasso, two coffees immediately."

Vasso: "Immediately."

She gets up and goes. Isaac's tone becomes intimate.

Isaac: "I have made up my mind."

Stavros: "Yes, father?"

Isaac: "We are going to send you to Constantinople."

Stavros: "What did you say, father?"

Isaac: "Our family is going to leave this place. You will go first."

Stavros gets up slowly and moves towards Isaac.

Isaac: "You will take with you everything this family has of worth."

Stavros kneels and takes his father's hand as if it were a holy object, bends over and kisses it.

Isaac, trying to go on: "You will take with you ..."

He cannot continue. He is very touched by his son's expression of love for him.

Isaac: "You will ... I said ... everything of worth this family has."

Vasso and her eldest daughter, sixteen-year-old Athena, are in an upstairs bedroom. The girl has been working—when her household duties permit—on a hope chest to take to her husband when the day comes. Most of this dowry consists of small handcrafted objects. One corner of the bedroom is filled with a small loom. Athena is on her knees taking a blanket off the frame. It is rather inexpertly woven, but it is dear to the girl. She rises and goes to Vasso and gives it to her, then brings up a couple more from a neat pile under the loom.

Vasso comforts the girl: "This winter I will come here at night and we'll weave together. By the day of your wedding you will have all the blankets you need."

In another bedroom, the youngest girl, Fofo, thirteen, is at the mirror, slowly removing her earrings. Her eyes are filled with tears. She has not taken these earrings off since the day her ears were pierced. Vasso enters, crosses to her, waits for an instant. Fofo gives her the earrings. Vasso kisses her and exits.

In the far corner of the cellar, Stavros and Isaac are on their knees, Isaac holding an oil lamp, Stavros digging with a small pick.

Isaac: "From time to time, I've had to do things that—well—we live by the mercy of the Turk, But, Stavros, I have always kept my honor safe inside me. Safe inside me! And, you see, we're still living. After a time you don't feel the shame."

In a corner of a back bedroom, the two aunts are giving up their wealth.

Vasso: "Anna, what will you do with them, little dearie, make yourself pretty? It's too late little dearie, it's too late."

She takes the lace collars. The aunt breaks into tears.

Stavros is still digging in the corner of the cellar. Isaac takes a letter out of his pocket.

Isaac: "So yesterday I had this back from Our Cousin in Constantinople." He reads: " 'Beloved Isaac: I will be honored. Let Stavros bring money to put in my business and I'll make him my partner.' You know he has a prospering establishment there, you'll see a prospering ..."

Stavros: "But father ... will it be better for us in Constantinople ... ?"

Isaac: "Yes! It will be!" Then, "Where can we go? It's our last hope."

It is not *Stavros'* last hope. He resumes digging.

Outside the main house is a small outbuilding where the family smokes its meat. Vasso and two of the brothers wrap slabs of this "Bastourma" in cloths.

One of the Brothers: "What are we going to eat this winter?"

Vasso: "When didn't you eat, fatty?"

The Other Brother: "The Chinese eat dog meat."

In the corner of the cellar, Stavros is still at work.

Isaac: "You will take with you all our smoked meat. You will take the two rugs on the floor upstairs. In fact everything you can sell, our donkey, you will take our donkey. Goochook, and sell him when you get to Constantinople. You will take the jewelry in this box."

Just then the pick hits the top of the box. Stavros and his father begin to pull it up.

Isaac: "The jewelry which came with Vasso when I took her for a wife."

Upstairs, the family has gathered around the box which Isaac is opening. As the top comes off ...

All: "Oh! . . . Oh!! Oh!!!"

Vasso pulls up a gold chain and locket.

Vasso: "This was my mother's. See! She's wearing it there . . ."

She points to an old picture hung on the wall. Its subject is a woman dressed in the style of the early nineteenth century. Vasso's mother was a proud woman with rather Mongoloid features. She is wearing the chain and locket.

Vasso: "I was going to give it to you when you got married."

She turns and looks at Stavros.

Athena: "It's better this way, mother."

On the eve of Stavros' departure the family gathers with greater formality. Isaac is conducting an historic meeting.

Isaac: "In time you will bring your three sisters to Constantinople. As the eldest, it is your responsibility to see that they marry well."

Stavros looks at his sisters solemnly. The girls look especially plain. Stavros smiles uncertainly.

Isaac: "Then in time, as your business prospers, you will bring your four brothers out and to your side. As the eldest it is your responsibility to set them up in business."

Stavros looks solemnly at his brothers.

Isaac: "Then it will be your mother's turn. It is your responsibility to make her final days happy ones."

Vasso: "Isaac, let's not ask too much!"

Isaac: "Vasso, there's a right way and a wrong way."

Vasso: "Yes, Isaac."

They both look at their eldest. The full load of responsibility is now on Stavros' back.

Later, with the ikons and candles prominent, the family sits, heads bowed, at prayer. But Vasso sits apart from them, sewing furiously on Stavros' coat.

Isaac: "My God, King Christ, gentle Lord Jesus, Who rose from the dead to look after mankind. We now commit our eldest son to Your loving care. Watch over him. He is our hope."

Vasso moves over close to Stavros.

Vasso, a heavy whisper: "Did you hear that?"

Stavros: "Yes."

Vasso: "He's trusting you with everything this family has. You realize that???!!!"

Isaac, sharply: "Vasso!!"

Vasso: "Forgive me, Isaac."

She resumes her sewing in silence.

Isaac: "Gentle, Holy Child, teach him that the meek shall inherit the earth."

The old uncle sneaks over to Stavros' side.

Old Uncle, whispering: "Except in this country!"

Isaac, aware of this interruption, is unable to bring himself to scold the old man. He simply waits.

Then Isaac continues: "Teach him that all men are brothers!"

Old Uncle: "Nevertheless, trust no one!"

Isaac: "That a gentle word and a Christian smile will turn away wrath."

Vasso comes alongside Stavros with the coat.

Vasso: "I have sewn the money into the lining. Feel it? Here! And in this little sack—the jewelry. Keep this coat on at all times. Are you listening? Even when you sleep."

Old Uncle: "Sleep with one eye open."

The uncle illustrates, closing one eye, waggling the other from side to side, pointing also with his finger from side to side.

This time Isaac speaks with all his authority.

Isaac: "Vasso! Be silent!"

Vasso drops her head. Then suddenly turns it away as an emotion overwhelms her. Isaac now speaks to her, more gently.

Isaac: "Vasso . . . what is it?"

Vasso: "My God! If you send him to the baker to bring bread you're never sure he'll come back. And now—Constantinople!! Look at him! Look at him!"

She begins to sob bitterly. The family has never before seen this woman cry. The children are awe-struck.

Isaac waits out her bitter sobs. Then he speaks, offering no comfort, only the truth as he sees it.

Isaac: "Vasso, if you and I have so brought up our eldest son that at this moment he can fail his family, we deserve to go down."

All turn now and look at Stavros. He sits there, the entire burden on his back. Then he gets up and goes to his mother, standing now awkwardly before her. He speaks, meaning it with all his heart.

Stavros: "I won't fail you."

Suddenly the mother and son embrace, she finally accepting him in his new position as head of the family.

A cluster of people, the Topouzoglou family, stands on a little mound, looking out at the vast Anatolian plain. Far, far in the distance, just mounting the first swell of the prairie, are two tiny figures, the boy, Stavros, and his heavily laden little donkey. At the crest he stops and turns. The boy is dressed in the coat his mother prepared for him. Under it, he wears a wing collar and tie. On his head is Vartan's fez. Now he waves goodbye. Then he turns his back on his family and speaks sharply to Goochook.

Stavros: "Come on you! Let's go you!"

He and the donkey go over the crest and are almost out of sight.

The family has seen him for what may be the last time. They turn and head back toward their city. The boy and his donkey are the tiniest figures on the vast plateau. Behind them, the sun sets.

2

The Kizzil is not a big river as rivers go, but it is the largest one in this part of the world. Stavros and Goochook are being ferried across it on a flat-bottomed boat. The ferryman works a single sweep.

The ferryman lays down his oar and the boat begins to drift in midstream. Stavros looks back nervously. So does Goochook. The ferryman begins to rock the boat vigorously. Stavros lets out a cry of fear. Country boys from the interior cannot swim. And the donkey, under his heavy load, would certainly not have a chance. Goochook begins to bray.

Stavros: "What are you doing?? You?? You?? I don't swim—YOU! What are you doing??? Allah!!"

The ferryman rocks the boat. The donkey panics.

Stavros: "Look out! The donkey! What do you want? I'll give you whatever you want. I'll give you more money!"

The ferryman immediately moves toward Stavros with his hand outstretched. Stavros hesitates. He looks at the distant shore, then at his overloaded donkey. He considers. Then he takes out a change purse which holds his small money. The moment the purse comes into view, the ferryman snatches it and takes all of its contents.

Stavros: "God will punish you."

Ferryman: "God knows my particular problems." He returns the empty purse. "Be grateful I'm not looking into what's on the donkey's back."

Even before the boat touches shore, the ferryman leaps off and runs. Stavros is hard after him. But behind him, the boat drifts from shore and the donkey begins to bray. Stavros has to run back. He shouts to the world in general, "Thief! Thief!"

As if in answer, a large swarthy Turk rises from under some rocks.

30

Holding onto the boat, Stavros shouts. "Catch him! Catch him!" The ferryman's path of flight takes him past Abdul, the Turk. Abdul seizes him.

Abdul is large and the ferryman small. Abdul has him by the collar and is shaking him, dragging him back to Stavros.

Abdul: "Oh you mother-seller!" He calls out to Stavros: "I have him. Don't worry. I have him."

Later that day, Abdul and Stavros are on the road to Ankara. Stavros is walking behind Goochook. Abdul, a man without baggage, rides his own animal, his long legs extended, heels scraping the dust. He carries a cane. He is swarthy, in his mid-thirties, weight two hundred odd pounds, and is a psychological enigma.

Stavros: "How will I ever thank you?"

Abdul: "It is I who am fortunate. After all, this road to Ankara is the home of every mother-selling bandit bastard in Turkey. What good fortune is mine to meet a brother on the road! Brother!"

He rubs the sides of his forefingers together, a gesture he is to repeat many times.

Stavros: "I beg you. It is my good fortune not yours."

Abdul: "You have such a sweet smile!" He speaks with passion. "You and I! Brothers!" Once again he rubs his forefingers together. "Anything I have is yours, just as I know that everything you have is mine."

Stavros gives him a sharp look. But Abdul is so open and so brotherly that Stavros' suspicion is laid to rest.

Time passes. It is midday and very hot. All are weary. Goochook stumbles a little. Abdul stops.

Abdul: "Brother, my heart aches when I see that animal of yours struggle under the load you have put on his little back. I'm sure that, at this very moment, Allah, who sees all, is saying to himself, 'When will that good man who's always smiling' "—Stavros stops smiling—" 'finally become aware of the pain he's causing that dear little beast?' Do you think that is possible, brother?"

Stavros: "No. I mean . . . yes . . . yes . . . I suppose . . ."

Abdul: "Then, much as he'll balk, we must insist that my animal share the burden."

Stavros: "Oh, no!"

Abdul: "I insist. That smoked meat is heavy."

Stavros: "But then you'd have to walk too."

Abdul: "So!?" He dismounts quickly. "Come! Since we are brothers of the road, our animals must be brothers as well. Here. Help me."

He starts to untie the ropes which hold Goochook's burden.

Both donkeys are now burdened. They go on.

Later, as the sun sets, they stop on a hill overlooking the town of Mucur.

Abdul: "My brother, I know that town well. I have been the helpless victim of many a bandit in the town of Mucur. We'll camp here tonight on this hill."

Stavros: "If you advise. But what will we do for food?"

Abdul can't help looking at the smoked meat. Stavros notices.

Abdul: "I know what you're thinking. But I won't allow you to do it. I'd rather go hungry. Word of honor!"

They make a roadside camp and build a fire. Abdul eats heartily of the smoked meat with the greatest appreciation of its savor. Stavros watches him.

Abdul: "Eat, brother, eat. Food is strength. We have nine, ten days long journey to Ankara. And then ... you go on?"

Stavros: "To Constantinople. Our Cousin has a prospering rug establishment there."

Abdul's mind has moved on to another interest: "I notice you didn't remove your coat all day. Aren't you hot?"

Stavros: "Well ... no ... a little ..."

He starts to take his coat off then doesn't. Abdul smiles, rubs his forefingers together, winks.

The heat of the midday sun beats down on the road to Ankara like a huge fist. The men are dusty and weary as they trudge up a rocky hill. Abdul stops.

Abdul: "I can go no further."

He sits down and pulls off one shoe painfully.

Abdul: "They say the Prophet walked barefoot, but it must have been over different roads than these. Look!"

He puts a finger through a hole in the sole of his shoe.

Abdul: "I thought this damned pair of shoes would last the journey. But then I expected to ride the entire way. I wasn't prepared for all this walking. What do you think?"

Stavros: "Well ..."

Abdul: "Oh, no! Oh my God, no! I see that look on your face: 'Abdul, the son of Abdul, is going to be a burden to me!' I would rather stay rooted to this spot for the rest of my life, word of honor!"

At a shoemaker's in the marketplace of the next town, Kursehir, Abdul is trying on a pair of new shoes. It is a rather flashy pair, not ideal for a long journey by foot over rough terrain. Abdul is berating the proprietor as Stavros stands by helplessly.

Abdul: "Aren't you ashamed! You would rob your mother! Just consider one thing, I beg you, my brother here has sold a side of smoked meat, one of the delicious pieces that his family entrusted to . . ."

Proprietor: "That is the price!"

Abdul turns to Stavros: "I've done my best!!"

Stavros doesn't answer. He wishes he had never hooked up with this man. After a moment he reaches into his pocket.

They are again on the road to Ankara. The day is hot. The road is hard under foot. Abdul is limping. Stavros is trying desperately to find a way to lose this man.

Stavros: "How are the new shoes?"

Abdul: "They pinch! My feet are covered with boils and sores."

Stavros: "Perhaps you should stay in the next town for a few days and rest?"

Abdul: "Oh? And you?"

Stavros: "I would go on."

Abdul: "Oh, no! I couldn't leave my brother. Don't fear. I'll never abandon you."

He limps along. Then stops abruptly, dramatically.

Abdul: "But brother, I must have a drink. My heart is dry! My spirit thirsts! One swallow of raki I must have!! You could not deny me one drink?"

Stavros and Abdul sit at the table in an outdoor cafe in Zordagh, a juncture point for camel and mule traffic. Here are ample provisions for everything that a mule or camel driver might look for after a week's journey over the burning plateau. It is a wild town.

Abdul is getting drunk. Stavros, his victim, watches him, still looking for a way to escape. A thunderstorm can be heard approaching. A waiter brings Abdul another raki.

Abdul: "Brother, I confess I cannot pay for this one."

Stavros: "You didn't pay for the others!"

Abdul: "Brother, it is not necessary to remind me that at this time I am less fortunate than you. After all, in friendship, there is only one rule. What is mine is yours and what is . . ."

Stavros, bursting: "But you have nothing!"

Abdul is patient with him: "As the Prophet said: 'Who can place a price on wisdom?' "

Stavros: "Despite the Prophet, this is the last I pay for."

Stavros becomes tense and silent. Abdul tries to get his attention. He rubs the sides of his forefingers together flirtatiously. He gets no response. Then Abdul burst into tears.

Stavros: "What is the matter now ???"

Abdul: "You wish you had never met me. Admit it. Admit it."
Stavros will not respond. "For some reason you cannot speak what is
obvious. Well . . . I had hoped to have my brother with me for the entire
journey. Only last week a man was murdered between here and Ankara.
As a matter of fact, not far from this town on the road to Ankara."

He drinks. Suddenly the rain comes down hard.

Abdul: "Behold! Allah weeps for me!"

It is a cloudburst. The two men run to find shelter for their donkeys.

They find an inn and secure their beasts in a low shed. The rain is
beating down hard. Stavros runs into the inn. Abdul makes as if to
follow, then runs back to the donkeys. He rips off the pack on Goochook
and heads off in an opposite direction.

Later, inside the inn, Stavros sits at a window, alone, watching the
rain, waiting. Abdul enters with two women. He holds a bottle. The
women are plump, decidedly hirsute. With them is a small bear on a
chain. They have all had—including the bear—a good deal to drink.

Abdul: "Brother, I have decided not to leave you!" Stavros glares at
him. "You don't seem to be as happy about this as I am. Where is your
famous smile??" Stavros doesn't answer. "A confession! I sold the rest of
the meat."

Stavros: "You sold the—!"

Abdul: "I did it for you! I swear. There is a saying, 'The rope drawn
too tight will snap.' So behold, Chingana!" A flourish towards one of the
women. "Chingana is yours! I don't know this other beast's name. But
we will find out the facts about her before too long. The bear, I believe is
also female." He bursts into song, dances. The bear dances.

> "Oh pity the man without a woman
>   Aman!
> Pity the man without a mate.
>   Aman, aman!
> A garden without water.
> A meal without wine.
> The sky without the moon.
> The face without the eyes.
>   Aman!"

Something snaps in the boy. He throws himself at Abdul. There
ensues a quick and decisive engagement. Abdul knocks him cold with
the back of a chair. Then he contemplates his victim with generous pity.

Abdul: "Poor thing, poor thing. Come, Chingana, take his legs. He's a good soul, a good boy. Come."

All three carry the boy upstairs.

Later, in a bedroom upstairs at the inn, Abdul and Chingana, drunk, are shaking Stavros.

Abdul: "Brother, brother. Don't worry! You are asleep but I am awake. I am looking after your precious possessions. I have brought them up out of the rain."

Stavros wakes up with a vengeance.

Stavros: "Allah!"

He leaps up and starts to look around.

Abdul: "They are all here. Every beautiful item!"

Stavros: "My sister's blankets, where are they?"

At this moment the woman Abdul calls "the Beast" makes an entrance from an adjoining room, clothed only in one of Athena's hope-chest blankets. She does a little belly dance.

Stavros is horrified: "What are you doing!!"

Abdul grabs "the Beast" and holds her lovingly, squeezing her soft parts.

Abdul: "Brother, while you were asleep, this woman has given me unspeakable pleasure. Ach! Ach! Aman!"

"The Beast" is drunk. Her hair is in disarray. her long yellow teeth glistening, her eyes bloodshot. She sways seductively, with only the blanket around her, trying her best to be ladylike at the same time.

Stavros is frantic, furious: "Where is my coat??"

They all burst out laughing.

Abdul: "You are wearing it, brother."

Stavros feels through the lining quickly. Abdul is really hurt.

Abdul: "You insult my father, brother, when you do that, you insult my father who taught me right from wrong. I am a patient man, brother, but you insult my mother, poor thing, long dead."

Abdul begins to blubber. Stavros is gathering his possessions.

Abdul: "But I forgive you! Now just look here. I can understand that this person must look to you like a beast. But do not go by her appearance. Penetrate to her soul. Take her into the other room."

He suddenly leaps up and grabs Stavros in a bear-like embrace.

Abdul: "I have never met a more generous and brotherly person than you. This trip has been a landmark in my life."

He starts to kiss Stavros violently. Stavros shoves the drunken man away.

Stavros: "Where is my other rug? The small one?"

Abdul, hurt: "Brother, I beg you, don't use that tone of voice with me!"

Stavros: "Never mind my tone of voice. Where is my mother's little rug?!"

He throws himself at Abdul, clutching him by the neck. Abdul, shaky with drink and weak from love-making, cannot defend himself. The women scream.

Stavros: "You animal! Where is my mother's little rug???"

Now in rushes the proprietor of this miserable inn, and, following him, a hamal (a porter) and a couple of camel-drivers from across the hall. They pull Stavros off Abdul, but the boy keeps calling out.

Stavros: "Where is my mother's rug?"

Abdul points to the proprietor: "I gave it to him."

Stavros: "To him? You gave my rug to him! What for? What for?"

He turns on the proprietor. This is a tough man. He has to be to run a place like this. He shouts his own outrage.

Proprietor: "What? What for?!"

Abdul now has to restrain the proprietor from attacking the boy. Meantime he is admonishing Stavros.

Abdul: "Brother, brother . . . shshsh . . . brother! Courtesy! Reason!"

Proprietor: "What for? To pay for your night's lodgings. What for!"

Abdul turns to the proprietor: "Shshh! We're all gentlemen here." Then to Stavros: "Brother, I am at fault in this."

Stavros: "Give me my rug."

Proprietor: "Then pay for your room in cash money. What do you think that rug is anyway? A silk Keshan? It is a rag that I'm ashamed to have my friends see, so I put it on the floor of the toilet to soak up droppings."

During this speech, Stavros has been frantically gathering up the rest of his possessions. Abdul falls on his knees before him.

Abdul: "Brother, only I am at fault here. I beg your forgiveness. I cannot live without your forgiveness."

He tries to clasp Stavros around the knees, but the boy dodges him and continues to bundle up his possessions.

Abdul: "Before all this company, I beg for your forgiveness. Brother, don't leave me here on my knees! Don't insult my soul!"

Suddenly, Abdul's voice has a new note in it.

Abdul: "Brother, I have never before been on my knees before a Greek!"

Stavros pays no attention, starts out with his belongings.

Abdul, still on his knees: "Brother, I warn you! With a Turk there can either be brotherliness or its opposite. I warn you."

Stavros is gone. Abdula gets up slowly and dusts off his knees. He is suddenly cold sober.

Abdul: "Too bad! Ach, Ach, Ach! Too bad. So! Now!"

He looks demonic. He has been telling the truth: he did like the boy—and he has been mortally insulted. He rubs his forefingers together, sardonically, then draws one finger across his throat.

The next day. The sun is shining. Stavros and Goochook have walked all night on the road to Ankara and are exhausted. There is a single railroad track along the road. A very small train passes by. Stavros doesn't look up.

From a window of the train, Abdul has spotted his victim.

Late that afternoon Stavros and Goochook are coming into the outskirts of a town called Soosehir. Stavros, half asleep as he walks, looks up and sees two uniformed men—rural police—watching him.

Stavros, driving Goochook before him passes by the police. Suddenly, they move in on him. He struggles a little, but his protests are useless. They drag him off.

Stavros: "What for? What for??!! What did I do???"

The process of justice in this town is conducted in a dusty and very shabby room in the judge's home. The judge sits cross-legged on the floor behind a low table. A familiar voice is heard.

Abdul stands there, the very picture of outraged justice.

Abdul: "Your honor, I made an exact list of every particular."

Stavros, between his guards, screams out: "Lies! Lies! Lies!" The rural policeman who is standing next to him backhands him across the mouth and knocks him off his feet: "Sssutt! Thief!" The judge gives the incident only the most perfunctory attention. He turns to a shabby clerk who holds Abdul's inventory.

Judge: "Read!"

The clerk reads. As each item is particularized, the policeman checks it.

Clerk: "One Hamedan carpet. The color of roses and the blue of midnight. A corner well worn."

Abdul: "Behold!"

Policeman: "As described."

Judge, half to himself: "Beautiful rug!"

Policeman: "One blanket, the color of peaches, woven at home by my dear sisters."

Abdul looks at Stavros indignantly. Stavros is standing with his head bowed, half turned away. No one there can see that he has opened the lining of his coat and is quickly swallowing coin after coin after coin.

Clerk: "Then! In the lining of the coat."

Stavros stops swallowing.

Abdul: "Your honor, make him take my coat off."

Judge: "Take off the coat."

It is a windy day. Stavros, without a coat, without donkey, without possessions of any kind is walking slowly into the low sun on the road to Ankara. He looks back and sees Abdul coming up, riding Goochook at a trot. Stavros' hand goes to his dagger, stays there.

The donkey catches up to Stavros. Abdul, riding alongside, addresses his victim in a friendly, chatty tone.

Abdul: "After you left I had a terrible time. Those policemen are not honest. And the judge! Aman! Aman! He offered to divide my new possessions with me. And then, when I declined, they all helped themselves. The judge particularly wanted the rugs. The law in this country needs considerable reform." Stavros does not answer. "Look! I'll show you what I have left!"

He holds out his hand with the sister's earrings, the locket, and a single coin. Stavros, his hand still on his dagger, doesn't turn his head.

Abdul: "Nothing! You see! Nothing!" No answer. "But there are some coins missing. About six of them by my estimate. I came to the conclusion you had swallowed them. No? I saw you do it. At the time I thought to myself, let him have something, poor thing. But now the situation has changed." He holds out his hand again. "You see! I cannot be so generous." No answer. "I admit you've been patient with me. If I had been you, I would long since have taken out the blade you hold there and put it to its proper use. But we Turks are primitive, while you Greeks are civilized. I envy you. You have learned how to bear misfortune, swallow insult and indignity, and still smile. I truly envy you." He looks at him, appraisingly. "Well . . . the coins? Eh? Anything happening yet? Not yet, eh? How long do you suppose?? God knows, eh? Eh? So . . . a drink?"

Stavros makes no sign of having heard. Abdul lifts his bottle and takes a long, long swig.

It is sunset. Stavros sits with his back to some wild rocks. Abdul sits in the foreground, now quite drunk and completely unmasked.

Abdul: "You're really such a coward! Imagine what I would have done in your place!"

Stavros' face burns with shame.

Abdul: "All you can do is smile and swallow. Just a bag of guts. I've killed men like you and it's no different than killing a sheep. One clean cut almost anywhere and the life flows out. A twitch or two and it's over. Have a drink! No! Of course! You don't drink. You don't fight. You've no use for women. What kind of a man are you?" He yawns, stretches. "Well I can't waste more time over you. Unfortunately I haven't a weapon. I'll have to borrow your knife. No? Yes? What? Why don't you say something? Are you afraid to talk? Do you value your life? I don't know what you people are? Are you different from sheep? They won't fight for their lives either. It's getting dark. It's almost time for our game. Well I'll give you a few minutes. I'll do my evening prayer. And then."

Abdul gets up, spreads his prayer rug, and begins his ritual of prayer. Stavros knows it's now or never. His hand is on the dagger.

As Abdul kneels and bends to pray, Stavros, with the speed of youth, is on Abdul's back, driving the dagger home again and again. Abdul lets out a terrible cry. Goochook, startled, bolts.

Stavros stands up, trembling. He looks around furtively to see if there were any witnesses.

The donkey is galloping away as if it were running for its life.

Stavros, calling frantically: "Goochook!! Goochook!!"

Stavros sees his donkey disappear for good behind a rise. The little animal's panic communicates itself to him. He starts to run. Then he stops, turns, walks back toward the body of the man he's killed. Something is beginning to toughen in the boy. He bends over and goes through the dead man's pockets. He takes his jewels and all the money he can find, straightens, looks at the coins in his hands. He makes a sound: pain, anger? Disgust at himself. Then he puts the money into his pocket and walks off. Without knowing it he has resolved that this will never happen to him again.

Finally, wearily, Stavros reaches the ancient, huge, crumbling stone gate at the entrance to what was the citadel of Ankara. Here is a watering place for donkeys and camels. Also a market with the usual flamboyant peddlars and the legion of beggars with their spectacular ailments. Through the arch can be seen the setting of the sun.

Stavros, covered with dust, is older looking, tougher.

He finds the railroad station. The sign reads: ANKARA. The boy takes out his remaining funds, a palm full of small coins. Then he makes up his mind and approaches the ticket window. There is a poster of the North German Lloyd Line advertising passage to America. It shows a steamboat going by the Statue of Liberty. Stavros looks at this for an instant, then he says to the ticket vendor, "Constantinople!" He puts his entire wealth on the ticket counter.

3

Stavros has arrived in Constantinople. He gazes in wonder at the six minarets of Santa Sophia. Soon we find him taking in the Golden Horn, the famous inside harbor of Constantinople. It is the busiest place in the city during the day. He watches the ferryboats in the harbor, the little water taxis, then he hears the sound of a big boat—a heavy steam whistle. His head jerks around. A large cargo ship is loading at a dock. An endless line of porters, at least one hundred men, go in, come out of the ship's hold.

Stavros hurries toward the ship. Then he looks up. The ship is flying the American flag.

Some American officers are supervising the loading from the rail of the cargo ship. They have open, decent faces. Stavros suddenly begins to call out.

Stavros: "America . . . America . . . eh? Eh, eh?"

The officers at the rail pay no attention to him. They're looking at the line of hamals loading the ship. A man, too old for his burden, buckles and falls. His burden falls to one side. Three men on the dock start for it.

Stavros, almost on instinct, unexpectedly even to himself, also goes after the load and the job. There is a terrible fight. All four men desperately want the job. Stavros fights like a wild beast. All his pent-up anger explodes. He lays about him with fury. In a few decisive seconds, he has the fallen man's load and his job. He snarls as he hoists it up on his back, then triumphantly starts up the gangplank.

The American officers have been watching the fight. As Stavros goes past the officers, he carries his burden proudly.

Officer in Charge: "Hello, kid!!"

Stavros struts and whistles, makes faces, proud of winning, dancing off under his load. Three big blasts of the ship's whistle are heard, as if it too were celebrating Stavros' victory.

It is dawn when the freighter, fully loaded, heads out to sea. A couple of hundred yards from shore, the whistle sounds again three times, "Goodbye," from a distance.

The dock is empty now, except for a solitary figure. Stavros is watching the freighter go. He has touched his dream. And now—he turns sadly and goes off.

The "closed" bazaar is made up of street after street of small, tightly packed store fronts, "closed" because all of them are under a glass arcade. It is the popular hour for buying, so the place is fantastically crowded. Fiercely competing vendors fill the middle way, their goods spread on paper laid on the paving.

Stavros holds a slip of paper in his hand, asks a direction, is given instructions, and goes on. The noise is overwhelming.

Around a corner of the bazaar, everything is suddenly much quieter. Here are the rug stores. Stavros consults the piece of paper in his hand. Then he walks along the front of a row of rug stores, reading their numbers and their names.

These stores are very quiet indeed. Stavros stops. He has found the Topouzoglou Persian Carpet Company. Stavros inspects the front of this small, dark store. The inside is quiet as a tomb. Stavros is disappointed. He expected a "prosperous establishment."

Stavros enters. Stops. No one comes up to him. Silence. Then the sound of a powerful rhythmic snore. Stavros looks for the source.

Our Cousin lies on top of a small pile of folded carpets, peacefully asleep. An old porter, wearing slippers, comes up to Stavros.

Stavros, with obvious disappointment: "Is this the establishment of Odysseus Topouzoglou?"

The Porter: "Yes. Welcome, welcome."

Then he takes a good look at the visitor and sees how bedraggled he is. His tone changes.

The Porter: "What do you want? We want nothing."

At this moment Our Cousin stirs, and then emits a marvelous variety of sighs, groans, and grumbles.

Our Cousin: "Ach! Ach! Ach! Tstststststststtt! Tststst! Aaachh!"

Stavros: "What's he saying?"

The Porter: "He's forgiving God for bringing him into such a world."

Stavros: "I'm his cousin. When will he wake?"

The Porter: "When business comes." He looks at the floor, at Stavros' feet. "Look at the dirt you brought in here. Who'll have to sweep again? Me!"

At this moment something wakens Our Cousin. He looks around, smiling vaguely. His mouth is sour. He rubs his gums, goes "Ach, ach."

The Porter: "Topouzoglou, effendi. This man says he's your cousin."

It is a dark establishment, and the old man's eyes aren't too good. Also he naps with his glasses off. Now, as he approaches Stavros, he first chortles.

Our Cousin: "Oh, ohh, oooohhh, welcome, welcome."

His glasses on, he now takes a good look. And *his* tone of voice abruptly changes.

Our Cousin: "What happened to you?"

Stavros: "I . . . I had a bad journey."

Our Cousin: "Well, well, poor thing, poor thing!" He turns to the Porter. "Artin! Run, run, two coffees. Immediately!"

Artin, walking off slowly: "Immediately."

Our Cousin: "I've been waiting and waiting. Welcome! Here, come, come in the back of the store. I have clean linen. Then I'll buy you lunch."

Our Cousin takes Stavros to a restaurant overlooking the harbor. Fired with the dregs of his energy, he is putting on a good show. Stavros is ravenous, even eating the fish heads.

Our Cousin: "So, what we need is more stock."

From across the harbor, the sound of the whistle of a large boat. Stavros' head swings around, listening.

Our Cousin: "What?"

Stavros: "Forgive me. I was merely going to remark that you don't seem to be selling what you have."

Our Cousin: "You are very sharp! Another mullet? I beg you. They are so small!!"

Stavros, ravenous: "Since you insist, I will. Thank you."

Again the sound of the whistle of a large freight boat.

Our Cousin: "You see I have the wrong goods for the market as it is today."

Stavros hears only the whistle.

Back at the Topouzoglou Persian Carpet Company, Our Cousin is showing Stavros his stock of rugs and carpets.

Our Cousin: "What I will do, as soon as you know the business, is to take the money you have brought, go to Persia and buy the kind of goods that . . ." He notices Stavros' silence. "What is the matter, cousin?"

Stavros blurts it out: "I haven't brought any money."

Our Cousin: "You ...?"
Stavros: "I was a fool and I was robbed."
Our Cousin: "You're teasing me."
Stavros: "No. I'm ashamed to face you."
Our Cousin: "But your father—?"
Stavros: "I'm ashamed to say it."
At this moment Our Cousin seems to have a heart attack. He clutches his breast, moans, groans, and carries on.
Stavros: "Cousin ... Cousin ..."
Our Cousin, suddenly shouting: "Then why did you eat my lunch??!!"
Stavros: "I was hungry."
Our Cousin is shouting when he isn't groaning. "Go, go, go out of my sight." Stavros starts out. "No, no, don't go. Sit down. For God's sake, give me a chance to swallow this. Why did you eat my lunch? Two of everything! Two of everything! The day of my ruination!"
An hour later Stavros is sitting alone in the front of the store. Our Cousin approaches, carrying a broom.
Our Cousin: "Here! Ruination! Sweep!"
He hands him the broom and Stavros begins to sweep.
Our Cousin: "I will write your father. He's a good man and ..."
Stavros drops the broom and rushes to Our Cousin.
Stavros: "No, listen, NO! He must never know what happened. Promise! Not a word. Promise."
Our Cousin: "I only meant to say that in time your father will ..."
Stavros: "Do you want to kill him? He put everything on me ... everything!!! It will kill him if ... I am going to make it up to him. I have big plans. They will be proud of me. But now, now, nothing. Hear? Promise? Nothing!"
Our Cousin: "All right. I promise!" Then, "Go on. Sweep! My ruination! Sweep!"
Stavros starts again to sweep. Our Cousin walks to the window and looks out on to the street.
Stavros vows to himself: "They'll be proud of me!"
Our Cousin at the window, indicates the street: "Look! The rich come to work after lunch, in a carriage, while I ..." Suddenly he seems to have an inspiration. "Stavros. Listen!" Stavros stops sweeping. "God is fertile! Behold!"
Ouside in the street a carriage has drawn up in front of a large establishment. A prosperous, extremely well-fed rug merchant is getting out.
Our Cousin: "Behold Aleko Sinyosoglou! A man with a great deal of money, a very large stock, and four daughters, one plainer than the

other, so much so that day by day he is losing hope of ever becoming a grandfather. You understand??"

Stavros: "No."

Our Cousin: "God solves all problems! We must not at this moment forget that you are a young man, even handsome, and if properly dressed . . . do you understand now?"

Stavros now does: "No." He turns away in complete disgust. "Allah!"

Our Cousin looks at the recalcitrant. Now he's peeved.

Our Cousin: "Never mind! You! Sweep! I'll arrange a meeting . . . and you'll see . . ."

Stavros begins to sweep. Then suddenly he flings the broom away, almost hitting the porter who leaps from behind some rugs like an animal flushed from hiding. Without a word, Stavros exits from the store.

In the window of the office of the North German Lloyd Line, along with the usual posters and displays, is a model of the passenger liner *The Kaiser Wilhelm*, which makes the Constantinople-to-New York run.

Stavros strides into the office. At the counter the boy speaks to a clerk.

Stavros: "What do I need to go to America?"

The clerk looks down his nose at this frantic young man.

Clerk: "Money."

Stavros: "How much?"

Clerk: "You mean third class of course. One hundred and eight Turkish pounds."

This is to Stavros an astronomical figure.

Stavros: "One hundred and eight—! Allah!" Then, "All right."

The clerk looks at him scornfully and begins to move away. Stavros reaches across the counter and holds him. With his free hand he points at the Assistant Manager.

Stavros: "Is he American?"

The Assistant Manager is very American. He wears a straw hat indoors, and is very much admired by some employees who work there. "Completely," says the clerk, speaking as of a god.

Stavros, his face pure jealousy and longing, takes in the American.

Stavros: "I'll be back."

And he exits from the office abruptly.

Back in Stavros' home, his family is at dinner. Isaac is reading a letter to the family—to Vasso, the children, the aunts, the old uncle.

Isaac: " 'And now I don't know where he is. At any rate he didn't bring me a single penny. Nothing! He says he was robbed. I tried to talk to him, Cousin, as is my place and duty. But suddenly he threw a broom at my porter and ran out of the store, his eyes on fire.' "

Vasso groans. The old uncle bursts out laughing.

Vasso: "What is amusing you, idiot?"

Isaac picks up another letter.

Isaac: "Now listen." He reads from the second letter. " 'Father, I couldn't trust our money to him. No one ever comes into his store. He sleeps all day on a pile of rugs. So I told him I was robbed. Meantime I have a new plan, a big idea! I'll have news for you very soon. I have already found another line of work. One that is much more active, in truth very active.' "

Vasso: "Well, that's good, anyway."

Old Uncle: "God knows what's going on."

Isaac: " 'My health is good. Tell mother that one way or another I get what I need to eat.' "

Vasso: "One thing he could always do."

Old Uncle: "Eat!"

Isaac: " 'So don't worry. One day you'll be proud of your son. That day will come, I promise you, you'll be proud of me!' "

4

Back in Constantinople, fifteen empty crates can be seen, one on top of another, jogging down a narrow, crowded street. If somewhere under them there is a man, we cannot see him.

Soon, however, it can be seen that it is Stavros who is carrying the crates. It is a hot summer's day and he is wringing wet and very worn.

In the shade of a warehouse, the hamals, or porters, are eating lunch. Stavros, who has no lunch, watches the others eat. One of the hamals, Garabet, has had enough of his bread and starts to throw it away.

Stavros, quickly: "Don't throw that away!"

He grabs it and wolfs it down.

Garabet: "Why don't you spend a few coins for a bread?"

Stavros smiles. But there is something manic about his smile now.

Behind a restaurant. Night, early Fall. Stavros and a couple of poor people have been waiting for the garbage to be put out. As soon as it is, they begin to pick it over. A dog tries to get in there, but Stavros drives him off.

Garabet watches him. He is an intellectual among hamals, a man of fifty, cynical, wise, sour, tough. Stavros fascinates him.

Garabet: "Say . . . you!"

He points.

Along the street comes a mother donkey followed by her newborn foal. Their owner goes into a doorway for a moment.

Garabet, mocking: "Milk!"

Stavros pulls a little battered tin cup free from his belt, and starts toward the mare.

Months have passed. It is a cold, rainy November. Stavros and

Garabet are working. Garabet has attached himself to the boy now, and they work as a pair. Stavros is tough as leather.

It is the end of a long dark day, and time now for the hamals to be paid off. Some young whores wait nearby. Garabet catches Stavros looking at them longingly. One of the whores, passably attractive, looks at Stavros.

Garabet: "I'm cold. I need a woman tonight. Want to come?" Stavros shakes his head. "I'll pay for it." Stavros shakes head again. "You need it."

Garabet makes a vulgar illustrative gesture. Stavros won't look.

Stavros: "I need nothing."

Garabet: "Did you ever have one?" Stavros shakes his head. "Don't you want one?"

Stavros: "My father wouldn't approve."

Garabet makes a vulgar gesture relative to Stavros' father. At that moment Stavros is paid and starts off.

Garabet: "Where are you going?"

Stavros: "I have another job."

Garabet: "Now? Another job? At night?" Stavros nods. "Here." He offers him his cargo-knife. "Kill yourself with this. It's easier!"

Stavros' night work is in the kitchen of a large restaurant, a noisy place, full of filthy steam. He is washing dishes. His face is white as soap. A kitchen maid, a child of fifteen, flirts with him. He sticks to his work. She gives up, eats something.

It is dawn and snowing. In a low shed, the man-drawn carts used to carry produce from market to market are stacked one atop another. Garabet walks up to one of them. He reaches under some burlap and shakes someone. Stavros bolts upright, drawing his knife, a wild animal, ready for anything.

Stavros: "Oh. You. There are thieves everywhere here. Like cats! What time is it?"

Garabet: "Get up. It's the hour. They're working. Aren't you cold?" Stavros shakes him off. "Come sleep on my floor tonight." Stavros shakes him off. "You need a good night's sleep."

Stavros: "I need nothing."

Then with a sudden gaiety he leaps out of the cart.

Stavros: "Allah! Come on you! Let's go, old man!!"

Stavros and Garabet pull two of the carts through the snow, side by side.

Garabet: "How much for a ticket?"

Stavros: "One hundred and eight pounds."

Garabet: "Aman! And by now you've brought together—?"
Stavros: "What do you care?"
Garabet: "How much?"
Stavros: "Four pounds and a little. So?"
Garabet: "So how long do you expect to live?"
Stavros doesn't answer, whistles madly. Garabet looks at him.
Garabet: "Your harness is coming apart."

The seasons change. There is a lemony sunshine in the market square. It is spring. A squabble is taking place. One of the hamals has rejected a load as too heavy. He throws it down.
Hamal: "That load is for an animal! Get an animal!"
The loader in charge looks for the man who never refuses a load.
Loader: "America America!"
Stavros, sitting on the ground repairing his hamal's harness, hears himself called, stands, puts his hands and arms through the loops in the harness, hitches it up onto his back, and goes trotting off in the direction of the loader with little coolie steps. In his patchwork clothes, he has to run the gauntlet of the other hamals, who resent him for accepting loads they have refused. "America America" has become his nickname and is now directed at him with scorn as he goes by.

Time passes. It is summer again. Garabet, in the marketplace, steals a melon from a passing cart. He walks to Stavros, who is sleeping in a mess of vegetable garbage. The boy hugs his hamal's harness, as if it were all he had in the world. His face, in the sunlight, is pale and worn. He is on the verge of final exhaustion.
Garabet looks down at the boy and puts the point of his shoe in a delicate spot, wiggles it. Stavros awakens with a jolt. He seems overwrought.
Stavros, frantically: "What time is it?"
Garabet: "You have time."
He breaks the melon and offers part of it to Stavros.
Stavros: "I can't stay awake! I keep falling asleep."
Garabet: "Don't worry. You'll be dead soon." He raps Stavros' middle. "What's the baby weigh now?"
Stavros: "What? Oh. Seven pounds and a little."
Garabet, devouring his piece of melon: "Small money! There are two kinds of money. Small money and big money. Small money is a whore. Look at a coin. She's been in everyone's hands. You wake in the morning, she's gone. Now then, there's big money. Like what you need ..."

Stavros had fallen asleep again. Garabet takes the other piece of melon from his limp hand and begins to eat it.

Stavros and Garabet are taking in the sunset over the busy harbor. The dock is a lovers' promenade. A pair of girls go by. Garabet notices Stavros looking at them with intense longing.

Garabet: "Behold! You're human!" Then he gets back to his favorite subject. "Now big money! Now big money is fertile! It procreates—how I don't know, but it reproduces itself. Every time you look—behold, more! There are only two ways for men like us to get big money. Steal it. Or if you're young, marry it. But you can't get it by work. Study me. Worked like an animal from the first day I could walk and carry! So? Behold! The lowest form of life."

He looks at Stavros, who is still watching the girls.

Garabet: "Oh! If I were you! There are some very ugly girls with very rich fathers!"

A couple of men pick the girls up. Stavros drops his head. In some odd way, he is disappointed.

Garabet: "Let's get ourselves a couple of those little mousetraps ..."

He grabs Stavros in a vulgar mocking lover's embrace. Stavros pushes him off. Then Garabet speaks in simple friendship.

Garabet: "Come on, boy, you need it." And he shows him what he needs, wiggling his shoulders and so on.

Stavros: "I need nothing."

Garabet: "You need it! After work, come to my place. I'll have one there for you ..."

Stavros hesitates, comes close to Garabet and whispers: "I ... I've never ... I wouldn't know—exactly—what to do."

Garabet: "Oh ... they show you all that."

Garabet's room is a hovel. The spill of light from the opening door reveals a young woman. We can't see her too well.

Stavros is at the door. His face is starved for human warmth.

Girl's Voice: "Yes, yes, come, close the door."

Stavros starts for her.

Afterward, Stavros lies on top of her in an absolutely dead sleep. Both are naked. A ragged burlap partially covers him. Nothing could wake him. He is in absolute exhaustion. She is not. She finds his money belt. Her fingers extract the coins, one by one.

In the market place at dawn, hamals are loading up for the day.

Loader: "America America!"

Garabet looks around, but there is no sign of Stavros. A checker assigns Garabet his load. But he drops it and runs off. In the background we hear, "America America!"

In Garabet's room, Stavros is ripping up everything in sight, looking for his money. Garabet enters.

Stavros: "Garabet!"

Garabet: "What happened?"

Stavros: "My money ... the girl ... where is she? I have to find her. Where do I ...?"

Garabet: "I don't know."

Stavros: "I have to find her. Nine months, nine months I worked! Where did *you* find her? Who is she?"

Garabet: "She's my daughter."

Stavros: "Your ... ? Allah!"

Garabet: "Yes."

Stavros: "Well then, well then ..."

Garabet: "I don't know where she is."

Stavros: "Well, how did you ...?"

Garabet: "I passed her on the street last night."

Stavros: "Where does she stay?"

Garabet: "Where they all stay, I suppose. There's a quarter."

Stavros: "Is this the way she lives—by selling herself?"

Garabet: "Are you a child? What else has she got to sell?"

Stavros: "Garabet! Garabet, I worked nine months!"

Garabet: "She did you a favor."

Stavros: "What?!"

Garabet: "I said she did you a favor!"

Stavros hits Garabet with all his might. Stavros is now very strong and hard-fisted. Garabet hits the wall, comes back, knife in hand, going for Stavros' throat, his free hand holding Stavros by the hair. He barely restrains himself. He's suspended for an instant, blind with rage, just under control.

Garabet: "I should kill you. You know? I don't like you that much. You're not a boy, you know? You know? If you do that you have to be ready to go on. You know?" Then, challenging: "I said she did you a favor!" He waits. "Do you imagine you could have brought together one hundred and eight pounds the way you did the seven? That way? The human body—it hasn't that strength!" He glares at him. "I should really kill you." Then, "So. Come."

He starts out. Stavros follows.

Vartuhi is a whore. Her room is above a cabaret where Turkish cafe society comes to hear music and to dance. Her room is not large. But the bed, behind a curtain of beads, is. Vartuhi occupies it now with a customer. A single lamp burns oil.

The door bursts open and in comes Garabet, followed by Stavros. Garabet goes right to the bed and seizes his daughter. The customer jumps out of bed and begins to run from side to side, shrieking like a cornered chicken. Stavros stays by the door, blocking it. We cannot hear what Garabet says to his daughter, but it is all curses. He beats her. She screams.

Garabet: "Who did you give his money?"

Vartuhi: "Stop! The patron. Downstairs. Stop!"

He smacks her again. She screams.

Vartuhi: "He was going to put me out! On the street!"

Garabet drops her, starts out.

Garabet, to Stavros: "Come."

They exit.

Vartuhi runs to the door, calling after him: "You want me out on the street? Without a room and a bed, what am I? I'm an animal—without a bed and a room!"

The patron, a large bulky Turk, is at home in his quarters. He is entertaining two members of the Municipal Police in full uniform. They are all eating pastries, dripping honey over their chins, and drinking hot sweet tea out of small glasses. Garabet and Stavros have just come in.

Policeman: "If you go to whores, you must expect to be robbed."

Patron: "Your daughter! Three months she didn't pay!"

His wife—three hundred pounds—enters from the kitchen.

Wife: "She'll owe him again next week. Next week! He's the saint of patience with them, the saint of . . ."

The policeman suddenly makes a terrible sound: "Aahahahhhc-chchhh! We were enjoying ourselves here." Then, with a violent gesture. "Go on . . . get out . . . go on before I . . . go on, get out!"

Garabet turns and puts it up to Stavros.

Garabet: "You want to say something?"

Stavros: "Allah!"

He walks out, beaten! Garabet follows.

In a corner on the waterfront Stavros finds a place to weep. Garabet, in his own way, is trying to comfort him.

Garabet: "I'm still angry you know." Then, gently: "I should still kill you. A fact! I should kill you!" The boy can't stop sobbing. "You hit me! Very hard! Very, very, very hard. You're a strong boy."

This doesn't work so he tries another tack.

Garabet: "You want to kill her? Go kill her. I won't stop you."

This doesn't do any good.

Garabet then speaks with gentle concern and real sympathy: "Anyway it's time for you to grow up and see the truth." He imitates him: " 'Big things ... Big Things!' " And then, mockingly: " 'They're going to be proud of me.' "

Stavros yells with pain: "Don't do that!!"

Garabet, now cruelly mocking: " 'They're going to be proud of me! Some day they'll be proud of me!' Hah!"

Stavros: "They will be."

Garabet: "You're nothing now and you never will be!"

Stavros: "I will, I am, I will, I am, I will. I'm going to leave this place. There is a better place."

Garabet: "It's all the same. Tell me. Since you left home, have you met among Christians, one follower of Christ? Have you met among human beings, one human being?"

Stavros: "You!"

Garabet: "Me! Didn't you look in my face?? You don't know me. You don't know what I am ..."

In a cellar, a secret political group is being addressed by Garabet. He is one of the leaders of the underground. Stavros is in the audience.

Garabet: "I have one idea for this world. Destroy it and start over again. There's too much dirt for a broom. It calls for a fire. It needs the flood."

Another meeting. Another cellar. Another night. Many of the same men are there. And Stavros also. He seems exhausted, deeply discouraged, and here at this place only because he doesn't know where else to turn. The atmosphere in this second gathering is more conspiratorial. The conversation is in whispers. Attention is directed toward a door. They're waiting for someone.

Man: "I'll say this: the main victims of the Turkish Empire are the Turkish people. One day Turkey will be a great nation."

Stavros: "After I'm dead, I'm not interested."

Garabet explains, mocking the boy: "He still thinks there's a clean life somewhere, eh? America, eh?"

A ferocious-looking man—in some way crippled—comes out of a corner.

Cripple: "Don't tell me about America. I was there. I helped build one of their buildings."

He lifts his shirt, revealing a long, ugly scar.

Cripple: "I fell—and then? No one needed me. If you have money in

America you're somebody. If you have no money, it's just like here. Life is for the rich!"

Garabet, speaking for Stavros, mocking: "He still thinks the same."

Stavros manages the faintest smile, the slightest nod.

It's not that he's lost sight of his objective. It's simply that he doesn't know, at the moment, how to go about reaching it. Suddenly everyone is silent. A man has entered, walks to the position of authority, and now speaks.

The Leader: "Anyone who's going to go, go now."

Garabet makes a little gesture suggesting to Stavros that he go. Stavros only sinks lower down in his chair. Behind them the door is locked. The meeting starts.

Later. A bomb is being concealed in a hamal's harness. The group around the bomb whispers.

The Leader: "Again! After the explosion, we separate. We meet one month from today. On the street you don't acknowledge each other. Is that clear?" All nod. Stavros nods.

At this instant the windows are suddenly filled with police and guns. The single oil lamp is shot out. Volley after volley. Screams of pain. The cries of the desperate. Then the shots stop. The door is broken in, admitting a kind of light. The smoke is settling. The carnage is terrible to behold. The dead in their last struggle. Then all is quiet, except for the final sounds of the dying.

In a military hospital, two army doctors are walking through a ward. They stop over a pallet and look down.

First Doctor: "It's too much. Look at him. A boy! All he wanted was something. What? Freedom. What?"

Second Doctor: "Shshsh!"

He indicates an orderly coming up. The tone of the First Doctor becomes traditionally autocratic.

First Doctor: "Here! You! You know when a man is dead?"

We see Stavros on the pallet. He is barely alive. A scar is burned into his forehead. He will never lose it.

Orderly: "I can tell when a mule is dead."

Doctor: "It's the same. With this one it's a matter of hours. There's a wagon full of them back of the kitchen. Go on—throw him in. He's finished."

The wagon of the dead is being driven through the countryside. The bodies are covered with a tarpaulin. Then one body, as if in a gentle slow-motion fall, emerges from under the tarpaulin and reaches the ground in the wake of the moving wagon, somehow, without a jar.

The body has life in it, but not much. A desperate effort and it reaches the side of the road. Then Stavros rolls over into the ditch. The effort has exhausted him. He lies there, straining to breathe. A mongrel dog comes up.

A cliff by the sea, a sheer one hundred and fifty feet into the blue Sea of Marmora. Soldiers are throwing bodies over the precipice.

Garabet's body goes into the sparkling blue water, breaks through the kelp, rises, floats, then is engulfed. On the cliff, a few scattered people, Vartuhi among them, stand at a little distance from the soldiers. She turns, starts off.

The people on the road back to town see something, hesitate, then walk around and past it. The something is Stavros, trying to make his way back to town on his hands and knees. His head is bloody, his clothes indescribably disheveled. He falls, struggles up, falls.

He lies in the middle of the road, waiting for a few drops of strength to come back. Vartuhi's feet come into his view. She stoops and helps him up.

Back home, the Topouzoglou family sit in their garden under a vine. A letter has arrived with bad news.

Isaac, reading: " 'I don't know where to look further, dear Cousin, I have looked everywhere. He's disappeared from the face of this black world.' "

Isaac puts the letter down. The family sit in silence.

In Constantinople, Vartuhi's room is stifling hot. Her "patron" is at the door.

Patron: "If you're married, go elsewhere. We're in business, here."

Vartuhi: "But he doesn't stay here any more. He's gone."

Patron: "I can smell him!"

He walks into the room past her. And after an instant's search in the tiny room, he throws open the door to a small and shallow wardrobe. On the floor is Stavros. His eyes shine like those of a trapped wild animal. He is soaked with perspiration. One hand is out of sight.

Patron: "Now hear me. Tomorrow. Tomorrow I'm going to see some money from you. I haven't had a copper in three weeks. So tomorrow! Eh?! Final."

He walks out, the door shutting behind him.

We hear Stavros in a frantic whisper: "Ssst! Ssst! Vartuhi, come here!!"

Vartuhi comes to him, sitting on the floor. He seizes her arm with demonic strength. The hand that was concealed comes into sight. It holds his grandfather's knife.

Stavros: "Don't let him frighten you. I just need a few more days. I'm getting my strength! My strength is coming back."

Vartuhi, thoroughly frightened: "Yes, yes."

Stavros gives her the knife: "Here, take this. Sell it and bring me food!"

Vartuhi: "Dear . . . dear little thing! Why don't you go home to your family??"

Stavros, an earthquake: "Go on. Get out. Bring me some pieces of meat! Some bread, some meat!!"

Vartuhi: "Yes, yes. Listen, do you think you're strong enough to take a walk this afternoon? The sun is shining. Go sit by the water this afternoon. When you come back, I'll have a little money. And piece by piece I'll pay you everything. I promised my father, and I promise you, everything."

Stavros: "Never mind that! I don't need small money now. I need a suit of clothes. A blue suit of clothes."

Vartuhi: "Well . . . I do have a friend . . . you know . . . an old man who comes here. He makes suits for men and . . ."

5

A Green Orthodox church, Constantinople. The service is in progress. The men of the congregation stand in a body in the nave of the church. The women sit in a pew at the side. The service is sung. Stavros and Our Cousin enter, light candles, and stand among the other men. Stavros wears a blue suit and wing collar, and has not shaved his upper lip. He looks pale but very handsome.

Our Cousin, out of the side of his mouth: "Where did you get the beautiful suit??"

Stavros doesn't answer. There is something new, formidable about the boy! Ungiving! Our Cousin's attention goes to the Sinyosoglou family, a model of bourgeois prosperity. The five Sinyosoglou brothers are in their middle age and are all in business together. Here they are, on Sunday, standing in a line, their hands folded across their abdomens. Their women, sitting at the side, are indistinguishable one from another.

Our Cousin whispers to Stavros, points to the prosperous Sinyosoglou men. Stavros looks at the Sinyosoglou women, models of devout propriety. Then both he and Our Cousin look at a very plain young woman, with a long nose and a sallow face. Her name is Thomna. She is the heart of the matter. Stavros makes a sign of assent.

The men of the Sinyosoglou family have noticed Our Cousin's attention and also that of the young man with him. They nod. Our Cousin returns the nod. Then he nudges Stavros. Stavros now nods, proudly, even haughtily. Thomna Sinyosoglou gives Stavros one lightning glance. Then she drops her eyes demurely.

The living room of Aleko Sinyosoglou. Present are Aleko and his four brothers, and the guest of this occasion is Our Cousin. They are seated in a line. Each brother has the top button of his trousers unbuttoned and has so released his belly to protrude in comfort. Two women of an indefinite age are passing Turkish Delights, heavily dusted with sugar, and glasses of cool water on a tray to wash down the sweets.

A conference is in progress, which, despite its dulcet tone, is "strictly business."

Our Cousin: "He's the eldest son of the finest family in all that part of Anatolia. You must have heard of them: the Topouzoglous?"

Aleko, the father of the girl: "Yes, yes of course. Nevertheless, there remains this question. Is his father able to bring with the boy a substantial amount of money?"

Our Cousin, after a tiny pause: "You're talking about money?"

Aleko: "That's something we must talk about."

Our Cousin: "We have questions, too."

Aleko: "But you know our business."

Our Cousin: "Still you have four daughters. There is the necessary division."

Aleko: "For each there will be enough. Now—I don't remember your telling me what business the boy is in."

Our Cousin: "Well . . ."

Our Cousin's game is to stall till Thomna meets Stavros. His hope is that when this happens, the matter of dowry and bilateral endowment will seem less important than the happiness of the two individuals whose fates are being discussed.

At the front window, some boys, cousins, whatnot, have been waiting for the arrival of Stavros. And now . . .

Boys: "He's here! He's here!"

The door to the kitchen swings open, and the opening is filled with the anxious faces of the Sinyosoglou women. Among them, Thomna.

Outside of the Sinyosoglou home, a carriage is releasing an elegantly dressed young man. Stavros pays the driver off with a flourish. He carries a cane.

Two of the plump brothers are at the window now. They turn from the impressive spectacle of Stavros stepping out of his carriage and nod approbation at Aleko.

In the kitchen Thomna's mother, her aunts, and her three younger sisters are fussing over her.

Anoola, her mother, speaks with a slight impediment: "Your figure looks very nice when you stand up straight and give it a chance."

Thomna: "Oh, mother, you're never going to be able to make me pretty, so give up!"

Aunt: "Stop frowning . . . you're going to get a line there . . ."

Other Aunt: "You better get married soon or you will grow a moustache!"

The women all laugh.

Aleko's voice: "Thomna!"

The women are immediately silent. Thomna goes to the door.

Thomna: "Yes, father."

Aleko's voice: "Our guest will try your coffee." Then to Stavros: "How do you like it?"

Stavros' voice: "Without sugar."

Aleko's voice: "You hear!?"

Thomna, turning back, whispers: "He has a very strong voice."

The women all giggle.

In the living room, Stavros is eating a Turkish Delight with all the condescension of an affluent young man born to means.

Stavros: "Very nice, very nice."

Aleko: "And this is my brother Seraphim."

Stavros, very traditional: "I kiss your mother's hand."

Aleko: "And this is my brother Protermos."

Some of the girls are peeking from out the kitchen door. They go back in the kitchen to compare opinions. A buzz is heard.

Stavros: "I kiss your mother's eyes."

Aleko: "And this—" He stops and suddenly calls off in the direction of the kitchen: "Anoola! Keep those women quiet in there. We can't hear each other with all that mzzzmzzz!"

Several anxious female faces look out the door, make gestures of servility and compliance, and so withdraw.

Aleko: "Women! God made the mistake of giving them tongues!"

All laugh as the tradition demands. Meantime the men are appraising Stavros and comparing notes.

The coffee is ready in the kitchen. It is poured into cups and put on a tray, which is then given to Thomna to bring in and serve to the men.

A Sister: "He is handsome, Thomna, I took a good look at him and he is handsome. Oh Thomna!"

Aunt: "Has he money?"

Thomna: "I don't know."

Anoola: "Your father will find that out."

Thomna carries the tray into the living room. She walks slowly up to Stavros and serves him. The game is that neither lets it be seen that they are inspecting the other. He is, after all, talking about more important things with the men. She is ever demure.

Stavros: "Oh, my father? My father is in various lines, different businesses."

Stavros and Thomna, deeply aware of each other, show nothing.

Aleko: "Fine, fine, a great variety of enterprises is wise."

Stavros takes a coffee from the tray Thomna extends to him. "One goes down, the other comes up!"

Thomna takes a swift look at Stavros. From the kitchen one hears the polite laughter of the women. Stavros takes a swift look at Thomna. As she hurries off, Thomna gives her father a lightning glance ... assent! Meantime ...

Uncles, a murmur of bees: "Exactly! Exactly! How wise! Yes ... yes ..."

The women are waiting anxiously. Thomna enters the kitchen with the biggest news of the decade!

Thomna: "He has a moustache!!!"

And she begins to cry. The strain.

Anoola: "Thomna dear, dear Thomna, many men have moustaches."

Thomna, crying: "I like it, I like it!"

In the living room the men talk.

Stavros, innocently: "That was Thomna?"

Uncles: "Yes ... yes ..."

All look to see what impression she made on Stavros.

Stavros seems pleased, even pleasantly surprised. "Oh!—oh! ... Oh!!"

Aleko gives an almost imperceptible nod of approval to Our Cousin. The deal is on! Everybody knows it. A general murmur.

Aleko: "Perhaps on one of your father's business trips here we can have a coffee together and ..."

Aleko is suddenly minimizing the matter of money. Impulsively he throws his arm around the boy's shoulders.

Aleko: "At last I'm going to have a son!!"

General laughter.

Back home a letter full of good news has arrived.

Vasso: "Look! Look, her picture!"

All rush to see. A long look.

Isaac, the best he can do: "She must be a very good cook!"

Aunt: "They say that a long nose is a sign of virtue."

Old Uncle: "With a nose like that, virtue is inevitable."

Vasso: "They have money though. Listen to this." She reads: "They insisted I give up the work I was in and—' " She stops. Suspiciously, "Did he ever say *what* work he was in?? No!" She continues reading: " 'And so—what could I do? I accepted a position in their firm.' "

The Sinyosoglou Carpet Company is clearly a prosperous establishment. Like Our Cousin's, it is located in an arcade, a large one, a street roofed in glass. Soft, grimy daylight filters down to the various commercial enterprises. Standing in front of the store is Stavros, the model now of the prosperous young businessman, again wearing wing collar and frock coat.

In the back of the store the brothers and Our Cousin are in hot negotiation. Stavros cannot hear their words.

A beggar comes by, solicits a coin from Stavros. Stavros ignores him. As the beggar moves off, Stavros notices his shoes. They are the ones he gave to a beggar long ago on the road outside his village.

Stavros looks up. It is indeed Hohanness. He is on the verge of collapse, hungry, sick, exhausted. He leans against a store front for a moment. It is the window of the store next to the Sinyosoglou Carpet Company, and the porter in charge comes out and drives him off. Stavros catches up with Hohanness. Hohanness, thinking Stavros another enemy, cowers, covering his head. Stavros lifts Hohanness' head gently.

Stavros: "Don't you remember me??!!" He points to his feet. "Those are my shoes!!!"

Hohanness, hazily: "Oh! Yes . . . yes, I remember."

And then some emotion he can't understand takes hold of Stavros. He embraces Hohanness passionately, wildly, as if the boy were in fact the only friend he had in the world.

Stavros whispers hoarsely: "You made it to here . . . Allah!" He comes closer. In a fanatical, conspiratorial tone: "See! We're going to get there!"

Hohanness: "I don't know. I used to think so, but . . ."

He has a fit of coughing, through which he smiles apologetically.

Stavros: "Don't give up! Don't give up now! You're just hungry. Are you hungry?"

Hohanness smiles, gently, warily: "I'm always hungry."

Stavros: "Come."

He takes Hohanness' hand and leads him off. Within minutes they are in a restaurant.

Stavros: "Eat, eat! I have money. Another?" He shouts imperiously. "Waiter! Bring another of these. Immediately. And more bread!" Then he leans forward, whispers: "Put some bread inside your shirt. Here! Here! And another piece. Go on, you'll need it later. No one's looking." And now even more confidentially: "You have to look out for yourself in this world, you know. The only bad times I've had was when I was—well, soft! You can't afford to be. People take advantage. For instance, you! You smile all the time. People take it—forgive me for saying so—people take it as a sign of weakness. Now, suddenly, people respect me more. Even you do. Right? You respect me more. Don't you? Eh? Eh?"

In the back of the Sinyosoglou Brothers' store, the five brothers, Stavros, and Our Cousin are gathered.

Aleko: "So I have decided. My daughter shall come to you with five hundred Turkish pounds."

Stavros: "I do not accept."

There is a moment of bewilderment. The boy has spoken abruptly, absolutely, and even with some arrogance. Aleko, puzzled, tries hard to be patient, understanding.

Aleko: "Why, my son, why, what do you want?"

Stavros: "One hundred and ten pounds."

All burst out laughing. Except Our Cousin. But his protests are lost in the burst of amusement and surprise.

Aleko studies the boy. "There's something about you I don't understand." There is a little anxious moment of silence. "Have it your way. So—one hundred and ten it is. Satisfied?"

Stavros: "Yes, that is satisfactory."

Aleko: "Well, then, smile! Don't you ever smile?"

Stavros smiles. They all laugh. The meeting breaks up. Aleko goes to Stavros and walks off with him, arm around him. The others follow.

Aleko: "So when will it be? Two months?"

Stavros: "The sooner the better."

Aleko: "So, two months! Good! And one small thing—it is our understanding that you will live here with us. You will not take our daughter away from us."

Stavros answers without hesitation: "I will not take your daughter away."

It is several weeks later. In the Sinyosoglou apartment, Thomna can be seen coming through the door from the kitchen carrying a tray which holds six little cups of coffee. She goes to a coffee table and sets it down.

It is a Sunday afternoon, right after dinner. The five brothers and Stavros are sitting around the coffee table, stunned by the impact of the meal they've just devoured. The women, who by tradition eat much less, are in the kitchen doing the dishes and cleaning up.

Aleko releases a sort of sigh: "Ach ... ach ..."

Other Brothers: "Ach ... ach ... ach ..."

Aleko: "Too much. Too much!"

More sighs. Then, one by one, they undo the top buttons of their trousers, and thus ease out their bellies.

Aleko: "I tell those women don't put so much food on the table, but they don't listen."

Suddenly he seizes Thomna and takes her off into the farthest corner of the room to a large overstuffed armchair. Aleko falls into it and pulls his daughter down onto his lap. She puts her head on his shoulder. He embraces her lovingly.

Stavros' face is a mask.

Aleko: "So! One more week and I lose my daughter." Thomna buries her face in his shoulder. "Happy?"

Thomna: "Baba, I'm frightened!"

Aleko: "Naturally. But you like him?"

Thomna: "Oh, yes, yes—but he's so mysterious!"

Aleko: "Maybe he's frightened too. What does he say when you're alone?"

Thomna: "Nothing."

Aleko: "Nothing?"

Thomna: "And we're never alone."

Aleko: "Well, I give you permission. Just be careful."

Thomna: "There's nothing to be careful about. He sits there and looks into space, says yes, says no, says nothing. It's as if he has a secret."

Aleko: "He's never talked to you?"

Thomna: "Never. Yes, once. He showed me some pictures in a book."

Aleko: "Pictures?"

Thomna: "A city in America. Very tall buildings. And he told me about them, how tall they were and all that as if he'd been there."

Aleko: "Oh well . . ."

Thomna: "He said he once had a dream to go there. I didn't know what to say."

Aleko: "Oh, all boys have dreams. I had the same dreams once. To go to a new land, start again. But people think one way when they're penniless and another way when the money comes."

Thomna: "Oh, Baba, Baba, I wish he were more like . . . like . . ."

She kisses him, tears in her eyes.

Aleko: "Well no one's as good as your Baba!" They enjoy a good laugh together. "We'll make him forget all that other. I'll give him money and you give him babies. And your mother flesh to put on his bones. And, so, he'll grow up and be a man!!"

Thomna: "Oh, Baba, yes, Baba, yes. Oh—I feel better!"

Aleko pulls her closer and whispers: "I have a little surprise for you both this afternoon. You'll see!" He looks towards Stavros. "Look! Look at him. See!"

Stavros is unbuttoning the top of his trousers. Then he catches Thomna and Aleko looking at him and quickly rebuttons. Aleko and Thomna laugh. She again embraces her father happily.

Aleko: "Go on, go on! It's no shame. Let the stomach out. It's natural!!"

Stavros is embarrassed, shakes his head.

One of the Brothers: "He's shy."

They all laugh, their bellies shaking. Anoola comes out of the kitchen to see what's up.

Aleko: "Anoola!! no supper tonight! I shall not eat again till tomorrow!"

Anoola: "You'll feel different in a few hours."

One of the Brothers: "Maybe in an hour." All the brothers laugh.

Aleko: "I don't want to see food again today! That's final!"

Katie, the youngest sister, is showing Stavros a book of photographs. She is about thirteen.

Aleko: "Katie, what are you showing him?"

Katie: "Pictures of the island."

Aleko: "Yes, the island. We have a beautiful place there, my boy. This summer we'll go there. We have two donkeys. We'll pack them and go for a picnic."

Anoola: "He's talking about more food already."

Aleko: "By next summer I will have digested this meal. Yes, there are some beautiful places there for a picnic." Anoola says something. "What? Oh. Anoola doesn't like flying insects." Anoola makes a sound of disgust. "So we'll have the picnic on our porch. It's screened. Any king would be lucky to have it. And you and I will sit there, Stavros. Plenty of women to look after us. And we'll wait! The years will pass." Anoola says something. "What? Oh. I know it takes only nine months. Whatever it takes, we'll wait. Nine months, ten, so long as it's a boy. A son. Then another. Two sons first. After that, I don't care." Anoola again. "What? I know you can't order what you want. Who should know better?" Then to Stavros: "But give me two sons and I'll give you my business. Everything! I mean, my share. My brothers are there, of course. But there is plenty for everybody. Just give me two sons. Then watch the years pass. The winters here. The summers on the Island. Before you know it, Stavros, your eldest will come to you and say, 'Father! I have found a girl. I want to be married.' And you will say, 'How much has she got? What dowry will she bring?'" All laugh. "And you'll get heavier and Thomna will get bigger, certain places especially, like Anoola."

Anoola squawks. "All right, Anoola, I didn't say where. And watch the years pass! And you'll be old and I'll be old and we'll sit here together and drink and eat and undo the tops of our trousers and take a nap right here, side by side, a little nap and the women will 'mmzzmzzzmzzz' from the kitchen. Then we'll wake and play backgammon. And then all of a sudden it will be time for a little Ouzo and some olives and cheese and all my children and all your children will be here together." He sighs, "Ach, ach, aman!"

They all sigh: "Ach ... ach ... ach ..."

Aleko: "And only you and I will talk, Stavros, because I taught my women *respect!* And when you talk everyone will keep quiet. And when I talk even you will keep quiet. And when we die, we will die properly! Surrounded by women looking after us! How does that sound to you?"

Stavros' eyes are half closed, but they are moist. The goodness and the warmth of this family has affected him deeply. Thomna is watching him anxiously.

Stavros, softly: "It's all a man should want."

The girls come in, finished with the cleaning up. Aleko suddenly rises.

Aleko: "Come on, now, get up, everybody get up. I've got something to show you. Come, come, Stavros, everybody!"

There is a general babble. The sisters are singing softly. Others join in. The group follows Aleko out of the apartment.

Aleko leading, the group comes out of the Sinyosoglou apartment, some singing, some humming or laughing. It is family life at its most seductive.

As they follow, Thomna does something which is, for her, very bold. She puts her arm around Stavros' waist. Aleko leads the way up the stairs.

Stavros: "Who lives up here?"

Thomna doesn't know. She is singing but makes a sign to say it's all a pleasant mystery to her. At the landing above, Aleko takes a key out of his pocket and opens the door of an apartment. He throws the door open, then turns, full of his happy surprise.

Aleko: "Stavros! Here!" He turns and gives the boy a key. "Go on in, it's yours! Thomna! Go on!"

The gift apartment is entirely furnished and ready for immediate occupancy. In fact, it has the stuffy, overcomfortable look of an apartment that has been lived in for years by a home-loving couple with a habit of collecting things. Anoola and the girls have been working on it for weeks.

Everything that is happening makes it tougher for Stavros.

It is a complete surprise for Thomna also. Her eyes fill with tears, and she turns and rushes to embrace her father. At this there is a hubbub. Katie is crying, the uncles laughing and examining things. Anoola rushes to Stavros.

Anoola: "See this . . . this . . . it was my father's . . . when he died."

Stavros: "What?"

Aleko: "Everything here belonged to someone in the family who later died! I don't know what she's trying to say about it, but don't bother!"

Thomna: "Baba . . ."

She goes close to whisper.

Aleko: "Yes, my heart."

Thomna: "Oh Baba, thank you, but please, take everyone away now, please. I want to find out how *he* likes it."

From the door, Katie and Stavros are looking into the bedroom. Katie is making her first experiment with the opposite sex:

Katie: "Oh . . . this is the bedroom . . ."

Stavros: "Yes."

Katie blushes. From a distance, she hears her father's voice. At the door of the apartment. Aleko is gathering his family and ushering them out.

Aleko: "Katie! Come on now, stop bothering Stavros." Then he turns on the others: "Go on, go on, go on."

As she goes, Katie whispers to Aleko.

Katie: "He likes me."

She exits. Aleko throws an apprehensive look back at Thomna, then exits too. The door closes. Thomna crosses to the door and locks it. Then she goes to the bedroom.

Stavros is at the window of the bedroom. The sun is coming through. Thomna moves softly to her husband-to-be and looks at him. It is the first time they've been alone, the first time she has looked at him as directly as she has wanted to, her first chance to get close to him. Stavros has been very affected by the warmth and the generosity of the Sinyosoglous.

Thomna, softly: "Stavros."

Stavros: "You have a fine family. Your father is a king. A king."

Thomna: "But sometimes I think we are too many girls. May God forgive me, I have often wished my sisters were brothers."

She laughs nervously.

Stavros: "I like your family."

Thomna, daring: "Do you like me?"

Stavros: "Yes."

Thomna: "Would you tell me if you didn't?"

The question is so simple and direct, yet so probing, Stavros can't but tell the truth.

Stavros: "No ... I wouldn't."

Thomna, after a pause: "Well ..."

Stavros: "But I do like you."

Thomna, daring again: "In the way a husband should like a wife?"

Stavros: "Well ..."

Thomna: "I'm sorry. You don't have to say anything to that."

An awkward pause.

Stavros: "Shall we go?"

Thomna, quickly: "No, let's stay here. I've never talked to you without my family."

Stavros: "Oh, yes. We have."

Thomna: "If you say so. When?"

Stavros: "Several times."

Thomna: "Yes, of course."

A silence.

Thomna: "Stavros!"

Stavros: "Yes, Thomna?"

Thomna: "Is there something you want to say to me?"

Stavros: "No."

Thomna: "Please don't take offense at what I'm about to say. I've often felt that you have some worry, some secret that you're not ..."

Stavros: "No, no."

Thomna: "Not that I'll expect you to tell me everything. Or anything, if you don't want to. I want everything to be the way you want it to be. Do you hear?"

Stavros: "Yes, Thomna."

Thomna: "I wish I were prettier for you."

Stavros: "Don't worry about that."

Thomna: "But I'm a good girl. You'll see. I'm a good girl. You just tell me what you want me to do. I'll do whatever you tell me."

Stavros: "Yes, Thomna. Don't cry, Thomna, don't."

Suddenly a crack in the wall around his tension.

Stavros, sharply: "Don't cry. Thomna, stop crying!"

Thomna: "Stop ... Yes ... Yes ... I have."

Stavros: "What's the matter?"

Thomna: "I'm frightened."

Stavros: "Of what?"

Thomna: "Of your silence. Say something!"

Then she practically screams.

Thomna: "Say something! Say something! Say something, something, something!"

She recovers. Or seems to.

Thomna: "I'm sorry. I've felt nervous all morning. I had a dream last night. May I tell you?"

Stavros: "If you like."

Thomna, almost hysterical again: "Do you want to hear it or don't you? Do you want to hear it?"

Stavros: "Would you like a glass of water?"

Thomna: "No." She recovers somewhat. "Oh, I'm ashamed of myself. I'm ashamed ... silly, silly ... I'm acting like a ... young girl. And I'm three years older than you. They didn't tell you that."

Stavros: "It doesn't make any difference."

Thomna: "I dreamt that we had a child. He looked like you, fuzzy brown hair all over his head, and so soft everywhere, and the back of his neck straight and proud like yours. And the little thing was hungry. So I opened myself to feed it, and it came with its mouth to me—and there was no milk. I had no milk. It pulled at me and pulled at me ..."

Stavros: "Don't worry, you will have."

Thomna: "I don't know if I can tell you the rest."

Stavros, touched by her now: "Of course, go on."

Thomna, laughing nervously: "Turn your head away a little. ... It had teeth. And the teeth hurt. The baby child turned into you. I mean—it was you. And you pulled back and looked at me with such disappointment. And then you walked away and I never saw you again."

Stavros: "Oh."

Thomna: "Do you believe in dreams?"

Stavros: "Yes."

Thomna: "Are you going to do that?"

Stavors: "Yes."

Stavros absolutely didn't expect to say this. The question was put to him quickly and suddenly, and his answer popped out spontaneously. At that instant, he was full of feeling for Thomna.

She is speechless. Then ...

Thomna: "Stavros? Stavros? What did you say? Stavros?"

It's a question she's frightened to ask, but must.

Only now does he realize what he has revealed. He is stunned by the sudden confrontation of what he is and what he has done.

Thomna: "Stavros ..."

Stavros: "This—I did this—because—" He can't go on. "Count yourself lucky. You won't see me again."

Thomna: "Stavros ..."

Stavros: "One hundred and ten Turkish pounds is the fare to the United States of America."

Thomna: "America? America?"

Stavros: "By the first boat."

Thomna: "I don't understand." Then she begins to. "Oh .. America?"

Stavros: "Yes."

Thomna: "And you—?"

Stavros: "Yes."

Thomna: "Oh." She can't speak for a moment. Then, "I still don't understand. You wanted it so much that . . .?"

Stavros: "You have to be a person like I am to understand."

Thomna: "What will you do now?"

Stavros: "I don't know. I don't care. Something."

She goes towards him.

Thomna, gently: "If you want to take our money and . . . go . . . to the United States of America . . ."

Stavros: "No."

Thomna: "I'm yours. What I have is yours."

He can hardly believe his ears.

Stavros: "How can you be like that?"

Thomna: "I have no reason to live except you." She looks at him lovingly—nakedly. "I wish I were prettier for you."

Stavros: "How can anybody be like that?"

At last he thinks of her.

Stavros: "Thomna, don't trust me. For your happiness, don't trust me."

Thomna: "You're all I have."

Stavros bows his head: "Don't trust me!"

Now Thomna, for the first time, goes to him spontaneously.

Thomna: "But Stavros, my soul, it will pass. Baba said so! It will pass like a sickness. When we once have children you won't feel the same, you can't, how could you??" She notices some reaction, goes on: "What? What?" There is no answer, "Stavros, it will pass, I know. I'll count on it."

Stavros: "Don't count on it."

A pause. There is something terrifying about the boy's silence. Abruptly, now, he gets up and starts for the door. Thomna cries out: "Where are you going?"

He stops and waits, but without making connection.

Thomna: "A year. Wait a year. Then if you . . ."

Pause. No answer. He is completely back in his shell.

Thomna: "Well, it's for you to decide. I'll not say anything to my father. I'll wait."

He exits. She sits there, alone, in their apartment.

6

The next day, in the Sinyosoglou Carpet Company, an event is taking place. Mr. Aratoon Kebabian, one of the big buyers from America, has come to Constantinople to make his season's buy. A business like that of the Sinyosoglou Brothers is built upon the favor of a handful of big buyers, mostly from America. Everything is done to win their favor.

Stavros and some porters are carrying a folded Sarouk carpet. Stavros is tense and silent. A porter scolds him.

Aleko: "Come, come, come, hurry, hurry." He turns to Mr. Aratoon Kebabian, selling hard: "I saved these thirty pieces of Sarouk nine by twelves just for *you!* Ask the boys! Boys! "

Porters mutter: "Yes, sir."

Aleko: "In the back of the store! Like eggs under a hen!"

He grabs a corner of the rug that Stavros and the porters are unfolding and drags it over to Aratoon Kebabian, where he is seated, a king in a straw hat. At his side has been placed a small table which holds sweets and a nargileh, a water pipe, from which he takes an occasional puff. He is a man of seventy-two but looks a little younger—except in the morning when he looks considerably older. He carries amber beads which keep running through his fingers. He dresses as if he were going to his seat in the enclosure at Belmont Race Track.

Aleko: "You know rugs better than I. You know you've never seen anything like these pieces! Here! Butter! Feel, feel!"

Suddenly Aleko changes his course. Taking the Sarouk by the corner he drags it with the aid of Stavros and the porters to Mrs. Kebabian.

Aleko: "Mrs. Kebabian, I beg you, put your hand on this Sarouk."

Aratoon: "She doesn't know anything about the rug business except how to live off it."

Aleko: "Only for her pleasure. Feel it!" He turns, sharply, to Stavros.

"Stavros, will you for God's sake wake up and bring the rug here! What's the matter with you today?"

Sophia: "Please don't inconvenience yourself. I don't like rugs."

Since she is not interested in rugs, Aleko brings her Stavros.

Aleko: "Mrs. Kebabian, may I present the future king. One day all this will be his. Stavros Topouzoglou, my future son-in-law. Come Stavros, kiss Mrs. Kebabian's hand."

Sophia Kebabian is a woman of forty-four, dark, slender, elegant, worldly, remote. She has the high coloring of the secret drinker. She notices that Stavros is all charged up.

Sophia: "You don't have to kiss my hand, boy."

Aleko: "Oh, of course, of course, in America they don't do that. Show him how they do in America, Mrs. Kebabian. Believe me when I tell you that this boy's *dream* is America!"

Sophia: "Mr. Sinyosoglou, don't sell me, sell my husband."

Stavros likes her. Her mood fits his. Aleko laughs uncomfortably. He is not used to women "talking back."

Sophia continues to Aleko: "He is going to buy. He's only first torturing you a little."

A tray of drinks is passed. Aratoon anxiously watches his wife to see if she takes one.

Sophia: "Oh, no, no, no, thank you."

Aleko: "Show him how they do in America. Go on!"

Sophia: "Well . . ."

She extends her hand. Stavros takes it tentatively.

Sophia: "No, not that way. Take hold of it. Good! Now shake it. Like this!"

Stavros: "You do this? In America? I mean men to women?"

Sophia: "Of course."

Aleko, glad she likes the boy: "His whole dream—to go to America. Imagine!"

Sophia: "Well—people have done it."

Aleko: "But not a boy like this. Men!"

Stavros almost turns on him. Sophia marks this. Then Aleko notices something behind him, turns and runs to Aratoon, who is preparing to leave.

Aleko: "Aratoon! Where are you going?"

Aratoon: "Time to eat. My stomach is my clock."

Stavros, quietly to Sophia: "You are American?"

He has never seen an independent, sophisticated woman before. He studies her, fascinated with her manner, her stance, her clothes, her perfume. She *is* America to him.

Sophia: "Yes. I was born here, but Mr. Kebabian brought me to America twenty-five years ago when we married and I . . ."

She raises her veil. She looks at him. He looks at her.

Aratoon: "Sophia, are you coming?"

Sophia: "No, I'm not."

Aleko: "Oh, you must. They're waiting for us at Abdullah's. I spoke to the chef myself. You should have seen his face when I said Mr. and Mrs. Aratoon Kebabian." He turns to Aratoon. "Everything you ever ate and remarked on there is ready. She must come!" Then to Mrs. Kebabian: "You got thinner."

Aratoon: "She doesn't eat. I married a *woman*. *Now* look!"

Sophia: "I don't enjoy eating when I'm not hungry."

Stavros smiles at her—a fellow rebel.

Aratoon: "You see how she talks back! They ruined her. The day she became an American citizen—ruined!" To his wife. "The Declaration of Independence was politics! Only! Not for women!!" Then to Aleko: "Come. No hope for her!" To his wife: "I'm leaving the carriage."

He starts out.

Sophia has been shopping and has many packages.

Stavros: "May I help you carry them to your hotel?"

Sophia: "Why, yes, yes, why thank you."

Sophia and Stavros enter the Kebabian suite in the Pera Palace Hotel. She is exhilarated by the prospect of some kind of adventure, playing the part of a gay, sophisticated woman of the world. They are met by a German maid.

Sophia: "Bertha, get Mr. . . . ?"

Stavros: "Topouzoglou."

Sophia: "Some lunch."

Stavros: "No, don't trouble."

Sophia: "Bertha!"

Stavros: "No, too much trouble."

Sophia: "No trouble."

Stavros: "I don't enjoy eating when I'm not hungry."

Sophia: "Well, all Greeks are taught to refuse twice. I won't believe you till you've refused three times. What can I get you? You were so kind."

Stavros: "Nothing. Well . . . Nothing."

But he makes no move to go. A hesitation. He smiles nervously. Bertha is fussing with a wardrobe trunk in the background.

Stavros: "That is a whole bureau? A whole bureau! And it travels with you? May I . . . ?"

Sophia: "Yes. Bertha, show him."

Stavros goes to examine the wardrobe trunk.

Stavros: "America, America!"

Sophia smiles. The boy kneels before it.

Sophia: "And down there, you see, for shoes."

Stavros: "Do you have any magazines from there? Pictures? Newspapers?"

Sophia: "Yes. Would you like to look at them?"

Stavros smiles, nods.

Stavros: "Can I?"

It is much later. Sophia is in the bedroom, lying down, drinking. Bertha comes in.

Sophia, in a whisper: "Bertha."

Bertha: "Yes, Mrs. Kebabian."

Sophia: "Is he still here?"

Bertha: "Yes, Mrs. Kebabian."

Sophia gets up and crosses to the door between the bedroom and the parlor. She opens it very cautiously. Stavros is sitting on the floor still going over the magazines. Now he sees one of Aratoon's straw hats. He goes on tiptoe, puts it on. He looks at himself in a mirror and winks.

The boy affects Sophia. How? She doesn't know yet. But he awakens something in her long given up for dead. She drinks, then crosses to the mirror of her dressing table, sits, and looks at herself. If a look could speak, we would hear, "I am still a very handsome woman for my age." She drinks.

Stavros is back on the floor, looking at magazines, when behind him the door of the suite opens and in comes Aratoon Kebabian.

Aratoon, as he crosses into the bedroom: "You still here?"

The boy doesn't know what to say. But Aratoon has not waited for an answer, is already in the bedroom.

For some reason Stavros feels guilty. And a little frightened. He listens apprehensively.

Aratoon: "He's still here."

Sophia, lightly: "Oh yes, he's having dinner with us. He's going to show us some dancing."

Stavros looks up. Sophia comes to the door of the bedroom.

Sophia: "You know some place where we can see some dancing? You do, don't you?"

Stavros: "But of course."

He smiles. Now he knows she likes him.

Later, in a night club, some of the male patrons are taking turns dancing in front of the line of musicians. At a ringside table, Sophia is drinking. Aratoon is eating as if he hadn't had lunch. The music comes to a pause.

Sophia, to Stavros: "I'd like to see you dance."

Stavros smiles. Then without a word, he walks towards the dance floor. He throws some money onto the musicians' platform. As they play, he begins to dance alone.

Sophia watches him. Aratoon finishes his food, looks at his hands which are covered with olive oil and meat fat, and decides to go to the washroom.

Stavros dances up to the table where Sophia is now alone. As he dances before, her, in little rhythmic breaks, he makes slight hissing sounds, directed at her, seductive, insistent. Her cheeks burn. She covers them with her hands. Tears come to her eyes. She drinks.

Later, a lone musician improvises on the bouzouki. Aratoon has fallen fast asleep at the table. Stavros and Sophia, seated on either side of Aratoon, talk across him. Sophia is drunk now, but gently, soulfully. There is an element of bitter humor in what she says.

Sophia: "I was eighteen when my father said, 'Marry him!' " She indicates the sleeping Aratoon. "I'd never been permitted to see that wonder, a man, alone. Not till him." Again she nods a little sardonically at her sleeping husband. "The day after the wedding—*tack!* He took me to America. And before I knew how, I had two sons. And after that— what? He had what he wanted. And there I was—an old woman or so with two sons and a husband with a good business, who played cards every night. I've never known a young man. I never lived my twentieth year. Or my twenty-first. And my twenty-second year is still inside me, waiting like a live baby to be born, waiting inside me, you know? How could you know?"

She can't go on for weeping. Stavros looks at her with compassion. She looks at him—a longing, dependent look. He leans across the table, takes her hand, turns it open. Then he buries his mouth in the palm. He gets up, starts moving away, then puts his hand on her shoulder close to her neck.

Sophia is on fire for the first time in her life. Her eyes close. Her whole body trembles in a deep convulsion. She tries to pull her hand free, can't. Then she gives in to the paroxysm for a moment. Now she's out on the other side, weak, remote. She gently pulls her hand free.

Sophia now looks at Stavros—resentfully? She's never been in anyone's power before. And never expected to be. She turns to Aratoon. Some of the long strands of hair which he uses to cover his bald top have slipped. She replaces them gently. The bouzouki! She looks at Aratoon with a gentleness and a kindliness she's never felt before. She's free of him. She smiles, then turns to Stavros—now with him, therefore direct, even brusque.

Sophia: "Let's take him home."

In the office of the North German Lloyd Line, a ticket is being stamped with a quick forceful stroke of mechanical validator. The official at the desk hands the ticket to a clerk, who gives him some money. Then the clerk takes the ticket and, crossing to the counter, hands it to Stavros.

In his hand at last, a ticket to America! Suddenly some pellets of paper hit him on the head. He hears laughter behind him.

Crouched against the wall behind him are eight boys, all in a row, all sitting upon their haunches, all about the same age and in the same condition of poverty and hope. They're grinning like little apes.

Stavros' anger these days is close to the surface. He spins around. Then he sees that one of the boys is Hohanness, who gives a little wave. Stavros goes to him.

Stavros: "You! You're going!—Eh?" Hohanness nods. "Didn't I tell you, don't give up?? Tell me, come tell me what happened?"

Hohanness: "That man—he's taking us all."

A portly man, Mr. Demos Agnostis, is at the ticket counter buying steerage passage for the eight boys.

Stavros is unexpectedly agitated: "You're all going?"

Hohanness: "He has a place to shine shoes in New York City, and—"

Hohanness has a fit of coughing, can't continue.

One of the Boys: "He pays our passage. *The Kaiser Wilhelm.*"

Stavros: "And what? What do you—?"

The Boy: "We work for him. Two years without pay."

Stavros: "Oh?"

Some painful struggle can be seen on Stavros' face. Envy? Regret? Why did his heart sink?

Stavros: "Tell me ... would he take another?"

Hohanness: "No, he'll only take eight. I came by the store once to tell you about it. I saw you get into a carriage with some rich men." He makes a graphic gesture in the neighborhood of his abdomen. "Plenty to eat! Plenty to eat! So I thought ..."

Suddenly Stavros' mask of self-sufficiency is up again.

Stavros: "Well, of course! Two years without pay! That is slavery! What do you think I am? Allah!"

Hohanness: "For me, it's all right. Well, anyway, I see you're going."

Stavros: "Yes, don't worry about me. The same boat too! On the same boat!"

Hohanness: "How did you get the money? Well, of course—you have rich friends!"

Stavros, tough: "Yes. I have rich friends."

The room where Stavros lives is extremely bare. Some burlap thrown in a corner serves as a bed. There is no other furniture. He is crouching on the floor against the wall. He doesn't move from this defensive position. In front of him are two objects: a bundle of clothes, wrapped and tied in a throw rug, and, alongside, his hamal's harness.

Thomna: "But your soul, your everlasting soul!"

Stavros: "Rot my soul!"

Thomna: "Stavros, it's wrong. It's a sin!"

Stavros: "That right and wrong business is for the rich. You can afford it. I can't."

Thomna: "Stavros, you come from a good family!"

Stavros: "Yes! All now waiting for one piece of good news, at last—one piece of good news."

Thomna: "But your father? What will—"

Stavros: "I don't want to be my father. I don't want to be your father. I don't want that good family life. That good family life!" He is raving. "All those good people, they stay here and live in this shame! The churchgoers who give to the poor, live in this shame. The respectable ones, the polite ones, the good manners! But *I am going!* No matter how! No matter, no matter, no matter how!!"

He stops finally, recovers, speaks gently, firmly.

Stavros: "I wrote you to come here, because I wanted to speak to you the truth before I left. The truth of what I am, so you don't go on thinking about me."

She doesn't answer, looks at the objects on the floor.

Thomna: "What's this?" She indicates his hamal's harness. "Oh. You're taking this with you?"

Stavros: "Of course. You can't count on anybody or anything. With this, in America, I can always make to eat."

He fusses with the harness affectionately.

Thomna speaks gently now. She has given up: "Christ arisen protect you!"

Stavros: "I know that I'll never again find anyone like you."

Thomna, weeping: "Stavros, my heart, my soul, my very own soul, what will hapeen to you?"

And now for the first time in months and months Stavros softens; he too speaks gently, wistfully.

Stavros: "I believe . . . I believe that . . . that in America . . . I believe I will be washed clean."

7

The prow of *The Kaiser Wilhelm* heads into a heavy sea. A massive wave breaks over the bow and flings itself on the foredeck.

Steerage. At the very point of the prow, looking ahead for land that will not appear for days, stand Stavros and Hohanness.

Bertha emerges from a companionway, followed by a sailor. They have traveled this route before. The sailor spots Stavros and approaches him. The ship is tossing. The steerage passengers huddle behind the deck machinery in little wet clusters.

The sailor has the working man's scorn for anything less than "honest" manual labor. He walks up to Stavros and stands in front of him, grinning.

Sailor: "Madam wants her bonbon."

Stavros, by now an expert at masking his true feelings, gives no recognition to this challenge. But the boy is beginning to feel the humiliation of his position. Hohanness doesn't understand quite what's happening, but he does see his friend's intense humiliation.

Stavros: "What are you looking at me that way for?"

Hohanness, softly: "Do you have to go?"

Stavros, tough: "I *want* to go." Then relenting, "I'll bring you some candy again."

Stavros feels criticized by the whole world. He assumes a defiant nonchalance as he starts off in the direction of Bertha. It's the only way he has found to live through his present circumstance.

The procession—Bertha, Stavros, and the sailor—arrives at the doors to the Kebabian suite. Bertha knocks softly on the first door. An answering signal. She turns to Stavros, speaks practically.

Bertha: "Madam prefers when you smile."

She opens the door deftly, admits Stavros, then proceeds to the next door, Aratoon Kebabian's bedroom, and enters. She closes the door swiftly and tiptoes to the bed. Aratoon is snoring heavily but quietly, an old man. Bertha sits in a chair by his bed, picks up some needlework, and begins to embroider.

The next day the sea is calm. The prow parts the waters. At the bow Hohanness is looking at Stavros. The "tougher" Stavros gets, the more understanding Hohanness becomes. He feels the other boy's shame through his mask, loves him for it.

Stavros, defiantly: "Stop looking at me that soft way all the time."

Hohanness turns away, embarrassed. Then he begins to cough. Each time he can't control his cough he looks around anxiously at Mr. Agnostis, nearby on the desk.

Stavros: "How long have you had it?"

Hohanness: "My cough? It's the first thing I remember."

He leans forward and whispers, touching his chest, smiling gently.

Hohanness: "I know what I have."

Stavros: "Quiet yourself." He tries to divert him. "They say tomorrow we see land."

Hohanness: "But before it eats me, if I can ... Did I tell you?"

Stavros: "Another time ... shshshsh ..."

Hohanness: "At home every morning I go for water. And it's a walk. You know water is heavy! Well, now—I'm the only child—my mother goes. So every morning I think of her making that walk. So before this eats me," he touches his chest, "I pray ... to earn enough to put a well down for her."

He is getting excited and begins to cough, looking around to see if Mr. Agnostis is within earshot. A sharp whistle is heard.

Through the companionway comes the sailor for Stavros. Stavros goes a few steps toward the waiting sailor, then suddenly turns and comes back to Hohanness, speaks, for once, free of his mask of defiance.

Stavros: "At home I have three sisters and four brothers."

Hohanness doesn't get the point: "Oh ... oh ...? Then ..."

Stavros: "One by one, I'm going to bring them over. You'll see. You'll see."

Hohanness: "Well, naturally ... that's the important thing. That's the only important thing ... naturally."

Stavros in his most cocky manner now turns and goes toward the sailor.

By now Hohanness loves Stavros.

Hohanness speaks to himself: "What's more important? Naturally!"

Screaming sea gulls fly around the mast of *The Kaiser Wilhelm*. In the distance, coming out of a mist, the shore of Long Island. Hohanness, at the prow, turns, calls.

Hohanness: "Stavros! Stavros!!"

But Stavros is not there.

The steerage passengers come to take their first look. Heads appear in the portholes. These people are very poor and from every country served by the Mediterranean. They are still in their native clothes, their possessions bundled and always at their sides. Italians. Romanians. Albanians. Russians. Serbs. Croats. Syrians, Bearded Orthodox Jews. Fanatics. Men alone. An occasional child with a tag around his neck.

In his cabin, Aratoon Kebabian awakes. Bertha is at his side, working on her embroidery.

Aratoon: "What's the disturbance?"

Bertha: "Long Island."

Aratoon, dismissing it: "Oh, well. How long did I sleep?"

Bertha: "A couple of hours."

They hear a low commotion from Sophia's room. Stavros, despite objection from Sophia, is preparing to rush up on deck.

Bertha, quickly: "I'll tell Mrs. Kebabian you're awake."

She goes to the door between the two staterooms and enters Sophia's room as deftly as she can. Aratoon listens.

Bertha: "Mr. Kebabian is awake."

Whispering, footsteps, the door to the outer corridor opening, and closing. Aratoon enjoys an immense yawn. Bertha re-enters.

Bertha: "She'll be in as soon as she's pretty."

Aratoon: "I have a long wait." Now he fixes Bertha with his eye. "Bertha! Bertha! Now come, Bertha!"

Bertha, facing him: "Mr. Kebabian I try hard. I try hard to be for her and to be for you. You know how she is. You know—how she is."

Aratoon: "I also know who pays your salary. Do you?"

Bertha: "Yes sir."

Aratoon: "Well then, let me hear. Order me some tea, some English tea, and then let me hear."

On the front deck, Stavros runs up to Hohanness. The other boys and Mr. Agnostis are also there.

Hohanness: "Stavros! Look, look! Mr. Agnostis says that is the city of Coney Island."

Stavros: "Those curves! What are they?"

Hohanness, authoritatively: "The Americans build roads through the air."

Stavros and Hohanness look at the promised land. Then Hohanness begins to cough painfully. He is instantly apprehensive that Mr. Agnostis will notice. He throws his whole face into the hollow of Stavros' shoulder and smothers the cough. Stavros is slightly embarrassed at the embrace.

He makes a face. He tries to quiet Hohanness by diverting him as one would a child.

Stavros: "Here. Here, Hohanness, stop it. Look, here. I brought you some candy again. Here."

Hohanness, with difficulty: "One thing ... that lady ... friend of yours ... has the most wonderful candy!"

He takes a piece.

Elsewhere on the deck, a number of the older passengers, including family groups, some women holding babies, are singing a Ukrainian song, full of longing.

Hohanness has recovered. He and Stavros drink in the shore line.

Night falls, and Hohanness and Stavros are just where they were. But the deck behind them is almost deserted. The two boys are singing a song for each other. It comes to its end.

Hohanness: "We'll always be friends."

Stavros: "Life's not like that. It's all meetings and partings."

Hohanness: "My father liked this one. Every Sunday, 'Hohanness! Come! Sing!' "

He starts to sing the song which Vartan and Stavros sang at the beginning of this story, on the mountain side. Stavros joins in, and as he sings, he takes off Vartan's fez, which he's worn all through, looks at it, and then drops it into the water of the bay.

Stavros: "First thing tomorrow, I'll get one of those straw hats the Americans wear. Tomorrow!"

Aratoon has wrung the story from Bertha, and the time has come. In his bedroom, still in bed, he is cutting Stavros down.

Aratoon: "So tomorrow, since you are without protector or guaranteed employment, the authorities will ship you back, back where you came from. And now may I give you some advice? Go fall on your knees before Aleko Sinyosoglou. Shed a tear or two, however false, kiss his hand, and so on. He'll take you back. His daughter is so ugly he has no choice. Well?" Stavros is silent. "And from this unpleasantness, learn a lesson—when you force a woman to choose, she will choose money. Well?"

Stavros: "She's a good person."

Aratoon: "She's in the next room now, her ear to the door, hearing every word. Why is she silent? Well?" Stavros is silent. "What are you going to do now? Eh? You know I've never seen a face like yours except in a cage. I have a feeling there's nothing you'd stop at. Is there? Anything? Have you any honor?"

Stavros: "My honor is safe inside me."

A sadism emerges in the old man.

Aratoon: "What? What? Safe inside you?? Boy, whatever you ever once were, you are now a whore! A boy whore! For sale! You understand? Stop that humming! I've seen hundreds like you. Boys who leave home to find a clean life and just get dirtier and dirtier. Will you stop that humming! And tell me: Have you looked in the mirror recently? Truthfully, do you suppose if your father saw you at this moment he'd recognize his son? Would he know who you are?"

Choked cries of pain escape the boy's tight mouth, but so wretched, they afford no relief. The door of the bedroom is flung open and Sophia rushes in. Bertha stands in the doorway.

Sophia: "Stop it! Stop it!"

Aratoon: "Go back in your room immediately."

In the corridor outside, two stewards and a sailor have been placed on guard.

Sophia: "Stop doing that to him. Stop doing that! He did more for me in two weeks than you did in your whole life!"

Stavros leads Sophia back to the door.

Stavros: "Sophia, go on. Go on now."

Sophia: "He's not going to do that to you."

Stavros: "It's all right. I'm this far. Thank you for bringing me this far."

He closes the door and faces Aratoon. In a way he is relieved that it's over, even though once again he has to find a new way for himself.

Stavros: "Mr. Kebabian."

Aratoon: "Ah! He's going to speak."

Stavros: "Yes sir." There is a pause. "I have nothing to say."

Aratoon: "What can you say? The truth is the truth. You know what you are."

Stavros: "Yes sir. Except ... Mr. Kebabian, I've been beaten, robbed, shot, left for dead. I've eaten what was thrown to the dogs and driven the dogs off to get at it. I became a hamal and—"

Aratoon: "NOOOOWWW! Now you understand yourself—a hamal!"

Stavros: "Yes sir. But now, I'm here. I've seen the shore and their city in the distance. Do you imagine anyone will be able to keep me out?"

Aratoon: "I'll see to it."

Stavros: "I'll find a way, I'll find a—" He stops, realizes what the old man has said. "What did you say? What?"

Aratoon reaches for the bell to summon the steward.

Aratoon: "I said I'll see to it. *I'll see to it that they send you back.*"

Stavros leaps on top of the old man, one hand covering his mouth, the other at his throat before he can ring the bell. Bertha enters from the other room.

Stavros: "Swear! Swear you won't say or do anything, anything!"

Bertha has crossed to the corridor door and flung it open.

Bertha: "Help! Help! Help!"

The stewards and the sailor rush in. Stavros is pulled off Aratoon. Blows, curses, commotion. And all through, Bertha screaming: "Swine! Swine!"

Aratoon: "He attacked me! He tried to kill me! Intent to kill, intent to kill! He's a criminal!"

The two stewards and the sailor drag Stavros through the cabin door. Aratoon follows.

Aratoon: "This is America, hamal! Do you hear? This is America! What will you do now, hamal? What will you do now? Eh, eh, hamal?"

In a sudden last desperate explosion, the boy turns on his tormentors, punching, scratching, biting, kicking. And this time they beat him into final submission and drag him off, limp and silent.

The ship's doctor is a small, worn German, wearing a soiled white jacket. He is soaking a cloth in antiseptic. Now he carries it to where Stavros is lying on a cot in the Ship's Hospital, third class. Hohanness is there. Stavros winces as the doctor applies the cloth.

The Doctor: "A man shouldn't be hit on the head. It's not as hard as it feels. Let him sleep."

Hohanness: "I'll stay with him."

In the middle of the night, Stavros has his first nightmare. Hohanness is on the floor beside him.

Stavros, whispering: "Hohanness!! Hohanness!!"

Hohanness: "Yes, yes, I'm here."

Stavros: "Is my father still here?"

Hohanness: "Your what? What? Oh, no, no."

Stavros: "Isn't that—? Who's that?"

Hohanness: "The doctor."

Stavros: "Is he listening? Can he hear us?"

Hohanness: "He's asleep. Don't worry."

Stavros, conspiratorial: "My father said: 'That's enough. I'm ashamed of you. I'm ashamed of what you've made of yourself. Come back, you must start again!'" He bursts out laughing. "It hurts when I laugh. But can you imagine? Making this journey all over again? Allah!!"

Hohanness: "Shshsh. That was a dream. Go to sleep."

Stavros: "Allah! Hohanness, can you imagine?" Again he laughs, again it hurts. "Hohanness, stay with me."

Hohanness: "I'll be here when you wake."

Stavros is almost asleep now. His face darkens, he looks troubled.

Stavros: "You know the truth? The thing I'd like most in the world *is* to start this journey over. That's the truth! Just to start it over, all over again ... oh ... oh ..."

Hohanness is very moved. Suddenly he has a terrible fit of coughing. His eyes swing around to the doctor, who is awakened by Hohanness' cough.

Doctor: "How is he?"

Hohanness, frightened: "He's imagining things."

Doctor: "Well, no wonder! He was hit on the head once too often. You better watch over him. Stay close to him."

Hohanness: "I will."

Doctor: "He's liable to do something crazy. Goodnight. That's a bad cough you've got yourself. Better not let the Americans hear that tomorrow. They'll send you back."

On the front deck the next day, one sees very little for the fog. *The Kaiser Wilhelm* is moving slowly forward. The usual harbor noises. Out of the fog, as if coming toward the ship, is the Statue of Liberty. As they see it, the passengers stand. There is a sound—is it imagined?—of a general sigh.

A large motor launch is coming alongside. Officials of the United States Health Service prepare to board ship.

Stavros wears a bandage. There is about him the manic desperation of the suicide-to-be.

One of the shoeshine boys has been sent to fetch Hohanness. He calls him, waves, calls again ...

Hohanness starts off. Stavros pulls him back and, in whispers, gives him his final instructions.

Stavros: "It's the excitement that brings on your cough. So, close your ears. Imagine you've just put down your well. And your mother and father come to you in gratitude. Can you imagine that scene?"

Hohanness: "Oh, yes, yes!"

Stavros: "I'll wait for you just down the corridor. The instant the inspection is over, run to me."

He indicates to Hohanness he can go, pushes him off, but the boy comes back.

Hohanness: "But you, what are you going to do?"

Stavros: "I have my own plans."

Hohanness comes close, whispers.

Hohanness: "What?"

Stavros makes a subtle proud little gesture which says, "Over the side and swim for it."

Hohanness: "Can you swim that far?"

Stavros turns his face away: "They say a man learns what is necessary to save his life."

Hohanness: "Stavros, if you can't swim, you can't swim."

Stavros: "You better go. Go on, go on."

Hohanness: "And if you go down?"

Stavros: "Better than going back." He pushes him off. "Go on! They're waiting."

Hohanness seizes Stavros' hand and kisses it.

Hohanness: "I'll pay you back, some day. I'll pay you back . . ."

Stavros, tough: "Let's speak the truth. We'll never see each other after tomorrow. You'll forget me. And I? I'll be where I am."

The shoeshine boys are all gathered in their little cabin, sitting on the edge of their bunks. Mr. Agnostis and the Public Health official are in the middle of the floor.

Mr. Agnostis: "Same as last year. Eight fine boys."

Hohanness is following Stavros' instructions. One side of his head is pressed hard into the pillow. A hand covers the other ear. He is imagining the scene at the well and his parents' gratitude.

Mr. Agnostis: "All from fine families. Perfect health. Employment guaranteed. Nothing to worry. Everything under control!"

At the end of the corridor, Stavros waits.

Hohanness' eyes shine with his imaginings.

Health Official: "OK, OK."

He comes out of the shoeshine boys' cabin and heads in the direction of Stavros, behind him the first buzz of celebration.

Stavros waits for the official to pass him. Behind him sounds of the boys celebrating are heard. Then suddenly we hear, dominating all other sounds, Hohanness' terrible cough. Stavros hears this, and suddenly he has an impulse to stop and delay the official so that he too will hear the cough. Then, just as the official gets real close, Stavros turns and faces the side wall of the corridor. He has controlled his impulse to betray his friend. He now flattens his face against the wall. The health official passes by Stavros, entering the doorway behind.

Stavros, face to wall, still shakes from the excitement of what he almost did. Hohanness, wildly elated, runs out ot the cabin and comes towards Stavros, hysterical with delight and relief.

Hohanness: "Stavros! Stavros!"

Then he begins to cough, this time beyond control. At the moment he gets to Stavros, his cough overwhelms him. He falls into the arms of his friend, in total collapse.

The door into which the health official disappeared was that of the Ship's Hospital, third class. Now attracted by the terrible coughing, the health official comes to the doorway. Behind him appears the Ship's Doctor. There is no longer any doubt as to what Hohanness' fate will be.

Stavros holds Hohanness. He looks at the official.

In the shoeshine boys' cabin, a conference is going on. All are present. Mr. Agnostis is talking to Stavros.

Mr. Agnostis: "I tell you *I* take you. But read! Here! U.S. Government paper. Where is your name here? Where? You want me in jail?"

Silence. They all sit in silence.

Hohanness: "Take my name. I beg you. Take Hohanness Gardashian."

Mr. Agnostis: "There can't be two of you!! There can't be two Hohanness Gardashians. Give up. Go back together. Keep each other company."

That night celebrations break out all over the ship. Disembarkation is at seven the next morning. It is the last night for the shipboard friendships.

At the prow, Stavros and Hohanness huddle together, their arms around each other's shoulders.

Hohanness: "When?"

Stavros: "As soon as everyone's asleep."

Hohanness: "I won't let you ..."

Stavros turns and smiles at Hohanness, a smile superior and determined, half scorn, half affection, unswayable.

A swirl of First Class passengers rush to the prow of the ship. The women are in long light-colored dresses.

A Girl: "Oh, Third Class is so romantic!"

Man: "They've got the best part of the ship."

Hohanness: "I mean it. If you go, I go too ... And I can't swim. I'll hold on to you. I'll call out. I won't let you go. I won't!" He pleads with his friend. "Stavros, please, please don't be crazy. Don't be."

He is weeping.

The celebrants have brought musicians with them, who now strike up. The First Class begins to waltz.

Stavros is full of envy, anger, and revenge. He leaps up and into the middle of the dancers, doing weird, manic leaps and turns.

Man: "Say, look out there. Look out!"

Stavros leaps and kicks out into the air like an insane man. Savage, uncontrollable cries escape his mouth. All the pain that's been stored up in him for months and months!

Hohanness watches Stavros with absolute love. Now Stavros begins to whirl like the dervishes of Konya, around and around, head tilted on one side, his eyes shining with a fanatical light. Hohanness, never taking his eyes off Stavros, rises slowly. Stavros dances wilder and wilder. More and more desperate! Hohanness turns abruptly and looks over the rail. A sudden impulse. He sees the black water of the bay. Each time this boy has said, "Before it eats me!" he has gently touched his chest with the palm of his right hand. Now he makes this gesture for the last time.

Stavros has won the admiration of the celebrants. They cheer.

Unseen, Hohanness goes over the rail and lets himself drop into the black waters of the bay.

The First Class passengers applaud and cheer Stavros. The moment they do this, he stops. He doesn't want anything from them, not even their admiration. He looks them over with fantastic hostility. Then spits out his "Allah!" and struts off.

Terror overcomes Hohanness in the water. He begins to cough. He goes down, comes up, coughing, his strength ebbing fast. He goes down.

The celebrants follow Stavros, begging him to dance some more, the girls beguiling, flirting with this wild boy, not letting him go.

In the black waters of the bay there is no longer any sign of Hohanness.

Stavros pushes off the celebrants, walks up to where he left Hohanness. He looks around for him, calls softly: "Hohanness, Hohanness!" Softly, gently, "Hohanness."

The First Class is disembarking. A band plays a gay exit march. The Third Class watches. Their turn will come later.

The eight shoeshine boys, now with Stavros instead of Hohanness, are looking up at the passengers of the First Class leaving the ship. Sophia and Aratoon disembark from the gangplank. Neither looks back. Stavros expected no goodbye. A tap on his shoulder.

It is Bertha, in a hurry. She extends a paper bag and an envelope.

Bertha: "Here! From Mrs. Kebabian."

She turns and goes. Stavros takes out of the paper sack a man's straw hat. He looks at it, smiles, puts it on. Under his breath he says, "Allah!" Then he opens the envelope. It contains a piece of paper money. Nothing else. Mr. Agnostis and the boys gather around.

Mr. Agnostis: "Ooohhh! Fifty dollars! OOOOHHHH!!!!"

In the immigration shed on Ellis Island, three long lines of people lead to three desks. At one of the desks, the eight shoeshine boys, led by Mr. Agnostis, come up for their turn. Stavros is wearing his straw hat.

Mr. Agnostis has papers in hand and now presents them to the Immigration official at this desk. The official has seen Agnostis before.

Official: "Oh, look who's here! And eight more little ones! They keep coming, they keep coming! How are all your little slaves?"

Mr. Agnostis' laugh is a nervous one. The boys stare anxiously.

Official: "Scared to death." He turns to the official at the next desk. "Jack! Who was that fellow—a Greek—we're watching for? Criminal assault was it?"

Stavros watches intently. Mr. Agnostis bends over, pretending to tie his shoelace. He has palmed a ten dollar bill and is preparing to slide it towards the shoe of the official, who raises it ever so slightly off the floor. Meantime . . .

Jack: "On the yellow sheet—that's it."

Stavros is watching the ten dollar bill and the foot of the official.

Stavros: "Allah!"

It's not much of a sound. It's rather a kind of growl. But it does voice protest. His dream is being shattered.

The official looks at Stavros. Then he smiles in a peculiarly combative manner. He picks up the yellow sheet.

Official, mispronouncing it of course: "Stavros Topouzoglou. Any of you go by that name?"

Mr. Agnostis: "That fellow died last night."

Official: "You? What's your name?"

He is looking at Stavros again.

Mr. Agnostis: "Hohanness."

Official: "Not you, *you!* He talks doesn't he? What's your name?"

Stavros now has the idea: "Hohanness Gardashian."

Official: "You want to be an American?"

Mr. Agnostis: "Oh yes, sir. Yes, sir."

Official: "Well, the first thing to do is change that name? You want an American name, boy?"

Mr. Agnostis is indicating to Stavros to agree, but Stavros doesn't quite understand.

Stavros, vehemently: "Hohanness Gardashian."

Official: "I know, I know."

Stavros, almost a shout: "Hohanness!"

Official, quickly: "That's enough! Hohanness. That's all you need here."

He writes something on a piece of paper and hands it to Stavros.

Official: "Here! Can you read?"

Stavros, of course, cannot. Mr. Agnostis comes up and reads: "Joe Arness." Then he gets it. "Hohanness. Joe Arness. Hohanness." He turns to Stavros. "Joe Arness. Joe."

Stavros, repeating: "Joe."

Mr. Agnostis: "Arness."

Stavros: "Arness."

Mr. Agnostis, points to him: "Joe Arness."

Stavros, nodding acknowledgment: "Joe Arness."

Mr. Agnostis, to official: "Good!"

Stavros, to official: "Joe Arness."

Official, full of the pride of authorship: "You like it?"

Stavros nods, makes signs, etc.: "Joe Arness, Joe Arness, good, good!"

Official: "Well boy, you're reborn. You're baptized again. And without benefit of clergy. Next!"

Mr. Agnostis and the eight boys leave for the ferryboat to Manhattan. The Ellis Island immigration shed is empty now except for the three officials. They are looking at one object: Stavros' hamal's harness.

Second Official: "What the hell is that?"

Official: "Oh, something one of them left behind."

On the ferry.

Stavros: "So . . . it's the same here! He took money!"

Mr. Agnostis: "People take money everywhere. But did you see him jump when you spoke? Did you see him jump?"

Stavros: "Yes. Allah!"

Mr. Agnostis laughs. And now Stavros joins in, the first full, simple, free laugh heard from the boy since he left home. Now the others join in, all laughing.

Down the last gangplank come the eight boys and Mr. Agnostis. Stavros first. He falls on his knees and kisses the ground! Then he lifts up and releases a tremendous shout of joy.

8

The first thing we're aware of is an echo, many times magnified, of the shout that Stavros released on American soil. The Topouzoglou family, in Anatolia, is gathered around Isaac. The family has shouted as one. Then the sense of caution that is always with them.

Isaac: "Shshshh! Shshshsh!"

He looks around to see who's within earshot.

Isaac: "Shshsh." Then, almost a whisper, he says: "And here is fifty dollars."

Vasso whispers: "How much is that? Fifty dollars?"

Isaac: "In Turkish money that is ... that is ..." He gives up trying to compute. "How did he ever earn so much, so quickly?" Then he answers the question. "America, America!"

Vasso: "Read it again—the last part."

Isaac: " 'In some ways it's not different here—' "

Vasso: "Shsh, not so loud!"

Isaac, looking around: "There's no one."

Vasso: "You never can tell. Go on."

Isaac starts to read again in a cautious tone: " 'It's not different ...' " He puts the letter down. "How quickly he's forgotten what it is here!" He reads again: " 'But let me tell you one thing. You have a new chance here! For everyone that is able to get here, there is a fresh start. So get ready. You're all coming. I'm working for that. To bring you all here, one by one.' "

Eight boys shine shoes in the Agnostis Shoeshine Parlor in New York, as customers wait. Stavros expertly snaps his polish cloth, a signal for his customer to step down. Stavros is wearing his straw hat. As the customer steps down, Stavros subtly intrudes himself, so that the customer can't avoid tipping.

Customer: "Here you are, Joe."

Stavros grabs the dime, throws in into the air, bounces it off the back of his hand, catches it, squeezes it, pockets it. Then he sings out.

Stavros: "Next! Come on you, let's go you! People waiting!"

In Anatolia, the entire family is leaning over the top of the wall in front of their home. They are all looking up the road, all looking in the same direction.

Suddenly, at full gallop down the road in front of the Topouzoglou home, a squadron of Turkish cavalry raises a heavy dust. For a moment, nothing can be heard except the thunder made by the horses.

The family is all there: Isaac, Vasso, the four sons, the three daughters, even the aunts and the old uncle. They watch as the cavalry rides by and is gone. And then there passes between the members of the family the most subtle and intimate smile. For they share a secret and they share a hope that no one else in this world has. And they all hear in their imaginings, nearer and nearer, louder, Stavros' voice: "Come on you! Let's go you! People waiting! People waiting!"

We see their waiting faces.

And then, at a distance, Aergius, the huge still mountain with its peak of eternal snow.

The end

FROM *The Arrangement,* CHAPTER *4*

FLORENCE had fallen into a fine sleep, but I lay there as if I'd been hit on the head. I was at the top of a psychic slalom, beginning to go down, but with no way of anticipating how fast and how irreversible the descent would become. I didn't yet know that there are no markers—and only very short distances—between what is called normal behavior and what is labeled mental illness. I've since come to believe that both these labels are useless. There are only human beings in various developing conditions, all continuations of what has been there all along unnoticed.

That night with Florence was my first experience with the true dilemma of "both." I'm not talking about an arrangement, the technique of keeping one woman in place while you temporarily carry on with another. What struck me as I lay and listened to Florence's even breathing was that both acts, the one with Gwen on my way to work that morning and the one with Florence, while coming hard upon each other, seemed perfectly natural and oddly equal. That shocked me. Not the fact that I had had sexual relations with two women on the same day—I had often done that and never felt a qualm. But I had made a genuinely loving connection with two different women, one right after the other, and I was not prepared by my training and tradition to believe that possible.

I couldn't lie there any longer with Florence's head on my shoulder and her leg over mine. Ever so gently I began to extricate myself. I didn't want more talk with Florence right then, so I was very careful not to wake her. She murmured a few times as I disentangled myself. Then she was again safely asleep, and I was out in the hall.

I wanted to go down and brew myself some coffee, but I heard Bartok. That meant that Ellen and her boy friend Roger were down there with the lights off. So I couldn't go down. I wonder how far they went. Bartok was coming to one of his half-assed climaxes. I wondered if they were, too. No. Florence had assured me just a couple of weeks ago that Ellen was intact.

Anyway, they were doing something, because I couldn't hear their voices. I sat on the steps. I didn't want to go back in the bedroom, and I couldn't go downstairs, so I sat there.

The human cock, I reflected, is the most honest part of man. I guess the human cunt is the same, though I'm considerably less sure of that. The cock I know more about. The great thing about it, the thing that makes it so completely moral, is that it doesn't pretend to any morality.

For instance, I thought, the cock would never use the words "ought to." And never the word "should." Right there, what a load to lose! All the Bird knows is "I want." Or, to be more exact, "*Now* I want." None of that forever-and-ever shit. Which has brought more people to early decay than any other sentiment. As well as to destructive acts against their fellow men and women. Most evil is done in the name of good.

I WANT!

Come to think of it, that phrase, "I want," expressed precisely the humanness I had lost. I simply didn't know what I wanted any more. I couldn't make a choice; I was swamped in unresolved boths. I was not doing anything for the simple reason that I wanted to. The simple, pure, direct, human, downright babyish "I want"—where had that gone?

Long lost. I sat there on the top of those steps and thought, long gone. I'd lost the knack. I'd killed the gift. I didn't know what I wanted any more. I felt only that I *must* do this and *should* do that, and I was *expected* to do such and such, and it was my *duty* to perform this-a-way and my *obligation* to see this thing through, and it was demanded of me to *fulfill*—always—what other people wanted of me. I didn't even know whether I wanted Gwen any more. I hadn't called her up, thought I should, had no expectation I would, thought it might be too late if I did, hoped it would, was anxious that it should not be, and so on.

The worst of it was a whole other set of imperatives that I had allowed myself to become subject to. These were the Expedients. Again not what I wanted, but what was useful at a certain time in any situation. "Expedient." The word written on the tomb of our generation. They did what was expedient.

Especially me.

But just plain, raw, meat-handed I WANT? What had happened to that? Long gone!

Those shoulds. They kill you, those shoulds.

Well, to go back to Peter. One-eye Dick is free of shoulds. And oughts. And all the troubles deriving therefrom. The Erect One has one eye on top of his head; he sights what he wants, takes aim, and charges straight for it. In the spirit of the great Teddy Roosevelt, he calls for all forces to get behind him and charge the hill. And the body, recognizing Tumescent Teddy's pure want, gets behind him and charges with all it's got.

Here's another thing I respect about the Joint. You can't quite make him get up and pretend. If he doesn't want to, you can beat him and scold him, but he won't go. El Conquistador will lie there and sulk. A soft-on is a reproach to its owner. It says, you're lying, kid. Later, when the false occasion has passed into history, the Member will sit up and look around, then stand up pretty as a tulip and say, like the comedian, "Wha' Hoppen??"

Not that the Root has to want a *lot*. But it has to genuinely want some. On the one hand he doesn't need, nor does he fall for, that no-one-but-you shit. His point of view on that subject might be expressed thus: Quote. You neurotic son of a bitch, why must you pretend or require that all desire be perfect, complete, and forever? Or the greatest? The girls made up that "forever" shit and that "greatest" shit and that "only-you" shit over the centuries to protect their fading years. You can't blame the girls for that. Their fading is fast. But why do you pretend? Close quote..

Now they say a stiff prick has no conscience. But let's face it. It's the honest part of us all, men. And the most democratic. It doesn't differentiate between rich and poor, and it draws no color line. Our brothers in our southern states profess to draw the color line everywhere. But Big Peter never went along with that color-line, and there are millions of witnesses to that.

Old One-eye, like all pure things, tends to be naïve. And wherever you find something pure and naïve, you also find someone trying to corrupt it. So the Mindless One is often the unconscious tool (and victim) of the corrupt mind and spirit of the person to whom he is attached. Men try to use their better part in so many different ways they shouldn't. To put girls down, to put other men down, to show off, to bully, to compete, to make up for defeats in other arenas, to revenge themselves, to collect scalps, and one of the worst, to satisfy idle curiosity. God knows there are hundreds of variations of perversion. Like the very ethical, very famous public figure I know who could do it to his wife only when she was asleep. We take out so many of our sicknesses through our Little Friend. But you can't finally corrupt the Shiny-Headed One. He will come back, see something he wants, and just naturally go for it. What could finally be more innocent?

With Florence that night, Peckerstiff was more honest, more gallant, more kind, and more human than I was prepared to be. He felt for Florence, responded to her clear and urgent need. And where my mind was all messed up with conflicts and blocks, the Bird found his nest, didn't pretend he was going to stay there forever, but entered, dispensed his grace, and left to rest. Love and kindness are the finest mixture.

CHAPTER 8

I STAYED in my little fortress most of that afternoon. When it came up five o'clock, I had no choice. I had to go back into the big house. I found Florence drying her hair. Her party clothes were laid out, so I gathered she was going with me. Just to make sure, I asked, "What am I supposed to wear tonight?"

"Call Olga Bennett," she said, then, "Oh, balls, Evans! Stop acting like a baby. When I wear a short dress, you wear a blue suit. And since we've been called together to celebrate your recovery, why don't you make some effort to be on time?"

We didn't exactly chat our way over to the Bennetts. But Florence did make one request. "Considering the way you behaved during your convalescence, I think Olga and Dale fantastically generous to throw you any kind of party. But Dale considers you one of his close friends. If you've got a defender left in this community, it's him. I know that doesn't mean anything to you now. But Olga *is* my best friend. So I wish you wouldn't be insulting tonight. Do you think you might manage that? As a parting favor to me?"

"A parting favor?"

"Well, we're separated, aren't we? Let's get at least that much settled."

I didn't answer.

"Silence? O.K. Let's see how you like the game when it goes the other way."

End of conversation.

What a strange phrase that is, I was thinking—"close friend." I had known Dale Bennett for seventeen years, played tennis on his court countless Sundays, had dinner with him and his wife Olga at regular intervals. But were we really close friends?

We met right after the war, when Williams and MacElroy first opened a west coast office. I would have sworn then that I was in advertising only temporarily. I was very busy looking around for what might turn out to be my real career. For a couple of years I became interested in films, thought of becoming a screen writer. It looked easy—especially when you met the men who did it for a living.

It wasn't. During those two years, I sold exactly one original story. It was called *The Red Arrow,* and it came out of some of my war experiences in the Philippines. Dale Bennett, then a recent Academy Award winner, was assigned to make it into a screen play with me, which, everyone told me, was a great break, because it gave me a chance to learn my trade from the then number-one man in the field. I must have had a premonition though, because I held on to my advertising job and moonlit the script. Dale preferred working at night anyway.

He was some five years older, and immediately took a fatherly interest. I, in turn, paid him all deference, kneeled and knuckled. From the time I was a kid, I'd found that the best way with anyone I felt I had to please. Dale and I always agreed. I saw to that. When I didn't agree, I swallowed it. That was our working arrangement.

Five months of work and Dale's best efforts succeeded only in revealing the basic weaknesses of *The Red Arrow*. Finally Dale felt he had to recommend that the studio shelve the property. He observed, in his funeral oration, that I had a lot to learn about story construction. He did not encourage me to continue in the field. I said, as we cleaned out our desks in the Writers' Building, that my basic story had never been really sound. I could see that now, I lied. All of which left the failure mine, and made Dale feel warmly towards me. So our relationship began, a social habit like dogs running together. Actually I didn't agree with him on politics, prejudices, taste, what a nice day was. He even found Gwen unattractive when I introduced her to him.

As Dale got older, fashions in screen writing passed him by. In fact he had had trouble, the last few years, getting decent assignments. But very recently this had changed in his favor and for a very odd reason. The party he was throwing that night had little to do with celebrating my recovery. What Dale really wanted to celebrate publicly was a killing he had made in the stock market with a company organized to manufacture birth control pills. He had got in with a buy of ten thousand shares at, I think, two. A week ago when he had decided to throw the Welcome-Back-Eddie party, the stock was at seventy-six and going up, which gave him a paper profit of almost three quarters of a million dollars. The odd part of it was that, whereas everyone had come to think of Dale as an old-fashioned hack, when the news of his killing got around, Dale was once again, as he had been fifteen years before, one of the most sought after screen writers in the industry.

I was thinking, so I missed the Bennetts' turn-off. Florence called this to my attention with a minimum of sarcasm.

"What's the film tonight?" I asked.

"You don't have to make conversation," she said. "We're almost there."

"I'm not making conversation," I lied. "I'm curious."

"I doubt that. But if I knew, I couldn't tell you. It's a surprise, for you, Olga said."

End of conversation.

Nearly all Hollywood parties climax with the showing of a film, usually one that hasn't yet hit the theatres. The film saves the evening as the conversation crumbles. As soon as I walked into the Bennett home, the surprise was revealed. The film we were to see was *A Cry From the Steeple,* a *cause celèbre* before its release. Its director was the soft mountain of man I could see on the sofa, pontificating to the people around him.

Dale rushed up and greeted me ardently. "We've been waiting a long time for this, you and I." He took me over and introduced me to Gottfried Hoff. Dale and I had talked about Gottfried Hoff for over a decade, but I had never really met him. Close to, now, he reminded me of the beached hulk of a great ocean liner.

Dale and I had first become aware of Hoff a year or so after we quit on my story; Dale had taken me to a literary party, and there he was, drunk and sounding off that all Americans are cultural savages, which sounds twice as mean when said with a German accent. That night he was surrounded by lefty intellectuals, amen choristers to everything he said. I'd come back, not too long before, from the Pacific, where I'd seen a lot of fellows die in a war that one of his countrymen had started, so I resented him immediately. Dale, who had been in London in 1941, wanted to kill Hoff on the spot. He vowed we'd get him.

A mutual enemy is strong cement. More than anything else, our unfriendly interest in Hoff kept our relationship close over the years. When we drifted apart, I'd forget about Hoff until Dale would call up with a fresh bit of gossip about him. Dale never forgot him.

We started off by finding out all about Hoff's past. He had made some fine pictures in the Germany of the twenties and early thirties. Then, comfortably anticipating Hitler's take-over (that's how Dale described it), Hoff got himself to southern California. There he enjoyed the war years. (I was slogging from Hollandia to Biak to Tacloban to Luzon. Dale was ducking the V's, one and two.) Hoff made some films, but spent most of his energy going to parties and accepting tribute. His chief exercise was bowing from the waist. He also had the pick of the crop of sunkist girls. (I had the Asiatic crud, Dale the Piccadilly clap.) Hoff soon established himself as king of the satyrs. For many years it was considered statusy among the local ladies to have been had by Gottfried Hoff. His arrogance was his lure. At regular intervals over the years, Dale used to call me and tell me with absolute astonishment the details of Hoff's latest conquest. More often than not it was a very "nice" girl, a very prized girl. Hoff, it seemed, never missed. His unfailing success further sharpened our appetite for revenge.

Hoff, of course, had not gone back to Germany as had other artistic *émigrés.* "The son of a bitch's got it too good here," Dale once said to me. "A house on Pacific Palisades, a nisei couple, a wife who's a perfect servant, the kind you can't find any more, and all the tail he can handle. That kraut bastard won the war for a fact."

Now at Olga's party he was riding the obsession of his life, the injustices committed in this country against his talent, his work, his self. Clearly he had extremely high blood pressure. His face was doused with perspiration and very red. His wife, who wore what can only be described as a small black tent, sat next to him and mopped his forehead with a man's handkerchief. She did not speak, smile, or frown. Hoff was her total field of vision.

Dale leaned over the back of the sofa and took the empty out of Hoff's hand, replacing it with a full. He either didn't notice or chose to ignore a request from Mrs. Hoff's eyes that he not give her husband a fresh drink. Hoff was talking about the outrageous treatment he had received during the production of *A Cry From The Steeple*.

Anyone who read the columns knew all about that film. The story was what is known in the trade as an inspirational subject with (in Dale's words) "this Jesus-type leading man, Mexican but clean." Dale's brother wrote for *The Hollywood Reporter,* so Dale was able to give me, in regular installments, the goodies of Hoff's squabbles with his producer. The first time Hoff had shown his version of the completed film to his producer, he had brought to the projection room, as his guest, his pet monkey, explaining that he wanted to see what the animal's instinctive reaction to the film would be. Since the producer was notorious for bringing his wife to the first public showing of each of his films, notorious, too, for following her "instinct," he called it, he naturally resented Hoff's swipe. (Even Dale had to admire Hoff for this one.) Well, after the film had been run off, the producer took Hoff and his monkey aside and officially informed the maître that he was not at all satisfied with the way the film had been put together. Which was not only what Hoff expected, said Dale, but what he obviously wanted: another international scandal of culture, another chance to publicly scorn the U.S.A.

Hoff called a press conference the next day. Every representative of the foreign press was there and delighted. They would trumpet again how Hollywood was ruining the work of this unique genius. Hoff concluded the conference by saying that under the circumstances, he had no hope for the film and would never see it again.

How Dale had managed to make Hoff change his mind was Dale's secret. But there he was now, about to see his mutilated film for the first time.

"How did you ever manage it?" I whispered to Dale. (We were standing right behind the sofa where Hoff was holding court.)

"I did it for you," Dale answered in a normal voice. I remembered that Hoff was partly deaf. "All for you."

Actually Dale's interest was his own. You might think, now that he was rich and in demand again, he'd have everything he wanted, but not so. He desperately wanted the recognition of the "in" crowd. Of course he would not admit this, especially to himself. But he had read what *Cahiers du Cinema* and *Sight and Sound* said about his films. He knew there wasn't a chance that he'd ever get favorable recognition from them. So the next best thing was something he could get—revenge. Hoff was one of the chief darlings of the "in" crowd, and *A Cry From the Steeple* was, by all gossip, a disaster.

Dinner was announced. Mrs. Hoff began the labor of getting her husband to his feet.

"I've put you right next to him at dinner," said Dale. "Keep his glass full. When he sees what that producer has done with his film, he'll blow. I want the blast-off to be worthy of the preparation."

Then he took Hoff by one arm, and holding me by the other, walked us into the dining area.

I immediately noticed how many of the guests were in on the deal. As the meal progressed, they pretended sympathetic interest in Hoff's stories, the while making snide remarks just below his hearing. It became a game to see how close you could come to being detected. As for Mrs. Hoff, they behaved as if she wasn't there.

Florence had caught on to what was going on, and I could see she didn't like it one bit. But her polite efforts to change the subject, or put a pleasant cast over it all, simply didn't work. The guests would not be pulled off their fun.

I was sitting right next to the target, and I caught it all: the salivating of the sadists, what they said that he heard, what they said that he missed. Predators around a wounded animal. To my surprise I began to feel for the man, I suppose because he was the underdog. He was so conceited, so self-centered, he was absolutely unaware he was being set up for slaughter. And this, what was in effect his naïveté, also began to enlist me. In some totally unexpected way, he was innocent.

Dale was looking at Hoff's empty glass, then at me. I pretended not to see. Dale finally had to say, "Eddie, Mr. Hoff's glass is not full." As I obeyed, I felt ashamed and resentful. Mrs. Hoff was giving me the same pleading look she had given Dale earlier. But it was too late. I was filling the glass.

And my own. From that moment, I matched Hoff drink for drink.

I remembered the stories I had heard of Hoff's great drunks, how he would hole up in a hotel suite for a week with a case of booze, Mrs. Hoff sleeping across the threshold of the locked bedroom door so her husband could not get out without her knowing it. In this way he would manage what was apparently necessary for him periodically: to disappear from the face of the earth. Looking at him now, with his uneven complexion, his gross fleshiness, his baggy black suit, those fabled drunks struck me in a different light. They were the actions not of a proud but a shamed man. What made Hoff sweat was not arrogance as much as violent self-disgust, an emotion I now knew well. He was gulping his food like an animal who had stolen a carcass and had to defend it till he had it all down.

When I didn't finish my venison, he asked me if he could. And he quickly did, perspiring all the time.

I suddenly had an impulse to wipe his perspiring forehead. Mrs. Hoff had been placed at the opposite end of the table from her husband, so he was without an attendant. I took out my pocket handkerchief and mopped the massive moist dome. Hoff acknowledged my service with a side-flung look that contained no thanks. He merely accepted the attention of a newly acquired slave. He was hard to take, Mr. Hoff.

I poured us both another.

Then, somewhere betwen the Brie and the baked Alaska, it happened. The bating of the man had become bolder and bolder, and suddenly I had had as much as I was going to take. "Oh, knock it off," I said.

The table conversation went on for an instant before people realized I had done something extraordinary. Then the whole room was silent. And I said again, this time directly at Dale, "What do you say, Dale, let's knock it off, kid."

Dale looked at me quite a while. "What was that, dear boy?" He'd called me "dear boy" for fifteen years, and I suppose I had always thought it patronizing, but I'd never said anything about it.

"What I said, Dale, was let's cut it out."

"Cut what out, dear boy?"

"You know damned well what," I said.

"No, I really don't. Be more specific, if you're able to be. Also think very carefully before you go on with this."

"I've been thinking about it for quite a while, and I'm asking you, since I'm the guest of honor and this pigsticking is being staged to entertain me, I'm asking you to turn the victim loose."

"I don't quite get what . . ."

"You get it. I want you to stop fattening this Berliner pig for the slaughter. You know damned well what you're doing."

"And what's that?"

"There's a word for it."

"And what's that word?"

"You know the word."

"No, I don't. I'd like you to say it."

"Well, it smells of sadism to me."

"Oh, it does?"

"That's right."

"And you don't like it."

"I don't like it one bit."

By now I regretted ever having started. After all, I didn't have the flimsiest friendship for Hoff. But once I started, I couldn't cop out. And why the hell should I? The hell with Dale, I thought, it's the truth. What's all this close friend routine anyway? I was now pretty drunk and said to myself, "You have no right to blame Dale. You had no business pretending to be his friend all those years. You're as responsible for all this as he is."

Dale Bennett turned to Hoff and, indicating me, said, "Gottfried, do you feel like a pig being prepared for slaughter?" At which the whole room laughed.

For the moment the tension was eased. Hoff, the rat, said, "My dear friend." (He was speaking to me.) "Don't be a child. What are you talking?" I thought the "dear friend" extravagant, and since he had often said publicly that all American men were children, I didn't particularly care for that designation.

So I said to myself, the hell with you, too, brother, and I determined to shut up and be a "nothing" the rest of the night, and maybe go home early.

Florence was the first to leave the table, followed by my agent, Mike Weiner, who had been sitting next to her.

I caught Bennett measuring me. I guess he was trying to figure where to gaff me first. As we got up from the table, he tossed off, "Speaking of sadism, dear boy, what have you been doing to Florence lately?"

"Why?" I said, real nothing.

"Because she looks terrible. I must tell you we like her a hell of a lot better than we do you, and, dear boy, now that you have officially recovered from your accident, I think you might give her an occasional thought."

We got separated in the crush going downstairs. The guests were being herded into the rumpus room, a big cellar fixed up Wild-West-saloon style, with a long bar at one end, and the entrance to the Ol' Crick —that is, the swimming pool—at the other. There were a lot of toys for adults in the room, including a stand of one-armed bandits, some old-fashioned flip-card movies featuring naked women of a bygone age, a row of pinball machines with all the little signs rewritten cleverly for local allusion, and a dart game with the head of Castro for a target. Painted on the barroom floor were the faces of the hosts' dearest friends. I was featured, an enormous Zephyr cigarette in my grip.

Some of the men immedaitely sat down at the barroom table and began the inevitable gin game. Among them was Hoff, who could hardly see by now. Even sober, he was a notorious pigeon.

Bennett followed me. When I sat down, he sat down next to me. "Now is the time," I said to myself, "for that famous silence of yours."

"Dear boy," said Bennett, "I can't help wondering why you're so worried about Hoff."

I noticed people moving closer. Quarrels, after all, are still our best entertainment. Dale began speaking partly for the benefit of his growing audience. "After all, he's nothing but a cultural Commie, with the psychology and manners of a storm trooper. He's been in this country since 1940, made a fortune by pissing all over us in his films; we've discussed all this a hundred times in perfect agreement, Eddie."

I held my mouth closed.

Dale was smiling. "What do you say?" Everybody was waiting for me to say something. Dale continued, "You gave me reason to believe you'd be absolutely delighted to see him finally getting his lumps."

I smiled my nothing smile, whistled my nothing tune.

"So what happened, Eddie?"

By now my silence was choking me to death. I'd gotten a taste, during my convalescence, of blurting everything out. I hadn't forgotten how good it felt.

At that moment, there was a wave of new entrances, the after-dinner crowd. Dale had to go greet them.

It's interesting who smells a fight coming first. Now gathered around me, waiting for Dale's return, was a la-de-da clothes designer, a man who had done a lot of Florence's clothes; you wouldn't think him blood-thirsty, but he was, ravenous. With him was his dykish wife, who doubled as his business manager, and she had that ringside look, too. There was one of the really big agents in town, a leader in the agents' take-over of the film business, a man with one of the greatest collections of French impressionists in the world, but personally a hood. With him was his wife. Also with him was his girl friend. There was the disappointed and abandoned second wife of a very well-known producer. And there was the disappointed and abandoned third wife of the same producer. They were given to attending wrestling matches in each other's company, al-ways in the front row, side by side. There was the aging ingénue star who still managed to play bobby soxers but was threatened with premature baldness, as anyone could see when she stood with a light behind her. At her side, as always, was her husband, the scion of the Willingham hotel empire, which his father, at his death, had left in perfect working order, so perfect that all the scion had to do all day was sit by the pool of his country club and make sure no Jews got in. Next to her was the queen, Emily Adams, the leading lady critic in town. She wore a heavy gold cross on her well-braced bosom. With her was her husband, a cretin. All these people had smelled a fight and moved in from nowhere like a circle of hyenas. Joining them were some of the kids, the latest squab come to town on the Greyhounds, and the wolves who had scouted them out and were presently showing and giving them the works. They just wanted excitement.

"I wish I felt free," said Emily Adams, "to tell you the names of some of the gals this man has hurt and hurt badly. If you knew some of the inside I know, you wouldn't permit yourself to be quite so sympathetic."

I was just about to say something to this bitch that would have busted up the evening and good, but I stopped myself in time, got to my feet, and from habit went looking for Florence.

She was sitting with a man I had never seen before. Florence was doing all the talking, her new admirer paying devout attention. I could see the route she was going.

Since Florence was occupied, I sat down next to our hostess and said, "Olga, hold my hand, will you? Your husband wants to pick a fight with me, and I really don't want to."

"Then go tell him you're sorry." "For what?"

"Eddie, what's the matter with you? Have you lost your mind? You called Dale a sadist in front of the whole dinner table, and in his own house. Do you expect people to take that? Since your accident, you've gotten away with insulting everyone who came to see you, including many of Florence's best friends, saying any malicious and irresponsible thing that came into your head. We all made allowances because we were loyal to Florence. But Eddie, the accident is over. That's really why we threw this party, to draw a line. Anything you say from now on you have to mean. Put up or shut up. Because Florence forgives you everything doesn't mean the rest of us have to. If you and Dale weren't the oldest and best of friends, he'd have had you out in the back yard by now. I wouldn't respect Dale if, the next time you make one of your cracks, he didn't bop you, but good. I'm sick of *that* you. So is everyone else here. I'm sick of hearing you knock this town and knock these good people. You're in God's clover here, and if you think it's poison ivy, don't bitch about it; move!"

She started to walk away mad, then came back. "Eddie, Dale's the best friend you've got in this community. You better find your senses again." She took my hand and began to pull me over to where Dale was. I was going to apologize, too.

Apparently it hadn't required a pistol in her ribs to persuade Emily to go into the details of Hoff's sex life. Olga tried to get Dale's eye to make him aware that I had something to say to him.

"Oh, Emily," he was saying, "dear Emily, you're so refined. I'm sure that's why your column is such a success. But we're among friends tonight, so let's speak plainly. Mr. Hoff's taste is distinctly for the rounded heel, for the simple reason that's all he can now get. His latest, I understand, was something sorry named Gwen, I believe Hunter, and she had an opening the size of the subway entrance at Forty-second Street and Broadway. And quite as many people had used it. And the price, if I may stretch the parallel a bit further, was just a token. Olga, did you speak to me? And who's that with you?"

Olga was not so sure, now, that she wanted to bring us together.

Gwen, of course, had never met Hoff.

Dale got up and began to work his way through the crowd to me. I was waiting for him.

Just then a servant came down the stairs and said to Olga, "Mrs. Bennett, the film is ready upstairs." Normally it would have been another hour before Olga led her guests to the projection room. But she sized me up and sized Dale up, then she raised up on her toes, and belted out, "Show time! Movie time, everybody!"

There were groans from the gin players who had just begun to get into Hoff. But Olga got even more insistent. "Get up, get up, everybody!" She pulled me toward the stairs, calling back over her shoulder, "Dale, darling, will you bring Mr. Hoff along?"

My head was full of blood. It beat so hard it hurt.

Olga never let go my hand.

Everyone wanted the seats near Hoff. Dale put him down in the very front row, and everyone who could crowd around him did. The rest tried to find seats at the side where they could enjoy his reactions.

The lights went off.

It didn't take long for the sport to start. The under-title music was not what Hoff had caused to be written. "This is not my music," he mumbled. "What have they done to my music?" he said more urgently. "I cannot permit this." Everyone laughed. "This is schmaltz!" he said with a thickening German accent, "Yiddisher schmaltz!"

He was hard to take, Mr. Hoff.

"My vision didn't need this schmaltz!" he said with his knockwurst accent. Everyone was laughing now. The evening was going to be a success.

The film itself started. Of course it had been considerably rearranged. And provided with an opening narration that underscored the Biblical parallel. "Schtinks!" said Hoff. "Gabidge!" Then on the sound track came a genuflection to organized devotionalism, spoken in unctuous tones by a famous TV personality, whose voice no one could fail to recognize.

"I piss on that bastard," growled Hoff.

I must say I felt the same way.

But others didn't. Along with the laughter, there were some hisses. I could particularly hear Emily's, "Will you please keep quiet, Mr. Hoff, so those of us who want to can enjoy the picture?"

At this moment Hoff discovered that one of his favorite shots—an establishing long shot that covered 360 degrees of Mexican desert littered with cadavers, skeletons, skulls, and other symbols of death, the whole composed to represent the "Waste Land which is the culture of our time" (quote from Hoff to the foreign press)—this shot was cut.

"Where is my long shot?" bellowed the drunken genius. He addressed himself directly to the people assembled there. He was standing now, and pointing in the manner of an Ernst Toller hero. Again there was a hostile reaction. "Will you please shut up . . . sit down . . . shshsh!"

But Hoff wasn't about to. "What have you done with my long shot?" he bellowed at everyone. He had described this shot in detail to the foreign press. "Three hundred and sixty degrees, all back lit; how I did it is my secret." He had promised them that they'd see at least that much of his vision intact. Now, caterwauling pure pain, he rushed up the aisle and into the projection room, from where he could be heard accusing the projectionist of having jumped a reel.

"Dale, would you send that man home immediately," said Emily, the gold cross heaving on her pink bubs. "I like this picture, and I will not sit here and . . ."

Hoff rushed back into the room. "I will sue him!" he announced to everyone. "If there is still a law in this country, I will bring this filthy little tradesman to his knees." Some people thought he said the word "Jewish." I didn't hear it.

"Who is Hitler's victim talking about?" a man whispered to Olga.

"His producer, I believe," she whispered. Then she turned to me and said, "And you have sympathy for that man, Eddie?"

The Jesus type, Mexican but clean, had come on the screen now. It had been Hoff's intention to introduce his hero at a high moment when he is driving the money changers out of the temple (a Mexican provincial cathedral). Apparently the hero's tell-off speech had been completely rewritten by the producer. The gossip, as Dale had passed it on to me, had the producer commenting on Hoff's original, "Mr. Hoff seems to be saying that people are bad simply because they are rich. I don't think this idea will find general acceptance in America." He wasn't kidding either. "Furthermore," he had gone on, "I noticed that when Mr. Hoff and I were having our salary discussions, he squeezed for every cent. He even demanded a secretarial job for his wife, who still can't write her name in legible English. Publicly, Hoff scorns money, but in fact he is a formidable trader, with a very solid feel for a dollar."

Whatever the truth of this, the producer had the speech completely rewritten, and had directed the new version himself, "So that Jesus would come out more Christian," he had said, "and less of an out-and-out Commie."

When the rewritten scene came on, Hoff stood in the projection beam, flailing his arms around and screaming, "Drek! Take it off! This is not mine!"

It was at this point that Emily stood up, all her jelly atremble, and said, "Dale Bennett, either he goes or I go. Take your pick." Now other people began to talk back to Hoff. He was yelling at the projectionist, right through the wall, "Take this off! At once!" (Et vunce!) There was an avalanche of "Et vunce's," riding on hysterical laughter, and at the same time, some very angry talk.

"What are you laughing?" demanded Hoff now, directly at the audience. "What are you laughing, you pigs?" (You had to admire his guts.) At which everybody who was laughing laughed louder. A male voice yelled at Hoff, "I'm going to kill you, you Nazi bastard!" People were restraining Mike Weiner, my agent, because they knew if he got to Hoff he would indeed kill him.

Nothing fazed Hoff. The man was ridiculous, preposterous, shameful, despicable. Though I knew he was probably everything Mike Weiner wanted to kill him for, I still couldn't help being enlisted by his pain. "This is desecration!" he announced to everyone in the room. "Where is your humanity? They have killed a piece of my life, you murderers."

The mask of levity was dropped now. Hoff was facing a roomful of jeering people. And he did, I suppose, the only thing he could to stop the film. He picked up a letter opener from the magazine table, rushed up to the screen, and ripped it to bits.

Then he pushed his way up through the aisle of jeerers, waving his hands, accepting their insults as if they were tributes. Someone tripped him. He got up, and smiled, and made a deep bow of gratitude. You just had to like him a little for that. Then he was out of the house, his wife following, head down and silent, looking as if she had never expected anything better from Americans.

Amidst the hysterics and laughing, there was another reaction, quieter, more sober. "It's our fault," said an old Western star—a dignified old man he was—"for letting people like that make films for us." This analysis drew a chorus of approbation.

The lights in the room were turned on now. The projectionist came out, looked at the screen, talked to Olga about getting a bedsheet and putting it up with thumb tacks.

The people who had been laughing most, the good-natured majority, headed for the big bar downstairs. The haters stayed. The room was suddenly very quiet and very tense.

I felt at bay. I was all alone up front. Olga had left with the projectionist. I took a quick look around for Florence. She had disappeared. I looked for the man who had attached himself to her. I didn't see him. Everyone who was still in the room had gathered at the back. They were talking intently. I couldn't hear what was being said, but I got the idea.

I felt like an enemy spy in a foreign country. I also felt very very weary, like the time in the spring of forty-five, after fifty-two days on the Villa Verde trail in Northern Luzon, the campaign in which the Red Arrow division lost one thousand and eighty men, I found myself in a front-line emergency hospital, watching them take shrapnel out of a boy's leg, the metal bits dropping into a pan, ting, ting, ting, and over the Armed Forces Radio came V-E Day, the big announcement. It was over in Europe. But no one gave a shit. All anyone could think was "When do I get out of *here?*"

I could feel a migraine coming. I had also drunk too much, and that was beginning to hit me. I sat there, my head in my hands. I just wanted to be forgotten.

But Dale Bennett hadn't forgotten me.

"Eddie, what do you think?" he said.

"About what?"

"You were defending Hoff before. What do you think now?"

Dale wanted me to crawl.

I had a headache now, definitely.

"Come on, Eddie," Dale persisted. "What do you think?"

"I don't think Hoff's worse than any of the rest of us. I think it's all the same here."

Dale took it calmly. "What do you mean *here,* Eddie?"

"Just what I said."

"You mean here in America, or here in California, or here in the industry, or here in this room—where here?"

I got up and started out. "I'm going home," I said.

They came down on me like wild animals. It sounded like one long garbled sentence spoken by many people: he got just what he deserved, that moral leper . . . no wonder our town is in trouble when reprobates like that make our pictures . . . European decadence doesn't go here; that's why no one goes to the movies any more in this country . . . our industry is built on the home . . . men like that bastard glamorize infidelity . . . all those Berlin sex perversions and all that running wild our kids are doing—that's where they get their ideas . . . it's our own fault because we give them all our prizes . . . show those New York critics decadence and they cheer . . . what happens to the picture of just an ordinary decent American family . . . Bosley Crowther's ax is what happens to it . . . this is still a Christian nation, isn't it?

My head was throbbing like I was going to have a stroke.

It wasn't that I wanted to defend Hoff. I just didn't want to shame myself. They wanted me to crawl.

I didn't want to shake up my hurting head. I sat down in the middle of them, and I talked to them the gentlest way I knew how. I did it quietly, but I tried to tell the truth. Why not, I thought; I'm finished here anyway.

"*I* just don't think any of us in this room should heave the first rock," I said. "Because I've led a fucked-up life, right, but I've led some of that fucked-up life with some of the fucked-up girls in this room. Haven't I? Well, you remember, Betty?" I was speaking to a woman, the wife of a TV producer, everyone knew had been around; I was making no revelation to anyone. Even now, pushing forty, she was on some bachelors' calendars. "You know, Betty?"

Then I turned to one of the other women; she had been a slim thing when I knew her, but now she was built like a cop. I was going to recall some history to her, too, but then I said, "Well, let's stop with the names. I mean we all live by forgetting, so let's all take the fifth. I've been with an awful lot of you girls here; now you remember, don't you? We all played the same stands, so I can say who did and when and where and how often, and what the bedroom Nielsons were. I'm sorry I mentioned any names, Betty. But maybe we shouldn't put on this big moral show-show tonight. Or maybe we should; probably we have to pretend like we do—all of you girls with your husbands for instance—because if we had to look at ourselves every day the way we really are, who could take it? The only thing I'm saying is, I think we should be kind to the other grotesques like this Hoff. Because I don't think any of us are any better than him.''

They were furious. But not one would speak, not even Emily. When I first came to California, Florence had stayed in the East, to get rid of our apartment and the furniture, and I had a chance to sample the stuff. I made the same route everyone else was making. And among the station stops we all hit was the one called Emily. She was just beginning to climb then, and she climbed the familiar way, but covered her tracks more cleverly than most. So now suddenly she wasn't talking either.

The picture saved them all. The projectionist had put up the sheet, and the adventures of Jesus *au sombrero* were rolling again. The Rurales were chasing him through the cactus, and El Jefe was a bastard named Pilotes for Pilate, get it? Suddenly everyone was very interested in the film.

The oddest reaction of all was Dale's. He just sat there, studying the face of his close friend. He kept his gaze leveled on me. I knew it was time to go. I got up and nodded at him.

He didn't give a sign.

So all this would have passed into history, too, except that as I was leaving the room, at the very door, Betty's husband—the Betty whose name I had mentioned like a damned fool—this man came after me. He was a TV producer, and right behind him was his agent, an Italian fellow who had once been a fighter, sort of. This agent didn't rank high in the cadre of the agency, but was carried for laughs, the joke being that he was head of the procuring division for visiting exhibitors. Well, this twosome got to me, and the producer grabbed me by the lapels, like they do on his television shows—a case of life imitating art it was. And he said, shaking me, that he hadn't at all liked what I had implied (implied?) about his wife Betty. So I apologized. But I must have smiled or maybe laughed when I did. Well, this got him. He refused to accept my apology. Besides, there was his agent right behind him, and this gives strength. He said my slur was a malicious lie, or my life was a magnificent slur, or something; I had stopped paying strict attention by then. He was storming, for the benefit of everybody in the room, how I had been allowed for much too long to get away with it. He went on and on. I couldn't figure why he felt he had to go through all those heroics; all he really needed to do was hit me a couple so his wife's honor, that old thing, would be publicly reconstituted. I was going to let him have a shot or two at me; what the hell, he was in the right. But he kept slapping me, and my head ached like one big tooth. So finally I closed my left hand and stuck it right in his nose. He sat backwards, plop, into the arms of his agent, who then put his client down gently and came for me. He did revenge Betty's honor, so notably, in fact, that she later rewarded him personally in the way she knew best.

All the time, the film was rolling. Now some people turned in their seats and watched the fight—if that's what it was, with me doing all the catching. They watched as if it was, for the time being at least, the more interesting of the two shows. They didn't try to stop it any more than they would have tried to stop a film. Because, after all, it wasn't happening to them. They weren't hurting. These people, I thought, are trained sideliners. Murder for them is a spectator sport.

But then, even as I was taking my shellacking, I saw that maybe some of them wanted to intervene. What stopped them was the severe way Dale Bennett was watching what was happening to me. He was presiding at a tribunal of justice.

The agent punching me didn't know who he was hitting or really why. He certainly didn't care about Betty's honor. And he had nothing against me. He was simply implementing what he took to be the general will. That was his profession; he was the agent for all of them. He was doing what they, for certain reasons of civilization, could not do themselves: the ten per cent dirty work.

I noticed the agent was beginning to puff badly. I got a spurt of strength, enough for one punch anyway, and I clouted him right in the Caesar salad. It may not have hurt him much, but it sure as hell surprised him, because he drew back for one big look, long enough to allow Mike Weiner, who was then coming down the stairs, to come to my rescue. And me to get out of the house. I never did find out what happened between Mike and the Italian guy. But the affair ended fitly: two agents fighting for their clients.

A ball hammer was beating in my head. I couldn't remember where I had parked the car. I could think only of one thing: Dale's cold eyes holding back everyone in that room from their humanity. They had sat there, ready to acquiesce to my murder.

The cold damp air made me feel better. The hell with them all, I thought. They're not going to kill me, any of them, with their wishes, conscious or unconscious, or by their indifferences either. Because the only one who has the power to kill me, and is liable to kill me, is myself. And not in my Triumph or my Cessna either. In some invisible way, much more silent, but also much more lethal and much more terrible. Like my fourteen years silence with Dale. That's self-betrayal. That's self-murder. Denying myself! And last night, that with Florence, that's denying myself, too. That's self-murder.

I suddenly saw the whole incident in bed with Florence quite differently. I saw that when I turned on my stomach and denied the evidence that I was still alive, when I squashed that down, I was only doing what I had been doing for years: denying my own life's expression, saying that I must *not* feel such and such a way, and that I *must* feel such and such a way, when I clearly no longer did or could. And above all, saying this thing with Gwen or whoever should not be and therefore wasn't. Like the old Leadbelly song, I was denying my name, and so murdering myself in a way much more lethal and final than the accident. They picked me up out of that accident, living. But I had been squashing life out of me so long that another few months and I would have been dead for good. I'd really had a narrow escape.

I remembered now where I had left the car. But it wasn't there. I supposed Florence had gone home in it. I didn't know where to begin to get a cab, except by going back into the Bennett house and calling for one. So I thought, maybe it's a mile; I'll walk it. But I was pretty wobbly. The cops said later that when they found me, I was walking the center stripe on Crescent Drive, shaking my fist at something they couldn't see. They tried to question me, find out who I was, but I didn't know. They went through my pockets. I don't carry a wallet. When they asked me where I was going, I said I had to find a catastrophe that might save me. When they asked me where my home was, I said I didn't have any. I kept saying through it all, "I'm through, I'm through here!" Those cops certainly were patient with me. They said, almost apologetically, that all in all it might be better if they took me in to cool me off, and later somewhere for observation.

On the way to the station house in the patrol car, I slept. Later I was in a room with some other men, and I slept there, too. Then there was a man calling out, "Anderson? Is there an Edward Anderson here?" I gave myself away, they told me later, by saying, "No, he's not here." Florence said, "That's him."

When we got home, Florence woke me. She said that the very first thing I had to do was call my brother Michael in Westchester. He'd been trying to get me all night; it was urgent. By that time, she had him on the phone. Michael was just about to leave for the hospital. He told me that my father had pneumonia. They had caught it in time, he said, except at that age everything is serious. But he was full of miracle drugs, so don't worry. There was one other thing. My father's arteriosclerosis, he said, had progressed, and this, in turn, had increased his hallucinating. The last couple of days he had repeatedly asked for me, believing all the time that I was just outside in the hospital corridor. Several times he had addressed me as if I was there in the room with him. Once he had even asked Michael to leave, so he could talk to me privately. Apparently he had something he urgently wanted to tell me. Could I, asked Michael, who was very impressed with my position and activity, could I come east, maybe immediately, if it was at all convenient; it would be wonderful if I could. If I couldn't not to worry, because there was nothing seriously wrong, not immediately—and so on.

Well, there, I thought, I have my catastrophe. Not one I'd want, my God! But there it was.

I made a reservation on the first plane I could get on, the one leaving at noon. The sun was well up now. The smog seemed to have blown elsewhere. I walked down to the pool—my farewell visit it was to be, but I didn't know it. I took off my shirt, lay down on the diving board, and fell asleep.

CHAPTER *14*

MY skid into a mental institution was by way of a series of discoveries. All the way down I kept having that wonderful sensation: at last, I've found it, the key to everything. But each day the insight that explained it all was not the insight which had explained it all the day before. And the more I learned about myself, the further out of line my thinking became; and the stranger my thinking, the stranger my behavior.

For instance, that day I had made a shattering discovery. I wasn't content to say to myself, "Kid, you learned the art of disguising your truest feelings with your mother's milk, and from that day you have lived your life in one disguise or another." I went on to think of everyone as living in a disguise, the particular disguise necessary to get them what they wanted. I began to think of all appearances, including that of things—of clothes, cars, food packages, public buildings, in fact just about everything that hit my eyes—as false fronts, as techniques of advertising. I began to think of our entire civilization as poses and attitudes, masks and simulacra.

Well, it's harmless enough to think of things that way. The trouble starts when you begin, as I did, to let these perceptions influence your behavior. They say a man is nuts when he begins to live in a world which doesn't correspond to the world everyone else is inhabiting. Such a person behaves from one set of premises and by one set of rules, while everyone else is behaving according to a totally different set of rules and premises. That is when you have to begin to think about society's right to restrain.

I had to walk to the railroad station. I didn't mind. It was one of those damp cool nights I like. Besides, the brown grocer's bag I was carrying, though it looked bulky, was in fact quite light. A word as to how I had suddenly acquired a brown grocer's bag.

Michael and Gloria and their two sons live in one of those long, low apartment houses presently being put up in the suburbs. They are called efficiencies. And they certainly are efficient. The front yard consists entirely of a parking lot for the residents of the building. The apartments run from one side through to the other. The prospect from the back windows is the parking lot of the efficiency apartment building next down the road. You can tell, however, that you are in Westchester and not in Queens or the Bronx, because there are some trees coming through the edge of the macadam of the parking lot. And because traffic gets quiet around nine-fifteen at night. The stores close. You can't get a taxi.

The tenants in an efficiency apartment are required to do certain tasks which janitors do in non-efficiency apartments. For instance, each tenant is expected to carry his garbage out to a shed at one end of the parking lot. This shed, built low so it won't be an eyesore, is made up of a row of numbered bins, each just high enough to house a large garbage can. You have your own bin and can, which is very good, because you never find yourself with no place to put your garbage.

On this particular evening, Gloria had given me, as I left, a brown grocer's bag containing their garbage for that day, and asked me to put it in their bin. But when I found their numbered alcove, the can was full. Since the bin was built just high enough for the can, I couldn't jam Gloria's brown paper bag on top of the rest of the stuff and still close the lid.

For a moment, I considered putting the paper bag in someone else's bin. But there were a rather authoritative-looking group of people on the stoop of the end apartment. The men looked like cops off duty. They pretended to be sitting there innocently, listening to the Met game on a very small transistor. I was convinced they knew what I had in mind, and didn't want to take a chance that I might put my bag in their bin and face a fuss of some kind.

So I turned into the street, still holding the grocer's bag full of garbage, and headed toward the station.

I have never gotten over my fear of policemen. There are days and particularly nights when I become obsessively aware of how many of them there are. Most people say there aren't enough around. But on certain nights I see them everywhere. I guess since I spent a year on a newspaper, I recognize plain-clothes men where most people can't. I even see them where they aren't. It's not because I feel guilty or anything like that. I have never committed a crime. I never even committed a misdemeanor till later that very night. But I have often felt like a spy in a foreign country.

This feeling was not eased by my four years in that Ivy college. I felt like a white nigger there, disorientated and separate from everyone else. Well, it wasn't just a feeling. I was.

But this is the odd part of it. When it came time for me to buy my clothes, I bought them at the same place where the fraternity boys bought theirs, J. Press, or A. M. Rosenberg's. Later, when I came back from the war and went to work for Williams and MacElroy, I went to Brooks Brothers, which is the same. The fact is that then and at college

I wore a disguise. I didn't want to look outside like I felt inside. I wanted to be indistinguishable from "them."

I have long felt that the ordinary male attire, what is called a business suit, is a garment conceived and tailored to deceive people. It's like the facade of the modern bank building. This neo-neoclassic architecture is the way it is for one reason only, and that is to inspire confidence in the honesty and durability of the institution housed therein. That is also the purpose of the business suit; it is an advertisement for the man, and sometimes, as in the case of many ads, it is misleading. It says, "You can trust this man in a business deal." The clothing of the contemporary male is not designed for comfort or protection or adaptability to various kinds of weather. It certainly isn't for beauty. It's made to suggest the opposite of deviousness. It is a do-business suit.

The funny thing is—I was thinking about all this as I walked to the railroad station—that even when I joined the Communist Party in the days of the Popular Front, I still wore the honest three-button Brooks Brothers. This wasn't accidental either, because it was important, in those days, for the Commie to represent himself to be just like everyone else, a little ahead, maybe, but not too much, and never as a person dedicated and determined to bring down this body politic. So the disguise was the business suit. On June 23, 1941, the day after Hitler invaded Stalinland, the comrades rushed out and bought themselves honest cloth in a respectable cut. It was a great day for tailors.

Another policeman passed me. I had the feeling that all the cops were out tonight. Even when I finally got on the train, there was one walking up and down the aisle. You could see the bulge of his concealed pistol, for chrissake. Some plain-clothes man! Why was he riding that train? Did he look at me strangely as he passed? Did I have too much to drink at Gloria's? I was still carrying the brown grocer's bag. Perhaps he was concerned about that. I better put that bag on the floor, out of sight. I had forgotten I was still carrying it. But now suppose someone questioned me, how could I explain it?

In the seat behind me two men were discussing the A.T. and T. stock split.

Actually, about my own clothes, I had a model. His name is Brooks Atkinson, the famous man who used to pass judgment on the season's plays for the New York *Times*. I used to study his photographs. He wore these little suits; whether they were gray or not I don't know because I have never seen the man in the flesh, but they gave off gray. Then he wore those button-down shirts like they wear at Harvard and Williams and Amherst and even Yale. He preferred little flat bow ties, the ones without flare. The whole effect was one of fantastic honesty and superlative modesty. I had the research department at Williams and MacElroy get me some pictures of this man, and I studied his secret. How confidence-inspiring, I used to think, how trustworthy-seeming. Still, I knew from reading the man's reviews that he was as human as the next fellow. His teeth were as sharp, and he liked the salty taste of blood just as any other animal does. He even had his human share of venom and vanity. He enjoyed power to the point of publicly stating he wished he didn't have so much. In other words, he was a descendant of the hunter-ape, as we all are.

Since he was about my size and weight, I took on his image. Of course I'm olive-complexioned, and at first I thought that would be a problem. But once you get the rest of the junk on—the glasses, the bow tie, the vest and all—there isn't much olive to show. About the glasses, I remember well, I had all my glasses changed one week to the little steel-rimmed kind that Mr. Atkinson wears. What the hell, why fiddle around with what's perfect? Everyone else at the agency wore those tortoise temple grippers, but I went in for the old-fashioned kind that Mr. Atkinson wore, the kind that curl behind your ears. I remember I also changed my hair-part that same week, moving it much closer to the middle of my head, where it was less dashing, true, but much much more trustworthy-seeming.

I guess I wanted people not to see the turbulence inside me. I wanted them to think of me as they did of him, decent, selfless, civilized. None of which—so I was fast finding out—was I. In other words, I disguised myself, quite consciously.

I never felt more grateful to Mr. Atkinson than when I walked through those motel lobbies in downtown Los Angeles to my assignations with Gwen Hunt. The desk clerks used to nod their heads as if I was in fact Brooks Atkinson. Then we'd lock the door, and there'd be chaos for a couple of hours. But, after, on would go the button-down shirt, the trim little bow tie, the three-button suit with the modest lapels, and the part in the center of my head. And out I'd prance, modest, even mouselike, but prance I did through the lobby, home free, with the clerks again nodding respectfully, as well they might.

That goddam plain-clothes man came back from the smoking car. He was carrying a briefcase now, but that didn't fool me. They all look like junior executives today. The F.B.I. started that. But I'm on to them. I barely restrained myself from slapping him where his gun bulged. I gave him a real cool little smile and a nod, as if to say, "I know who you really are." And he gave me the same back, as if to say, "I know who you are, too."

The train was slowing down for the stop at 125th Street, which is not where I had intended to get off. But I had an impulse to go look at the neighborhood where my parents lived when they first came to America and where I was born. Gwen would just have to wait a little longer, that is if she was still waiting at all. For the moment, I didn't care.

I knew that neighborhood was part of Harlem now, but forty years ago it was a district for up-and-coming whites. I had always wanted to go back there, walk the streets where I had played, and look at the changes. But year after year, coming to New York for business, I had not had the time. I always scheduled myself for everything except the things that really concerned me. If *I* was interested in it, it had to be less important.

So I started to leave the train and got just to the end of the car, when there was a call from behind me. "Hey, fella, you forgot your package." The conductor was holding up the brown paper grocer's bag. "Oh, thanks," I said, laughing nervously, and hurried back to get it.

On 125th Street, I decided to walk a bit. I also decided to carry the brown bag for a while. I had begun to have an affection for the thing. I held it in the crook of my arm like a big football.

Gloria's drink was wearing off and I didn't want that to happen, so I went into the first bar, Black and Tan. I had a jumbo beer for fifteen cents. Then a shot of rye, then a foot-long hot dog, then another shot, then another beer. That brought me back.

There was a commotion at one end of the bar. Someone had come in off the street and quick-sold a vacuum cleaner to one of the bartenders for fifteen dollars. Inspection showed it to have a prominent brand name, and no motor. The seller had disappeared.

I sized the place up. What the hell was I doing here, a stranger within a stranger, a disguise over a disguise?

I remembered when I came back from the war in '45, how unrelated to me everything seemed. Were these my people? Was this my fatherland? Why did I have so little sense of loyalty or patriotism, I, a twice-decorated soldier? I had fought for this place, seen men die for it. But now, looking at it, I wondered, why did they die for this? I'm not talking about the idea. I'm talking about the place, the way it actually is.

"But," I said out loud, "the whole thing doesn't have to be this way."

The fellow next to me, without turning his head, commented, "No. It doesn't."

"I mean the whole damned thing." I didn't turn to look at him either.

The bar has taken the place of the church. It is the only place in America where men examine their souls.

The fellow next to me said, "I know what you mean." I still didn't turn to look at him, nor he at me.

I had another boiler-maker. I remember I thought then, "This society is insane." I meant all of it—the customs, the clothes, the work, the hours devoted to work, the way people spoke to each other without looking, the homes they lived in, the streets they walked, the air, the noise, the filth, the bread—all the basics. But the real thing that bothered me was that this country, despite all the talk about happiness—was in some pervasive way anti-pleasure. Oh, I know we're always stuffing something into our mouths —a drink, a cigar, a piece of nickel candy. And we're forever riding here and there. There's music everywhere, even in the elevators, and you can see old movies day and night on TV. "But," I said, "where do you go to really have a good time in this city?"

"What kind of a girl you looking for?" said my elbowmate.

I took a quick look. He was a plain-clothes man, no doubt, offering to pimp for me. A trap. I had a double shot and got out, clutching my grocer's bag tight.

Christ, was I seeing straight? I didn't used to see the world around me this way!

"Of course not. You were part of it, then, so how could you see it?" I said out loud.

Once I did. At college. I felt everyone there was my enemy, and that I had to conceal my true feelings. I behaved as if I was a spy in a foreign country.

I started to run in and out of the crowd like a broken-field runner, holding the brown paper bag in the crook of my arm.

I was spoiling for a fight. About anything. With anybody.

At Lex, I turned downtown. Yes, I thought, this is how I felt in '45 when the atom bomb had cleared Hiroshima off the face of the plain, and then, since twice is better than once, Nagasaki. I remembered then that I felt as I did tonight. Once home, I got me a job at Williams and MacElroy, put on my nice-guy disguise, and twenty years passed like one of those time-passing bits in the movies, the leaves flying off the calendar in the studio-made wind.

I went into a bar on 116th Street, full of Puerto Riquenos far from the clear sea water and the rain forest. And Negroes with no home to be far from. This can't ever be their home, and that other too far back. The whole bar looked like one of those rooms under the concrete risers of a stadium where fighters wait before they go into a ring. It was full of fear and murder. I felt at any minute we'd all drop our disguises and slug our neighbors without turning to see whom we were hitting.

"The whole thing doesn't have to be this way," I said sternly.

My elbowmate at the bar said, "Go and fuck yourself, mister."

I looked at him. He was a Negro. He'd decided not to wear his disguise that night. He was himself.

"It doesn't have to be this way, any of it," I said again. "We just got off on the wrong foot, at the very beginning. So we can't see that any other way is possible."

"Will you move away from me," said my neighbor. He had a bad lump over one eye, and a long welt where someone had tried to cut his throat. He wasn't a cop, I could see that.

But I felt trusting, not threatened. He wasn't a cop, I could see that.

"You see we're not wrong," I said, "it's all the rest of them out there."

"You're full of shit, mister."

"No, I'm not. You know what I'm talking about."

"If you don't like it here, why don't you haul ass out?"

"Where could I go?"

"I don't care where you go. Stop bugging me. What are you, a cop or something? You're a cop, aren't you?"

"Did you know that A.T. and T. split its stock today?"

He took a transistor radio out of his pocket, and turning on a comic real loud, held it flat up to his ear. Then he moved down the bar away from me.

I followed him.

"Will you stay away, you got nothing on me."

The bartender came over. "What's the matter?" he asked.

"This cop is bugging me. I didn't do nothing."

"I was just trying to talk to him," I said.

"What for?" said the bartender.

That wasn't easy to explain. The bartender staring at me didn't make it any easier.

"Everybody's getting along good in here," he said. "You see anybody bothering anybody?" His tone was most respectful.

"I don't even see anybody talking to anybody."

"So we're A1, what do you want?"

That was hard to explain too.

He continued, "Would you mind doing your drinking somewhere else? If a cop drinks in a place, it keeps customers out. No offense. Would you mind?"

"O.K.," I said. "Give me another belt and I'll go." He did, on the house, and I left.

It had begun to drizzle. I felt loaded for trouble. It struck me as strange, because I'd spent so much of my life in a disguise for the purpose of staying out of trouble.

I was now at 112th Street, where we lived forty years ago. There was nothing there now. Six, seven, eight big co-op apartment buildings. Uniform. Disguises all. Incognito architecture.

A cop walked by. In uniform for a change.

"Where's everybody?" I asked.

"What?" He looked friendly, which was a sure-as-hell disguise.

I said, "Where's everything?"

"Where's what?" he said.

"Everything, everybody." I was pretty annoyed and sounded so.

"Inside," he said. "You better get in, too, before you get into trouble."

Then he walked off and up to another man, a plain-clothes man by the look of him, and said something. They both turned and looked at me.

"Well all right," I thought and I walked up to the cop and the plain-clothes man. I'd never done anything like this before.

"What do you mean by telling me I better get in before I get into trouble?" I demanded.

The cop and the plain-clothes man looked at each other and began to laugh.

"What's so funny?" I said belligerently.

"Just move along, will you, mister," the cop said.

"You move along. Go about your business, and stop following me."

By God, they walked away!

A third man, another plain-clothes man obviously, came and stood in front of me. This guy was really disguised. The son of a bitch spoke French.

"*Parlez vous français?*" he said.

"*Oui,*" I said, "so don't give me that."

"*Comment?*"

"Speak English," I ordered. "Just cut it out . . . the three of you." I looked around. The other two had disappeared. But I knew they were in a doorway, around a corner, somewhere, watching me. But this last one, the son of a bitch, just stood there.

I walked away, or rather turned away and towards a wall of planks and old wooden doors around a co-op that had just been completed, and I walked smack into a poster for Zephyr cigarettes.

The poster showed a medical type, very WASP, could be a doctor with that white coat, and behind him one of those skinny models with built-up tits watching him with polite lust and—now I remembered. That's my poster! I'd written the copy: SMOKE ZEPHYR. THE MEN YOU TRUST DO. THEY'RE CLEAN AS A BREEZE. Our answer to the cancer scare.

"Pure shit!" I said.

"*Comment?*" the plain-clothes man, whoever he was, said. He seemed nicer now.

I decided to trust him. I smiled at him, first tentatively, then without caution. He smiled back. Whatever and whoever he was, he had a nice smile.

I bowed and said, "What can I do for you?"

Then he said, "Thank you very much. Can you please tell me where I can urinate myself in this city?"

I didn't have an answer. Big question. The housing development was all around me. Suddenly I had to go, too. Christ, I thought, the honor of America as a civilization is hanging on this very simple question. A proper culture should certainly provide a place where a man could pleasantly relieve himself every so often.

I turned to the Frenchman. I was pretty sure by now he wasn't a plain-clothes man. He was just a fellow, like me, in a foreign country. "It's like Paris here," I said. "You look for the advertisements, and when you see one, like this one *ici,* that's the place! Except here we do it right *on* the advertisements. *Regardez!*"

I took the thing out and pissed all over where it said, "The men you trust do."

He watched. Men are interested on a comparative basis in each other's roots. I was waiting for him to take his out. I'd never seen a French one. I pointed to where it showed this semi-coed type with the "D" cups having her polite sex fit over the doctor type in the white coat. I said, "This is your part. Let her go!"

The Zephyr people, I remembered, had decided to try this campaign in limited areas to get a testing.

Well, that was when the real plain-clothes man and the cop moved in and we had our little fracas.

I enjoyed the ride in the police car. In fact, I was so relaxed I fell asleep on the way downtown. When I woke, it was all pretty hazy. I remember someone roughed up the Frenchman just outside night court, and I didn't like it. In fact, believe it or not, I dumped somebody who sure as hell was a plain-clothes man because all the loyal plain-clothes men hopped me and muscled me a bit. They couldn't, however, do the job they'd like to have done, because we were in the night court building by then. Besides, I gave them what Godoy gave Joe Louis, the top of the turtle to hit at.

Next thing I remember we were in front of a judge I couldn't see clearly. I put the brown paper bag gently down on the court stenographer's table, and I said to this judge I thought there were too many plain-clothes men around the city. I had a grand moment when I said, "Do you, your honor, know where a visiting Frenchman who is not familiar with our city and customs can urinate on 112th Street and Lexington Avenue, in the middle of the night?"

This stumped the judge, I guess, because he turned and whispered something to the plain-clothes man behind him. "He doesn't know, your honor," I said, "I asked him."

At which the judge pointed to me and said to the plain-clothes man on my right, "Bring him to my chambers."

Then I spoke out again, "I don't go to anybody's chambers unless you let this Frenchman go." The plain-clothes man who was holding my arm twisted it a bit.

"Ouch!" I yelled. "Has this man the right to twist my arm?"

The judge ducked my question, as well he might. He turned and said to the Frenchman, "You can go."

"I think we owe this man an apology," I said.

"Don't push your luck," said the dick.

"I think you owe him an apology," I said. "Suppose you were in Paris and this happened to you. You'd be screaming for the one hundred and first airborne."

The judge rapped his gavel. The cops took the Frenchman away. I never saw him again.

The next thing I remember I was in a dingy little room in the back somewhere, and this judge was taking off his robes. He lit a cigarette, turned and looked right at me, and said, "Don't you remember me?"

I looked at him, and as I did, something of authority and disguise fell off, and there was Beetle Weinstein, or as he came to be known, Ben Winston. "Beetle," I said. "For chrissake, it's the Beetle!"

"Yes," he said. "Me."

"You had your teeth fixed," I said.

He acquired the name Beetle because of the hang and the weight of his lateral incisors.

"Yes," he said, "and that's the least of it."

"What the hell are you doing here?" I asked.

"What the hell are *you* doing here?" he said. "And let's have a drink." He reached into the space behind some law books and pulled out that fine square bottle.

A drink put me right back on top. "I've been wanting to do that for years," I said.

"What?" he said, lifting his glass. "To the day!"

"Piss on my ads!" I said. "Tell me, Beetle, how do you take it?"

"How do *you* take it?"

"Stop answering my question with a question, you Hebe bastard, now answer my goddam question, how do you sit up there and represent it?"

"What?" he said.

"You know goddam well what. IT! All of it. The general fraud."

"Patience, my friend, we wait."

"Bullshit, judge. It all doesn't have to be this way."

"All of what?"

"All of any of this, all of IT!"

"Are you all right?" he said.

"Yes. But I'm nearing a crisis. I'm not just drunk, you know. This is a hell of a lot more than that."

"I can see that," he said, "a hell of a lot more."

"And there's no end to it, Beetle."

"What happened to you?"

"When?"

"Since I last saw you?"

"IT happened to me."

"What's IT?"

"Were you in the war?"

"I enlisted the day after Hitler sent Runstedt across the Polish border. Didn't you?"

"Well, you remember when you came back from the war and everything looked insane? I mean literally, the whole civilization, didn't it? Judge?"

"Yes, it did."

"Well, that moment is when you were thinking straight. Then they got around you with the promotions and the money and that robe you just took off. But you had a week or two of sanity back in the summer of '45. Do you remember it? Give me another drink."

"Help yourself."

I did. We sat there for a moment. I was breathing extra hard.

"Are you sure you're all right?" he asked me.

"I've never felt truer. I want to send two telegrams tonight. You will have to help me."

"Sure. What are they?"

"I've got two professions, and I'm going to formally and finally quit both."

"Why don't you do it in the morning?"

"I won't be thinking as clearly in the morning."

There was a knock on the door, and he muttered something that gave one of those plain-clothes men the right to come in. He was, now that I saw him in a different light, just a big Irish kid. He was holding my brown grocer's bag.

"I thought you might want to see this, Judge Winston," he said.

"What is it?" said the Beetle.

"Take a look inside, sir."

I said nothing.

The judge looked inside. "I still don't get it," he said. "What is it, Officer?"

"Just a mess of garbage," the plain-clothes man said. "But when Detective Shepley tried to take it away from him, the prisoner knocked him down."

"He knocked a police officer down?" asked Judge Winston.

"Yes, sir."

"Tst, tst, tst," I said.

The big Irish kid glared at me, then continued. "Just thought you might want to see what he thought was so precious, you know what I mean, Judge? I think it's significant."

"Thank you, Officer, you're right, it is significant."

The plain-clothes man nodded and walked out.

The judge looked at me. He looked more like a judge again.

"Eddie," he said, "what are you carrying this around for?"

"Is it against the law?"

"Stop being so belligerent! I just wondered why you were carrying it around with you."

I thought for a long time about that one. With my new devotion to the truth, I made an effort to clear my mind and answer truthfully. I thought, should I go through the whole goddam story? If I did, would that explain it? Finally I said, "I can't explain, your honor, why I'm carrying that brown paper bag full of garbage around with me."

There was a pause. Then he put his arm around my shoulders and said, "Never mind that 'your honor' poetry. Listen, maybe you ought to not do anything decisive about anything, including your jobs, till you take a long rest."

I got up.

"Beetle," I said, "thanks. But I never felt truer in my life. There isn't a damned thing wrong with me. Everyone else is wrong. And now, speaking as offender to judge, are you going to hold me?"

He looked at me very sad and very concerned. "No," he said, "I'm not going to hold you. You're free."

"How do I get out of here?"

"I'll walk you to the back door," he said. Then he reached for his robe. "I'm afraid if I don't have this on, they won't let me back in." He laughed and I laughed. But he meant it.

"One for the road?" he asked.

"Don't need it," I said. "I feel fine."

"Then one for old time's sake."

"For the old days, yes, that, yes," I said.

He poured.

I was in the Communist Party for a fast ten months. When I went to their Twelfth Street H.Q. to report for my unit (a group of newspaper men doing "united front" speeches and articles for the Party), the man with whom I'd make contact on the 9th floor was Bennie Weinstein. He had a soft spot in him, you could tell even then, so it didn't surprise me that I never heard of his rising higher in his cadre. He was o.k. for the Popular Front days when everyone was friendly. After the war, when things got cold and hard again, he wasn't the right casting.

When I got back from the war, the C.P. meant nothing to me. I wanted to make up for lost time, and make a life for myself. Which I did. From the looks of it, he had too.

"To the old days," he said again, "the real days!"

We drank to that. He put the bottle back behind the law books and showed me out the door. We walked through some corridors, past various attendants. The black cloth received its tribute. The judge nodded and grunted, didn't give much back. He had the authority game down cold.

The passages through the cellar could have been painted by Hopper. The bulbs were unshielded forties. The inhabitants, all in some way connected with administering justice, seemed drugged. They were standing at intervals that didn't relate to function or intention. Perhaps because the building's source of heat was just below us, these nether regions were overheated. The accommodations for the jailors were no better or different than those for the jailed.

Judge Winston (Weinstein) opened the back door. It was still drizzling.

"Nasty night," he said. Then he looked at me anxiously and said, "Everything in the family, right? About the old days and all that? You know?" He was not telling me, he was pleading with me. How rickety was his security, I thought. "You know," he continued, "there aren't many of us left."

"Us what?" I asked.

"Us old rebels," he said.

We stood there for a bit looking at the drizzle. I suppose he was wondering what I thought of him. But when I dared look at him, he smiled and said, "Where you heading for now, old buddy?"

"Guess I'll go get laid," I said, "if I can."

"Gets harder every year, doesn't it?" He laughed, and added, "I wish I could go along with you—oh, not just for that, though I'd like to break out, haven't in a long time. What I meant was that being together has brought back so many memories."

I remembered his wife. She had been the pistol of that family, had gone to Cuba twice, the first time with Clifford Odets, whose girl friend she was that month, and the second time on her own. That time she had stayed there and become a *soldadera* to one of the men who fought in the hills—this long, long before Castro. When this man had been trapped and shot by Batista . . . or was that what had happened? I didn't remember clearly any more.

"Where's Elizabeth?" I asked.

"Oh," he said, "remember her?"

"When did she die?" I said.

"She's not dead," he said. "We're still together. We've been together damn near thirty years now." He droped his voice. "Did you know that she was once the mistress of Clifford Odets?" Was he boasting? "Then, after that, she lived with one of those real hill *campesinos,* the real thing, buddy my boy, shot by Batista! An American-made bullet right between the eyes. Shame on us. Bastards! But they didn't get her. How she ever got back into this country, don't ask, it's thirty years ago. You'd never, never guess what she's doing now."

"What and where?"

"A stock market analyst on Wall Street. Works for an investment banking firm. Of course, with nearly every hot tip on the street crossing her desk, and with the kind of market we've had for ten years, and never forgetting her thorough knowledge of Marx—that sure comes in handy— she's made us a small fortune. I could quit any time."

"Why don't you?"

"And do what?"

"There's a lot still to fight for, isn't there?"

"You can't do anything today, buddy my boy, you know that, because baby, these are what that fellow called the Years of the Toad. Where are they all today? Mexico. Underground just like you and me. We're all underground in this country. No one knows who's where. Like you. Advertising. A whore's trade. When you're drunk, you feel like quitting; when you're sober, you don't—that's it, isn't it? Because, hell, you're sitting there waiting just like I'm sitting here waiting. Maybe once in a while we do a little something. Like tonight. I bet you were glad it was me at the other end of that gavel."

I didn't answer.

The drizzle showered jewels through the funnel of the street lights. "Well," I said, "guess I've kept you long enough."

"Don't say that," he said. "It's not every day that I meet one of the old ones." He tightened his belt. "You put on weight sitting on that goddam bench every day, looking at the refuse of this filthy society, the sellers and the sold. Man, I could write a book. And I will, some day, I will; I promise you that, Eddie. Hold me to that. Will you hold me to that, Eddie?"

Then he did the last thing I would have expected of him. He reached out and gently touched my cheek in as near to a caress as he was prepared to give another man. "You're going to get laid now, are you? You son of a bitch."

"Well, I'm going to see about it."

"You've kept alive some way. Maybe it's the fucking. Goddam you, you still look as—" he hesitated, "as unreliable and crazy, as hungry and wild and mean as you did twenty years ago. And that's a compliment."

Then he spoke some lines with a pounding rhythm.

> " 'Love which is lust is the lamp in the tomb.
> Love which is lust is the call from the gloom!'

"Remember that? Henley?"

"Did Henley write that?" I asked. *"That* Henley?"

"Yes, buddy my boy, that old Invictus fellow. See, you never know. Remember what Marc Laurence told the Un-American Activities. . . . They asked him why he had joined the Communist Party, and Marc says, 'Because you meet so many pretty girls at their functions.' " He burst out laughing; then he looked over his shoulder again. "You could, too. That's where I met Elizabeth. At a function. They were raising money for the Scottsboro boys, I remember. She was beautiful then. Oh, yes, Elizabeth! You should see her now! A market analyst! Odets told me in 1937 that she had the prettiest pair of cup cakes he had ever seen . . . Were you ever with her? Back then? I know you knew her. Tell me. I don't mind."

"Yes I was. You know, just once . . ."

"I don't mind," he said.

"Well," I said, starting to go.

"I imagine it must still be going on, all that kind of life, somewhere."

"Oh, sure, same game, different players."

"You ought to get yourself a pair of rubbers. I mean your feet. You'll catch cold."

"Well," I said, "so long."

"You know you gave me a lift, you did. I sit in there day after day, I begin to feel like a bug in a box. And . . . well . . . she was good, wasn't she, Elizabeth, in bed?"

"Wonderful," I said, "but she would never see me again. It was just one of those accidents, you know, just once."

"Oh, sure, sure, don't worry. I understand . . . but she was . . ."

"Wonderful," I said. I started to go again.

"Well, take it easy," he said, "and be careful."

"Of what?"

"I'm in a precarious position here. Nobody has the least idea who I am! You know?"

"I know."

"So everything in the family? Right?"

I reassured him, waved, and walked away. When I looked back, after a few steps, he was still in the doorway. He stood there alone, no longer thinking of me. Then he entered the heavy building with its barred windows. The door was metal and heavy, and you could hear that when he shut it.

I walked into the cool night.

"AAAAAAAAAaaaaaaah!!" I said, out loud, clearing something within me. "Aaaaaachch ahhhhh!" blowing out the congestion of hopelessness Beetle Weinstein had left in me. Everybody around me was in disguise and dying, dying in disguise. But tonight, with the warm drink and the bright cool pins of drizzle, I was exhilarated. I had lived through it, I was the sole survivor of a gigantic shipwreck. I had escaped. At least I had postponed extinction. I was fed up with death, fed up with the silent slow surrendering all around me. I had left that behind me. I could see from Beetle Weinstein just how far behind.

"I was that way once!" I shouted. And then, "It doesn't have to be this way!" Out loud, all this, because I was also fed up and for good with my own secrets and my own front, my disguises and my pretenses. I was fed up with "Brooks Atkinson." The drizzle had fogged my glasses, and I took them off and looked less like him. And suddenly, for no reason, I was suddenly fed up with the New York *Times,* too, fed up with the "best" of our civilization as well as the worst. I felt like a foreigner in the whole life around me.

"I'm not part of this," I said. "I'm out of it."

Then I thought, where can I go? What can I do?

Start with a negative. At least I know what I don't like, what not to do. Because what I had been doing had just about killed me. I'd barely escaped with my life.

Love which is lust is the lamp in the tomb!

Well, I don't know about that, probably true, "tomb," yes, that part is true. I was in and now I'm out, and most everyone else is still in. Is "all that" still going on somewhere, Beetle had asked. Is it? Has to be, if it's going on in me.

And lust? Yes. The only thing that had kept me alive through all the years of my success were my indecencies, my infidelities, my "bad" side, my outrages. My decent and faithful, fair, orderly, and considerate side was a mask, and that mask, like the one in the old fairy story, had tightened around my face and my mouth till it just about choked me to death. Where I had lied and sneaked and cheated, it had been to escape the regimen, the terrible *order* that had been killing me. And damned near did.

Walking down Broadway, which was just as crowded with the sellers and the sold as Judge Winston (Weinstein) had said, I took a damned oath that I would suit myself from then on, no matter what the consequences, even if it brought me face to face with my own worthlessness and the scorn of the rest of the world. Perhaps it would bring me some whiff of my own identity. I would not disguise myself from myself again. I would not be law-abiding in respect to conventions and covenants which I had not made or agreed to.

I had a premontion, right there in front of the Astor Hotel, that I was about to pull out of the wall every hook from which I had hung my life. I was returning to the morality of the nipple and the mouth. It would bring down on me disapproval and reprehension. Still it was the next move. That was for sure.

Self-disgust is saving my life, I thought.

My only dignity, I thought, is my self-disgust.

Then I remembered a line, or a paraphrase, perhaps that's all it was, from the Bible. You have to lose your life to save your life. Whoever said that had it right. You have to die before you can live again.

The Paramount Building tower is the ugliest building I have ever seen. Its clock said ten of one. I hopped a cab.

It's totally illogical, I know, but I did expect that Gwen would be there waiting for me. Because, I thought, she is the same as I am. We're different in every way except the essential way; she's also an undigested stranger lost in the streets of this nation of identical streets. She'll be there, and she'll be waiting for me.

And, of course, when I got to her apartment building, the buzzer from above opened the front door immediately. The door to her apartment was ajar waiting for me. Gwen was sitting in a chair knitting. And lying on a sofa reading *Sports Illustrated* was a man she introduced to me as Charles.

FROM *The Assassins*

Cesario had a favorite picture of himself, taken in Panama City twenty-six years earlier by an army staff photographer. It made front page on the post paper, had showed the winner of that Friday night's fight, not in the ring, but out of it, being restrained by four M.P.s. There was a big hole in his face—his grinning mouth, from which blood roiled like tomato soup. Cesario had won that night like he'd won other nights, by catching everything his opponent could throw for the first five, six rounds, taking it all till the other man thought he had the Mexican ready for the kill in a matter of seconds, another flurry or two.

That's what he was most proud of in those days, his ability to take punishment. When his opponent finally punched himself out, couldn't hold his arms up, Cesario began to come on. Having eaten more fist than any normal man could, "Loco" walked out for *número siete,* crossing himself, and bit by bit paid his opponent back in leather for what he'd whispered in the clinches, and for what his twin brother and bunk buddies in the front row had never stopped shouting from the rail underfoot.

It wasn't a matter of race—well, that was part of it—but mostly because they all had their pay riding on the other guy and were watching it go.

Cesario enjoyed the last round most. He had his man staggering every which way, one eye closed, the other fluttering. Every time he was about to fall, Cesario would let up so he could recover enough for Cesario to begin to punish him again. The end of the fight was perfect, and Cesario recalled it now as he drove to the address on Queen Street that Colonel Dowd had given him. Just as the final bell rang, the man fell on his face, out! At this, his partisans in the front row decided to climb into the ring themselves. But they didn't have to because Cesario was over the ropes and among them like a badger, going for their vitals with foot and fist, in any direction there was belly and balls.

It had taken four M.P.s to break it up. When they were finally holding him back, that's when the picture was taken.

As he drove up to the house on Queen Street, Cesario was primed for that kind of encounter, himself alone against a houseful of the freaks he'd seen around Juana that night at Bennie's.

The single-story house, windows to the floor, a lawn with pepper trees, didn't look bad.

When he got out of his car, he left the curbside door open for a quick getaway. With his heart pounding the inside of his ribs like a baby's fist, he hopped on the porch, ready for anything.

He tapped on the door, waited, got no answer. He hit the door a solid shot, waited. He heard music, but no one came.

He tried the handle. It wasn't locked. He opened it a little and called in, "Anybody home?"

The music was that stuff Juana liked.

Now someone was coming.

The door opened farther, and a boy, not over fifteen, inspected him—and his uniform—for a few seconds.

"I'm looking for Juana Flores," Cesario said.

The boy called back into the house, "Michael, somebody's looking for Juana."

There was an answer Cesario couldn't make out, but the boy turned to Cesario and said, "She's not here."

"Are you sure?"

The boy called back into the house. "He wants to know if I'm sure."

Again he got an answer, again turned to Cesario and said, "Yeah, I'm sure." Then he closed the door on Cesario.

The hell with this, Cesario thought and walked into the place.

The room was dark. The only light was from the Joan Crawford oldie on the tube. Cesario saw Garfield and Crawford's lips moving, but what he heard was rock. When the film cut from a night scene to sunrise over the city, Cesario was able to distinguish two people, a girl lying on the floor, not looking at the movie, the top buttons of her jeans unbuttoned, held together with a ribbon. Pregnant?

The other person was a boy in his late teens, sitting at the end of a long sofa. He wore trousers only. The upper half of his body was so thin his ribs showed. He smiled up at Cesario, a gentle offer of welcome, then turned back to the old movie.

They were smoking a twisted cigarette. Cesario knew what it was. The boy pulled on it, passed it to the girl lying at his feet. She held it at the very end, drew in, passed it back to him. The exchange was unhurried and did not interrupt their preoccupation, his with the screen, hers with her thoughts.

The music was reaching a climax. When it was done, the thin boy looked up and smiled at Cesario again. There was something about this welcome that threw Cesario off.

A quick look around the room showed there was no one else there, no gang of freaks. The boy who'd come to the door was not in sight.

"I'm Juana's father," Cesario said.

The girl looked up at him, then dropped her head back on the floor.

The record stopped, the arm swung out of the way of the disc about to drop, and in that silence Cesario repeated, "I'm Juana's father. Where is she?"

"Out in the desert," the boy on the sofa said.

Garfield began to play the violin, but what they heard was Jim Morrison singing. The thin one nodded his head in rhythm.

"Where abouts?" Cesario asked. "Can you tell me where?"

"Sure," the thin boy said. "It's hard to describe. In the hills back of Saint Ignacio Mission, know where that is? At the near end of the reservation? You know where Father Felipe Pass is?"

"Yeah. Near there?"

"Back of there. It's not on a road, though."

He's being evasive, Cesario thought.

"We're going up there in a little while," the boy said, "if you want to come with us."

There was something about this young person that deflated Cesario's anger. He smiled at Cesario; nothing mocking about the smile. Metal-rimmed glasses added to his innocence.

"When you going?" Cesario asked.

"Soon as she decides something," he indicated the girl lying on the floor at his feet. "I want her to come with me, she's making up her mind."

He fussed with a small brass pipe, filling it with crumble, lighting it. He took a couple of pulls, then offered it to Cesario. "Want some?"

Cesario shook his head. "I thought Juana lived here," he said.

"She does. But sometimes she goes out there."

"Where's her—boyfriend?"

"Vinnie? Had to go to San Francisco. So when some of the kids decided to go out to the desert, she went, too."

"Where does she stay when she's here?"

"Like to see?"

"Is it all right?"

"Come on." He got up. "You sure you don't want to try this?" He offered the pipe again. "It's really good."

"No, thanks. Thanks, though." Cesario followed around to the hall at the back of the house. A naked man, just about awake, was coming through. He looked at Cesario without surprise, then went to the refrigerator and looked in.

"Michael," he complained, "no more beer?"

"Guess we're out," Michael said. He touched Cesario gently on the elbow, led him down the hall to where two rooms, doors open, faced each other.

In one of them the boy who'd come to the door was sitting on the floor busy at something Cesario couldn't make out.

Michael pointed to the room opposite. "She stays in there."

The entire floor space in this small bedroom was taken up by two large mattresses, neither of which was covered with a sheet. Crumpled at the head of one of them was a Basque striped blouse that Cesario had first seen in a store window and bought for his daughter.

He looked at the other mattress. Someone, boy or girl, was asleep, almost entirely covered by a blanket. The man who'd gone for the beer came back and, lifting the blanket, got in next to the sleeping person.

Cesario felt he was intruding, turned and looked for Michael. He wasn't there. The people under the blanket rustled around, then fitted together spoon-style and were still.

Cesario backed out.

His eyes, now opened to the dark, could see what the boy on the floor of the room opposite was doing. He had a pile of dried weed in front of him and was breaking off twigs, then crumbling the leaves onto a flat sieve that was propped across two cinder blocks.

The fifteen-year-old dealer looked up at him, lifted a leg, kicked the door closed.

"He thinks you're a narc," Michael laughed. He was kneeling on the floor close to the girl, whispering to her.

Cesario heard her say, "Right, right, I don't own him."

Michael stood up. "We're going, Mr. Flores," he said.

"I'll leave this here." The girl shut what looked like a home-stitched leather satchel.

"How you all going out?" Cesario asked.

"You won't need it out there," Michael said to her. He was putting on a long-tail shirt of thin white cotton. "We'll get a ride," he answered Cesario, "sooner or later."

"I got my car," Cesario said.

Michael smiled. "Then we can take some stuff out." He turned to the girl. "You got any money?"

The girl shook her head.

Michael nodded a few times as though her answer was the one he wanted. "This is Rosalie," he said to Cesario. "She used to be with Vinnie—before Juana."

As they left the city, Cesario stopped at a supermarket. "How many people out there?" he asked Michael.

"I don't know," Michael said, as if that was a helpful answer. "Get a lot of beer and some Fritos and cheese, you know. And some oranges." Then he turned and looked at Rosalie lying across the back seat. "She's asleep," he said, looking at her fondly.

"Whose kid is that she's going to have?"

"I didn't ask her. I suppose it's from Vinnie."

The shock pulled Cesario back to what he was there for. He'd begun to enjoy the experience; it had become an adventure! Now he was burning.

He stayed in the store till he had control of himself again, buying enough for a dozen people. He had to keep up the friendly front until he got hold of Juana.

When he finally came out, a full bag in the crook of each elbow and one between, he saw a policeman bent into the car, questioning Michael, who was looking at the policeman with utter friendliness.

"That's all right, officer," Cesario said, coming up.

The officer straightened, took in the air force sergeant, then looked back at Michael smiling at him from the front seat of the official car. It occurred to Cesario, now that he was back in the world of straights, that Michael was a pretty weird sight, sitting in the front seat of an air force car, his long hair falling over his shoulders in heavy curls, his face emaciated to where his cheekbones shone through the skin like amber, his soft, dark beard setting off his teeth as he laughed at the cop's bewilderment. For the first time, Cesario noticed a small aqua stone in one earlobe. And his voice—!

"He wants to know whose car this is, whose is it?"

"U.S. Air Force. I'm Sergeant Flores. Want to see my I.D.?" To his astonishment he found himself protective of Michael.

"I guess not," the cop said.

"Open the door, will you?" Cesario said, half an order.

The policeman obliged, then walked away.

As soon as they were in traffic, Cesario asked, "Does what's his name, Vinnie, know it's his?" He was whispering, but it wasn't necessary; Rosalie had slept through the encounter with the cop.

"You never know what Vinnie knows."

"Because maybe if he did, he wouldn't leave her like this."

"He didn't leave her, exactly. Your daughter's a very aggressive person, did you know that? She made up her mind to take Vinnie away from"—he indicated the sleeping girl—"and she did. Rosalie told him, any time you want to go, go. But her feelings were hurt. That's why she didn't want to move back."

"I don't believe that—about Juana being all that goddamn aggressive!"

"Well, okay," Michael laughed.

"She'd never even been with a man before."

"Okay," Michael laughed.

"What the hell are you laughing?"

"If you say so. Anyway, it's no put-down."

"Well, she hadn't. Don't you believe me?"

"If you want me to, sure."

Cesario, on the verge again, again held back.

They had come to the last cluster of stores before the climb up to Father Felipe Pass. Cesario stopped the car in front of the liquor store and went in for a fifth.

"That stuff's no good for you," Michael advised. "It'll rot you out."

Cesario didn't answer. Look who's talking! he thought. He felt better with the bottle in the car.

Cesario drove up the long, winding roads that were the way to the top. He wanted to change the subject, and Michael was very ready to talk about himself.

"I was in chemistry, can you believe it? The University of Pennsylvania, I was becoming an industrial chemist!" He laughed. "How to make new synthetics. For a while I was good, too. Straight Bs. But I could see most of what we were working on had to do with killing, insects or men or the earth, anything for big profits. I used to sit through those classes in a daze. People thought I was cracking up, talking to myself out loud, I couldn't hassle that scene. Because I was asking myself, is this the way I'm supposed to be? Like these people?

"So I began to read, not what the teachers told us to, but the hidden histories, the beliefs and ways of savage tribes. I found out it hadn't always been this way. What we are is recent as time goes. Other ways men live, that was what I wanted to learn more about. So I transferred out here, to this university. I began to study anthropology, that's their specialty, they got Indian ruins all around. The point of anthropology is that ours is not the only possible way. But the teachers were all apologizing for the old ones, calling them primitive, like you had to get into their houses by climbing down smoke holes and all like that. But they didn't seem primitive to me because they were what it's all about, and ours is about money, right?

"So I quit here, too. I sure have quit a lot of places!" he laughed. "I just decided to sit real still, live inside myself instead of inside a house, you know what I mean? No? Anyway. I sold my books and my clothes, let my hair grow out, like saying I was not for sale, and I began to look for my own way. I didn't do a thing except I believed in it, which means I didn't do much, right?"

"What did your father say?"

"I never found out how to talk to him. I wrote him a letter, thanks, goodbye, that was all."

"What did you do about the draft?"

"Oh, that was funny!" Michael laughed. "When they finally found out where I'd moved to, they invited me to come visit. So I did. They took one look at me—one good listen—I got this high voice, you hear, though I'm not a faggot, though I wouldn't care. Anyway, they took one look, and they could see I was telling them the truth. I told them I'd never shoot a gun at anything, not a man, not an animal, not a bird, nothing. If they sent me

over there, I told them, I'd sit down between those armies and do my postures and my yoga breathing and my *asanas*. They asked me what that was.
So I got down on the floor and I was standing on my head"—he couldn't
control his laughter any more—"and they were all around looking at me
and calling other soldiers in to look at me. This is a posture of relaxation,
I told them, I can stay up here for fifteen, twenty minutes. They declared
that wasn't necessary and that I'd be hearing from them, which I never did."

Michael laughed without end, and finally Cesario couldn't help joining
in.

"You're Mexican, right?" Michael asked.

"Mexamerican, Chicano."

"Part Indian?"

"Who isn't?"

"Why don't you come with us?"

"Are you kidding?"

"Maybe we have the same path, how do you know?"

"Are you kidding?" Cesario threw him a scornful look. "I was born in
Sonora, but we moved—ever hear of McAllen, Texas?"

"No. I wish I were Mexican. Do you know this one?" He began to sing
in a thin sweet voice.

"Sure—my father used to sing it. 'Adelita.' "

They sang together all the way to the top. Different songs, the first time
Cesario had sung since he got married.

The place called Father Felipe Pass is a saddle. On each side is a hump
of reddish-brown rock, covered with the thorny growth of the area and a
scattering of old, soft boulders. The prominences rise perhaps five hundred
feet above the plain, and between them is the pass, discovered by an intrepid
churchman, where the wagon traffic used to move. Now it's a place to park
for a view of the desert below.

"It used to be a lake," Michael said, "you can tell! See? The bottom of
a lake?"

"A lake? When?"

"What would you say to two hundred million years ago?"

"That was a lake?"

"You know Kansas? That was a sea!"

They walked down off the top of the rise and stretched out, and
Michael told Cesario about the life that was once on the hot muck of this
earth, about the Diplodocus and the Brontosaurus as high as a three-story
building, about the dinosaurs who fed on vegetation and were so big they
had to eat all day without stopping just to stay alive, and the Tyrannosaurus
Rex who fed on them.

"You hear that silence?" he asked. "That comes after something has
disappeared forever. They were here and they're gone and now there's si-

lence!" Cesario noticed his eyes, how soft and kind they were, and he stared at them till Michael had to ask, "Why you looking at me?"

Cesario had brought his fifth, opened it and had a long drink, and then for no reason that he understood he thought, My wife's trying to kill me. This made him feel even closer to Michael, and that was puzzling, that he could be fond of someone like this boy.

They rode over the flat, through the thorn bushes and past the saguaro. "Those things are full of water," Michael said, "and those—their fruit is good. You could survive here without food and water, if you needed to."

Then Rosalie woke and leaned forward in the seat and put her arms around Michael's shoulders, and Michael kissed her hands. Cesario couldn't remember when he'd last been the object of any such tenderness. Except from Juana, before all this.

"You ought to buy her a gift," Michael said. Cesario was startled. Did the boy know whom he was thinking of?

"You know what she'd like?" Rosalie said. "A rabbit."

"Where the hell am I going to buy her a rabbit?" Cesario asked.

A few miles later, Michael told him to turn off past a sign that read McIvers, and they went back to a clump of feathery Australian pines, and down under them was a little house and a big barn, and there they bought a small white rabbit. While Cesario was paying for it, Michael washed Rosalie's face in the water that flowed out of a length of pipe. There was no pump in sight.

Cesario didn't know how to hold the animal, so the girl did.

As they were getting into the car, a pair of fighter-bombers, wings almost touching, passed low over their heads, and the sound following made the earth quiver. They watched them disappear, then got into the car.

"You see," Michael said, "since our civilization is a failure, we're looking for another model."

"Who says it's a failure?"

"We all know that," Michael said gently. "You, too." Then he reached into his pocket and pulled out a little earthenware object. "Here," he said, "I want to give you this."

Cesario took it. "What is it?" he asked, turning it over.

"I found it out where we're going. It's an Indian whistle. Blow in there." Michael took it from him and blew into an opening, and there was a thin, plaintive sound.

"There used to be birds nesting under the roof of the house where I was born," Cesario said.

They had turned off the road and onto a dirt trail. Then that came to an end, and Michael told him to stop. There was another car standing there, an old Chevy without a top.

"We walk the rest of the way," Michael said. "It's the other side of that rise."

It was very hot now, and Michael took off his shirt and Cesario started to take his off, too, but decided not to. He had plumped through the middle and didn't look as firm as he'd like people to see.

There were a couple of hours of sun left, the hottest part of the day with the wind down to nothing. Michael, carrying two of the bags, led the way, then Rosalie, then Cesario with the ice-cold beer, now warm as broth.

When they trudged over the dirt rise—it wasn't sand, it looked like it had once been the bottom of a lake—they saw the house. It was something that had grown in stages, a stone cabin, added to in dobe, then finished with a wooden addition. There was no door, no window frames in the openings, but that side of the hill was already in shadow and it was very dark inside, so dark that at first they couldn't see the single person there, a girl sitting in a corner at the end of an old automobile's front seat. Michael put his packages down on the floor, greeted her as "Sandy." She seemed barely aware of him, stared through him, still held out her hand. When Michael took it, she squeezed, but didn't say a word.

From somewhere they could hear sporadic rifle fire.

Cesario put the beer down. He could see more now, but there wasn't much to see; the place was unfurnished. There was a large fireplace with a grill in it and some pots alongside, including a large enamel coffeepot.

The rifle fire stopped, and they could hear distant voices in dispute. Cesario walked out into the heat again, and in a minute, Michael followed, stood next to him.

"Where's Juana?" Cesario asked him.

"We'll find her." Michael began to walk in the direction of the rifle fire, which had resumed. Cesario followed, sweating. "Why don't you take off your shirt?" Michael asked.

In the next hollow there were four young men firing carbines at beer cans. The one with jump boots waved to Michael, then he saw Cesario and stared at him as if he recognized him.

Cesario had never seen the man before. He was black, his hair grown out Afro-style, and he wore glasses. As Michael approached him he turned his back to Cesario and whispered to Michael. The other men, laughing and fussing, paid no attention.

Rosalie, who had changed to shorts, came up to Cesario.

"What are they doing?" he asked her.

"Learning how a gun works."

"But there's no dangerous animals around here," he said, "are there?"

"Come on," said Michael trotting up, "we'll find Juana. Isn't it great here?"

They walked along the ridge into the glare of the sun.

On the last high point they came on a man entirely covered by a heavy, coarse blanket except for his head, which protruded from a small hole in the center. He was staring into the setting sun. Michael and Rosalie didn't speak to him, and he didn't take his attention off whatever it was fixed on.

The shooting began again.

Cesario, for some reason, perhaps the candor with which Michael had answered any question he'd put to him, decided to ask again, "What are they doing?"

"Learning to hit a target. They have the idea it may be necessary."

"For what?"

"Self-defense," Michael smiled and nodded a few times.

They walked up to an enormous cactus. Its main organ was twenty or twenty-five feet high. "Some of these hold as much as two tons of water," Michael said. "And their roots run off, just under the ground, sometimes for half a mile. A big one like this sucks up all the moisture round here. You notice there aren't any others around it. Survival in the vegetable jungle!"

"Hey, I think there's Juana." Rosalie pointed to a bra and dungarees on a bush. "Juanie," she called.

Juana raised up. She must have been sunning herself; she was naked.

"Your father is here," Rosalie ran and sat next to her on the ground and embraced her.

She's telling her it's okay what happened, thought Cesario. What the hell kind of people are these?

The whispering and embracing over, Juana looked around at Cesario and waved. She was putting on her pants, back turned to him. Michael was standing right over her. Juana grabbed her shirt, and, holding it in front of her breasts, ran to her father and embraced him, kissed him. Cesario hadn't held her so unclothed since she was an infant.

Without another word, he and Juana walked away from Rosalie and Michael.

"He bought us some food," Rosalie called out after her.

Juana held on to his arm and looked at him. She's really glad to see me, he marveled.

"You're sweating," Juana said. "Why don't you take some of all this off?" She led him to a declivity, a cup in the hill. He sat in the shade, she in the clear.

The sun was beginning to set. "Isn't it beautiful here?" she said.

"Who owns this place?"

"I don't think anybody does. Michael says some man bought it because he thought the city was going to grow out this way. Then it didn't, so he just forgot about it. Michael fixed the roof, and now they come out even in the rainy season."

"How do they—I don't see any wires."

"There's no electricity," she said. "Candles."

"How do they cook?"

"There's a fireplace—we make out. How are the kids?"

"They're okay. They miss you."

"I miss them, too. But these people—they're like a family, too. Don't you like them? Michael?"

"Yeah! You know I like him!" Cesario didn't control the surprise in his voice.

"And Rosalie?"

"She's pregnant—you know that?"

"I know. It's wonderful!"

Cesario decided to lay it on her. "She's got your boyfriend's kid in her."

Juana lay out flat in the dirt and looked up at the sky.

There wasn't a sound. In the distance, Cesario saw the men who'd been at target practice walk slowly up the hill, their carbines pointed to the ground, then down into the shadow and out of sight toward the house.

He wished he hadn't said it, not that abrupt way. "You didn't know?"

"No." Whatever Juana was feeling, she didn't let show. "I don't care," she said.

Cesario couldn't think of anything else to say. He watched the sun go down.

A man dressed in a suit without a shirt under the jacket was walking toward them. Cesario watched him approach. Juana must have heard his footsteps, but didn't move. The man, Cesario could now see, was an Indian. He carried something wrapped in newspaper, blood-stained. "Hello," he said. "Where's Vinnie?"

Juana shaded her eyes and looked at him. "Oh, hello, Arthur." She was still flat on the ground. The man squatted on his heels next to her.

"We killed a deer yesterday, and I brought him a side. It's a young one, tender."

Juana didn't speak. The man asked, "Where's Vinnie?" again.

"He had to go somewhere."

"I know he likes venison. He be back soon?"

"He went out of town."

"Didn't say where?"

"No."

"I brought him something else." He held up a little brown paper sack, the kind used to hold bits of candy or items of hardware in a general store. Juana took it.

"You gonna see him again?"

"Yeah, sure."

"Give him those. He knows what they are."

Juana nodded. He made a sign and walked away.

Juana covered her eyes with her hand. "That's the way Vinnie is," she said.

"Michael says he went to San Francisco."

"He has to go there sometimes."

"You know he deals in drugs? You know that?"

Juana didn't answer.

"Juana?"

Juana didn't speak.

"That's how he makes a living."

"I don't care," she said and got up. "Let's go back to the house. It gets cold pretty quick here, and you're sweating."

"Not any more, we can stay a while if you want."

She looked at him, and he seemed so kind. "You're a sweet man, damn fool daddy." Then she embraced him.

Cesario held her in his arms. "I can't stand for anyone to hurt you."

"He's not hurting me, daddy, what's the matter with you? He's helping me. I didn't know anything before him. About anything. He's teaching me who I am, daddy. Come on, let's go down—"

But Cesario wouldn't let her out of his arms. "I'll kill him if he hurts my girl," he said.

"Don't talk that way, daddy."

"I mean it."

"You probably would. You're a wild man."

She was standing in his arms and looking at him with everything in her face that he could ask for. He thought of the Virgin in the old church and thanked her.

"You see," Juana was saying, "you're really like these people here, but you've forgotten what you are, which is a goddamn Mexican and not made to act so G.I. all the time."

"What do you know about anything?"

But she was saying what he'd been thinking.

Everybody in the house was turning on to grass. There was a stack of Rolling Stones on the portable, nothing else, and everyone was turning on to the Stones.

Cesario was turning on, too, halfway down his fifth, remembering the days when he was young in Sonora, before his family was pushed out by the then Mexican government. "The goddamn Mexicans!" he said.

Juana was standing, holding her arms out. He was proud of her, the way she stood waiting for him with her arms out. "Get up, daddy," she demanded. She was the best girl there.

He did what she said, got up, held her close, began to move. He hadn't danced like that in years, not since he was in Panama and had his big strength, took it all, and was still starved for it after. He held her against his body now and he moved, holding her and moving, not far or much, mostly in place, like a bear in his heavy rhythm.

Everyone watched, even the black boy half-hidden in the corner.

"They teach you to dance like that in the air force, daddy, that where you learned to—?"

"Hell, no, hell, hell no!" Cesario said. He bent over her and laughed and held her harder and moved sideways, then forward, then sideways, and back and—

Sandy, the girl they'd met when they first arrived, was sobbing uncontrollably. Everyone looked at her, but there wasn't much you could do about the pain she was in. Rosalie went over to her.

"What's the matter with her?" Cesario asked Juana.

"She dropped some acid, she's having a bad trip."

Michael walked over to Sandy, and the girl rose and embraced him and began to sob. "Michael," she said, "Michael?"

Cesario didn't want to watch any more. It frightened him, not only because some time or other Juana might have been in that condition but because the anguish of the girl was so awesome, so uncontrolled.

Outside he crouched against the wall of the house, sitting on his heels, his back to the dry dobe, and he prayed.

"What are you doing here?"

Cesario raised his head. It was the black boy in the paratroop boots.

"You CIA or something?"

"No."

Michael came out of the house. "He's Juana's father," he said. "He's a friend of mine."

"I want him to know," the young black said, "if he's CIA or something, he's not jiving me—maybe you, not me." He turned and went into the house.

"Don't mind him." Michael squatted next to Cesario. "He's been hiding out here for five weeks, and he's beginning to freak out—when he saw your uniform, you know?"

"He doesn't bother me," Cesario said. "How's the girl, the one who's busting up in there?"

"She's on a real bummer, a lot to work off."

"Who is she?"

"You heard of the—?" he stopped. "Oh, what's to hide?" he said. "She's the daughter of—" Again he stopped. "What's the difference? She's rich. Her family. See what good it did her? She's out there all alone like everybody else." He laughed. "Her grandfather, that old man don't know it, but he's been supporting the revolution in this state, like for those carbines. And he's always good for bail. 'Call Sandy for bail!' She's way into all that— like the guns. All right, this," he touched the stripes of Cesario's sleeve, "that has to go, I mean all of it, there has to be a silence again. Like we heard on Father Felipe Pass, then a new thing has to come to be, right! But for me—what happens outside—I'll just watch that. I decided I'm going to explore my own space, inside me. Like that shooting. I was into it, too, but now I look at things different. I got to go someplace and listen to myself. You know? Instead of hating other people, I got to like myself. It's a whole different route, right? You see the difference there? No? Well, you will. I want to say something to you."

Cesario nodded.

"About Juana. Get her away from him. Vinnie, he don't stay with anybody. Never has, can't, he's way out, like in orbit, alone, that's the way he is, moving out, way out—"

"Food, daddy! Want something to eat?" Juana looked frightened. The girl inside could still be heard.

The venison was from a young animal, and there was a lot of it because Michael and the older man whose meditation they'd come on didn't eat meat. It was mostly knuckles and joints, but the meat between was sweet and good, and Cesario enjoyed it. Besides, he could see it was happening; Juana was going to come back with him. He chewed at the ribs, and he sucked the meat from between, and he washed it down with the rest of the whiskey. He didn't even mind the young black—what was he, a deserter?— staring at him.

"What are you looking at?" he finally asked.

The black didn't answer, just kept looking at him.

"What the hell you looking at?" Cesario asked again, now laughing.

I'm going to pick me a fight with this fucking black boy, he thought. He felt like he used to feel when he was a young man, before he joined the air force, when he was just a Pfc. in Panama and used to fight for the hell of it when there was no other entertainment, like he used to before he got married and learned control. He could feel the strings loosening, the knots becoming undone.

"You black shit-head," he said, "what you looking at?" Then he took the bones that were on his plate and shoveled them on the boy's plate.

"Daddy, don't do that!"

"Well, he keeps looking at me, that's not polite. You trying to ruin my meal? I'm enjoying it. What the hell you looking?"

"I'm looking at who's helping the Man kill his own people."

"My own people!"

"Black people."

"I'm an American, fellow."

"You're a murderer, fink!"

"Let's cool it," Michael said.

"Cool what? I told him I don't want to eat with a murderer."

Juana was holding his arm.

He smiled at her. She's with me, he thought, and he didn't care to fight the boy. "Okay," he said, "you don't want to eat with me, don't eat with me."

The boy got up and walked to the fire and lay down near Sandy. She looked at him, then took his hand and held it over her chest. Her eyes were out like a frog's.

"The U.S. Army and the U.S. Air Force and the U.S. Navy and all the U.S. people in U.S. Washington," the black boy said, "they're racist murderers, all of them, and you've got your brown tongue up their brown assholes, so that's what you are, too. So I don't eat with you, see?"

"Good," Sandy mumbled, "that's good." She tried to get up, fell back.

Cesario, full of flit and very ready, felt Juana's hand on his arm and tried to say what he had to say in as controlled a way as he could. "You can talk all that about the air force and the navy and Washington because we protect you. We protect you so you can curse us and do your let's-pretend target practice. You can peddle your drugs and live like this in someone else's house and eat the food and drink the beer someone else bought because you know when you get into trouble there's always grandpappy to come running with the bail money and pull the pig off your ass. Revolutionists! You ain't gonna revolution shit, and you ain't gonna shoot shit either because this country's strong enough to let you play your games, so go ahead!"

Cesario walked over to where the boy lay with his hand on Sandy's chest and said, "Don't worry, buck, I won't tell anybody about you, because nobody's worrying about you, boy, no one's scared of a nigger who—"

The black jumped to his feet and began to flail at him like a faggot— Cesario saw that right away—and Cesario crossed himself quickly like he used to before every round, then moved in and laughed and laughed, he was so exhilarated, picked off a couple, then stepped inside, then back, then in again so that the black boy's arms went around him, and Cesario was laughing all the time, which made his assailant all the more frantic to kill him. Cesario felt like in his younger days, when he thought for a bit he might really become a pro, he had some kind of gift and took a hell of a punch, people who knew fighters said that little Mexican cock sucker, he could be another Carmen Basilio. Oh, God, it felt good! He muscled and shouldered and blocked and slipped and when he was inside the boy was hitting him everywhere except where it might hurt and Cesario himself didn't throw a punch, he knew he could take the boy out any time he wanted, but let him punch himself out, he was beginning to hang his arms and Cesario decided to finish it a different way. Being inside, he said to the boy, "You better quit, nigger, you gonna get hurt!" But the boy was out of control, had to kill or be killed, only way he could stop. Cesario feinted with his hands and the boy stepped back off balance and Cesario put his right foot behind his left foot and gave the boy a quick shove, with one hand, that's all it took since he was off balance, and the boy fell over backward, his head hitting the floor just hard enough to stun him and stop the fight.

Cesario looked down at him, then at the others, and he said, "Revolution! You can't even put me away, twenty years older than any of you, it would take every man in this place, no, not all of you together, want to try?"

Michael was sitting with his back to the wall, petting the rabbit Cesario had bought for Juana. He held it up now and said, "Look at this, Mr. Sergeant Flores, come over here, please, and look at this animal. Because there's something I'm wondering."

For a reason Cesario didn't understand, he did what Michael asked.

"Here, take it," Michael suddenly put the rabbit in Cesario's hands. "Look in its face," Michael said. "Could you kill it? Then how come you kill human beings? Because you don't have to look in their faces?"

The rabbit moved, and Cesario had to look at it.

"You're right about this country being strong," Michael said, "so why do we fear everybody? And you're right some of us come from money, so we had everything, right? And didn't want it."

"You're all sick!" Cesario said.

"Maybe. But since you're healthy, answer me this. Has there been a year since your Christ died that somewhere on this earth Christians haven't used their best knowledge and their best sons to kill other Christians? And now we've refined the art, we don't even have to look at them, press a button, that's it! Like you! Can you look that rabbit in the eye? Cross yourself, Christian, like I saw you do before, then break its neck? With your hands? Looking at it, can you do that?"

Cesario couldn't look at the animal.

Now Michael's voice was so quiet that Juana had to come close to her father to hear it. "Tomorrow, go sit in the desert, sergeant, like the saints, the saints started as murderers. Go where there's nothing around you but the cactus and the snake and ask yourself, Mr. Sergeant Flores, aren't you what he said, a murderer?"

"No, he isn't!" Juana stood up. "I know him," she said.

"All right, Juana," Michael said.

"He's my father, don't talk to him that way!"

"All right, Juana, all right."

That was when Cesario knew for sure that Juana was coming with him.

In the desert the stars still have their fire. Juana and Cesario lay out in the sand, side by side. They heard a coyote. The wind was right, and the lean animal soon passed just above them and looked down at the house, smelling the smoke and the meat in the smoke.

Cesario took Juana's hand so she wouldn't move and wouldn't be afraid, and they watched the animal trip nervously back and forth, take a few quick steps toward the house, then change its mind and lie down, then get up and trot back into the darkness.

"I've got a transfer. To Spain, I think."

"Spain!"

"You're a grown girl, and you can do what you want, but I wish you'd come with us."

"I love you, daddy. Don't mind what Michael said."

"I mean what happened with you and—Vinnie. Well. Maybe you made a mistake, that's part of life, that happens."

Juana didn't say anything.

"I know what you're worried about. Your mother."

Juana nodded.

"She's just a worried woman, and she gets frightened. Can you blame her? I don't want you like that girl in there. I want you to have children. I'd like to be a regular damn fool grandfather, anything wrong with that?"

"No."

"So, I say, try it. Then—do what you want."

"All right."

"Did you say all right?" Juana nodded. "Well, then, we'll go back in the morning, okay?"

"Okay, only tell her—tell her—"

"I know what to tell her," Cesario said. "Where'll we sleep, it's cold out here." He got up.

When they went back into the dobe house, Cesario let Juana find their way to a spot on the floor. He rolled his coat up and put it under his head. Juana slept with her head on his shoulder. Cesario was as happy as he had ever been.

In the middle of the night, he guessed it must have been two-thirty because he had the habit of waking at two-thirty, he heard a rhythmic sound from close by and turned his head. Michael was on his back, and over him, Rosalie. Her breasts touched his chest, her belly curved to meet his. She was riding. There was longing on their faces, not diminished by the fact they were with each other.

Cesario turned away, remembering the way he and Elsa had been before they married. Long gone, he thought, and not about to come back.

Against the side of his body he could feel Juana's belly filling with breath, then emptying. He'd had that with Elsa, too.

He could hear them moving again, this time faster. Rosalie moving, Michael absolutely still.

Cesario looked again. Rosalie was holding Michael frantically, in that way that Cesario also remembered. Then it was over and she lay down on top of Michael and they were still.

Cesario now watched them without embarrassment.

In time she turned her head and looked at Michael, and there was something there that told him Michael was still distended.

I'm no killer, Cesario told himself. But I need what they have, I've got to have that because if I don't—

The life was still in him, he felt it now as hard as it ever was, and he turned away from Juana so she wouldn't by some chance move and become aware of what he had.

He turned his head, and there was Michael, looking right into his eyes. What he saw was a look of friendship, more than a look, an offer.

But it was too late. And it was too early. Cesario, when he looked at Michael now could think of only one thing—that Michael, he and that other one, Vinnie, had taken his daughter away.

So he stared at Michael, without giving. "I've got her back," his look said.

. ; .

"Want me to go in with you?" Michael asked.

Vinnie shook his head.

There was a stir in the doorway of the house before which they'd parked. In the dark they could make out a girl trying to come toward them and a man holding her, finally pulling her back where they couldn't see anything more. Then it was quiet. The man stood in the doorway, just behind the fall of light; they couldn't see his face, and he didn't move. Whatever the girl was trying to call out through the screened window, the fans in Chavez Ravine covered.

.

As Vinnie mounted the porch steps Cesario turned his head to avoid looking at him. But there was an impression on the periphery of his sight: How white the bastard's skin is! And another: There's something missing from his face. He looked quickly to see what wasn't there; the boy's eyes were invisible behind his dark shades. "Are you Vinnie?" he asked, looking away again. "I'm the one," he heard Vinnie say. Through the space between his cheek and the edge of his own glasses, Cesario could see Sergeant Jones moving up to the screen door. "Your friends want to come in, too?" Cesario asked, he didn't know why.

. . .

Vinnie walked in. Cesario closed the screen door, then the front door. He turned and looked at his guest again, his hair, his face, his chest, making a cop's identification, then lower, the bulge where the trousers met, extra large it seemed to Cesario, he'd broken into his daughter with what was there. Cesario thought of his own, how it looked as if it had been in cold water too long. He lifted his head now, couldn't see the boy's eyes, did see the hatred in the other features, the mouth, the way it twisted down, the lower lip, how it protruded past the hard-drawn upper lip. This boy was no saint— the pallor had fooled Cesario—or if he was, it was the saint who'd betrayed Jesus.

. . .

Standing in place, waiting for the thing to happen over which they had no control now, they spoke their words as if they'd been rehearsed.

"You're taking her over my dead body!" Cesario said, remembering the phrase from a TV program he'd seen, speaking in a voice audible to no one but Vinnie and in a tone that had no threat in it. It was simply something he said.

. . .

"Then that's the way it's going to have to be," Vinnie said.

. . .

The pathologist was to say that death came as a result of a single shot fired full into the boy's face from one foot away; there were powder-burn marks to indicate this. The tiny slug had passed through the top of the mouth and lodged in the cerebellum.

It was easy, Cesario thought, I never saw his eyes.

. . .

IN THE AIR FORCE, malcontents wear masks.

When Colonel Dowd came down to breakfast the next morning, his daughter Marian was there, and with her, his son-in-law, Alan Kidd. Lieutenant Kidd was on the judge advocate's staff, the base's legal department. He was dressed for tennis.

The way Dowd looked at the young man made Mrs. Dowd feel a defense was called for.

"We were having blueberry pancakes," she said to her husband, "and I remembered Alan particularly enjoys—"

"You playing tennis this morning, Alan?" the colonel asked.

"Try to every morning, sir." Alan was coating the last of his griddle-cakes with soft sweet butter. Dowd watched him. Alan noticed his hesitation, said, "Join us, sir." A gesture offered a chair.

"Have you read the newspapers?" the colonel asked.

"Try not to before I play. Does something to my concentration on the court. I did hear we had some violence on the base—"

"Are you trying to kid me, Alan?"

"I am. Yes, sir." Alan arched his back. He was a perfect six-foot, one-hundred-and-eighty-five-pound specimen, a Yankee classic, at twenty-five distinguished not because of anything he'd done but because of what he was, a man aloof, protected by his passivity. He had made no concession to the new full fashion in hair. His was blond, parted in the middle and falling just to the top of each temple. President William H. Taft wore his hair in this style; so had Secretary of War Henry L. Stimson.

"I heard you were in the base hospital last night," Colonel Dowd said, "just before me."

"Yes, sir, I heard all the commotion, took a stroll, and I did drop in there."

"It was you who brought Flores the ice cream—"

"Yes sir; that's right, strawberry he wanted. Curious."

Colonel Dowd looked at his watch. Alan refilled his coffee cup. "Only be able to play a couple of sets this morning."

The colonel gave up. To his wife he said, "I told you not to let me eat those frozen Mexican shrimps last night."

"They weren't Mexican."

"They were Mexican, and they were frozen, and they froze again in my stomach."

"He's quite right, Mrs. Dowd," Alan gently set her straight. "The Mexican variety, you should remember, have the larger fantails." Then Alan turned to the colonel and threw the largess of his approval from the other side of the royal carriage. "But I must say, sir, I find them delicious."

Muriel twinkled. Alan had a knack of making everyone grateful for his approval.

"Take a bromo, sir," Alan offered. "You seem a bit overwrought this morning."

The cook hadn't heard the news about the colonel's stomach, put pancakes in front of him.

"Not today, Mary," the Colonel said, "tomato juice today."

"I'll just relieve you of those, sir," Alan said, and did.

"How the hell can you play tennis with six blueberry pancakes decomposing in your stomach?"

"He does very well," Alan's wife, Marian, defended him. She was reading the morning paper, all about it.

"A full stomach never bothers me," Alan said. "That's one of those myths, sir." Having carefully buttered the six sides of the newfound cakes, he reached for the honey. It was Heidi-Heather, a great favorite of the base commander's, a delicacy which his brother, Bank of America in Holland, sent him from there. Alan spooned into it twice, scraping bottom.

"There's plenty of maple syrup," Colonel Dowd observed.

"Your Green Mountain Boy Maple Syrup, Colonel, under some pressure from the federal government, has admitted in the smallest possible type that it is composed nearly altogether of chemicals, sweetening, color, and flavor. Read the label when you have time, it's instructive."

Colonel Dowd had to laugh. Actually he liked Alan. On days when base H.Q. business was light, he often went out of his way to seek him out. On such days his son-in-law never stopped gabbing, overturning old mossy stones. But his jibes and jeremiads were gentle, passed for entertainment. And after a few late drinks, Alan needed only a nod from Dowd to sit down at the piano and sing in his modest tenor the good old tunes the colonel loved, "Drink to Me Only" and "The Blue Bells of Scotland."

Colonel Dowd felt very close to his son-in-law at those times. He had lived long enough in enough different societies to be suspicious of ambition when it was the central force in a man's life. In fact, Dowd had a streak of hedonism in him, now dead from neglect and the rigors of propriety. It had left a trail of memories. For no reason, now, he remembered the young mistress he had in Tokyo during the Occupation; he remembered her as he often did when he was unhappy, her silky, straight, and very black pubic hair; he recalled the stinging hot baths they'd taken together and how she'd ask, "Have I pleased you?" after they made love. He looked at his wife, Muriel, and his daughter, Marian, each a very handsome woman, each with a sizable piece of aristocratic flint in the middle of her face, past which they were now scanning him, trying to read his thoughts.

"I want to talk to you," Marian said. She put the newspaper down.

Alan finished what was on his plate.

Dowd said, "What about?"

"About what's on your mind," Marian said.

"How the hell, daughter, do you know what's on my mind?"

The cook hurried in. "Omaha on the phone!"

Colonel Dowd ran for the stairs.

"Get your breath before you talk to them," his wife called after him. Then she turned to her daughter. "Marian, leave him alone! You know he's in a bad mood."

"Mother, I am not in the air force, and I do not adapt my behavior to what his mood happens to be."

Alan stood up. "Think I'll run along," he said.

"Alan," Marian complained, "I want you to be here when I talk to him."

"Thank you for breakfast, Mrs. Dowd," Alan said, "I enjoyed it." He walked to the door, picked up his racket and a cable-knit white sweater.

"Alan! Please!"

He turned and looked at her. "Would you come here a moment," he said, "and excuse me, Mrs. Dowd?"

Marian walked to him like a child about to get a scolding she deserves. He looked down at her for an instant, smiled his Apollo smile, patronizing yet protective, then suddenly bounced the flat of his racket ever so lightly off her hairdo and, as the gut twanged, said, "I really don't want to be mixed up in this case. Let's not burden the base with my indifference this time, let's leave this opportunity for honor and achievement to hungrier men?" He looked at her, nodded agreement for her, then inclined his head gracefully as he did everything gracefully, kissed her lightly on the lips, and sauntered out, leaving her in love with him.

Nevertheless, she waited for her father to come down.

Upstairs in the bedroom, Colonel Dowd was lying on his bed, prepared for what he thought would be an extended conversation. But when he told his superior the news, all he got back was "Chu-ryst!!"

"What does that mean?" Dowd asked.

"We'll have to meet on it and call you back. Don't do anything till we have a chance to consult here. Meantime I want you to tell the automated recorder exactly what happened and what the considerations are as you see them. Try to essentialize, Frank. Now—when you hear the signal."

Beep. Colonel Dowd talked a précis of the night's events into the phone, laid down the facts, then summarized. "We can't win on this one," he said. "If Master Sergeant Flores, with our help, gets off, we will be reinforcing the impression general in our society that the air force, the navy, and even the army are privileged. On the other hand, if the man is penalized—and remember this is clearly a case of murder in the first degree—we will be outraging the community. They are fed up with these kids—hippies, I mean. There is another consideration on this side, even more serious. Either way —and this is why I say we can't win—we are leaving the impression that our highly trained personnel have been highly trained to solve their problems by the use of a gun. We are, are we not, trying to create the impression that our services are made up of decent, law-abiding citizens, repeat citizens, civilians! You can see the problem is complex, correct?"

"I need immediate, specific instructions. How do you want me to proceed? I will be under considerable pressure here from the media and the community, and this pressure is sure to increase. Please make every effort to get back to me with an early answer. Waiting. Over." He spoke his name, rank, and station and hung up, repeating, just before he did, "Urgent!"

Downstairs Muriel had cornflakes waiting for her husband.

Also waiting was the judge advocate on the base, Lieutenant Colonel Earl McCord. He had brought the late morning edition.

"What does it say?" Dowd asked. "Good morning, Earl."

"Could have been worse. Good morning."

"Have some coffee," Dowd said, asking for silence.

"Had some." McCord nodded thanks at Mrs. Dowd. Then he ventured, "I thought you might want to talk to me, colonel, before I go to the office." His eyes slid over to Marian, then back to Muriel. "I mean after you read these."

Well-trained Muriel got up. "I wonder if you'd excuse me," she said. "I'm leaving." She looked at Marian.

"I'm not," Marian said.

"I didn't mean—" McCord started.

"I know what you meant," Marian said to him. "Now if you will let me say what I have to say and pay proper attention, you'll be rid of me within a couple of minutes."

Dowd had taken in the front-page stories with a glance down, a glance up, and turned to the sports page.

"Daddy, pay attention, please."

"Marian, I have a crisis this morning."

"On the sports page?"

McCord chuckled to cover his embarrassment. He was glad he didn't have to handle women like these, especially the daughter. Lieutenant Colonel McCord had trained his wife not to talk in the morning. "Perhaps I'd better move along now," McCord volunteered, looking at his chief for instruction.

"Sit where you are," Marian said. "What I have to say involves you, too. Daddy!"

Dowd put his paper down. "Yes, Marian."

"I want you to give Alan a chance on this. I think you're misled, both of you, by his easygoing ways, and you haven't allowed yourselves to discover that Alan is an exceptionally—"

"Now, Marian, did I ever say he wasn't intelligent?"

"Daddy, Alan has never had a chance—don't look at me that way, Colonel McCord. I know I'm being personal. I'm his wife." She took an instant to quiet down. "Daddy, I know you're going to see to it that Sergeant Flores has every bit of protection the air force can give him—"

"My dear," Dowd said, "the air force doesn't yet know—"

"Daddy, that's pure bull. This could mean a lot to Alan."

"All right, Marian, we'll talk about it later."

"He has two more years to do. I should think you'd want him to go out of here with some sort of reputation, some sort of professional standing —listen to me!"

Lieutenant Colonel McCord reached for his cap.

"Colonel McCord, you've always treated my husband as a playboy when the fact is that he's really got a brilliant mind, far more interesting and original than your own, if you'll forgive me saying so—"

Dowd blew. "Marian, get the hell out of here!!"

"This is the first time I have ever asked you for anything, daddy," she said. "I know I'm making a fool of myself, but goddamn it—"

"I appreciate your loyalty, girl."

"This is going to get in all the papers and on television, and it's a chance for Alan. He's too proud to ask for it, so I'm doing you a favor, I'm giving you a chance to be a decent father."

After Marian had left the room, Dowd asked McCord, "Why don't you like my son-in-law?"

"Well sir, every time I assign him, he acts like he's doing me a favor to accept."

Dowd smiled.

"I like your daughter, though. I like it when a woman sticks up for her husband that way."

"You didn't answer my question," Dowd said.

"Well—are you serious?"

Dowd nodded.

"He's just not a soldier," McCord said.

"He wears a uniform."

"With moccasins."

"They're black. That's within limits. What do you mean, he's not a soldier? What's a soldier?"

"Well, I was raised on a post, Frank, and I suppose I'm as blind as any other lifer. Lieutenant Kidd's got all the civilian virtues. He's gentle, kind, amusing, agreeable, companionable, clean, tolerant, understanding, intelligent, I didn't mean to leave anything out. And he looks great. Okay. Now! How has he earned the right to behave so condescendingly?"

"He's the son of a famous judge. You've heard of Judge Nicholas Kidd?"

"I certainly have."

"And, well, he was brilliant in college and law school—"

"We are still preparing for the eventuality of a full-scale war, are we not? Can you imagine an air force of tennis players? Someday someone may have to stand up again and mean what he says again and die to make it stick. Lieutenant Kidd is above it all or—I don't know. Do you?"

Muriel found her daughter sitting at the window of the room she used to occupy before she married. Muriel was a sensitive woman, trained to accommodate herself to the mood of others. She went to a chair, the mate of Marian's, sat, and looked out the window, too.

They sat for a minute without talking.

"Alan," Marian started slowly, "is suddenly, totally without ambition. I don't know what to do." She waited for her mother's response.

"Apparently," Muriel said, "he has everything in the world he wants."

"Well, that's dangerous. He's in the air force for one tour, he has two years to go. What's going to happen to him when he gets out?"

Muriel thought a moment. "Men have stages," she said. "When your father came back from Japan, I thought he'd never need me again. But in time—"

"I keep wondering, is it my fault? He's like a car that's had a sudden loss of power."

"Well, he was always—"

"No, he wasn't!" Marian said. "Jesus, mother, he was 'most' everything in college, most likely to succeed, hardest worker, Phi Bete! Sometimes I think I understand what's tuned him out, but if I'm right, I'm part of it! It's like he was dying of some gentle but fatal disease, one he enjoys. Suddenly he's decided to quit on everything. That's why I thought if Daddy—"

"Does he still love you—physically?"

"Nothing like he used to. You notice how he was downstairs—detached, a little mocking, you can't quite touch him, godammit mother, he makes love to me like.he's doing me a favor!" Marian picked at the hem of her skirt. She made up her mind to raise it an inch and a half.

"I'll talk to your father," Muriel said.

Marian leaned over and kissed her.

Downstairs, Colonel Dowd had told McCord about the call from Omaha. "For the moment," he said, "there's nothing to do but wait to hear. Meantime, avoid the press. I've closed the base to visitors. How the hell did those hippies get through the gate last night?"

"Sergeant Flores passed them through."

"Apparently he was waiting for them. With a gun."

"Apparently."

"What's your judgment on this?"

"I've been trained all my life to do one thing."

"Enforce the law?"

"*Uphold* the law. The subtleties of public relations, I suppose they're involved here, not my field." The pipe had gone out, and he put a flame to it.

"But dealing with your field, upholding the law—?"

"There's only one answer. First degree. Deliberate and unequivocal. He's guilty."

"That's his opinion, too."

"He was in a position to know."

"You don't think he stands a chance?"

"That's not my point."

"What is your point?"

"I don't think we should defend him," said McCord. "I don't think we can—and be what we're supposed to be. Not really. We have to uphold a certain standard. We know what happened. And we know the law."

"But aren't there human considerations that—?"

"The law is what we have."

"You mean, you'd ask for his life for killing a couple of drug addicts?"

"I want you to know," McCord said, "I like Flores. He's a damned good soldier from what I've been able to observe—"

"But you'd—"

" 'Fraid so. Have to."

They were silent for a moment, then Colonel Dowd slid off with, "Well, let's see what they say in Omaha."

He got no help from Omaha. "The only instruction we feel sure about giving you is that it must be a civilian trial, no display of privilege. If he's guilty, he must be punished, just like any other citizen. Incidentally, how does he intend to plead?"

"Guilty. Says he wants to pay for his crime, seems eager to, in fact."

"What's the matter with him?"

"Religion, I think."

"Well, here's our feeling. You are there to protect the United States Air Force, and the services in general. You must bear in mind that at this time we are on trial with the American public; we have to watch every move we make."

"Peace is our ever-loving profession, right?"

"Frank, you have to look at this killing as if it happened on Okinawa. One of our men got drunk and killed a native. Remember how we bent over backwards there—?"

"Sergeant Flores is a good soldier."

"No privilege. Don't throw our weight around. You're head of an occupation army. If the soldier did it, he did it. Incidentally, who did he shoot?"

"Two longhairs."

"Well, could be worse."

"One was black."

"Oh God, I thought you said long-haired."

"You know, Afro, electric, something."

"What the hell did he go and do that for?" There was a silence, then, "There's nothing in our instructions, Frank, to prevent you from getting the best lawyer in that community and charging him with defending your man."

Colonel Dowd didn't answer.

"How's the weather out there?" Omaha asked.

"Oh, you know, it's the desert. That hot wind blows up from Mexico and we fry."

"Well, keep in touch." The phone went dead.

Mr. Don Wheeler, first partner of the biggest law firm in that world, rearranged his morning so he could sit down with the colonel immediately. He asked only that the base commander come out to his home. "We'll be able to talk without anyone informing themselves that you've consulted me. I can guess what it's about. The murders last night?"

Colonel Dowd made a sound for yes.

"I don't think I can help you," Wheeler said, "but perhaps I'll make a few suggestions. You remember how to get here?"

Two years earlier when Dowd had been brought back from Asia and put in command of the base, he had been introduced to the substance of that desert motoropolis at a series of social gatherings. The most important as well as the most convivial of these took place on Don Wheeler's hilltop, where his home, Points o' the Compass, extended its paws over four terraces. The party centered around an ox roast served from a reproduction of a chuck wagon. It started late in the afternoon so that Mr. and Mrs. Wheeler's guests could have margaritas on the west terrace and enjoy the sun setting to the music of mariachis. The party stopped rather early so that the male guests in ranch clothes, broad cowboy belts with heavily ornamented buckles cinched over desk-chair bellies, would be in good shape the next morning when, dressed for what they were, insurance executives, bankers, real estate developers, department store owners, mine owners, they redevoted themselves to the business of life and the life of business. Dowd remembered the occasion and the house very well. He pointed out the hill to his driver and told him to go to the top.

Dowd got a surprise. The house was full of packing cases. Three Mexican servants were packing up Mr. and Mrs. Wheeler, who were leaving for good.

"I'm going back to my cows," Don Wheeler explained.

"Ten years late." Mrs. Wheeler smiled and shook hands with the colonel. When Dowd had seen her last, she had looked to be maybe ninety-five pounds soaking wet. In the two-year interval, she'd lost weight, now looked twenty years older than her husband, a tiny, gracious crone.

Wheeler, on the other hand, had a "western" build, a solid six feet, broad across the shoulders, thick through the chest, tight in the waist and thighs, very long legs, longer for the boots he pulled on every morning. A slight swagger was inevitable. "Yes," he said, "Hope's right. I promised her—"

"You promised yourself," Mrs. Wheeler corrected gently.

"So I did. That when I was fifty I'd live out my life the way Hope and I like to live."

"He was sixty yesterday," his wife looked up at him as if he was a son of whom she was very proud. "He doesn't look it, does he? Give him a couple of months on a horse, and he'll look just like all the other hands." She patted his belly, ever so lightly. When she raised up on her tiptoes and stretched her neck and head to him, he kissed her, called her darling, and she left.

"No one knows exactly what she has," Wheeler said, "but it seems to be progressive. We've seen a lot of doctors."

The colonel didn't know what to say. "Where you moving to?" he asked.

"Two hundred thirty-nine miles due north. Got a couple of sections, half a mountain, one real pretty stream, full of trout, ranch house, outbuildings, bunkhouse for the hands, run a lot of cattle. But it's not a business. Like Hope says, how do you want to live? I propose to get on a horse every day. I do not propose to hear cars, sirens, typewriters, telephones, complaining, bargaining, bluffing, all the sounds of humanity at business. I don't understand the world now. What I do understand, I don't like. I'd rather see a rattler in the morning than most of my clients. A coyote sounds more brotherly than anything I hear in that city. And I don't know a friendlier sound than the one my cows make when they come in at the end of a day. Now air traffic is a problem. TWA goes over four flights a day, but they're at six miles and I can take that. You people fly one pattern over me that's a noisy bugger! But I figure you're protecting me from—what the hell are you protecting me from, please, sir? What? Huh?" He laughed and said, "You look worried."

Turning away from his guest, Wheeler slung his feet upon the arm of the chair next to him and began to shake out the base commander's memory. He demanded the precise sequence of events, time and geography, the smallest details, the contradictory versions. He seemed not to be listening to Colonel Dowd; often his questions did not link up to the answer he'd just received. Like all good lawyers, Wheeler had the knack of making the most innocent man feel a little guilty. Just when Dowd began to resent this, Wheeler turned and apologized. "I know I'm doing this like you were the fellow who shot him. Force of habit. I'm sorry." Then he looked at his guest and smiled.

But Dowd was not so much angry as fussed. Wheeler turned away, noting this, stretched his arms and yawned. Then he decided to satisfy his curiosity.

"I must admit there is one thing that puzzles me, and it hasn't a thing in the world to do with the case."

By God, Dowd thought, the son of a bitch wants to chew on me some more. "What's that?"

"I can't help wondering why you're so worked up over this." Wheeler let the question hang. The moment became uncomfortable. "You must be very close to this man," Wheeler continued. "He doesn't sound your sort at all. But here you are, and—"

"I rather dislike him, to tell you the truth," Colonel Dowd said.

"Then what?" Wheeler persisted. "It's irrelevant, of course, but this kind of trip is well outside your line of duty, isn't it?"

"Well, he's always been a valuable man at his job."

"So you're protecting a good soldier?"

"I can't imagine anything else. How did we get into this?"

Wheeler recognized that something he knew a lot about, his instinct for the jugular, was loose again. "I'm sorry," he said, then asked, as if Dowd had started it, "may we please just drop this? I feel I've embarrassed you."

"Oh, that's okay," Dowd said. "I'm just surprised you found me to be so—involved, so exceptionally—"

"It means your instincts are in the right place. I don't imagine there are many bits of brass who'd take the trouble to personally set up a defense for—what did they say in Omaha when you spoke to them this morning?"

"How did you know I spoke to them?"

"I didn't."

"They were—cautious."

"Look after the air force first, its reputation, its public standing?"

"More or less."

"But how do you best do that?"

"That's the question." Wheeler smiled at him, and Dowd tried again, feeling his way. "I'm still surprised by what you asked me," he said.

"There's a mystery in most human behavior. That's always been my interest in the law. Most of our work is for industrialists and real estate people, and to tell you the truth, I despise it. But this stirring around in people, I'll miss."

Wheeler smiled at him again, and now Dowd went with it. "How about some lunch?" Wheeler asked. "Huevos rancheros, some guacamole, we might even dip into an early margarita."

Dowd found that despite Wheeler's questioning, he was enjoying the man's company. Wheeler insisted that his wife make the margaritas herself, and she even brought them out herself, setting them down carefully so the salt around the rims did not shake loose. Then she kissed her husband's forehead—they were always saying goodbye, it seemed—and left. He watched her go, pausing to bend over some border flowers, pulling out three dead stalks with three quick plucks. Then she straightened up and didn't just then remember what destination she had chosen for her next trip, said, "Oh!" and set off purposefully into the house, light as a bag of feathers.

Wheeler found the eggs too bland and added chili till he liked them enough to order another set of twins. While he ate these he informed Dowd, "You don't have anything to worry about."

"I really don't know why I'm so wrought up over this," Dowd replied.

Wheeler was looking down into the valley where the city was laid out under a blanket of mustard smoke. "Would you believe it, when I first settled up here, the air was as clear as a mountain brook in the spring? Now I don't dare draw a breath when I go down there, wait till I get back up here to get my oxygen. The irony, of course, is that what you see down there comes mostly from copper mines, some as far away as one hundred miles, and they are our clients, I work for them."

"What's the solution?"

"I'm leaving the battleground in disorderly retreat. It's every man for himself now."

"Still—the rest of us—we haven't got a place two-hundred-odd miles north of here to go to."

"I'll take you with me. I got a couple of cabins up there, one five miles from my house, you have to get there on a horse. In the winter you can watch the antelope come down off the mountain, they go right by the front door; and any time you're liable to see wolves in packs or a puma alone, and eagles, they're still there, but you better hurry, they're going—"

"What did you mean I have nothing to worry about?"

"The air force is not going to have a damned thing to say about this. It's a community matter, and the community is going to protect itself."

"The murderer was air force."

"This community is not going to let your man pay with his life for something every single one of them would have done."

"But justice—"

"Fuck justice! You would have done the same thing if it had been your daughter, right or wrong?"

"Well—"

"Answer my question!"

"No, I don't think so."

"You would and you know it. I'll tell you something. If it had been one of my boys who'd shot one of those long-haired freaks, I wouldn't be worrying over it, no, sir, nor feeling as guilty as you—or I guess as he does."

"He doesn't feel guilty. He says he's ready to pay."

"I don't care what he says, it's out of his hands. This is frontier. We protect our homes, and we protect our women, the damned fools. I'll tell it to you plain. Your man did right."

"Well, perhaps he did—"

"No perhaps about it. My grandfather came out here, Bible and gun, from the state of Maine, and a meaner-looking son of a bitch you won't find even in the movies. He put four markers down, and that was it. No deeds, no grants, no favors. And brother, I'm telling you, if someone had fooled around with the sorriest of my five aunts—" He burst into laughter. "And if he'd been away, my grandmother would have taken care of it and without a whole lot of soul searching; she'd just put her pistol down on whoever. What the hell is going on—I'm going to be candid, sir—when you, the commander of Collins Air Force Base, are uncertain where the values in this thing are?"

He got up. "Come on, let's go down to my office. Ride with me, your driver can follow."

Just before they passed into the smog, Wheeler stopped the car. "There's one now," he pointed to a bird circling about a mile down range.

"Hawk?"

"That's an eagle. Don't know what the hell he's doing down here, looks like he don't either. Poor son of a bitch can't see through this soup to get himself a meal. Wish I could communicate with him. I'd tell him I got a couple of his cousins for neighbors up north, and he ought to come on up."

"Beautiful, the way he floats."

"He can drop like a big red rock! There isn't a damned thing man has ever made that's as beautiful as that bird. I'll tell you a story. When I was a kid I thought I'd get me a young eagle to train. So a buddy of mine—he's dead, went down over Bremen—we climbed a mountain, made fast a rope, and dropped me to the ledge where the nest was. Well, sir, the mother of that brood spotted me. I had looked around carefully before I went down and hadn't seen her. But I sure as hell saw her coming at me, and I'm telling you I was lucky to get out of there with my life. I never forgot how that lady defended her kids, I mean those are fundamentals. Mister, what happened to the fundamentals?"

Dowd had no answer.

"You wonder and quibble and consult about a man who finds his daughter's been corrupted by a worthless drug-consuming son of a bitch and does something about it. What the hell has this society lost when that bearded bastard whose picture I saw in this morning's paper is flushed down the toilet? Tell me that?"

"Not much, I guess."

"Tell me the truth, don't you admire your man for doing what he did?"

"Well—"

"That man has done us a service, Colonel Dowd, and while your mind won't let you admit it, your feelings, which are truer, they know it. And that's why you're here on an errand that a second lieutenant should be chasing out. You're paying the man respect by coming up here. You're thanking him. And believe me, the community will, too. Because whatever bad I say about this city and this area, I still know these are right-thinking people here, and they're not going to let your man die. So relax."

As they turned into the parking lot next to Wheeler's office building, he said, "I'll take the case. I mean my office will. I won't be around much, but I'll put a good man on it, and I'll be looking over his shoulder to make damned sure he does right. Okay?"

In Wheeler's office there was a saddletree between the two large windows and on it an elaborately worked Mexican saddle of golden-hued leather with brass fittings. Dowd admired it.

"It's been there fifteen years, lest I forget my cows." Wheeler leaned over the intercom, "Tell Gavin McAndrews to come in here." Then at Dowd, "You look like you got one thing more to say."

"Just this. The air force is extremely desirous of preventing any and all impressions that its members are privileged. When I spoke to Omaha this morning—"

"They'd rather see the man dead. I know."

"Oh, now, come on, they've got a point. We just can't be prominently involved in seeing to it that our man is let off easy."

There was a soft knock on the door, and Wheeler bellowed, "Come in here, Gavin!"

When Dowd saw the way Wheeler looked at young Gavin McAndrews, he remembered the moment on the terrace when Hope appeared in the doorway holding the two goblets of linda margaritas up in front of where her breasts had been, and Don Wheeler leaned over to him, whispering, "We have no children."

"Sit down, boy!" Wheeler said with surprising roughness, pointing to a chair. "But before you do, shake hands with Colonel Francis Dowd, you heard of him!"

"I certainly have, proud to meet you, sir."

Dowd noticed that Gavin had a slight limp.

"Read the papers this morning?" Wheeler asked the young man once he was seated.

"Yes, sir."

He's too young, Dowd thought.

"What I was referring to," Wheeler said, "and why the base commander is here—is the murder on the base last night."

"Yes, sir?"

Wheeler put Gavin on the spot. "What did you think?"

"I think," Gavin began slowly and thoughtfully, "well, I haven't met the man, but I'd certainly believe that he'd have an awful lot of sympathy behind him in this community. He certainly has mine. I hope to have kids and—well, what do I think? It looks like an open and shut case of first degree, but if the case is presented right, which means in its human context —the law, when you get down to it, colonel, is the most human of the professions—I believe your man might very well get off with manslaughter two." He turned to Wheeler. "Are we going to handle it?"

"You are."

Gavin looked at the colonel. "Is that all right with you, sir?"

"You're handling it for this office," Wheeler said. "Colonel Dowd is leaving it up to me, and that's my decision."

Then he looked right at Dowd and waited. If he was going to object, now was the time.

Dowd let it pass.

Wheeler didn't camouflage that the pause and the silence amounted to an acceptance of Gavin by Dowd. "Okay," he said. "Now Gavin, tell the colonel what manslaughter two means in terms of penalty."

"Five to seven, he might have to serve that much. Depends. Might get off with less. It's flexible. I'd say five."

Maybe it's good he's so young, Dowd thought, won't look like entrenched power at play.

"I'll do my best," Gavin said. "I surely will!"

"You better do better than that," Wheeler said sourly. Then he laughed, and they all joined in.

Gavin looked at his watch. "Well then," he said, "I think I'll high-tail it down to the jail and meet the man."

"He's not in jail," Colonel Dowd said.

"Where is he?" Gavin asked.

"He's on the base. House arrest. I spoke to the chief about it, and he said—"

"What the hell did you do that for?" Wheeler demanded. "Jesus, I thought you were so concerned about public—" Wheeler stopped. "I'm sorry," he said. There he was again, treating Colonel Dowd as a subordinate.

"I know," Dowd said. "It does seem wrong, but—"

"You did say you didn't want to create the impression air force personnel were privileged?"

"Now, calm down, sir, calm down," Gavin said. He often had a way of scolding his chief, a treatment that Wheeler loved. "I agree it was a wrong move, but we'll straighten it out. We'll have him in a nice comfortable cell for his supper—and—"

Any doubts Colonel Dowd had had about the young man were gone, not only because he saw the boy had poise but because it was clear that he could hold his own with Don Wheeler, something Colonel Dowd had not yet done.

"Mr. Wheeler," Gavin said, "what would you say if we wait for the county prosecutor's office to act on this one? Let them be the ones who throw our man in jail. Make them the guys with the big black hats straight off? Let's lose the first round, what do you say?"

Wheeler looked at him with the purest admiration. *"Muy inteligente,"* he said. Then, to Dowd, "Ain't he the shrewdest little son of a bitch?"

FROM *The Understudy*

Sidney Castleman, né Schlossberg, was an actor of vast talent who went on living after his star had died. On Broadway in our time, who needed a sixty-six-year-old potbellied Jewish bull for a hero? He was needed by the "I" in this story, who had once been Sidney Castleman's understudy and was now himself a star.

IN THE INSTANT you step from a night flight into the land of Kenya, you find a festering in the air and that the illumination is faint. Imagination, of course, livened by alcohol, but what I smelled that night were cannibal fires, and the light, feeble and spotty, was the light from those fires.

Inside Nairobi Terminal, the officials making entry difficult or simple were black. They were extremely courteous in a style out of fashion in our society and inherited from the colonialists they'd booted. But this show of manners made the power they had over me more threatening. They treated the white man as an equal, a terrible comedown for the Caucasian accustomed to favored-race status. Equality is not what he wants.

I'd been drinking. The only thing more salutary than being alone, I'd discovered, was being alone in alcohol. Now it suddenly concerned me that these health and security people might find my wobbly presence undesirable. I tried to control my sway and my totter. I needed help, but from someone who would recognize that my disarray was basically spiritual and that I might wish to enjoy it a bit longer.

Then there he was, a man who did. "I'm Piper," he said, "Jim Piper, your white hunter."

Quickly he spoke a few words of Swahili to the customs man going through my luggage. The black smiled, answered. They were old friends. Jim flipped my foldover bag, and the official, who now seemed charming, not threatening, blessed it with a chalk mark.

"All set," Jim said. "Right this way." He pointed the direction, then, with a deferential "If I may precede you?" gesture, led me, carrying the bag, my aluminum camera case, my hat and raincoat, and my in-flight reading, which I'd not cracked.

"Hope your flight wasn't too bad," Jim said over his shoulder with a perfect smile.

"A bit bumpy," I said, sure of his sympathy, so not asking for it. I'd once played *Journey's End.*

"Sorry about that, sir," he said as if he was responsible and had goofed.

"I know you must be very sleepy," he said as we got into a VW box. "We'll have you in your room within ten minutes. The hotel, Kimani," he said to the driver.

"The last time I came to Nairobi," I said, "it was also the middle of the night, and all I found was a note directing me to take a taxi to the New Stanley Hotel, where there was a room reserved. I was with my wife, and I—"

"How could anyone allow you to arrive in a strange continent at two in the morning and not be met?"

"What safari company?" Kimani turned to ask.

"Don't tell," Jim Piper said. "I don't want to think badly of our rivals."

"Is this room quite all right?" he asked. We'd not paused at the desk. Jim had registered for me.

"Oh, fine, fine." I was asleep on my feet.

"I'll have a peek at the bed. It's traditional, make sure the linen is—yes, it's fresh. Now, goodnight and thank you. I look forward so much to our days together. In this envelope"—he offered me a large English-style Manila-brown—"you will find three items, a map of the region where we'll be going, a sort of schedule of times, places, and distances, which please consider no more than something to depart from, and finally, here, a list of what I think you might want to have with you in the way of clothing and personal effects. I'm sure you've thought of them yourself, but just on the chance that you or your wife have overlooked something, there it is. I will be here at noon, and we'll go shopping for whatever you may want to add to your gear. That shouldn't take too long, so we'll get you a nap in the afternoon." He quickly pulled down both shades. "You've lost seven hours, you know."

He came by exactly at noon and had a second breakfast with me. He was tall, blond, and handsome. If that sounds like the hero of an old-time novel, that's exactly what he looked like, perfect in the same way. So were his manners, taught him at a guess by a maiden aunt who'd learned hers from a maiden aunt. Jim Piper did everything quietly and easily but with rigid attention to correctness. I used to make the mistake of considering an Englishman gay if his bearing was gentle and his manners irreproachable when all it had been was that they're bred to the graces, including a consideration for others we Americans neglect. Jim, for instance, asked if I wanted my rolls warmed and did I prefer cream to milk in my coffee. He made sure my eggs were as I liked them, sent them back when they weren't.

He informed me he no longer killed game, refused shooting safaris. "I regret every animal I've killed," he said. "I've done all I ever will of guiding people who come to Africa to get their Big Six and when they see a larger head than one they have, kill it too. I don't want this part of the world changed, it's the last of it, you know."

On the shopping go-round he made sure I wasn't overcharged or given inferior goods, offered recommendations which I accepted. I actually didn't need all the extra stuff, but I was enjoying his company and how he handled the Indian shopkeepers.

I noticed he wore sandals over bare feet, asked did I really need socks? He was very positive about that, thought I should have at least four pair, always a dry set available. The only real hardship in the Bush, he reminded me, was the ants. They'd crawl up a man's trouser legs if he stood still for more than an instant next to one of their marching columns. It was best to have long socks with elastic tops and keep them up and over one's trouser bottoms.

In the course of all this I dropped that my wife generally did my shopping and asked, "Are you married?"

"Oh, dear no," he said. "Almost once. Decided against it when I began to lose sleep over her. Haven't time for that."

Had I found a man without a "personal life"?

"If a woman wants to stay over at my place now," he went on, "I make it quite clear that I intend to get a full night's rest and if she wants to stay up and chatter to please look elsewhere."

That was the first time I noticed what I came to call Jim's voice of command. When he was recalling his conversation, imagined or real, with the young woman who wanted to talk after intercourse, he impersonated himself in that situation, not as he was with me, but suddenly very commanding, a person who protects his elite order by laying down rigid rules of acceptable conduct. Then he smiled at me, and there again was this comforting, companionable voice and his air of affable gentility.

He took me back to the hotel and, looking at his watch, said, "Now I want you to take your catch-up nap. Lack of sleep can make one a bit edgy in the Bush. Meantime I have to get together with Kimani and the other two boys. We have three hundred items to check and double-check before we set out. Why here"—he handed me two typewritten sheets—"suppose I give you a copy of our list, just for sweet curiosity's sake."

"God, you're organized," I said, after a quick look.

"There's no way to correct mistakes in the Bush, you know. Now one last thing. We generally try to provide some proper entertainment for our clients the night before we set out, a sort of get-to-know-each-other party, not that you and I need that any longer, do we?"

"Oh, no, but fine."

"Well, there's a rather nice place, Indian, of course, but clean. I'm confident you won't get any tummy trouble. Quite a nuisance in the Bush, that can be. Do you like curry?"

"I like curry and I like it hot."

"They'll make it as hot as you can stand. Well, now then, there's this other matter. I hesitate to bring it up because of the very affectionate way you spoke of your wife, but here! I am prepared to bring along two ladies, one young, the other less young, and if you care for either—they're not too bad actually and I know from experience that they're agreeable—" He stopped, seemed to have lost his way. "Oh, yes, if you care for one or the other—you see I was so impressed with the devotion you expressed for your wife—but this may be our last contact with whatever benefits urban civilization has to offer, and it's possible young women are one of those, would you say?"

"I imagine," I said, joining the conspiracy, "they can be quite a nuisance in the Bush."

"Indescribable. The mind balks at the thought." He came back to procedure. "Well?"

"You were about to tell me how I might indicate a preference?"

"Oh, yes," Jim said, "order the same drink the one you prefer ordered."

"I'll have a beer too," I said to the very swarthy Indian who was, Jim informed me, the owner as well as the waiter and the cook.

Then I turned my face to the sandy-haired, blue-eyed sabra, the excessively healthy employee of El Al Airlines, one of the two women Jim had brought along.

It was so simple, the first step out of my married bind. She looked so clean, El Al, nifty! Perhaps we would do nothing but talk. I've done that, I really have. No, I'd go with it, come what may. I was entering a new phase. Let Ellie go to Florida and lug Arthur's piano with her. El Al! She had blue eyes, looked very clean. I'd fallen into luck, and I had Jim to show me the way. He was, I could see, what I wished myself to be—unconnected.

"So, it'll be two whiskeys," Jim said to the owner-cook-waiter, "without ice, please remember, and two beers. I imagine the local will do." He turned to me. "I think you will find it acceptable. If not we will have a word or two with this gentleman." He smiled, a little threateningly I thought, at our host.

The tone of his instructions to the Indian, an older man of a sodden yellow complexion, brought back certain salients of British history and the sound of martial brass. But when he turned to me, his voice switched over to that of a member of our elite, clubby, softly spoken, almost girlish.

If Jim had any reaction, disappointment or pleasure, because I'd preferred one woman and left him the other, he showed it not at all. Actually the girl who'd become "his" scared me. Darkly handsome with excellent features and long chestnut hair, she would have been quite attractive except for her eyes. They bugged out of their sockets. This lady, perhaps thirty, was quickened by an excessive flow of thyroid that gave her the threat of instant hysteria. I'd had all I could take of that.

My sabra was as clearly uncomplicated, no threat of tears in the corners of those agate eyes, no lines of affront around their casings, no disappointment erosion tracks off the ends of her mouth. She wore a military skirt of the same sandy color as her hair and a blouse that was loose and light. Through its panels her breasts were offered. My sabra promised an evening of simple pleasure.

Nothing turned out as I'd anticipated.

In the first place there was no question of whether we would or would not, no problem of my place or yours. After the curry, Jim dropped us off at her home without asking either of us. He was riding a well-worn track.

Then? Nothing. I didn't turn on.

And El Al? She sat on the armchair, perched on the sofa, finally waited on the bed, like a fish on a plate, ready to be consumed, promising no resistance, looking at me with neither desire nor apprehension.

That became the challenge. Could I rouse this girl?

And myself?

Finally her indifference got to me. But—

When one caress didn't work, I tried another. When one area didn't yield a response, I shifted my efforts. I went lower. I parted the petals. When my hand didn't do the job, I used my mouth. When that failed, I introduced my member.

She didn't seem excited or repelled by anything I did. To judge by the expression on her lovely face, she might have been behind the counter at the El Al office.

When I came, if she was relieved to have it over with, that didn't show either.

"Don't you come?" I asked after she'd washed off my contribution.

"Of course," she said, "whenever I care to."

"How is that accomplished?"

"It's very simple, you kneuew." This was her only mistake in English pronunciation, this *you kneuew*.

"You mean you do it to yourself?"

She smiled, crinkling her eyes.

"Why didn't you give me some hint, a suggestion?"

"That wouldn't have accomplished anything."

"Then why did you allow me in the first place?"

"I wouldn't want you to go away disappointed on your first night in East Africa."

"Are you sure that you—?"

"Of course. I please myself. Very much."

"So then, you need no one?"

"I like the whole thing better that way. I don't have to douche or wash off. I don't have a big body pounding hell on me in a rhythm that has very little to do with my own and leaves me much too tired to do a good morning's work in the office. By God, I've seen some chaps who want to keep putting me on my back again and again all night and in the same way. I wonder what pleasure they think we—?"

"But still you do it?"

"A social gesture, you kneuew."

"It isn't that you like girls?"

"They're as bad as the men. We have very strong girls in Israel. They pound hell on you and, excuse me, chew on you, worse than the men. For longer."

"So then, all you really need is—yourself?"

"It's not a big problem, is it? Just a body function for you, so a body function for me. Alone I never have to plan it or go through a lot of nonsense first. Sometimes I take myself by surprise. Suddenly I'm playing there, and continue till satisfied. Then I sleep. Immediately. No damned neurotic woman with her stories of failures with men, no anxious man who wants me to wait till he's raised what's necessary to try again. That can be a long wait, you kneuew."

"Yes, I know."

"You're not offended, I hope. Some men take it as a slight on their—"

"Not me. I understand you perfectly. Thank you."

"How did you get on with El Al?" Jim asked the next morning as he helped me carry my bags to where our jeep was parked.

"Did you ever make it with her?"

"Everyone in our organization has. But if you mean shoot her down, no one has accomplished that. Still it's very nice to have that kind of person around, don't you think? She's quite companionable and certainly not tiring, and she can always get you on a flight, one way or another. You slept well, did you not?"

"Perfectly."

"What more can you ask?"

"And the other one, yours?"

"Oh, my God, she, how do you Americans say it, she flips her bloody wig as soon as you touch her. At first you get an overwhelming sense of potency, you find yourself as she finds you, irresistible, the completely exciting man. But after a while, all that becomes quite exhausting."

"So you're tired this morning?"

"Oh, God no," he reassured me, brother to brother. "I told you I do not allow any woman to trouble me. For instance, last night, she wanted to come to my place and so forth. But I—"

"But then you would have had her all night." Was I getting the idea?

"No, no, you Americans are so romantic, so polite. I would have told her the evening was concluded just when it was concluded at her place, after my second discharge. But at my place, I would have had to get up and be rather persistent that she do likewise. I can't stand last night's woman around in the morning. Can you? I would have had to dress her, that's a bit of a problem with an unwilling woman, don't you find? Then lead her to the street against her will, possibly with a bit of resistance to boot. I have no time for that."

"But at her place?"

"I get up when I'm ready, my car is below."

I'd cabled the safari company that I wanted to go out as simply as possible, with one man in one tent. But the jeep we were approaching had a trailer in tow which bulged with equipment and supplies, and I certainly had not anticipated that three small black men would come tumbling out to snatch up my luggage and call me bwana.

I watched Jim going over the trailer coupling, testing each rope and knot to make sure it was taut and hard. He had the massive forearms of a tennis pro.

Satisfied, he commended his crew.

Then we rolled out of Nairobi.

Street by street, the city shook off Europe. In Karen, the suburb named after Isak Dinesen, Jim told me there were still lion and, even closer to human habitation, leopard, heard at night, seen never. Leopard were the great adapters, he said, could live on anything, our cats and dogs, our leavings. They would survive men. Behind me the "boys" were laughing their assent.

"They understand more English than they let on," Jim said. "But say whatever you wish and quite openly. They're good boys."

"Kikuyu?" I asked.

"Oh, God, no, Kikuyu! Civilization has reached them. The Jews of Africa! Much too clever for their own good. No, these boys are Wakamba."

Then he made the introductions, a C.O. presenting his staff, Kimani the cook whom I had already met, Francis the waiter, and Obowatti the spotter, all smiling and I at them. They were packed into a space so full of baggage and gear, of extra fuel and hyena-proof lockers that I would have said there was no room for them except there they were, knees pulled up under their chins, looking like saucer-eyed bush babies.

"I thought the short rains would be over by now," I said an hour or so later. We were going down the side of a great escarpment into the Rift Valley, and a huge cloud, lowering its black belly over us, began to drop its load.

The boys were out before Jim stopped the vehicle, putting up the side screens.

"If you're tired," Jim said, "this might be a good time to nap."

"I don't want to miss anything."

While Jim, on request, was telling me about the Great Rift, what it was and how geologists say it happened, I fell asleep.

When I woke it was still raining and I spoke the thought that woke me. "About last night," I said, "what we were discussing, don't you think if you exclude from your experience all relationships that cause you pain or inconvenience, aren't you denying yourself the most real—?"

"What is real?"

"Deepest?"

"Because they hurt you, they're deep? My God, you're a Christian saint, complete with stigmata."

"They're bound to be painful often, yes."

"I've never had a deep experience with another human. I avoid that sort of thing. You have to be careful whom you admit to your life, wouldn't you say? I'm sure that sounds shameful to you, quite un-Christian."

He'd said precisely what I wanted to hear.

"Most of the women I know," Jim continued, "are pleased to have it brief and impersonal. The protestations of everlasting love I've heard are generally for quite a practical purpose."

"So we'll pay the bills?"

"For one thing. There's an awful lot of sentimental brush to clear away. Sexual pleasure, when you've tasted it for a while, is not that precious. To tell you the truth, neither is life. When you've lived in the Bush awhile—"

"But doesn't that way of living—leave a rather large hole in your life?"

"Which way of living?"

"The arm's-length way?"

"I didn't say that. I said clear away the false concerns, the sentimentality. Accept things as they are."

I was tempted to bring up Sidney.

"The deepest experiences I've had are not with women, what they call love. That's an American obsession, love. You're looking sleepy again. And just when I was getting to the deepest experiences of my life."

Jim would have forgotten Sidney years ago.

When I woke the rains had stopped, and I saw animals grazing.

"The gazelles," Jim pointed, "are Grant's. And there's a—"

"A Tommy." I remembered the little Thomson's gazelles with affection. "The cattle? Belong to the Masai?"

"Yes. We've reached the border," Jim said. "The meat producers for humans have begun to give space to those for cats. Oh look!" He pointed. "See. He's only got three legs."

The Tommy had lost one leg behind. He was grazing apart from the others, pulling up a couple of quick teeth-crops, then looking up, then down for more, then up, all the time his short white-tipped tail twitching nervously.

"How come he's separated from the herd? I should think he'd—"

"His fellows probably drove him off. He's bad magic, don't you know, a spook. Anyway, he's safer here with the cattle. The Masai hold off the lions."

We'd stopped so our boys could remove the rain panels.

Standing in the middle of the field were two very young Masai of the area whose ear lobes had been pulled down and opened into long loops. Their faces were daubed with reddish clay. On end, at the sides of their tall, slim bodies, were long spears. One of the boys, pre-pubescent, was naked.

Jim waved. The boys waved back, looking at us with neither deference nor hostility.

Ahead the plains rolled like the open sea.

"That's the way it all used to be," Jim said, "I can remember."

We were moving again.

"How does he survive, the Tommy, on three legs?"

"He does, as you see, for a while."

"Someone should take him in."

"How like a god!"

"What does that mean?"

"Forgive me, but that's what I mean by sentimentality. It's our special arrogance that we humans decide who survives, even who deserves pity. Nothing personal, but who are you to say that particular Tommy should be saved?"

"It's only an impulse to help the weak."

"That's very Christian and very dubious. You're an American. You know that the strong survive by killing the weak."

"You in favor of that?"

"Of course not."

"Against it?"

"Of course not."

"Then what? It's the law of nature?"

"The law of life. Every man for himself." He smiled at me.

"Actually I wasn't thinking of those less strong. I was wondering about—aberrations. I don't know the proper word applied to animals. For humans it's eccentrics, freaks. Did you say 'spook'?"

"Yes. They're killed."

"Why?"

"They threaten the rest of us."

"But why?"

"That's the unanswered question. The Greeks killed messengers who brought bad news. By killing the man you kill the news. Animals believe in the same kind of magic. They're no less savage than we are."

Midafternoon we came up to a complex of low-lying buildings.

"Keekorock Lodge," Jim announced, "part of Kenya's national effort to lure the dollar—well now it's the Deutsche mark."

"That where we're going to stay tonight?"

"We could. We could also press past here to the spot I have in mind for our permanent camp. It's about twenty miles into Tanzania, well off the road in an unmarked valley that—"

"Let's go on."

"I was hoping you'd say that, but before I take you up on it, let me warn you that this lodge is your last chance for a sitting-down defecation, and a bath with unlimited hot water. We have a shower, but theirs is better."

We did the twenty miles to the Tanzania border in silence. It was that hour of the afternoon when the predators begin to hunger and stir and, if they are lion, stalk off from their pride, their legs stiffened in the heavy walk peculiar to cats, their heads lower than their shoulders. We made a turn in the road, and there were three cheetah, a mother and two, Jim said, walking not trotting, business on their minds. They moved off the road for us, not hurrying, then watched as we passed, perfect beasts, the king's hunting companions of old, the frown of royalty etched into their face fur.

"Why are they traveling the road?" I asked. "Isn't that dangerous?"

"This is a photographic area. No shooting allowed."

"They know that?"

"Of course."

"Still, why on the road?"

"Small game stay close to where man is, feel safer there. So the cheetah—"

"Know that?"

"Of course."

Some ten miles later, Jim turned off the gravel road and into the

Bush. There was no sign anyone had gone over that ground before, open country without track, rut, or marker. Jim was navigating by a hill, a gully, a brook, a special tree, a great rock.

The jeep astonished me. It rolled over brush and small trees, climbed at sixty degrees, forded streams.

"It's a Toyota, actually," Jim said, "a Japanese copy of the British Land Rover, which, like many of their imitations, is better than the original."

I asked about a herd in the distance. "Zebra," Jim said, "and so, of course, lion." He pointed out a pile of white bones.

"How do you know, lion?"

"Hyenas don't leave bones. Leopards don't feed on the ground."

The area was an old battlefield littered with the final traces of those who'd perished.

The secret camping site was at the bottom of a long, even slope. A stream ran among heavily leafed trees, giants.

"Fig trees," Jim said.

He drove under the great boughs into the dark.

"Isn't this great?" Jim said, jumping out where it was most heavily covered. "Precisely the kind of place you want, I'm sure."

Behind us the light flared, then failed. Rain began to fall, but under the spread of trees it was still dry.

"It sure is," I said, wondering what it would be like at night.

I watched them uncouple the trailer, Jim moving swiftly here and there in a kind of lope, never seeming to hurry, still everywhere, pointing where he wanted our tents, where their kitchen, speaking his orders in that unchallengeable tone. It seemed perfectly in place here, his voice of command, not excessive or unnecessary. It was reassuring to hear.

"Come on." He started for the Toyota. "We'll look around."

Birds were scurrying for shelter.

"It's raining pretty hard," I said.

"Going to be a beauty. Great sport! Let's go."

"The boys have guns?" I asked as I got in my side.

"We don't carry guns on this kind of safari," he said. He spun his motor, shouted some final instructions in Swahili, and we drove off.

The rain was falling in glazed sheets.

Climbing, we'd reached a nob of high ground. Jim whipped his Toyota around like a movie cowboy his mount and flipped off the ignition.

"Now, will you please look at that!" he said.

I'd never seen the anatomy of a storm before. In open country a storm has dimensions and contours, it has movement. We could see where this one was going, and where it had been the light of the sun was again touching the earth.

Then the belly of the cloud came over us and gutted itself. We could see nothing, ahead or behind. A sheet of water covered the ground.

"How do the animals survive this?" I asked.

"They turn their backs," he said. "Isn't it beautiful? Don't you find it beautiful?"

"Yes. Even though it makes me feel helpless."

"Cuts you down to size, doesn't it?"

He was looking at me, appraising me. Then he changed the subject, questioned me about New York, knew street names, buildings, statistics.

I told him about the muggings, about the terror in which middle-class whites live and the poverty in which most blacks live, finally about Ellie and her karate class, about her determination to protect herself.

When I was through, he asked, "Why do you live there?"

"It's where my profession is. And it's my country. That's the way it happens to be now."

The rain was coming down even harder. Still we heard distant barking. Dogs?

"What do you consider your country?" I asked. "This one's ruled by blacks. You're merely tolerated here."

"The old man, President Kenyatta, still needs the white man's brains and knows it, so he's been fair to us, so far. But when he dies, I haven't decided where I'll go. I lived in Rhodesia for a time—"

"Rhodesia?"

"I was in their police. There's a lot I liked about Rhodesia."

"Of course you saw it from the police point of view."

"I imagine you must be for that since they're protecting your wife while you're here."

"My generation was brought up to disapprove of the police."

"Why ever?"

"I wish they didn't have to be so many and so—brutal."

"Brutal! You are a sentimentalist. Really! Forgive me, but—what do you think civilization is? Strength provides order. Nothing else can. Actually Rhodesia is the only country which will survive what's coming."

"Which is?"

"The holocaust, the great black revolution. This is Africa, and the savagery of our animals is nothing to the savagery of our natives when they're not controlled."

"I've noticed that when you talk to the boys your tone of voice is—"

"In Rhodesia the police are trained to be very definite and very loud, in that way exercising a sort of control by voice over our inferiors."

"Then it's an acquired thing?"

"I also come by it naturally. My father, deceased, was a general in the army when this was British East Africa. Our family went through the Mau Mau time, and while it wasn't as bad as your sporting novelists make it out, nevertheless the ones who were hairy-back came through while the sentimentalists perished or fled to the mother country. May I ask you something?"

"Of course."

"In the situation you describe, the one in the streets of your city, don't you feel at the mercy of your blacks?"

"I suppose I do. Sometimes."

"You can't possibly like that feeling."

"What would you do in my place?"

"Go to Rhodesia. Perhaps."

"If you liked it there so much, why didn't you stay?"

"There was a threat of marriage," he said. "I escaped. Are you getting hungry?"

He'd changed the subject abruptly.

"I am, but it's not important."

"Our client's comfort is always important," he said.

Apparently he'd noticed a diminution in the force of the storm which I had not. I wouldn't have moved on a superhighway, but Jim proceeded slowly yet without hesitation through what seemed to me to be a cloudburst. I could see no path, no marks, but in a short while we were rolling down that long, even slope, at the bottom of which I could see our camp. He put the Toyota right up against my tent.

"I imagine," he said, "since you're so happily married, a woman can't possibly seem a threat to you?"

"It's happened."

"I know you'll disagree with this, but here it is. I believe the wave of the future is the herd concept, not the family."

"Are you serious?"

"That's how most of us live now, isn't it?"

"And you're satisfied that way, to be alone?"

"Above all when I consider the opposite choice. The family, to begin with, is an invention of man. It's not natural, is it?"

He looked at me and waited, but I didn't pick up the subject.

"When you're ready," he said, "we'll have a drink."

I dashed through the rain into my tent and zipped the flap.

I hadn't exerted myself, but I was tired. I found a narrow cot made up with bulky blankets, and I fell on it. The only other furnishing was a small table holding a large field lamp. It was lit and hissed. The tent was made of a fine cloth which glistened, a synthetic. Waterproof, it also seemed airproof, a perfectly sealed container, like those small ones they use to pack frozen foods or those other enclosures where some of the sick spend their last hours.

I decided to have that drink. I jumped the puddles to the front of Jim's tent. The little waiter, Francis, came trotting through the rain to ask what I wanted.

"Whiskey, please," I said.

"With soda, sir." A statement, not a question. "And no ice."

"Actually I'd like it with hot water, but with the rain—"

Francis was gone.

From inside Jim's tent I heard BBC, the news. "They're having a freak snowfall back home," Jim called out. "Yours. That ought to cool those streets."

The rain was still coming down. "Under the circumstances," I said to Jim when he appeared, "I'd be quite content to have something cold and simple, like a peanut butter sandwich."

"I'm not sure we have peanut butter," Jim said.

Francis came trotting back with a glass containing three fingers of Scotch whisky and a small white pitcher full of steaming water.

"How do they heat the water?" I asked Jim.

"By fire," he said.

Francis's head was as wet as that kind of hair can get. He asked Jim what he wanted and trotted off through the break in the bushes. Jim had placed the kitchen so it was concealed. Almost immediately Francis reappeared with Jim's drink and a plate. He stood in the rain just outside the shelter made by the canvas overlap and reached in. The plate contained cashews, and they were warm and crisp.

"This is all very gallant, this running back and forth in the rain,"

I said to Jim when Francis had disappeared, "but why did he stand that way? Why didn't he come in out of the rain?"

"And get us wet? I wouldn't have cared for that." Jim passed the nuts. "They don't take rain the way you do," he said. "They live in the weather."

"How do they keep a fire going?"

"They do. Several. Please don't show surprise at what they're able to put on the table. At the end of the meal, if you feel so inclined, say a word of commendation. They'll merely nod, but a word like that, correctly spoken at the right moment, holds the whole thing together down here. It pays their pride."

"Which is all they have?"

"What more have you? Sorry."

The dinner was excellent. There was even a kind of béarnaise sauce for the steak and three kinds of vegetables. Considering the conditions under which it was prepared, the meal was a miracle. But I'd already learned to accept miracles with the same exaggerated casualness Jim did.

When it was over, I chose what I thought might be the right moment and spoke some words of praise in a tone as close to Jim's as I could manage.

Francis nodded and ran off. Kimani, the cook, who'd come to our end of the kitchen path, nodded, then turned back.

"Spoken like a true white African," Jim burst out laughing. "Now, let's have a liqueur. Francis!"

Francis was already bringing a tray of bottles from among which I chose Drambuie. As I sipped, I heard the first lion.

Jim didn't, apparently.

"He sounds hungry," I said, to call his attention to the distant roar.

"It's the rain," said Jim. "It makes them anxious and disgruntled."

"Will that go on all night?"

"Till they make a kill. When their mouths are full of meat, they don't roar."

"I'm perfectly safe in my tent, I know," I said. "But by what magic? It's a very light piece of cloth, actually—"

"No self-respecting gourmet lion would choose you if there was wildebeest available. We'll have some of that steak in a day or so. It's almost as good as British beef for flavor."

I had another Drambuie, just to keep up with Jim.

"Besides," he went on, "lions have nothing against humans at night. During the day they know we have guns and can see to use them. You can't like someone you fear, can you? But at night—"

"There's another one. Hear? Seems closer."

"He is. Tell me. Why did you come here? Particularly? I've been meaning to ask."

"Just for a vacation, a change. What do you mean?"

"People from superior civilizations keep turning up here. Some to experiment with danger, but most don't really know why. I can guess. The tension at home has become unbearable. The trap has been sprung, poor buggers. The least they can do is restore through this shock of the elemental—Africa!—some sense that life is not—their lives—bound between two converging steel rails which lead to the edge of a cliff. But I rather think you're like me. You pretty well know what you're doing and why."

"I did something just before I left the States I haven't yet figured out."

"Then there has been something on your mind, I was right."

I didn't want to talk about Sidney.

"Well," Jim said, "except for our neighborly lions, you'll have lots of peace tonight to puzzle out whatever it is."

"Are you suggesting I should go to bed now?"

"I've begun to recognize your sleepy look."

He walked me to my tent like a host should his guest, checked my bed, inspected the floor for ants, found none, showed me how to turn the hissing Gaz light off and on, said a perfect goodnight, and zipped me in.

Being alone was a new experience for me. That sound unbelievable? I've always had somebody with me, my mother, my first wife, Ellie and Little Arthur, the cast of whatever play I was in, my agent, the Lambs, the Players, Equity Council, the handball players at the West Side "Y," my tax man, my lawyer—and Sidney.

Work is my drug. Whenever I'm alone for more than a few days, I do something drastic, I get a job of some kind. When I'm working I have no time to wonder if I'm happy or miserable. That is why I never take a vacation unless I've a job to return to. I don't dare.

Now, here I was, as I'd wished, me and my Gaz light and a couple of books, *Future Shock* and *One Hundred Years of Solitude,* that I carry everywhere but never read and probably never will.

I heard the lion again. Another lion? The same? He sounded different, perhaps because he was closer?

A word about a lion's roar. It's not. It starts like a roar, then there's a succession of sounds you never hear in a zoo. It goes like this, in a sort of diminuendo, "I'm hungry, I'm hungry, hungry, hungry, hungry, hung, hung, hung, huh, huh, huh, hu, hu, h, h, h, h, gh." Finish. Silence.

What's he doing now?

The natives tell you the lion is saying "I'm boss," over and over. Maybe the fucking lion has an identity problem, has to reassure himself he's boss all the time.

The lion—or lions—I was hearing may have been uncertain, but he was—or they were—also advancing.

An actor is not a brave man. I suppose there are exceptions, but I don't remember meeting one. They're all very brave on stage and on the screen. Burt Lancaster has never lost a war. Kirk Douglas has never even lost a battle. John Wayne gets straight up after a heavy chair's been broken over his skull. Every picture since *The Great Train Robbery* has celebrated the courage of these men. They've been a great ad for our sex!

But in life, as I've known them, actors are rather cautious. They don't want their features mashed or misplaced. They don't even want their hair mussed.

For instance, I'm an absolute coward. Yet on stage, I play people of unwavering courage, not only physically dauntless, which is comparatively simple, but morally. I've played moral leaders!

Yet if I'm without a job or some close friends close by or a loving bedmate even for a day or two, I begin to wonder why I live.

Add an advancing lion to that and—

I sat up. Why the hell should I lie in bed with the covers pulled up over my head, trembling? If I couldn't sleep, I'd do what I do at home, read. I got the Gaz lamp going, although it hissed in a way it hadn't when Jim lit it, and found my place, the one I'd had for the last two weeks in *Future Shock*. I began to read about modular man.

Suddenly I put the lamp out. Why call the lion's attention to which tent I was in?

I'd spotted a roll of toilet paper on the bedside table. I pulled a piece loose and compacted it into a pellet. I stuffed the pellet into one ear, made another, plugged the other ear.

I still heard the lion.

I wetted the pellets with saliva, stuffed them back into place.

I heard the lion less.

I kept my fingertips in place behind the pellets.

I could not hear the lion.

Was he silently sneaking up on me? Did predators of that size come into camp? Did they smell the meat smoke from our dinner? Meat smoke! Christ! There were five very smelly humans in that camp, and the most powerful odor of all was the one from my frightened and disconsolate soul.

I turned over. The pellets fell out of my ears.

Fuck Sidney Schlossberg! I'd avoided thinking about him, and I would not think about the bastard now. I had no time for Sidney Schlossberg. He deserved what I'd done, and asked for it. I'd taken years and years of his shit and now—fuck him! Feel guilty? Why should I? All right, I do, a little. Ellie doesn't feel guilty. Myron his brother doesn't feel guilty. My producer, Mr. Sol Bender, who used to be his assistant stage manager, doesn't feel guilty. Adam, the first-time-uptown director, doesn't feel guilty. The president of Actors Equity, Mr. Frederick O'Neill, I'm sure he doesn't feel guilty. Cardinal Cooke, a real-life moral leader, he doesn't feel guilty. Why should I feel guilty?

Because I'm a goddamn freak, that's why. There was no reasonable basis for the guilt I felt.

And what the hell did it have to do with that lion outside, the one who was looking for me?

Imagine what Jim would say about Sidney! I knew goddamn well what he'd say. He'd laugh.

I'd make sure. I'd ask him in the morning.

That fucking animal was getting closer and closer. Hugh, hugh, hugh, ugh, ugh, ugh, gh, gh, gh, h, h, h, you ugly son of a bitch!

I tried the pellets once more, but they were dried and misshapen. I'd call Ellie in the morning and tell her to send me a box of those rubber things Brando wears in his ears. I read he wears them even when he acts so he won't hear the actors he's working with. So much for the Actors Studio.

With that, I fell asleep.

What phone? How could I call Ellie?

Which reminded me, I hadn't seen my agent before I left.

I woke.

No, the lion woke me. He must be right in camp, the sound was that close.

I listened for footfalls, didn't hear any. Of course not. Their feet are padded.

The rain was gentlenow, the storm had moved on. From a

distance came a crack of thunder followed by the barking of many animals.

Suppose I had to take a piss now. That would be something! Then I realized why I'd had that thought. Because I did. Have to piss.

I sat up. I really had a problem.

It was all that goddamn liquor I'd put down. What the hell did I drink all that Scotch for? And the Drambuie? Three shots? And Sanka? Why? To prolong the dinner, the time I'd be with Jim? To postpone the moment when I'd be alone in my tent? To make sure I'd sleep soundly, that was it.

Another theory shot to hell.

Outside someone, something had moved. Which is to say, some animal had knocked over—what? There was a washstand with a bowl on it at the entrance to my tent. I thought I'd heard the metal bowl ring. Now some heavy scuffling movement. Then silence.

I really had to go. The hero of stage and screen had to pee.

I put on the Gaz light, listened. I got out of bed. Slowly. Without, I hoped, a sound.

Suppose, I considered, I kneel at the entrance, zip up the zipper just enough so I could—no, that wouldn't work.

Note to my lady readers. The member tends to shrink when the bearer is frightened.

Also, I remembered a story Jim had told me about a tall "tripper" who'd fallen asleep with his feet outside the tent and lost one of them to a passing hyena. At one clomp! The pressure in a hyena's jaws, Jim had informed me, was equal to nine hundred pounds. Or was it seven hundred? What the hell's the difference?

Better a foot than my dear little friend.

I wondered what Jim would do? Why, he'd go out and do his business. He'd told me another story about going to our little canvas field toilet, there meeting a lioness coming out. Jim had laughed at the surprised look on her face. She'd run away, of course, but then Jim gives off confidence and I give off the opposite. "Never back off," was Jim's advice. "If you turn and run, you're finished."

What I finally decided to do was piss in a corner of the tent. This might occasion some embarrassing questions in the morning, but the hell with that. I'd be intact.

I was never more glad to see the light. I understood the birds, why their songs are so sweet in the dawn. Survival! They'd made it through the night.

I peeked out of my tent, and there was little black Francis running up with hot water as if he'd been waiting up all night for me.

When Jim appeared, it was in style. The zipper of his tent's front fold slid up, and there he was, taking his first steps of the day with that lordly vagueness he might have affected in his own home, where he, of course, was. Around his body he wore a midthigh-length robe of paisley cloth. He smiled at me in the manner of the host of a country estate and asked the ritual questions. I answered that I'd slept very well thank you, but he wasn't listening. It was much too early to listen.

Francis came running with the same little white pitcher, refilled with steaming water. Jim stirred his first cup of Nescafé while he issued his first orders of the morning.

"Mizzouri, bwana," Francis assented, then, "Mizzouri, Mizzouri," as he trotted off in the direction of the kitchen.

I heard him passing on the master's wishes, had a glimpse of him as he ran across the opening of the kitchen path, disappeared behind the bushes, reappeared at the canvas stall shower in the hollow where the wild fig leaves were heaviest.

"Forgive me," Jim turned in my direction, still balmy, still waking in his own time while servants scurried. "I've ordered a shower prepared." He sipped some of the Nescafé. "Of course it's for you. They'll have it ready in precisely the time it will take you to drop out of your clothes. You'll find the water quite hot and very refreshing."

Francis had lowered a canvas drum which had been suspended over the shower stall, and he and Kimani were filling it from one of the large fire pots. I could see the steam swirling up as they poured the water.

"I'll wait till tonight, Jim."

I don't know why I refused, perhaps out of deference.

"As you wish." Jim nodded pleasantly and had another sip of the Nescafé. "It'll be ready for you when we get back this afternoon."

Francis ran up with a large bath towel, stood at the ready while Jim emptied his cup. Of course Jim did not hurry. When he finally got up he smiled at all present, not in apology but in the sharing of pleasure, at me waiting for him to turn on my day, at Francis waiting with his towel, at Kimani waiting at attention beside the shower stall. Then he took the towel, said "Thank you, Francis," and strolled off, holding his robe closed in front, a crown prince of the days of empire who did not expose to gentry the royal organ which would continue the line.

There was nothing to do while he was gone but pretend to like Nescafé.

Fifteen minutes later he reappeared, rather more alert.

"Did I inquire," he said, "how you slept?"

"To tell you the truth, only pretty well."

"The lion can be a bother till one learns to ignore his histrionics. By the way, they finally made a kill about five or six miles down range. Would you like to have a look?"

"Oh, yes, yes."

Something about the way I responded made him smile.

"What amuses you?"

"People from the States are always so eager to witness a kill," he said.

"How did you know there'd been one? Where it was and how far off?"

"See those birds circling?"

He indicated the top of the long slope above our camp and past.

"No."

"Then I'm afraid you'll have to take my word. I've asked Kimani to pack us a picnic lunch, and we'll have a look at our noisy neighbors. Shall we?"

"Zebra," he announced. He'd stopped the Toyota and pulled a pair of Swiss field glasses out of his glove compartment. "They got a zebra."

Through the heat haze, I could barely make out a large herd of some kind, a couple of miles off.

He handed me the glasses, and it was what he said.

"These lenses," I said, "pull everything together. The lions seem to be eating the zebra right in the middle of the herd."

We rolled up slowly, making the least possible disturbance. The rain of the night before had left reflecting pools of water in which I could see the white clouds moving. Other places there was a skim of green over the water which made it shine. The whole country was emerald fresh.

It was the least likely setting for what we saw.

The survivors, about two hundred of them, were grazing not a hundred feet from where one of their number was being devoured by a small pride of lions.

Jim stopped the Toyota. "She was with foal," he said, giving me the glasses.

One of the lions had his head up into the somatic cavity of the dead animal. The front quarters of the mare and its head were still intact. I asked about that.

"They always go in the back. They love the vitals, the heart and the testicles, the liver, the sweetbreads—and the unborn young."

"Can we get closer?" I asked.

"Well, maybe, a little. I don't like to disturb them. This is their place, you know."

I was annoyed, controlled it. "What is?" I asked.

"This whole place. We're guests here."

He turned the motor over, slipped the Toyota into low, and began to creep forward as slowly as the vehicle would move until we were within twenty feet of the lions and their meal. One of the predators, a beautiful animal, looked up, its muzzle blood-soaked. Then, unconcerned, went back to feeding.

"See the little fellow's feet," Jim whispered.

They were delicately turned and very small.

"I imagine they're still soft, the hooves," Jim said.

"Horrible."

"There are men, gourmets, who consider unborn pig one of the great delicacies."

"The picture I'd like to get is the zebra's head, which is intact and rather peaceful-looking, as if it had no idea what was happening below, and the lions gorging into the rest of her."

Jim circled, slowly and carefully, then stopped.

"This is as close as we'll go," he said.

I took my picture but wasn't satisfied.

"Got it?" Jim asked.

"Yes, but it's not really what I wanted."

"I'm sure you'll have a very nice picture."

"Can't we get a little—?"

"Sorry, this is as close as we go."

We sat and watched.

There was no sound except slobbering as the lions pulled loose and gulped down the hunks of warm, moist meat. Occasionally there'd be a quick, angry snarl within the family circle, but there was enough there for the whole pride, so no cause for quarrel.

"How much can one of them eat?"

"Full grown, a tidy forty pounds, thank you very much. I've seen them after a meal when they couldn't run if they had to."

A lioness suddenly pulled away from the zebra and dashed at a hyena who'd come too close. She didn't catch the slope-backed animal. He cut off at a sharp angle, and she did not follow. The hyena came back to precisely where he'd been and waited.

Now I noticed the others waiting in circles of privilege, four other hyenas, barely able to contain themselves, trotting back and forth like kids who had to pee. They were next. Behind them were three light-foot jackals with lovely gold pelts and delicately pointed noses in contrast with the snouts of the hyenas. But they were there for the same purpose. Since they had longer to wait, they were more patient. On the ground and absolutely still was a college of carrion-eating birds, naked-necked vultures with feverish red eyes. They knew they were to be last and had no choice except to accept their place at the bottom of the brotherhood.

"These lions won't eat again till perhaps the day after tomorrow," Jim said, "more likely the day after that."

"And the zebras know?"

"Look at them."

Just thirty yards away they were cropping grass as fast as they found it. Occasionally one of them would look up at the lions devouring his comrade, but the look was brief and unconcerned and he'd return immediately to the food at his feet.

"Do animals have feelings?"

"Same ones we do, fear, hunger, sexual desire, competitiveness, anger—"

"Guilt?"

"Not guilt. If a zebra felt sorrow and guilt every time one of his herd went down, he'd crack up, life would be impossible."

"You mean to tell me the fate of their comrade does not interest them?"

"Oh, it interests them very much."

"How?"

"As a cause for rejoicing."

"Rejoicing?"

"In the animal world a survivor celebrates. When a lion dashes into a herd, what do they do? They get as far away from their weaker brother as possible, they particularly leave the incapacitated, in this case a very pregnant mare. Take her, they say to the lion, don't take me."

"So each day's ease is bought by the life of a brother or sister?"

"Did you hear them last night, barking, how restless they were?"

"I thought that was dogs, wild dogs."

"Zebra bark. They were barking on and off all night. They knew it was time for their pride to eat."

"*Their* pride?"

"Certainly. It's a very close bond, predator and victim."

"So the kill relieved them?"

"Obviously."

"Now you're going to tell me that they wanted the lions to—"

"Well, perhaps they did want to get it over with, one way or another. The proof is that if they kept still, and quiet, they'd escape notice completely. At night their disguise is perfect, and the lion is really a boob. But the zebra never stops barking and switching his tail, and the lion hears one and tracks it down till he sees the others and there you are. What do you want to do now?"

"Could we possibly watch a little longer?"

"Of course, of course. For how long? I ask only because I'm concerned."

"About what?"

"I saw you brought a white golfing cap along. Better put it on. The big heat of the day is about to come down."

"I was in the South Pacific during the war," I said. "I know all about the sun."

"I really wasn't trying to hurry you."

I put on my white cap.

"There's a great rock just off the road not far from here." Jim was pressing me. "It has overhanging trees, and there's a brook below. We can picnic in the shade, and then you may want to nap—"

"I want to watch until she's disappeared," I said quietly. "For some reason the dismemberment and consumption of this zebra fascinates me."

Jim burst out laughing. "Forgive me," he said, "but she'll be there, and the lions, too, a couple of hours from now. I really ought to insist we go, you are, after all, in my care, aren't you? Let's get into the shade and relieve your head of this heat."

"I'm perfectly all right."

"We're almost exactly on the equator, you know."

"I've been there before."

"But never, if I may say so, at sixty-five hundred feet. You are not feeling the sun, but it's pressing down just as hard."

"All right." I gave up. "let's go."

My wife, Ellie, would have warned Jim that when I give in to persistent hectoring, suddenly become agreeable and compliant, then I am at my most hostile and treacherous.

But once in the shade I enjoyed it. The picnic was delicious. Kimani had packed a cold bottle of Soave, and there were two remarkable salamis, one from Genoa, and the breast of a plump chicken and oranges from Spain and homemade bread and sweet British biscuits.

"I want to apologize to you," I said. "You were quite right about the heat. The only other time I've known it like this was in New Guinea during that other war, long ago. It was so hot then, I remember it felt much hotter than this, that it aroused the opposite sensation, a chill, a feeling of sudden cooling, like a fever does. Actually I had dengue fever in Manila in forty-four, and I remember how I shook with cold, then burned up—"

"I've heard of dengue. There's some down on the coast around Melindi. It comes back, doesn't it?"

"It did once. Anyway, the point is you were quite right, the shade is delicious and so was the picnic and I'm awfully glad to be here with you, O.K.?"

"Please don't ever feel you have to apologize," Jim said. "The heat makes everyone irritable, especially at first."

I liked him. A lot. He'd packed the remains of the lunch away, and we were lying on our backs looking into the foliage as it moved to the breeze, and I thought I was lucky to be with him.

"I'm going to make a confession," I said. "I had to urinate—"

"Francis told me."

"I'll tip him extra."

"Not necessary."

"You see I was too frightened to—"

"Please don't mention it again. You're not the first to do that."

"Suppose I'd been courageous instead of a miserable coward, and waiting for me in the WC had been the lioness you told me about, remember her?"

"Very well."

"And forgetting your instruction to show a fearless front, I'd called for help. I was wondering would those boys come to help me?"

"Would you have gone to help them, in the same situation?"

"I don't think so."

"Well, don't feel guilty about it. It's not natural to risk your life."

"You mean I should stay in my tent and rejoice that it was Francis or Kimani who'd met the lady in the WC and that I was safe?"

"I didn't say should, I said natural. The way it is."

"Would you have come to my rescue?" I asked.

"Yes," he said.

"Why?"

"Honestly?"

"Of course."

"Because you pay me."

A breeze had come up, fluttering the leaves above us and washing the rock where we lay. The film of moisture evaporated from my body, and suddenly I was very cool. It was pleasant there, and I was at home with Jim.

"God, ain't it peaceful," I said.

"It is." Jim was short. He wanted me to sleep. And I was going fast.

"Two nights ago I woke in the middle of the night," I remembered for him, "and what woke me was sidearm fire. It wasn't very far off. There must have been twenty rounds pressed off."

"In New York?"

"In the capital of contemporary civilization. Not two blocks from where my wife and I were in bed. Two blocks. Twenty rounds. Rifle? Sidearms, I thought. In the well-lit streets of that goddamn city."

"Who was it?"

"I don't know. I never left my bed."

"Didn't rush to the rescue?"

"Rolled over on my stomach. And now, my friend, I believe I am going to nap."

"Pleasant dreams."

"There was nothing about it in the papers next morning. No one considered it unusual, I suppose. It was like another time I remember, in Manila. They were shooting all over the city that night, snipers, you know, and what was left of their army. They didn't know the city had fallen."

"No?" He was careful with my sleep.

"They're probably still shooting in the suburbs."

"Yes, of course, the suburbs," he murmured.

"Of Manila. They may still not know." I laughed, but I was asleep really.

"Manila," I heard Jim say.

"Great sport! We were celebrating in the center and in the suburbs they were still fighting. And tough? Better believe it! Those
Japanese, I mean. I know I'm not making sense, it's O.K. O.K.?"

By then it was too much trouble to explain anything, it was all too
involved, went too far back, before Jim was born, no doubt, mean-
ingless now. What did it matter, that other war, that city's fall? The
invasion money, that Great New Eastern Brotherhood League paper
money, littered the streets like shredded carpeting. We'd scooped it
up in handfuls and thrown it up in the air. It was our night to
celebrate. Jim stuffed his pockets with it—

Jim? How the hell had Jim come into this? And perfectly in place?
"I can only suppose," he said, "they haven't heard that their officers
surrendered and that we've captured the Great Fat One."

On the way to the one street where everyone except General
MacArthur was heading that night, the city dark because the Japs
had blown up the power plant as they retreated, we passed the
stockade. There we had lights on the prisoners, had our own genera-
tors there. The Japanese soldiers watched us go by. Oh, they were
tough! And good fighters, everyone said that, even Jim. "I regret
having had to kill so many of them," he said. "I don't go on shooting
safaris anymore."

How Manila unbuttoned for us that night! Outside the big house
where we all went, there was a line more than a block long, and,
inside, every crib was busy. After he was through Jim said he
proposed to pay off in Japanese invasion money.

Well that Little Mother, she came screaming. "Madam,"
Gentleman Jim said, not using the word in the vernacular, "be
reasonable. You've been taking it from the Japanese for three years,
now I'm afraid you're going to have to take it from us."

Well, did she fuss and holler! Jim had to laugh, because she began
to look good to him. "I find your cussing most agreeable, Madam
Mother," he said, "so I'm going to do you, too. We rescued you from
your Japanese oppressors, as you say, so now, at least for a night, we'll
enjoy your gratitude. No charge. You won't have to pay me, dear old
bag, or I you. It will simply be friendly intercourse."

It was all in fun till she yelled out and this strong-arm young Huk
came running. He was dead and covered with a blanket before I got a
good look at him. "Jim!" I shouted, and Jim turned and shot him. It
was a reflex by then. Later someone said the boy was her son. While
he kicked the boy to make sure he was dead, Little Mother got a shiv

somewhere. We hollered so Jim saw it in time, let her pass, as Ellie had taught him, "Tai-saba-kee," then grabbed her wrist and twisted so the knife fell to the ground where the rest of us fought for it, a souvenir.

Meantime Jim had pulled her skirt up over her head and tied it off. The rest of her looked O.K., what you could see in the thin light. "Not too bad, actually," was how Jim put it. Then he let her go, "just to keep it all sporting." With the skirt bagged and bound over her, she looked like a hen running from the block where she'd left her head. Wherever she ran, we were there, turning her around. It was a game kids play. Jim was laughing so, he couldn't get it hard. Finally he did, and she gave up, lay on the ground, two legs, a belly and a bag. Jim did her in front of the rest of us. "Great sport!" he said and, as a mark of respect, wouldn't let anyone else at her though there were candidates. He cut her head free, formally thanked her, calling her "an exceptional person," and so adieu.

As we left, she screamed, "You're going to get sick, soldier. You're going to get what the Japanese gave me, because you're all the same, soldier. You're no damn good!"

But if she thought this would faze Jim, she was mistaken. "That's what I mean by sentimentality," he said. "All that justice crap. I ain't going to get no damn clap because you know why? Because I deserve it. Malaria neither," he said, reaching into the soup plate full of yellow pills that were on every table in our dining room to protect us from the fever.

I remember everybody was eating breast of turkey that night, and there was sweet rice wine to wash down the tender meat. I'll never get tired of breast of turkey. It's really for victors.

"Did you ever get the clap she promised you?" I asked, sitting up. "Jim?"

There was no one on the rock but me. The light breeze moved without a sound, and it was cooling. I lay down again.

It wasn't quinine, I remembered, it was atabrine, made you just as yellow though. Maybe it was good for malaria, but it was no good for what hit me, because two nights later, when we were done with the Manila celebration and getting ready to move north, General Gill commanding, onto the Villa Verde trail, where our spies and spotter planes told us the Japs had massed to defend their capital, Baguio, well then, just then, I came down with the dengue. Damn thing probably saved my life, because we lost one thousand and eighty men on the Villa Verde trail. That was the last fuck, that night in Manila, for many of our guys. I was left behind when they saw me crawling around the backyard on all fours like an animal, the conqueror of Manila puking prime breast of turkey, all white meat, I can never get enough of that!

I could still taste it, now in Africa, retching in my sleep. I must have fallen off again, because I heard myself saying, "Who the hell do you think you are, Jim, to shoot that young Huk and leave him with a whorehouse blanket covering him while you tie his mother's skirt over her head and fuck her in the chicken-yard dirt before the entire 32nd Regiment, Jim, who the hell do you think—?"

I'd thought it funny at the time.

It wasn't Jim, of course. Why now had I made it Jim? What was I doing making a villain of that very decent man who was taking care of me, even against my will, forcing me to protect my balding head from the heavy sun? Jesus, how unfair!

Jim came into sight over the edge of the rock. Behind him the green fields were glazed with heat. He'd made a little sack of his handkerchief, and it was full of freshwater crayfish.

"We'll have them tonight with our drinks," he said. "How did you sleep? You seemed to be having pleasant dreams when I left."

"My dreams? . . . were terrible!"

"Safaris do that. Want to go back to the kill, see what's left?"

On the way we encountered an old male lion, walking the middle of a buffalo path, his head down, his belly slung like a hammock and swaying from side to side.

"Now, there's a fellow who'll sleep well," Jim said.

Most of the lions had left. Two cubs were playing tug of war with a foreleg. Their mother was cracking vertebrae, the sound of hard candy. In a few minutes she stood, looked at the cubs, must have communicated something, because when she moved off they followed.

She wasn't fifteen feet away when the hyenas were all over the skeleton, rushing off with legs and pieces of the rib cage, all in different directions. Then the birds came down and at the same time the jackals dashed in. One against one, they were evenly matched, but the vultures were a flock and soon covered all that was left of the mare. The three little jackals were lucky to get what they got and be free of the loathsome mass of feathers, gristle, beak, and claw.

"I'll take that shower," I said.

It was waiting, the canvas drum filled with very hot water. When I was through, Kimani was waiting with a towel. Jim, having detected my anxiety, had told Kimani to stand by during my whole adventure with that canvas shower stall.

I'd have to find a way to apologize to that man for what I'd dreamed about him.

After the Scotch, we ate the boiled crayfish, husking them with our front teeth, then dipping the soft little bodies in butter and English mustard. We were happy and as silent as friends can be.

As I finished my Sanka, the spotter walked into sight at the head of the kitchen path, carrying a small bag.

"Obowatti is leaving us," Jim said. "I'm going to drive him back to the lodge, where he can pick up a ride home."

Jim waved a hand to indicate he was not ready to leave, and the spotter walked back out of sight.

"I was wondering what happened to him," I said.

"Not been himself," Jim said. "Now. About tomorrow, I thought I might take you to that private game preserve, remember?"

"I want to see the wildebeest migration."

"Oh, right, right. We'll certainly do that."

There was the sound of a ruckus from behind the bushes.

"Kimani!" Jim called in his full voice of command. The silence was immediate. Jim turned to me. "Obowatti's got a wife who's sharing her nights with Obowatti's brother."

"Oh, no wonder—"

"Obowatti's determined to kill his brother. I offered him money enough, it was Kimani's suggestion, to buy another wife. But apparently he's going to carry out his plan. I must say it seems to me that one woman, especially when she's quite plain and that black, is just like another. Too much religion, don't you know. These people were so much better off without civilization. Now they're becoming as neurotic as the whites."

Kimani came up, looking apologetic, and said something in Swahili.

"He said, 'What's the difference,' which is what I'd like to know. Let him do what he wants, Kimani."

"How long will you be gone?" I asked as Jim got up.

"An hour. I may bring back some company," he said. "Just overnight."

"A girl?"

"Oh, God, no!" he laughed. "Fine dinner, Kimani," he called as he drove away.

I decided to go to bed early. Francis lit the Gaz and provided the little pitcher of water for brushing my teeth. He'd placed an empty biscuit tin on the floor in a corner of my tent.

I couldn't sleep till the Toyota returned. There was a strange voice, then Jim's answering. As soon as I heard him, I fell asleep and, to my surprise, slept through the night. The lions of the area, I suppose, were sleeping too.

When I woke next morning, Jim and his guest were in earnest conversation, leaning toward each other over their coffee. The visitor's back was to me, and he didn't look around when Jim waved good morning, simply waited till he had Jim's attention again, then went on with what he'd been saying.

Francis came running with a table and chair and set them up in front of my tent. I was to have breakfast apart.

I sat with my back toward them, so I didn't get a good look at the new face in camp till later when Jim came to see how I was getting along and I turned and saw the man walking slowly toward the jeep with his head down. Then he stretched his neck in a compulsive and strained gesture, looking off through the trees to the field on the sunny side of our camp.

Jim's guest was an East Indian.

He was well dressed, in the clothes of a trader, gave the impression that he never took off his suit coat in public, put it on in his private chamber every morning, took it off in the same place at the end of the day.

Jim was extremely apologetic. "His car," he said, "is no good through open country. I'll have to take him back to the main road where we left it last night. Only be a few minutes."

I indicated the Indian. "Is everything O.K.?"

"Oh, that? Just a personal matter, trivial, so silly."

I looked at the Indian gentleman, and he was looking at me. Whatever their meeting had been about, it had not been trivial to him.

When Jim came back he had another Nescafé, seemed troubled and in no hurry to set forth. Then he noticed me looking at him, jumped up, and called out, "Let's go, let's go!" and walked quickly to the Toyota.

He didn't say a word about his visitor and I didn't ask. I was curious, of course. It was the first indication I'd seen that Jim had a personal life.

We headed in a new direction. Even heavier rains had fallen here. It was like riding a road of water-filled sponges. Then we began to climb, up a hill, then another, then over a ridge, and looking down, we saw the migration.

To say there were thousands of beasts in line would be untrue. "In line" would not be accurate, and "thousands" quite inadequate to describe the horde which spanned the horizons.

Leaderless, without guides or marshals, they seemed to be following instructions in an old memory. Their movement suggested a great crowd leaving the locus of a disaster and moving to a place where they'd been told they'd find safety.

Along the skirts of their path we saw piles of fresh-cleaned bones. Carrion birds circled, their cries the final rites.

To get a better look, I climbed up on the hood of the Toyota—we were down on the flat now—then jumped off and walked toward the herd. Jim had usually discouraged my going off alone, and I expected he would now. When he didn't, I asked, "O.K. if I go closer?"

"What lion would be interested in you?" he said with a smile.

I looked back after twenty steps. Jim was sitting on one of the mudguards reading a letter written on blue note paper.

I got closer to the herd. They did not notice me till I was twenty feet away then all together, at a signal I couldn't see or hear, they hobbled off in their lumbering stoop-backed trot just fast enough to keep a minimal distance between us. Heads bowed, without a sign of pleasure or hope, they were like the human masses of the Middle Ages.

I walked back to Jim, who was still on the jeep, cross-legged, reading. When he saw me, he stared at me for an instant, holding the letter in his hand as if he was debating giving it to me. Then he put it away and, with an effort, found another subject.

"You were asking me yesterday," he said, "what I wasn't indifferent to?"

"Since we're alike in so many ways, I did wonder."

"You know what a free fall is?"

"Yes. No. Not really."

"You fall out of a small plane and for sixty seconds you're free of everything."

"Say it again."

"You fall backward out of a plane, which is immediately not backward, because directions are the same in space. And for—"

"Sixty seconds. That seems a very long time."

"It is. At first you find it impossible to keep from pulling the cord even for three seconds. Then, it takes months and months to develop the control you need, you do twenty, thirty, forty seconds. One day you're doing sixty, and those sixty seconds seem like the only pieces of your life worth living, the only time you're entirely free."

"I don't think I could ever do that."

"It's a matter of control. You could do it, you're like me that way. But I've only found one woman who was able to do sixty seconds—"

"So you fell in love and—"

"Just the opposite. I couldn't stand her. She began to be competitive and make demands. She changed personality, and so I—"

"You left town, went out on safari."

"How did you know?"

"It's what I would have done."

"When I got back from one trip, she was married. She's pregnant now, but I hear she still goes up, against doctor's orders, of course. She really does it only to annoy me, but I have no time for that. Well, look, I think we have something going over there."

He pulled his Swiss field glasses out of the glove compartment.

"Wild dogs," he said, handing me his glasses. "We're in luck today."

I could see seven or eight mottled animals loping along the skirt of another part of the migration.

"What are they doing?"

"You'll see."

"They're just standing around. No, a couple of them are running. They don't seem very eager, whatever they're doing."

"They don't have to be eager."

"Now those two have stopped. Two others have taken it up."

I kept the glasses up as we moved closer. Now I could see that their casualness was confidence. They were skillfully cutting one of the wildebeests out of the herd. It didn't surprise me when I saw this animal's brothers and sisters and cousins edge away from him. What had horrified me only the day before, I was now taking for granted.

The Toyota stopped. I lowered the glasses. "Let's drive closer," I said.

"Wait till after the kill." He took the glasses from me.

"Are you sure there'll be one?"

"Wild dogs? They never miss."

"You admire them."

"Oh, yes. No hysteria, no eccentricities, absolutely efficient. And even though they eat their victims while they're still living, they are also the least cruel citizens of this world."

Jim gave me the glasses. "Look! Quick, or you'll miss it."

What I saw was one of the pursuers making a quick grab at the rear ankle of the chosen, at which the heavy animal spilled over. The pack was on him precisely as he hit the ground.

"It's just a matter of getting them off their feet," Jim said. "Then they're finished."

"You mean they're eating him now?"

"He'll be partly gone by the time we get there."

Jim stopped at a decent distance as he always did, but the glasses put me into the flurry of feeding. The dogs raised their heads and wagged their tails, then went back to their meal.

"That animal is still living," I said. "This is terrible."

"He's in a state of shock," Jim said, "not feeling much, really."

"Awful," I said.

"I'd like to die like that," Jim said, "heart beating fast, blood running. Now your lions, they grab the muzzle or the neck of their prey, clamp shut, then hold on—five minutes, more—till the animal suffocates. If you want to know the picture I have of civilization, that is it, slow death by suffocation."

There were nine dogs feeding and three pups, all tearing great mouthfuls off the wildebeest's rack, wagging their tails as they did, and the wildebeest still kicking his feet.

"Want to get closer?"

"I can see fine."

"You'll get used to it. You're used to a lot worse."

"Am I?"

"We all are. The higher up one goes in the order of beasts, the crueler they are. Man, of course, surpasses all. And women."

There was a strange sound, a sort of whirring and slapping. The vultures were coming down. I saw the hyenas arriving and the jackals. They all paid the dogs as much respect as they had the lions, even though these good fellows never stopped wagging their tails as they ate.

"They seem so friendly," I said.

"Why shouldn't they? They have nothing against the wildebeest."

One of the dogs suddenly turned and chased a hyena, nipping at his anus, as if for the sport of it.

"Would they have eaten the hyena if he'd pulled it down?"

"No," Jim said, "the hyenas would have eaten the hyena."

Suddenly I'd had enough of the spectacle, the wagging tails and the way Jim took it.

"Let's go," I said.

"They're not through yet."

Was he teasing me? His face was perfectly composed, deadly calm. I couldn't make out what he was feeling. "I've had it, Jim, thanks. Let's go on," I repeated. He nodded and started the motor.

When we caught up with the main body of the migration, Jim asked, "Still interested in this?"

"I imagine I've seen what there is to see. Tell me, is the grass greener and more plentiful where they're going?"

"It used to be. At one time it was thigh-high, very rich and very beautiful. But that's gone now."

"Then why do they go? Why does that animal go along that path to that place?"

"Because there's a lion waiting for him there."

"Oh, come on, Jim."

"True. They know how they're supposed to die, and they don't know a better way. Do you?"

"I'd turn around."

"And disappoint the lion? You wouldn't want to do that, would you?"

"Yes. I'd find a better way."

"You really believe there is one?"

"There has to be."

"Why? You don't even know why you're here. You told me so."

"Here on earth? Or here in East Africa?"

"Here in East Africa for a start. Sorry. No offense meant. I'm a little upset about—a personal matter."

"I know I'd rather be here than where I was."

"Well, that's something. And how about here on earth? Oh, of course, your career. You've found a meaning."

"To what?"

"Footprints on the sands of time, all that rubbish. Back in the Bush we know better. Tomorrow it will rain, and where will those footsteps be? Where do the bones go? The ants don't differentiate between saints and sinners, successes and failures, predators and victims. Who of this herd remembers the beast he walked alongside of yesterday? What male remembers the female he topped the day before? He forgot her as he got off her back. Oh, look!"

He pointed to a wildebeest calf toddling along, looking like a lost child.

"Where's its mother?" I asked. "Devoured?"

"I doubt it. The cat would take the calf first, much more tender."

"Then where the hell is her mother?"

"You don't see her looking for her calf, do you?"

"She should be."

"Should is a word to forget. It goes with hope and charity and love and all the rest of it, fidelity—forget them all."

"What's eating you, Jim?"

"I'm not myself. Please forgive me. I certainly don't want to intrude my personal—"

He stopped. Neither of us could find anything to say.

"What will happen to that calf?" I said finally.

"You will go out there, presently, and pick it up, and we'll put it into the back of the Toyota and take it back to camp, find us a baby bottle, fill it with cow's milk, feed it, continue to take care of it till it grows up, which means, for you, taking it back to the States. Wouldn't you like to do that?"

"Why would I?"

"Because you're precisely that kind of sentimentalist."

"Don't talk to me that way, Jim. I don't like it."

"No offense was intended. Just a confrontation with facts, which you seemed to want. Very well. You abhor my view of universal indifference. So tell me, where do you stop being responsible for your fellow man? Tell me that. That's what Mr. Gargi, the Indian chap, came to see me about this morning. Here. Look at this."

He pulled up hard on the hand brake, and the Toyota stopped. Jim reached into his pocket and pulled out the blue letter he'd been reading and handed it to me.

"See if you don't think this pretty damn cheeky," he said.

At the top of the blue note paper, embossed in white letters, was the word ANDREA.

"Who is Andrea?"

"Read the letter first. It's written to Marge, the girl I was with the other night. The girl you were with got the same letter. Frightened both girls a bit, let me tell you."

I didn't reach for the letter. He put it in my hand.

"Go on, read it. Only remember I did nothing to lead her on, absolutely nothing. And I had nothing to do with her being pregnant."

He protests too much, I thought. Then I read Andrea's letter.

Dear Marge, Please don't see Jim again. He's incapable of loving anyone, you know that. His heart is as cold as a stone buried in the earth. That's his curse. An occasional go with him can't mean anything to you. Please don't hurt me for an instant's distraction. My happiness depends on him. I'm ashamed of that. But it's true. Even now, after all he's done to me. Even though I don't respect him anymore. That's my curse.

I looked up.

"She's married to that Indian gentleman you saw this morning," Jim said. "Go on. Turn the page."

I have plans to reunite us. If anything goes wrong with that I will not want to live. Do you want to be part of what kills me? I can't believe you do.

I remember the night we met. Your eyes were soft and kind. I know you'll understand me. Read between the lines. And help me. Before it's too late.

Andrea

"What do you think of that?" Jim demanded.

"Seems a terribly unfair letter," I said.

"Insane, absolutely insane. We agree."

I'd lied. Immediately, instinctively, I was on the girl's side. Why hadn't I said so?

"The Indian gentleman?" I asked, carefully folding the blue note paper precisely where Jim had unfolded it. "He's—"

"Married to her, and she's pregnant and still goes up to free fall."

"Oh, she's your friend who did sixty seconds?"

"She would have gone ninety if I'd said go ninety. 'Ask me anything,' she used to say. 'My life belongs to you.' Well, I get along very nicely, thank you, without anyone's life in my hands."

"Is she the one you almost married? No, that was in Rhodesia."

"She followed me here. Then I couldn't get rid of her. When I went out with other girls she'd follow us. I'd come out in the middle of the night, and there she'd be, sitting in her car, smiling and waving. I finally decided to see her one more time and try to convince her the more she went on that way, the less chance there was of our ever getting together."

"But then, weren't you leading her on?"

"Most certainly not! I told her over and over again that we were finished. I left Nairobi, went on safari for weeks at a time, ignored her messages, didn't answer her letters. Now she writes these girls, threatening them."

"I didn't see any threat in her letter."

"Why do you keep taking her side?"

"Do I?"

"Yes. You do. Sorry. Well, then, I did what I hope is a kindness. When you see Andrea she looks ever so demure. I told Gargi about affairs she'd had before me that I knew about, all unhappy, all did not last. She's seen much action, as they say in naval communiqués. 'No need to feel responsible for her,' I said, 'she was that way long before either of us.' "

"Do you really think that helped?"

"Not at all. Made him feel for her even more. There are men like that, you know, saints in sackcloth, born to suffer. 'Walk away,' I told him. 'She'll get over it. People do.' "

"Always?"

"If they don't it's no one else's concern, is it? I resent when people try to put the full load of their lives on you. The least we can expect from each other is, 'I don't tax you, you don't tax me.' "

"I don't understand. Why did she marry him, the Indian?"

"To hurt me. But I wasn't hurt. As she found out. Still here he comes last night, clearly under her whip, to inform me she's pregnant and not by him. They're married, but she hasn't let him have her, he says. I find that a bit hard to believe, don't you?"

"As you say, I don't know her."

"You don't have to know her. It's ridiculous on the face of it. And what's the message this poor clod carries from Cassandra? She has made up her mind to wait for me. He will divorce her, he says, if I'll marry her. Isn't that outrageous?"

"True love. He must be terribly jealous of you."

"No, no, he's very fair, a perfect gentleman, no matter what those niggers in Nairobi say about him."

"Even a perfect gentleman has his breaking point."

"I had to tell him, 'Sorry, dear boy, but I'm not at all sure the child is mine and if by some chance it is, I advise you, and her, to abort at once and start over again."

"And what was his answer, poor clod?"

"It's against his religion to take a life, that sort of thing. So I said, 'Surely since you feel that way, it's your responsibility.' "

"How did he take that?"

"It's not a matter of how he took it. He said he understood how I felt and that he'd simply have to keep close watch to make sure she didn't swallow every pill in her collection, which is the largest in East Africa. Well, I'm certainly not going to be stampeded by that kind of emotionalism."

"Actually you are, just a little?"

"Not at all. By the way, what made you say that about a breaking point?"

"When he was in camp, he kept stretching his neck, like a heron. Remember? Then he shook his head as if it was a bottle and he was trying to shake something out of it."

"A crick in his neck, no doubt. No? Well, whatever it is, he brought it on himself. What astonishes me is how this very decent chap, educated, you know, quite civilized, I'd travel anywhere in his company, believe me, how he can tie up with a madwoman like Andrea."

"You did."

"I knew when to stop. You have to pull out of a situation like that when the moment comes."

"Do you really think you can just cut a person off? Cold?"

"To save yourself. Surely you must have been in that kind of stew. Everybody has."

I laughed.

"Are you laughing at me? Not that I blame you. All this fuss about a woman."

"Is she pretty?"

"I doubt very much you'd think so."

"She must have something. Beautiful eyes?"

"Eyes? Like Marge's, frantic. Make you uncomfortable all the time."

"Beautiful hair?"

"A scruff of the stuff you pull out of a carpet sweeper after it's been over an old rug."

"Then what the hell attracted you?"

"I cannot imagine. Chicken-breasted. The bones coming through the skin. A rocky ride, let me tell you."

"May I see her picture?"

"How did you know I had one?"

"Let me see it."

He reached into his back pocket and pulled out a worn lionskin wallet.

"You won't get anything from this," he said. "She's all covered up."

It was an old snapshot, cracked over its surface and frayed at the corners. Andrea wore a swagger suit lashed at the ankles over hard-nose boots. There was a pack on her back, the parachute, and on her head, unbuckled, an aerialist's helmet. Draped over her shoulder was an animal.

"What's the cat?" I asked.

"The cat is Andrea. The kitten is an ocelot. She had animals all over her place, even snakes." He laughed. "They'd leap on us at the most inopportune moments."

Andrea's eyes shot out a light that fired her face. The angle of the cigarette in her mouth defied the world.

"She's terrific," I said. "She's really something!"

"There've been days when I thought so."

"Her eyes? What's that light?"

"My father had a word for it, when he met her. Apocalyptic."

There was a tiny cry, and we looked around. The wildebeest calf was standing as if he'd been waiting for us. Then he began to trot.

"That little fellow will be dead by morning," Jim said.

"Let's take it back to camp."

"Now, really!"

"I know I'm behaving like a silly American, but I can't leave it here helpless. I mean, I can but—would it be all right?"

Jim smiled at me affectionately. "Of course," he said.

The little fellow was a born broken-field runner. We had great sport catching him. Jim finally brought him down, bound all four feet with one knot, threw him in the back of the Toyota, and told me to sit on him. As we rode home, the little wonder released a pungent yellow fluid all over me which made Jim laugh. "Excuse me," he said laughing, "do excuse me but—"

The tension was gone, but when I got back to camp my head

ached. "I think I'll take a nap before dinner," I said, touching my head.

"You left your hat off again," Jim said. "Take some aspirin immediately." I looked at the calf, and Jim said, "Don't worry about him. Lie down."

"I don't think he appreciates that we saved his life."

"They never do. Want some turkey broth?"

He brought it himself.

"I had a difficult time prevailing on Kimani not to butcher your ward," he said. "When I told him we wanted some sort of nursing device for the little fellow, he thought we were insane. Feeling better?"

"Oh, I'll be fine."

"I warned you that sun is treacherous. By the way, I'm fearfully embarrassed."

"By what?"

"By the way I—by what happened out there this afternoon."

"Oh, please don't be."

"Well, I am. Making you put up with all that, her letter, and—oh Lord! The only excuse for my behavior is that we seem to have become friends."

"We have."

Suddenly he reached for my hand and shook it. "Thank you," he said, "thank you very much." After he left, I thought that an intimacy.

Neither of us woke for dinner.

Jim had warned me the little calf's presence in camp would be quickly nosed out, but the lions I heard seemed to be far off, so did not disturb my sleep.

Then there was a sound which did, something between the one a rotary saw makes when it hits a knot in an oak plank and the scream of a child through the barred windows of a home for the deranged. It was answered from the opposite side of camp.

This conversation went on for a time. Then there was silence.

My head was banging. I got up, fumbled in the dark for the aspirin, swallowed four, fell asleep, woke, slept, not on and off, but drifting half between.

I was in that kind of a doze when there was a sudden commotion, terrible and swift. I thought I heard a tiny cry. Then I saw Jim's light go on, heard him curse. The flap zipper of his tent went up. Jim was walking out into what I never would have. I heard his voice, could not make out what he was saying to the boys. Then there was, most surprisingly, some laughter, more talk, more laughter.

In the morning my headache was mostly gone. I felt unsteady, a little testy, the natural result, I thought, of a bad night. I took two more aspirin.

"What was all the laughter about last night?" I asked Jim when he appeared for breakfast.

"You've been relieved of your responsibility," he said.

"The calf? How?"

"Leopard, I think. He's gone."

"Didn't they stake him down?"

"The practice here is to enclose a walking meat supply in a fence of thorn, a *boma*, very effective usually."

"Apparently it wasn't. What happened?"

"The boys believe in the magic of the leopard. It's the animal they respect most, trust least, same thing, I suppose. What they say is that a leopard leaped into the enclosure, then leaped out again with the calf in his mouth."

"Could a leopard do that?"

"Not even a big male."

"What's your theory?"

"Rather romantic. The wildebeest calf, hearing the leopard calling—you did hear the leopard last night?"

"Those screams?"

"Yes. The little fellow felt very wanted. Who can resist being wanted except a fool human—by the way, what did you think of the letter on further reflection, Andrea's letter?"

"I felt sorry for her," I said, glad for the chance. "Very sympathetic."

His face clenched, but he didn't speak.

"So what do you think happened?" I said. "To the calf?"

"It went looking for—for whoever. It got through the thorn enclosure some way, jumped, perhaps. How can you possibly feel sorry for her? That is a totally unfair and impertinent letter."

"I suppose it is."

"Suppose! Forgive me, but I can see you've never had an experience with that kind of person. People like that can be terrible bullies. Have you any idea what emotional blackmail she was demanding? Excuse me for speaking to you this way, but I'm out of patience with her, really."

"I can see that—about being a bully."

"I will not be moved by it."

"I suppose you're right."

"I know damn well I'm right!" He was breathing very hard. "Forgive me, but I will not be blackmailed—"

I tried to help him. "And the laughter"—I changed the subject—"what was that about?"

He looked puzzled. "What laughter?"

"Why were they laughing, the boys? After the calf—"

"Oh, the boys. The laughter was Francis and Kimani's tribute to the surpassing cleverness of their friend, the leopard. You're aware that they had no sentimental feelings about the calf. They regarded it as fresh meat, simply that. They think you're an absolute fool, excuse me, for being sentimental over that damned calf."

We drove up the long slope which hung over our camp, then across some stubbled meadows.

Jim laughed. "I have just broken," he said, "every rule of the Society of White Hunters. Again. Oh, dear!"

"Which only proves you're human."

"Well, you'll never be bothered with my personal life again, I can assure you. I will remain impersonal as we're supposed to be. At all times, O.K.?"

"I don't mind," I said, "either way."

The damned ache in the bones of my head would not go away. The sun was pressing down. I put on my golf cap. I felt edgy and a little cold.

"Today," he said, in his professional voice, "I thought we might have a look at the private game park of Monsieur Oscar Jamet. Will you be agreeable to that?"

On a terrace at the side of their long, low settler's house, M. and Mme. Jamet were entertaining a guest for breakfast. He was presented to me and identified as the game warden of the district. A plump black, spending his middle years in sedentary postures, he used the interruption of our arrival to protest a busy morning ahead, thank Mme. Jamet for her hospitality, and take his leave.

M. Jamet, dissatisfied with the conclusion of their conversation, accompanied the game warden to his car, while pressing a last point. M. Jamet was a huge, pneumatic man of perhaps fifty-five—an Alsatian, Jim had said—sprouting strawberry-blond hair from every ruddy aperture. Santa Claus in summer, he spoke perfect English.

Mme. Jamet twinkled off to make her staff attentive to our arrival.

"Sit here in the shade," Jim said. "Keep your hat on. I will explain."

I changed seats. As I did I noticed an eight-foot pyramid of skulls and skins at the top of a flower garden.

"That's from the animals they've lost to poachers," Jim explained. "They drive the animals into the fence Oscar put up. Easy victims. Oscar is very exercised about it, and I must say I can hardly blame him."

Mme. Jamet was back, followed by a black servant in a short white butler's jacket who offered us a choice of fruit punch or a Bloody Mary that tasted odd.

"*Marie la Vierge,*" Mme. Jamet explained in her twangy French accent. "We do not allow alcohol on the place. The blacks smell it out, break in like mice, lose all control with a single drink. It is impossible here, a normal life."

A cloud moved and the sun touched her. She was older than her husband, a woman thin the way Jacques Cousteau is thin, a variety of chic. She made a virtue of her raillike body, wore tight boots of glove leather and whip cords. A broad belt dramatized her wasp waist, a sweater showed no irregularities in front to mar the flow of green vicuña. A lesson in how to make an asset of a physical disaster.

The game warden's driver opened the car door for his boss. We heard a few words as M. Jamet's voice was raised in outrage. "Must I create my own police force?"

"The poachers," Mme. Jamet explained. "This government does nothing." She looked at the warden's car. "*Merde!*" she said.

The driver closed the door and the game warden sank into his tonneau.

"Oscar had to cut out tobacco, too," Mme. Jamet said. "A problem of circulation. Suddenly his pressure goes up to one hundred and ninety. But he permits me these." She was smoking a Dutch cigarillo, held elegantly between shell-pink fingertips. "Will you try one?"

The game warden's driver, on instruction, started his motor. This act tripped something in M. Jamet. He erupted, and we heard every word.

"Well, then, tell me, can I ever expect any assistance from your government?"

I couldn't hear the game warden's reply but couldn't miss the ambivalence of his manner.

Then the car drove off.

"M. Jamet," I said to Jim, "has your authority voice."

This remark, intended as a social joke, nettled Jim. He turned to M. Jamet who was returning to us and said, "Oscar, can you find a moment to inform this representative of the greatest democracy on earth what techniques the fact of being a white man in East Africa makes necessary?"

M. Jamet expressed his disgust in sounds without words. Then he shook my hand and said, "It's so good to see an American face."

Our breakfast was brought to table, and I was served.

"Here, here." Oscar took my plate. "Come on, sir, ranch style. Let me put a piece of this impala steak under your eggs."

"No, thanks," I said. "I was up with a headache most of the night."

I'd felt the nausea again as soon as the meal was served. Perhaps it was the presence of all that meat. There was fat link sausage as well as the impala steak and hand-cut hog's bacon.

"I will have that last piece of toast," I said to the butler, who was carrying off the silver toast holder to have it refilled.

"Zoo-zoo!" Mme. Jamet trilled for his attention.

The butler kept a course for the kitchen door.

"Attention!" Oscar shouted. "Where are you going with that?" Then he added something in Swahili, an elaboration which made the butler recover from his start and laugh with relief.

Everyone joined in except me. I didn't know the joke.

Oscar noticed I wasn't smiling.

"My client," Jim explained, "doesn't like the way we talk to our blacks."

"I'm certainly on his side in that," Oscar said, "but there is no other way, as you must have observed, to get their attention, not their obedience, simply their attention."

During breakfast, Oscar Jamet told us of his efforts to preserve one tiny corner of East Africa as it was. "Do you think that is appreciated here? I give employment to more than thirty of these people, pay them better than they pay each other. Am I showered with gratitude? I no longer expect it. What I am concerned about is the animal life here, to preserve it. Come, let me show you what I've created."

Reaching out a huge hand, he pulled me out of my chair.

We went to the game preserve—the Jamet home was outside its cable-link fence—in two vehicles. Oscar asked me to go with him, and on the way he told me the story he must have told hundreds of times, his success story.

"In June of 1940, German tourists wearing helmets and riding tanks rolled into our country," he said. "Soon afterward, some of my friends were invited to join the Wehrmacht. They took me too, a mistake because I am a practical man and value my life. As soon as I found myself opposite an army known to take prisoners, I surrendered. To the Americans."

"At that time there were no sleeping facilities or dining accommodations for prisoners in France, at least not on the level of comfort you Americans choose to provide your guests. So your generals, excellent fellows, sent us to the States. There I found my ideal, particularly admired your business methods and your films. I worked behind the cigarette and candy counter of the prison camp's PX. There I learned English, polished it at the cinema. Now they tell me I speak rather like Bing Crosby. Also I read your magazines, discovered that many of your big men were born on the wrong side of the Atlantic. This taught me hope."

He was pushing his open Land Rover at nearly sixty miles an hour.

"When the day came for us to be returned to our motherland, I had my big idea. I opened a small plant to manufacture a confection, called it Bonne Nouvelle. You've seen it, no? An exact imitation of the most popular American candy bar. My only innovation was to use American methods of marketing and advertising—in France. I had learned what you have to teach. How you sell is more important than what you sell.

"Five years after the first Bonne Nouvelle appeared on the market, I sold my entire operation for twenty-two million francs, not French, Swiss."

The jouncing had me dizzy.

"Now I wanted the Garden of Eden with sanitary facilities," he laughed. "I found this place. I doubt Adam's preserve was any bigger."

I was about to beg him to drive a little slower, and a little more smoothly, when we came to a nine-foot fence surmounted by three strands of barbed wire set at an angle pointing out.

"I have sixteen thousand acres inside this nine-foot fence. I live here as if this is all there is to the world. I don't know who the president of the United States is now."

"It's—"

"Don't tell me. I don't care to know." He seemed to be very worked up, either in exhilaration or anger. I imagine nothing exhilarated him like his rages. "The wonder of it is," he said, "that all this comes from a bar of candy."

"I'd like to taste a Bonne Nouvelle."

"No, you wouldn't. Anyway, you can't. I don't allow it in the house."

We'd arrived in front of a large sportsman's lodge. Oscar stopped the car and jumped on the steps, taking a keyfold out of his back pocket.

His headquarters—a sign across the lintel of the front door so declared it—was on a corner of the preserve. On one side, I could look along what seemed to be miles of fence that went up a rise in a perfect line, out of sight over the top, then up and over the next rise of land.

"Come on in, friend," Oscar shouted. "Ah, it's so nice to see an American face again."

"What did this fence cost?" I said from the porch.

"Don't ask! An absurd expenditure. The fence was made in West Germany, excellent construction. You can imagine what I had to pay these Nazi bastards, but it gives me a completely controlled paradise in a world whose rapid disintegration I don't want even to hear about."

"Here you are God," I suggested.

He took this as a compliment.

"My only problem is a few poachers, but we're going to control them too, and pretty damn quick."

The walls of the room were weighed down with huge trophies, the biggest horned creatures still not extinct. A field telephone on the table screamed to be picked up.

"Oh, my God," Oscar said, "they found another poacher, at the other end of the—" He was out the door, moving like an elephant. "Come if you like, good way to see the place." I was running down the stairs, head banging inside. "Don't if you don't feel well, it might shake you up." I was in the jeep, and he'd started the engine. "Stay here and wait for Monique and Jim if you—" We were rolling.

Going up the incline we hugged the fence. Antelope looked through the mesh as if they wanted to join the animals on the liberty side. Oscar drove right through, scattering them.

It was a terrifying ride.

In the four or five years since he'd put up the fence, the strip of land along its base had sprouted acacia trees and thorn bushes, which Oscar simply rolled over, the young, resilient stems crashing along the steel underpan of the Land Rover, one after another, like heavy surf under a Boston Whaler.

"Hold on," Oscar shouted.

Suddenly I began to scream. At the top of my voice!

Everyone screams differently. I have no idea what mine sounds like. But for the first time since I was an infant I lost all control of my feelings, all caution about letting them be heard. I didn't give a damn how it would sound to the other fellow, what he'd think about me or say to others about me later.

The fact is Oscar seemed rather pleased. He gunned his Land Rover even faster.

We'd turned the crest of the hill, were heading down.

Later I found I'd been holding on so hard I had three breaks in the skin of my fingers around the nails.

I remember Oscar yelling, "Isn't this—? It's *formidable!*" as another tree and its heavily leafed top was swallowed under us.

There was a hammer inside my head, and it was trying to get out by beating a hole through the skull.

Once I almost fell out. We'd reached the corner, and as he turned he saw me going, grabbed me, and held on. He had a grip like a bear trap.

Then we stopped, and he jumped out of the Land Rover.

I would have puked, but I saw Oscar drawing a pistol out of a holster I hadn't noticed and advancing on a man a couple of his wardens in olive drab shorts and underwear tops were holding at gun-point.

It amazed me that blacks would turn in blacks. I had to ask Jim about that. How could they continue to live in that part of the country?

Oscar, giving orders in Swahili, held his pistol on the poacher as the pair of wardens bound the man's hands behind him.

"Come here, sir," Oscar said to me impatiently, "come here and look at this."

My head was throbbing like my heart's motor was in it.

The black kept his eyes to the ground, a captured animal.

Oscar was pointing to—it was a Grant's gazelle, the first time I'd been close to one, a perfect young animal, its throat cut. The wardens had come on the poacher as he was dismembering the animal. Its head was on one side, eyelids up, eyeballs looking straight at me. The two legs, cut free of the body, were tied together at the ankles. The animal had been skinned, and on the skin lay those cuts of meat the blacks liked best.

"They love the liver and the kidneys," Oscar explained, "just as the big cats do. They eat the heart raw." He turned and looked at the two wardens. "You can have all this," he said, indicating the meat on the skin, "but put the legs in my car." He turned to me, and I thought he winked. "We'll have them for dinner," he said.

The poacher was ordered into the back seat of the Land Rover, a warden on each side. Driving back to headquarters, I realized that running over small trees was not special to emergencies. Oscar ran over everything in front of him all the way back.

The area to the rear of the headquarters' lodge was a sort of hospital. Small cages and enclosures held animals, sick or wounded, which needed care. In one cage an ocelot ducked out of sight as soon as he saw us. In another cage, behind small mesh, a python was asleep.

Oscar ordered the door to one of the cages opened. Jim and Monique and some of the other wardens watched as the poacher was pushed into the enclosure and it was locked behind him.

"You all right?" Jim asked me.

"We had an exciting ride," Oscar laughed. "He almost fell out."

I couldn't take my eyes off the poacher. He was standing motionless in the middle of the enclosure, head down, waiting for whatever disposition Oscar would make of him.

"What are you thinking?" Oscar asked me.

"Nothing," I said, turning my head away.

The keeper of the little zoo came up with a small cage in the shape of a pail. In it were a dozen white mice. He saluted M. Jamet, then dropped a mouse into the enclosure where the python lay asleep.

"He ate yesterday," Monique said. "He may not today."

"Is something disturbing you?" Oscar asked.

I'd been looking at the poacher again.

"Nothing special," I said.

"That man," he said, pointing to the poacher in the cage, "is breaking every law, the law of the state, the law of humanity, the law of God, and he has no damn business taking my property. What would you do with this problem?"

"Oh, darling," Monique said, "they're just meat-starved. You have so much here, let them take a little."

The man in the cage lifted his head and looked at me. A new face? I looked away quickly.

The mouse in the python's cage was behaving in a way I hadn't anticipated. It was inspecting the eight-foot snake with its nose. The python opened its eyes without revealing the least interest in the small, clean rodent.

"What's he doing?" I asked. The mouse nosed around the python, who had again closed his eyes.

"Am I right, Oscar?" Jim said. "If the python doesn't eat the mouse, the mouse will eat the python."

"Eat the python? Where would he begin?" I laughed.

"Where he found the meat most tender. That's what he's determining now. Since the python doesn't show interest in any way, the mouse might even believe him dead, but dead or alive, he's meat."

The mouse's confidence was up. It was nosing the python's long body like a master chef inspecting a whole filet he might purchase for his kitchen.

Slowly the python woke, looked at the mouse, a fixed stare. He didn't move except his head. The mouse looked back at the snake, not the least bit intimidated.

"All right," Oscar exploded, "go ahead, let him out."

He did not wait for one of the wardens, went to the enclosure, opened the door, and, taking out his knife, cut the bonds around the poacher's wrists. "But for chrissake, this is the third time—" He was not addressing the poacher because he was not speaking in Swahili. He was addressing me. "So stop it. You're going to make a villain of me."

Oscar barked some orders in Swahili which the poacher understood. He ran and was gone.

Then I had this thought. I hope Ellie's safe.

The snake looked at the mouse with interest now. I was watching intently, or so I pretended.

"They're meat-starved, *chéri*," Monique said.

"Well, then, why doesn't their goddamn government do something?"

"They're trying to get them to raise cattle but—"

"*Merde!* They're too lazy." Oscar was challenging me directly.

When the snake struck, it was a move so swift I couldn't follow it. He had the side of the mouse in his mouth, and before I could see what happened, it had happened. He'd coiled his body around the clean little animal, and there was nothing to see but the head of the tiny white predator who a moment before had been enjoying great dreams of consuming the choicest part of the python.

"You know what the game warden's advice to me was?" Oscar

yelled at me. "Kill the next one. That, he says, is the only warning they'll pay attention to. And that warden, you saw him, is a black man."

"Then why don't you do it, *chéri?*" Monique said coolly.

The hospital attendant kept dropping mice into the ocelot's cage. The cat charged out of its little box-shelter, grabbed a mouse, and was eating it as it crouched back into cover. One of its legs was badly twisted.

"What happened to its leg?" I asked.

"A hyena," Oscar said. "Wouldn't you say, Jim?"

The ocelot was out again, grabbed another mouse. The sound it made was similar to the one a man would make eating an Oh Henry! bar, the bones as they were chewed up made the sound the nuts make with the candy.

"What will you do with it?" I indicated the cat.

"If I let it free," Oscar answered, "it would be dead in a week. He's there for life."

"Who would kill it?"

"Its brothers," he glared at me. "Nature has no tolerance for cripples and weaklings." I did think he meant me.

The ocelot was eating another Oh Henry!

"That damned head warden advising me to kill one of them. What do you say to that?"

I shrugged, turned away.

But Oscar came after me, and I had to face him.

"You have no right to come here judging me," he said.

"I wasn't judging you."

"He wasn't doing that, Oscar. Now come off it," Jim said.

"He doesn't have to live here and face these problems. He has no right to be morally superior to me. I do my best."

"Of course," I said.

"This is their place. They are more than ninety-eight percent here. They have the government. We live by their tolerance. If I killed one, I'd be stood up in a trial where I'd have no chance of mercy. They wouldn't do what I just did, would they, let the man go?"

"I understand that," I said.

He sighed with disgust. Then he said, "So tell me what you're thinking."

"I'm wondering," I said, "why one of these blacks hasn't killed you a long, long time ago."

I turned from his gaping face and walked to the Toyota.

A half hour out of that controlled paradise, I asked Jim to stop while I threw up Oscar Jamet's breakfast. After which I felt so much better that I resented Jim putting his hand on my forehead, that hand with the message, "Now calm down, little boy."

"I'm all right," I said. "Take your hand away."

"You have a fever."

Was he pleased or was I paranoid?

"You should be in bed."

"I didn't come to East Africa to go to bed. Let's see the sights."

"What sights? It's four o'clock."

"Make a suggestion. What sights are there at four o'clock?"

Now, why did I begin to needle Jim? I don't know. I can tell what happened. I leave the explanation to you. One last mystery, I did what I did for Jim's sake. It was an act of friendship.

"What are you so edgy about again?" I started.

"I'm really quite the same as always, thank you."

"Always when? Yesterday afternoon or when you met my plane? You're not always the same, you haven't been the same since I expressed some sympathy for the author of the letter you insisted on showing me, sympathy I still feel. You've been pissed ever since I said I felt sorry for that poor bitch, what was her name? I asked what her name was, Jim?"

Sidney would enjoy this, I thought. "My boy, when am I going to see your Rave Act?" Well, man, now!

"Andrea."

Jim was good and mad. It was oozing out of his face.

"Andrea! That's a beautiful name, you know."

"Suppose you tell me what you'd like to do, sir, and I'll do my best to oblige."

"Sir?"

"What would you like to see?"

"Let's get into something, I mean, really into something."

"What do you mean, into something?"

"Into. Close. Let me touch this goddamn continent, not just look at it."

God, that felt good. My control had been my curse. Now, sick and feverish, I was coming out, mean, nasty, my honest-to-Christ self.

"What sort of thing would you like to get into?"

"Into some of the wildlife I've seen on your gay tourist postcards. The bastards who took those candy-colored cards must have been closer to the animals than you've ever allowed me to be. They must have got off with their lives."

I could see the cables he'd wound round and round himself tighten and strain. I had to cut those cables, for his sake.

"Well, let's see," he said and stopped, his eyebrows up and stiff.

The man was just like me. I'd never seen such control. I had to push him over the precipice. I had to help him fall into that disgraceful human morass where I was now wallowing.

"Well, let's see now," he said, looking around, the poor catatonic son of a bitch, "let's see now," for the third time, his neck so clutched in that chronic muscular spasm he could hardly look right or left, his profile so veddy clean-cut, like those members of Yale secret societies who meet in club rooms without windows. "Well, let's see now," teetering on the brink, still like one of those Kennedy boiler-room studs, somehow the elite, "Well, let's see now," talking through his goddamn nose, the sound vaulting through the chambers of that high bridge and coming forth so special.

Then he broke out of it. Control won again. "I believe there are buffalo over there"—he pointed—"on the hill opposite."

He handed me his glasses.

"Please do not offer me those glasses again. I want to get close."

Where he'd pointed there were black smudges in the green.

"Well, then, suppose we have a look."

"I've really seen enough buffalo," I said. "Buffalo, I must tell you, were the major disappointment of my first trip. They are all, male and female, nothing but spooky black cows, lumbering, heavy-footed, spiritless, with shit dripping from ass hole to ankle."

"You're quite mistaken, you know."

"I'm quite mistaken, I know, but about what?"

"The character of the buffalo." He sounded so starchy again. I had to break this man down.

"Well, if they're not docile and boring and cowardly," I said, "if they're what they're cracked up to be in your tourist propaganda, then for goodness sake help me experience these marvels. Or else this whole goddamn trip has been like watching a TV show in your living room on a rainy Sunday afternoon."

I gulped. Some sour nausea juice had risen to the back of my throat. I swallowed it.

Jim noticed and smiled. "I think you should be home in bed," he said. "You are not yourself."

"All right! Let's see the fucking buffalo."

"I think you are not being sensible, but since you won't be, very well, we'll take a ride."

He threw the Toyota into gear, and we broke out over green cover.

"What is it the buffalo can't," I shouted, "see, hear, or smell?"

"They see, hear, and smell very well."

We hit some terrible holes. The bocci balls inside my head bounced and banged.

"Personally I think all their senses are dull," I shouted, making my head hurt worse. "Look." We were coming up the slope toward them. "They look so stupid, just staring at us."

"That's because they're uncertain about our intentions. Watch it." Another hole. "Wart hog!" Jim swerved.

I've seen Arabs in the Cairo market pounding copper plate. One of them had got into my skull.

"The fact is," Jim shouted, "they are very dangerous and completely unpredictable. You never know what they're going to do."

"When you know it's a milk cow!"

Many times at the seashore, when I was carrying a throbbing head, a quick jump into the surf had cured it. If you get the blood running fast, it will carry off the tension, therewith the pain.

"It's a large herd," Jim said, "bigger than I thought."

No doctor, no analyst, no wise man, no scientific spiritualist, no swami, no friend, boy or girl, no mother, no father had ever told me, "You have headaches only because you choke down what you feel."

"You get headaches?" I asked Jim.

"Never."

Another theory shot to hell.

"A very big herd," he said. "All through the Bush there. Here, take these glasses."

"No, thanks."

He stopped the Toyota. We were a hundred yards away.

I slyly felt my forehead in a gesture I hoped would pass for accidental. It was very hot.

"Let's get closer," I said.

"We might a bit," Jim said. He moved the Toyota twenty feet, pulled up the hand brake.

The animals stared at us. We stared at them.

"Nothing," I said.

"What do you mean?"

"Look at them."

"Very pretty."

Actually, they were, in a picture postcard sort of way, hundreds and hundreds of them, exactly alike, a mother couldn't have told which was her son. All had that same expression of undirected anxiety on their— "If you call them faces," I said out loud. "All their stupid expressions are the same."

They didn't move and we didn't move.

"How about it?" I said.

The only sound, a wind and its song, quickened the silence. Occasionally the soft end of a branch moved against the soft end of the branch next to it. I closed my eyes. My head throbbed.

I concentrated on the silence. It didn't help. "Let's go," I said, eyes closed.

He moved the Toyota another twenty feet, pulled up the brake.

The animals looked at us fearfully. Jim turned off his motor. It didn't reassure them.

"All boxers," I observed, "in their most formidable photographs look frightened."

"Don't know quite what you mean," Jim said.

"I mean that the stance of these black cow-asses may be aggressive, but their eyes are very, very scared."

"That's why they're dangerous," Jim said.

"Now will you move up a little, please?"

"I think this is as close as we should be."

"Well, I think we should be closer, so move it."

"It's really not advisable."

"Fuck what's advisable."

I was waiting for Jim to say "Fuck you!" but he couldn't make it, poor wretch.

"I'm asking you to move closer, man," I said.

"I'm sorry, sir, I must refuse."

"I don't think you're sorry, but if you are get over it and move. I cannot take a head shot from this distance."

"In that case I'm afraid you'll have to take what you can. Perhaps when you see them later, the snapshots, and remember the circumstances under which they were taken—"

"All I'll remember is that you refused. I'll give you one more chance, I ask you once—"

"By the rules of my organization, the Society of White Hunters, a decision of this kind is entirely mine."

"I came here to take pictures, and I will not take a single—"

"You should have brought a longer lens. Next time—"

"There will be no next time. I am formally asking you and for the last time—"

"Absolutely no."

"In that case I will have to complain to your superiors."

"They will maintain my position."

"Do you think I've been sounding like a typical ugly American?"

"I'd rather not say, sir."

I burst into laughter and he joined in. Then we stopped and stared at the buffalo and they at us. My stomach was souring again. I could taste it. My whole gut was beginning to go into spasm-cramps. I knew I mustn't let Jim see any of this or he'd go into his authority routine again and ride me back to camp.

Then he made conversation. "There's a cow," he said.

"So what?"

"She's got a calf. Look at the little fellow. Can't be more than three or four days old."

"Will you stop that old-maid's drool! 'Look at the little fellow.' It's revolting, really, stop it. Where is the little fellow?"

Jim pointed to a clump of very small trees, and in the thickly leafed center I could make out a black hulk.

"I see the cow," I said. "Where the hell is the calf?"

"If you'd use my glasses you'd see her plainly."

"But since I won't and I can't see the calf from here, will you move up, please?"

Jim dropped his head.

I had him going!

"What are you doing, thinking?"

Jim didn't answer.

I had him.

"Jim, will you please take me to where I'll be able to see what I came all the way from the United States of America at great expense to see?"

He looked at me and smiled. Nasty and very human. At last!

"All right, sir," he said. After another moment of staggering silence during which he seemed to be enjoying a joke of his own, he said, "I will do what you ask."

He turned the motor over, and when it caught on, he pulled a short lever near the floor. The Toyota was in four-wheel drive.

Slowly we moved toward the cow.

Jim didn't say a word. He held the Toyota in a dead line, straight for the cover where the beast and its calf were. His pace was slow, but it was even, and anyone would know, even a dumb buff, that Jim was not going to stop, that he was putting it up to the other fellow.

In the clump, nothing moved.

"Hold on," Jim said, his voice calm, nearly casual.

I took hold of the side of the Toyota's frame.

"Not there," Jim said. "Here."

Lightly, with one of his long fingers he touched the handle directly in front of me, over the glove compartment. "Both hands, please," he said.

Foot by foot, we moved forward.

There was a ravine on one side, and as we moved it got deeper. Jim was sizing it up, three feet deep, going on four, on five, on six. Now, there was no way out, not to that side. Jim looked in the other direction, straining up in his seat. Satisfied there was no obstacle there, he settled in again.

The cow, when it came, came out of the silence and through the cover like an explosion. She headed straight for us, looking bigger with every gallop.

Jim spun the Toyota, jerked it around. "Hold on!" he yelled. I held on with both hands, watched that big black cow coming for me with nothing between us except a little space and some steel made in Japan.

It was too late to avoid a collision, but the way Jim handled the Toyota, the animal's huge skull and horns caught us only a glancing blow. She slid off, scraping along the body of the Toyota, rocking it.

She'd hit right where my hand would have been if Jim hadn't moved it.

The cow, turning on dancer's feet, came at us from the other side. Her momentum was like that of a great boulder falling off a cliff, then bouncing down a long incline, throwing off mud and pebbles and smaller rocks and the sparks of its ferocity.

Again she caught us a glancing blow. Jim had seen to that.

She turned, at us before we were ready, coming from the other side, so our only escape was the ravine.

She was not to be denied this time. Charging with all her weight off balance, forward, she was going to destroy us this time, put our back on the ground, our four rubber feet in the air. She was going to turn us over so our soft, vulnerable parts would be open for her to horn, penetrate, rip, and destroy, sending our jangled junk flying in all directions. She was going to finish us with her horns and her great boned head.

No, this woman wasn't like Mrs. Rhino with calf we'd teased the day before. That housewife was only too glad to turn and waddle off, her child following. It was kill or lose her calf, the way this big black girl played it.

She hit us head on, cracked us low, cracked us hard, catching a place with her horn down and under our side, lifting the ton of Japanese metal off the ground on one side, straining, pushing with her hooves, making mud of the ground under her, wrestling, twisting to get her horns deeper up and in, again under, then deeper, under, deeper, lifting each time till we were on an angle, the last angle, I was sure, before she'd have us turned over.

When she gave her last heave, I would have fallen out except that Jim caught me. His grip wasn't gentle. I know from its feel that he thought I was getting what I deserved.

Having saved me, he headed straight for the ravine, our only way out, at a speed that would get us away from the buffalo, perhaps, but which might very well break the axle pin or that vulnerable place where the steering mechanism breaks into joints.

Just as we reached the ravine, just as we started down the incline at top speed, he slammed on the—

There were no brakes.

We hit that side a terrible galump, the chassis slamming down on the two ankles. Then we straightened up and out, turned, and started up the other side, and since we were headed straight for the lineup of buffalo which were till then watching, but would spook and come at us if they felt threatened, Jim turned the wheel sharply away, and it was then I fell over the side.

I was still holding the handle. Jim grabbed me by the top of my jacket and collar. He couldn't slow down, that had to happen by wheel friction, nor could he let the wheel go. He had to keep the Toyota going away from the buffalo. So I was dragged a dozen yards, my feet scraping ground, then a dozen more before he could pull me into place. He slammed me into my seat.

The buffalo cow wheeled in place—how beautifully she turned! —and trotted back to where her calf was waiting.

Jim kept his path, running over bushes and small trees like the mad Alsatian Oscar Jamet.

I looked at his face. It was angry but it was also pleased. I'd behaved like a prime number one U.S. prick, and I deserved what I got.

Jim down-shifted. Finding a little upgrade, he was able to bring the Toyota to a stop.

He was out of it in a second, found a buffalo skull, put it under a back wheel. Then he got on his back and took a long look under the car.

"We have no brakes," he said.

He got back into the Toyota, took out a butt-edge, shorthorn briar pipe I hadn't seen before, filled it with some scraps from the bottom of his pocket, lit it.

"Kimani is a good bush mechanic," he said. "If he can't patch us up, he can at least get us to the lodge at Keekorock where we'll get another vehicle."

"What happened?" I asked.

"She ripped up the brake rods on one side. We'll have to zigzag back to camp and try to avoid any steep downgrades. We may have some difficulty. How's your head?"

"Forget it."

He smoked.

"Sorry," I said.

He did not accept my apology.

We made very slow progress. There were places where I had to get out and put a tree bole under the wheels. We found we could brake the wheels with a rope around a tree and let the car down a grade. On upgrades we were O.K.

"I'm really sorry," I said.

He nodded.

"I was quite frightened, you know."

He had no comment.

Later when he saw me putting my fingertips to my eyes and pressing in, he asked, "How's your head?"

"Not too good."

My eyeballs were burning.

After we'd negotiated another long, difficult downgrade, he said, "I'm the one that needs to apologize. I should never have let you egg me into that foolishness. I know better."

"I sort of enjoyed it—"

"I doubt it," he said.

"I was scared, but I did enjoy it."

"I could get thrown out of the association," he said.

"Blame me."

"We are very strict. That kind of excuse is not accepted."

"The client is always right."

"The client is generally a fool. It is our responsibility to protect the client from himself."

At the top of the long incline into camp he hollered, and Kimani and Francis came running, and I got out, and we held back the Toyota as he let it downhill in low gear, four-wheel drive.

He dropped me in front of my tent. I said, "I'm not feeling too well, Jim, but I'd appreciate it if you'd proceed as if I was in perfect shape, which I am not, O.K.?"

He nodded. I thought about the expression on his face when I was lying on my cot. He was ashamed of himself. Poor soul.

Almost immediately I was in a kind of sleep, my body covered with dew. I was shivering, then shaking, then perspiring. I put my arms around myself and embraced my body. Hard.

There was a blizzard over the east coast of the North American continent. I wondered where Sidney was. I turned on my face, arched my back, trying to relieve that slugging in my skull. I pushed my forehead down on the cot cover. I pressed my eyeballs into my head with the heels of my hands.

There was no way to turn aside what was coming. I hoped only to get through dinner, then, zipped in my tent, let come what may.

New York City had eight inches. I could hear the sirens of the police cars, muffled by the heavy fall of flakes. Then everything was silent, as it is in a blizzard at night, and I heard the frantic bark of zebras. I knew what that meant. Where was Sidney now? Where was he sleeping? How was he making out? Probably blaming it all on me, the record heat, his mean, sweltering room in Harlem. Still, would I prefer to be Sidney's understudy again?

I only had a few minutes before dinner. I couldn't show Jim the least weakness. He'd stop the safari.

I got down off the cot and onto all fours. I swayed from side to side, crawled a few steps, rocked again. It was great to be on all fours. It had been my only relief that night in Manila, when the dengue hit me, to crawl around the rain-soaked yard of the hut on stilts where we were quartered. It was a relief to be an animal then, and now.

Jim pulled up alongside, signaled me to pull over with a jerk of his head, then pushed his motorbike off the throughway and turned off its motor. Slowly, deliberately, he dismounted, pulling a heavy leather-covered pad out of his back pocket. What was he trying to do, set a new world's record for how long it could take a cop to get off a motorbike? He was like a man free-falling through space. "You're going to have to turn in your license," he said in his biggest voice. "This trip is over."

I heard light, quick footsteps. Francis was holding the basin of warm water he provided me before each meal. "Dinner," he said, putting the water carefully on the little table outside my tent.

The warm water cooled my face. When I reached for the towel, Jim handed it to me.

"Those zebras are giving themselves away again," I said.

But Jim had gone. He was sitting at the dinner table, sipping his whisky and staring into the fire. He was not looking at me in a disapproving or superior way. I was grateful for his good manners.

"You look better," he lied when I joined him.

"I had a nap," I said. "That usually helps."

"May we get you a drink?"

"Whisky and hot water, yes, thank you."

"Francis!" Now he sounded like a cop again. "Bwana," then some sharp Swahili, then, "Whisky, hot water."

"What I said to your friend with the fence," I said. "I regret that."

"Oh, well, I suppose that's the kind of thing one thinks but doesn't necessarily say."

We dropped the subject.

They brought the meat, an animal's leg garnished with a mint sauce and flanked with greens cooked Chinese-style, crisp and unnaturally green. I was seeing the safari for its poetry, the sudden astonishing brotherhood of human creatures who would not otherwise have been together. There was a sweet murmur among us, Francis serving the table, Kimani in the kitchen, Jim talking. Then the blending aromas, the meat in its crisp-flaked skin, the delicate but insistent mint sauce, and the heavy, all-pervading odor of the rotting Bush. But above all there was my own fevered sensibility, distorting everything, the heat pumping through me, followed by the cool of evaporating perspiration, all making me open to feeling and wonder.

"I still don't see how they do it," I said, "prepare a meal like this in the Bush, particularly when it's raining."

"You O.K.? More or less?"

"For instance, the roast. Is that lamb?"

"Impala."

"Well, that needs an oven. The bread, another oven. The mint sauce, a slow burner, no? How do they manage it? The hot water for my whisky, a trifle, but it needs a burner too. Kimani must have, at the end of the lane through the Bush, at least eight adjustable burners."

"That is what he has, and as many more as he might need. And each burner is capable of infinite adjustments."

"Come on, Jim, stop being so mysterious."

"It's no mystery," he said. "They build a great fire, starting hours before so that by the time they're ready to cook, they have a huge heap of red embers, a flaming pile of jungle charcoal. The ovens are just pots. Are you listening?"

"Intently."

"They take shovelfuls of these embers and build any size and temperature and duration of heat source they wish. The ovens are the classic ovens of primitive peoples, earthenware—" He stopped.

"Go on."

"Air tight. The bread and the leg of impala are placed inside those pots, which are set on beds of embers. Then their lids are covered with shovelfuls of the red-hot coals. One shovelful will do under the small saucepan in which the mint sauce— Don't you really think we should get you back to Nairobi as quickly as possible?"

"No."

My head had nodded. I'd caught it at the last instant before it fell to the ground.

"Go on," I said. "I'm O.K."

"That's all there is to it."

He didn't know how to continue the pretense at conversation. There was a silence.

"By the way," he said, "Kimani's confident he can patch up the Toyota."

"I'm sorry I behaved like such a shit," I said.

"When?"

"Come on, Jim, don't tease me. This afternoon, all afternoon."

"Oh, don't concern yourself about that."

"Well, I do."

"You were simply not yourself. I've been aware throughout this trip—"

"Aware of what?" He'd stopped, hesitated.

"That you haven't been yourself."

"I was extra intolerable this afternoon, even for me. How did you stand me?"

"It is our profession to look after our clients, not to judge them."

"How could you be so controlled?"

"As soon as we get back to civilization and you've paid your bills, I will revert to my hairy-back self."

"I wouldn't blame you. You've been very patient with me."

"Because I was worried about you."

"No need. I've had this fever before. It comes suddenly, goes the same way."

"May I suggest once more—"

"That we cut this safari short? Forget it. I have engaged you and the boys and this little caravan of equipment for three weeks. Andrea will have to wait."

He laughed. "Oh, come now, it has nothing to do with Andrea. Andrea is nothing to me but a nuisance."

"If that were so, which it isn't, you would still have to— Imagine the conversation, if you have the courage, that must have taken place the evening of the return of the Indian chap. Can you hear the talk between that husband, no matter how mild, and his wife pregnant by another man who is white, a colonialist, a member of the master race, against whom the benedict doesn't even dare raise his voice, poor sod?"

I was raving again. The heat had come back, very hard.

"And this hero has nothing but scorn for the husband, scorn so deep that it has never occurred to him to fear the man's anger were it ever released, his revenge were it ever exercised. Scorn so great that he, the white master, can be polite and generous, drive him here, drive him back, share a meal, share a tent, conduct the whole episode with that well-bred smoothness, that stainless-steel control, the kind that he might show a well-hated brother back from overseas, instead of the husband of a woman whose life he has ruined."

"God," he said, "I thought that kind of romantic palaver had gone out with the ruffle."

"No. It's only that people since the last century have ceased opening their minds to the reality of torment when it's in another person. Someone like you, especially, has become so hardened to the pain of others, animal or human, that he pretends it does not exist. Christ! This goddamn head hurts."

Sweat was seeping from my hair roots into my eyes, stinging—

"You are getting yourself overwrought," Jim said. "And for nothing. You're right. I've lost the ability to have those feelings, but you have not. Congratulations."

"Why congratulations?"

"I wasn't angry at you this afternoon. I envied you. I think that is the best part of you, that ability to feel hurt. Are you really all right? I never met an actor before. I can't tell."

"Yes. What's for dessert?"

"Francis!" he called.

Francis came charging up the green chute, through the green bush, throwing off sprays of Swahili, frenzies of deference, fireworks of subservience, poor Francis, scrambling the dishes together onto a tray, rushing them through the bushes. He was gone, was back, was gone again.

Kimani brought the steam pudding himself. It was a perfect shape, a lactating breast, a soft bomb. He poured brandy over it, detonated it with a match. As the flames subsided, he sprinkled the confection, using both hands, confectioners' sugar from a large blue enamel shaker, cinnamon from its red mate.

The scent of of cinnamon filled the air.

"Cinnamon, Kimani!" I said.

"Mizzouri, bwana." Kimani was proud of his presentation.

Jim gave the delicacy the respect it deserved, cut into it slowly and carefully so it wouldn't crumble.

"We cannot undo the hurt we've done, said the prophet."

"What prophet is that?" Jim asked.

"So don't try. That's your stand, right?"

"More or less," he said. "We do our best. But I don't think we can be responsible for the pain we cause others. In the end it's every man for himself."

"Oh, fuck that," I said.

"Fuck what?"

"Fuck you, you arrogant, pseudocolonialist, master-prick!"

He cut the pudding into several slices. We only needed two, one for him, one for me, but he kept cutting it. God, so gently, not crumbling it, so exercised he was, yet so controlled.

"We are only two here," I said.

He gave me mine on a plate.

"Talk to me," I commanded. "Don't sulk."

No answer. He was pouring a white, creamy sauce the consistency of whipped marshmallow over my pudding. Again Kimani dusted it with cinnamon.

"I knew a girl once who smelled of cinnamon," I said.

"How fortunate for you! Her breath?"

"Not her breath, her being, her body, her most private parts, they smelled of cinnamon."

"How wonderful! Where is she now?"

"Lost in the herd."

"Too bad."

"I think I'll lie down."

"Do. Sleep will help you."

"I think I won't."

"Why in the world are you so miserable?"

"For the same reason you are. I betrayed a friend, I think."

"Oh."

"A close friend."

"Perhaps he deserved it."

"He did, but does that make a difference?"

I closed my eyes. I was dizzy.

Suddenly, to my surprise, I was telling him the entire story, in detail, slogging through the mud of memory with the last nits of my energy, pushing that great stone out of the swamp in which it had become mired.

After I'd finished, he said, "You're much too generous. You are nowhere at fault in this."

"Is that your only reaction?"

"Put him out of your mind forever."

"I haven't been able to."

"You haven't tried."

"All right then. I don't want to."

"Man is not, as the politicians and the priests, the prophets and the poets would have us believe, cruel to his fellow man. He is, as you are, generally too kind."

"You can't seriously believe that."

"And because of that false kindness, that destructive compassion, we have now filled our society with freaks and psychos, criminal assassins, all feeling they are justified for their crimes, all screaming as they wield a knife or point a pistol, 'What else could I do? Can't you see I'm really a saint? Pity me, forgive me, protect me.' "

"Instead of—what should we do?"

"Don't offer help. Don't save them. Let them die off. Because if you don't, the victim will not be them. He will be you. So you—stop."

"Stop what?"

"Stop feeling guilty about this Sidney."

"I am not."

"Then why are you crying?"

"Not about him."

"Then?"

"I was remembering the girl who smelled of cinnamon."

"Oh, that's different, that's all right."

"Except for one thing."

"Which is?"

"She's dead. And she was Sidney's wife."

"When? His wife?"

"Her name was Roberta."

"You believe in the sanctity of marriage?"

"No."

"She was probably leaving him, wasn't she? She'd probably been with others before?"

"Many, very many."

"The day before?"

"And the day after."

"So, you do believe in the sanctity of marriage."

"What I believe in is the sanctity of pain. We must respect pain. We must not cause it. That's what I did, and that's what I am ashamed of. That's why I wish so often that I was someone else."

"But we can't help giving each other pain, especially if we like each other."

He was still talking when I keeled over. The last things I remember were his mouth moving without sound and the taste of that steam pudding with its warm aroma of cinnamon.

Jim must have lugged me to my tent, undressed me and covered me, turned off that hissing air-sucker, the Gaz, lest I set myself alight, zipped fast the single seam opening of my envelope of synthetic cloth, left me entombed, thank God for small favors.

Now I let myself enjoy my fever. I was grateful for its heat.

I felt what Jim had described. I was falling free. I spoke a conjuration to drive out of my body and up into that flickering light those old ghosts who'd chewed my spleen, summoned before me the characters to deny whose threats I'd sculpted my stone mask. My eyes looked unblinking at the citizens of my hitherto secret state.

Particularly that preposterous one with the snap-brim black Borsalino hat. How absurd he seemed now.

But not as absurd as my obsession with him.

About what followed that night—I can't tell how much of it

happened, how much I imagined. I'm not going to try to convince you, for instance, that later that night I talked to an old male lion outside my tent. I remember thinking he looked like Bert Lahr and that I'd seen him at Equity meetings. I remember remarking to myself that the eyes of old animals, like those of old people, get smaller. They begin to peer. I remember how that old lion smelled. I can still smell him. No, not cinnamon, you fool. They mark their territory with piss.

I remember these details, so possibly it all actually happened. But I am not going to bother convincing you. Make of it what you will.

It started when I fell asleep, which was immediately, and the dream was there. It had been lying in wait behind a bush of the mind, or in a WC like Jim's lioness, and came busting out.

I was in the dining room outside the Polo Lounge in Beverly Hills, that favorite spa of talent brokers with its tables scattered through the trees in back of that old rambling luxury hotel. The foliage was not as heavy as in the East African hollow where I was going through all this. Still it was tropical, semi. I was feeling sort of feverish too, that day long ago, very wrought up, so the dengue fitted. This agent comes rushing up, late as ever, to "take me to lunch," and after the BS about how was my trip out, which I'm sure he didn't care about, he says something he means.

"I think something good is happening for us," he says, us being him and his client, me.

"That'll be nice," I said.

"I'm going to take you out to the studio to meet the director," he said, checking his wristwatch and throwing the waiter a "get moving!" look.

"Will Sidney be there? Mr. Schlossberg? Castleman?"

"Oh, sure."

"Because he doesn't know I'm in California."

"I told him."

"What did he say?"

"He said, quote, 'I'm glad you're trying to do something for the boy.' "

I snorted. He snorted.

Yeah, Sidney deserved everything I did to him that day.

When we got out to the studio, he was sitting in the director's office as if it was his. They were playing gin. When Sidney loses at cards, he makes it seem he is losing on purpose, a gift from on high to the poor clod behind the other hand.

"Well, look who's here," he said, "the mechanical rabbit."

Everybody laughed though they didn't know what Sidney meant. I did. He meant I was the kind of actor who went precisely the same route in a performance every night while he, impelled by that unpredictable thing, his genius, would take different courses depending on how he felt.

I was glad he lost the game. The director accepted his check.

An assistant of some kind came for him, looking rather resentful. Seemed Sidney was supposed to have been at wardrobe an hour ago. There was a camera crew waiting to test his clothes for the part.

"What the hell do I need another test for?" Sidney demanded.

"Just part of our routine out here," the assistant said.

"What was wrong with what I wore on stage?"

"They looked stagey, Sidney," the director talking.

I noticed there was an edge to the director's voice and it was sharp.

Sidney took no notice. "You should have brought my tailor out like I suggested and had him make my clothes. Your hack has made too many suits for gangster parts."

Sidney jumped up, hooked his arm through that of the assistant in a democratic gesture, and made an exit like the one he had in his last play, very gay, very gallant, very indomitable, waving his hand. You know! As he went past where I sat he mussed my hair and exited to general laughter.

Which stopped as soon as the door closed.

"If Mr. Sid Castleman would work at it," the director sighed, "he could develop into quite a pain in the ass. Even if he didn't work at it."

The director was looking forward to ten weeks of Sidney, and not with pleasure.

Sidney came back into the room. He always stretched his exits. "Meet me in the Polo Lounge at five thirty," he ordered. "We'll have a drink. Roberta is here. She'll be glad to see you, or at least she'll pretend." Then he turned to the director. "Now you find this boy something in our film, Eddie," he said. "His mother put him in my charge when she died."

He left again. The director sighed again. The thing about Sidney in these days was that he was always sure he overwhelmed people with his charm, when actually the opposite had happened.

The young agent who was shepherding me caught my eye.

The director was looking at me, carefully.

"He's quite an actor," the director said, jerking his head toward the door.

"Sidney's great," I said, "on stage. Of course I don't know any-thing about this medium."

"This medium is the most honest one in the world. The camera is a microscope. It reveals anything phony. If you're a goddamn ham," I thought he looked at the door, "that's what comes over. If you're a prick, you can't hide it from the camera."

He kept looking at me.

"Stand up," he ordered.

I stood up.

"Turn around."

I turned around.

"Take him to see Mort," he said to the agent.

We were out of the room without a wasted word. "He likes you," the agent said as he hustled me down the hall.

Mort Benesch was the producer on the picture. Sidney was in his office, too. I could hear him from the anteroom. He was complaining about the director, and the costumes.

"They make me look older than I am," he was shouting. "The idea of a costume, it's supposed to make you look younger. Your director, Mort, should know that. It's basic."

The secretary was an older woman and very experienced in her field, which was Mort Benesch. "I don't think he'd mind being interrupted," she said and called her boss on the intercom.

"Bring him in," Mort shouted, not using the intercom.

Sidney came up and threw an arm around me as I entered. "This boy has some talent," he declared. "Under the right direction he can be quite effective. Mort, I expect you to do everything you can for him."

Mort sighed. Sidney was causing a sigh epidemic.

Then Mort looked at me. Hard. "We're going to try," he said.

The young agent looked at me to say, "Did you hear that?"

Sidney finally left. His last words were, "I'll do the fitting in the morning. I'm going down to take a steam. Call down there for me, will you, Mort? Tell them I want the Turk, not your Swedish faggot. I don't like his hands."

Mr. Mort Benesch was exhausted when Sidney left.

Oh, yes, Sidney deserved all that happened to him that day. But, looking back, I prefer him to the men who were unloading him.

"I didn't realize he was that Jewish," said Jew Benesch to my agent.

My agent made a gesture meaning, "He's what you see."

"Or that hammy," Mort Benesch said in his chopped-liver accent.

He looked at me again, a long time. I felt I was expected to say something.

"I'm absolutely sure," I said, coming to Sidney's defense, "that a strong director can hold down Sidney's tendency to ham." If you call that coming to Sidney's defense.

"I don't know we got a director that strong," Mort Benesch said. "You want a schnapps?"

"No thanks," I said. "He's always that way at first, till he settles in."

"If he settles in any further, he'll take the studio over," Mort Benesch said. He yelled for a drink.

"He's really a great old man," I said.

"Yeah, he's too old," Mort Benesch said. "What the hell is your goddamn agency trying to sell us?"

The agent looked at me.

The secretary came in with a drink. "Mr. Benesch," she said, "they can hear you out in the hall."

Mort Benesch waved her off. "Get me Burt Allentuck," he said to her, "and don't criticize me."

"Yes, sir," the secretary said. "Mr. Castleman asked for a limo to take him back to his hotel as soon as he gets through in the steam room. Will that be all right? I've only got your car. The rest of the drivers are out on that Malibu location."

"Let him get his own car. Why the hell doesn't your agency provide your client with transportation?" he said to my agent.

"We did," the young agent said, "but he found fault with it."

"What?"

"Said the driver was insufficiently respectful."

My agent was a murderer. Too.

Mort Benesch kept looking at me as he talked to Burt Allentuck. He bawled Mr. Allentuck out as much as he dared. Mr. Allentuck was one of the important agents in town. No one trifled with him. Mort scolded, then complained, then softened altogether, looked at me and said, "He's in here now." He kept studying me and listening to the phone, and then he said to my shepherd, "Take him back to Eddie Diamond's office."

By then I had an idea what the score was, so I wasn't surprised when I got back to the director's office and found Head of Wardrobe there with a tape measure and his assistant to write down my sizes.

"How did it go?" Sidney asked when I walked up to his table in the Polo Lounge.

"O.K., I guess," I said, bending over and kissing his wife, Roberta, on the cheek she offered. "They took my measurements."

"Which part?"

"I don't know," I lied.

"They don't know what they want," Sidney said.

"Get up, Sidney dear, so he can sit between us."

I kept Sidney between us.

Even fully clothed in her light silk dress, Roberta gave off the fragrance of cinnamon. Most women smell of seafood mama, especially when they're caught unprepared. But I was never with Roberta when she didn't smell of cinnamon, not only between her legs, but wherever those particular glands are, under her arms, in the roots of her hair, her skin. Each time I was with her and long after she'd gone, I could smell it on my fingers and in the air where I moved.

Roberta had been an actress, too, and while Sidney's career had prospered, hers faded. She quite correctly felt that Sidney didn't give a damn about the career of another person even if she was his wife. Actors are more honest than other people.

The difficult part for Roberta was that when she and Sidney had come together it was she who seemed to have the big career ahead. She had a natural sexiness about her, something uncalculated, animal and innocent. She was absolutely open about enjoying her power to attract me, played the game of Changing Partners as if it was the only game that mattered.

"Are you going to be in the film, too?" she asked.

"They're going to give him a part, or I'm going home," Sidney said.

"Why don't you come live with us? We rented this Spanish mansion for six months. It's got a pool in back, heated and perfumed, and more bedrooms than I've seen yet."

"No thanks."

"I get it," she said. "You'll be having visitors. Well, we got a garage, and there's a lovely little apartment over it. It's supposed to be for the chauffeur, but we don't have one—"

"We haven't worked that out yet," Sidney interrupted. "The agency promised to get me a chauffeur. It's in the contract."

Sidney did not drive a car.

"If they don't, then Burt Allentuck's got to pay for it."

"Oh, Sidney—"

"I'm seeing him for supper tonight. I'll straighten the whole thing out."

"Will you take me to supper?" Roberta said to me, snuggling against Sidney. "Sidney won't!"

"It's not I won't take you. Burt Allentuck said we had some business to talk."

"Will you?" To me.

"No thanks."

"Why not?"

"Ellie's going to call. I've got to stay in my room."

"You mean it's that serious with the young lady—what's her name?—"

"Ellie."

"That you can't have dinner with the wife of your oldest and best friend?"

"I was up all night in the plane. I'm bushed."

The headwaiter, a man who looked like he played the violin, came up and said there was a phone call for me, I could take it in the booth just outside the Polo Lounge.

"Bring the phone here," Sidney ordered. "What's the matter with us? Everybody else got a phone at their table."

The headwaiter gave me a funny smile, shrugged, and left.

While I waited for the phone, I took in Roberta. She was sitting snuggled against her husband, kissing the side of his neck from time to time, which Sidney took as perfectly natural obeisance. She agreed passionately when Sidney called the director, whom she was later to bed, a knucklehead, joined Sidney in all the Broadway versus Hollywood snob humor current at that time—it's the other way around now—said what she had to say, which was plenty, about how stupid and corny and insensitive the people of this place were—"They've never offered her a job," I thought—and was making Sidney feel just fine with her body's pressure and her sharp wit.

While all the time, she was working me. I'd had premonitions in New York, heard she wasn't always faithful to Sidney. But this was the first time she'd come on that strong. When she reached up and tucked the fall of Sidney's side hair behind his ear and kissed his lobe, for instance, she looked straight at me without blinking.

I couldn't have said then if Sidney was unobservant or indifferent. It didn't occur to me that he was naïve, till now.

Finally they got the phone connected and in my hand. It was the young agent. He knew where I was and who I was with so he was careful not to require any answer much longer than a syllable. He said that things looked good, they wanted me to read some of the shit for them tomorrow, and not to worry about hurting Sidney Castleman because, even if it wasn't me, it wasn't going to be him. They'd had Sidney.

"O.K.," I said, "O.K. Yeah. Tomorrow. Any time."

"What are they bothering?" Sidney asked when I hung up. "I told them to find you something. Now that agent will take the ten percent for doing nothing. I'll tell Allentuck tonight that I should have the commission. Which part did he say they're giving you?"

"He didn't say. They just want me to come in tomorrow."

He believed it.

The phone rang again. I picked up. It was the young agent again. "Where will you be tonight, in case they want to see you, or talk to you?"

Roberta was looking at me again.

"I'll be in my room all night, 427, here, in this hotel, 427."

I remembered I said it twice, four twenty-seven, once for the agent, the other time for the wife of my friend.

I can still remember her face watching me through that phone conversation, a perfect mask. She was not innocent like Sidney, not good-but-foolish like Sidney. She knew all about betrayal, expected it, dealt it. Betrayal was her field.

"What did he really say?" she asked after I'd hung up the second time.

I was flustered. When I stalled, she said, "Sidney doesn't suck up, so people like that get sore at him. They think no one has the right to be arrogant except them."

She had a good idea what was going on. The thing that made her suspicious, she told me later that night, was that none of the wives had called her. When you're really in that society, the wives want to socialize. Roberta hadn't received a single call from a wife.

After I hung up, she kept looking at me with that mocking smile. Finally I said, "Sidney, ask your wife to stop staring at me."

"I can't control her," Sidney said.

"Sidney tells me you devote a lot of your time and energy to fucking the wives of your friends," Roberta said.

"Is that right?" I said, which is to say, nothing.

"Who is it tonight?"

"Do I look like the type who'd do that?"

"No, that's why I suspect Sidney is right."

Sidney's date with Burt Allentuck was at six thirty, the time at the end of the day Mr. Allentuck preferred for that kind of conference. If anything unpleasant happened, it would happen gracefully over drinks, or, as in this case, he would take Sidney to Romanoff's. Even Sidney wouldn't throw a scene in Romanoff's.

Roberta took her husband to the agency in a yellow cab, then herself back to the hotel and quick like a bunny into room 427, as if we'd made the date.

I pretended we hadn't, acted surprised.

She said I must not think because she'd come there she didn't love Sidney. Sidney doesn't have time for anyone else in his life, she said, "But I do love him, only him. I love him a lot."

She'd guessed everything. "I knew it when they kept making wardrobe and makeup tests," she said. "You don't keep pissing money away on stuff like that if you're sure. They're not asking you to do a lot of wardrobe tests, are they?"

"What do you mean?"

"Oh, come on, I'm not going to fuck you unless you're straight with me. I know why they brought you out here. Naturally, they have no imagination so they hear about his understudy, that he has a short nose that turns up. You know these rich Jews here. They're the biggest anti-Semites."

She was undressing all the time. How careless women are with their clothes when they decide to take them off! I had, I remember, folded my pants along the crease and laid them carefully over the back of the armchair, hung my coat on a hanger, my shirt too, spread my underwear, carefully, pulled my socks inside out so they'd cool and dry. I was controlled even at a moment like this.

But Roberta just dropped her clothes where she'd pulled them off, some on the chair, some on the floor, the dress in wrinkles, her underpants in a ball, the hose rolled and wrinkled.

"I don't like to do this to Sidney," I said.

"Christ, you're a hypocrite!" she said.

When she came to bed, she carried herself as though her disproportionately large breasts were not an awkward burden, as so many heavy-breasted women feel. She came bearing gifts, crossing her forearm under them, supporting them as she moved slowly toward me. Then she kneeled by the side of the bed, and before she kissed me or anything like that, she laid the Bobbsey twins on my chest, carefully and gently, laid them there, as if to rest them for an instant. Then she stroked them—Roberta's sexuality included herself—following along with her hand over my chest and onto my stomach and so on. It all came back to me with the smell of cinnamon.

When Ellie called from New York, I was in Roberta. Roberta looked up and waited and listened to everything, didn't pretend not to. I had the impression she enjoyed the scene. Later when I knew her better I knew that she was anxious to prove to herself and to everyone else that the world was all double-x.

Talking to Ellie I didn't hide anything from Roberta, told Ellie there was an excellent chance I'd get the part. She should be prepared to come out. We could get married out there, I said. I'd have real money for a change, seventeen-fifty a week, the agent was talking, eight-week guarantee, probably run over. Eddie Diamond, the director, usually did.

All through this—I remember how delighted Ellie sounded —Roberta smiled faintly, not moving, still hosting me.

Then there were tears in her eyes.

By the time I hung up I'd gone soft.

But it didn't take long to get it up again. Roberta took it as soon as she could get it, like she was starved, fucked with her eyes closed— both of us did—as if what she was doing had less to do with me than with someone else, the man getting the bad news at that instant, the fool still pretending, no doubt, that he didn't feel the pain of the knife eviscerating him.

Something born of guilt was running wild in us both. The usual controls by which people try to be passingly decent to each other were relaxed. For who can enjoy being a perennial understudy? Who wife to a man as self-centered as Sidney? We were both working it off, getting back at him, clutching at each other, the press of our embrace squeezing the cinnamon out of her body and into the air.

That night it was Sidney who was the proud person and Roberta and I partners to the guys with the knives who'd been ripping our friend all that long day.

That's what I hadn't got over. That's one reason I still felt guilty so many years later in that East African encampment.

Sure I could see Sidney sloughing it off, that big phony, pretending it was something he'd expected all along, smiling that twisted half-smile. But some of his life's blood spilled that night all over the floor of Romanoff's Restaurant.

And in room 427.

He called me about eleven. Roberta and I were fucked out, lying across each other, almost asleep. I said yes, I was asleep, and yes,

Sidney had wakened me. I must have sounded quite annoyed. "How the hell do I know where she is?" I said. "I'm not your wife's keeper. She probably went to a movie."

It was then, as Roberta moved close to the phone to hear what her husband was saying, that Sidney told me he'd withdrawn from the movie, decided he couldn't ever get along with that knuckleheaded pretend-director and that he detested Hollywood, more as he got to know it better not less as everybody had promised. Sidney even suggested that I try for the part. They'd probably give it to me. It was that unimportant, I suppose he meant, and they that stupid. Perhaps it would solve my money problems, Sidney suggested. Besides I had more tolerance for vulgarity than he did, and much more control of my temperament. Actually Sidney thought I didn't have any temperament, I could live through any humiliation. He wasn't far wrong about that. Anyway, he said, to sum up, perhaps I needed the part. He sure as hell didn't.

"I'm asleep," I protested.

But Sidney went on and on, making fun of the director, then turning his venom on Burt Allentuck the agent—what a phony he was, Sidney, laughing uproariously at his own jokes—then suddenly, saying as if it was I, his understudy, who was keeping him on the phone, "Well, I've got to get some sleep," and abruptly hanging up on me. And Roberta. Without saying goodbye.

"Why did you talk so mean to him?" Roberta said.

I'd hardly said a word.

"A baby," she said, "just a baby," and again there were tears in her eyes.

She dressed slowly, doing her best to smooth out her rumpled clothing. I got off the bed, naked, to take her to the door. She touched my penis goodbye, running her fingers over it, brought it half up again, saying, "You've got a pretty cock."

It was then I asked the question, "You like me better than him?"

I knew it wasn't a question to ask someone as hip as Roberta, but I couldn't help it. I just couldn't prevent myself from asking. "Do you like me better than him?"

"Oh, that's what this is all about?" she said.

I was pretty embarrassed, but that is what I wanted to know more than anything else. I wanted his job, I wanted his woman, I wanted to be better at everything than he was. Success to me, in those days, was beating Sidney. He was the goal posts and the finish line. When I got past him, I'd scored, I'd won.

Roberta, of course, didn't answer my question. All she said was, "You've got a very pretty cock."

I knew his from the Luxor Baths. It was long and spindly and freckled all over. I thought it ugly.

But I wanted her to say it.

I stood naked at the door of my room and asked her just before she began to walk down the hall, "When will I see you again?"

"I never plan ahead," she said.

Then she walked away, and I watched her go, standing bare-ass naked in the empty hall on the top floor of the Beverly Hills Hotel in the middle of the night, still without the answer to my question.

When Sidney abandoned town with Roberta the next morning, he left it to his agent to sublet the Spanish mansion. The agent, in an act of expediency, rented it to me.

A few days later I wrote Sidney a note telling him I'd been offered the part, "just as you said they would." I said I hoped he wouldn't be offended and then, butter for his ego, that they were rewriting the script according to some suggestions he'd made.

I had a telegram back. "Not offended in the least. It's a mediocre part. Know you'll do what you can with it. As for rewriting that script, it's like rearranging deck chairs on the *Titanic*. Call me when you get back. Sidney."

I loved Sidney when I read that wire—the big phony! In fact when I read it I began to cry with relief, but with love, too.

And that's what woke me that night years later. I was crying in my sleep. I wasn't even in bed. I was standing in my tent crying.

The fever was really boiling up.

I had to get on all fours again.

Then I was outside my tent that way, like an animal on the ground.

The wind, a whisper, stirred the fig leaves. The waning moon threw their shadows, a host of huge moths, onto the tops of our tents.

I was suffocating. I kept trying to fill my lungs.

My entrails were writhing like a snake on a gig.

My head was one of Kimani's little ovens, cooking my brain. My eyes were being pushed out of their sockets by the heat.

On all fours, swaying back and forth, I hit my head again, then again on the damp earth.

Oh the sounds! I had to control the sounds I made or Jim would hear me and the safari would be over.

In another minute I was going to vomit. The impala's leg, the Chinese-cooked greens, the cinnamon steam pudding were all going to come up. There was no way to make that silent.

Was there a breeze? My body shivered with cold.

I crawled to what was left of the fire. I could see better than I expected. I understood how animals get around in the dark, why they're more comfortable then.

My body began to burn again.

The sound of the brook led me toward cool water. Moving through the bushes on all fours, I found myself before a small tent. I could tell by the smell the boys were in there. A soft cry in Swahili, then some murmuring from inside. Laughter. Silence.

They thought I was an animal. Perhaps they were right. I'd known them by their smell. I'd frozen when I heard the sounds my enemy makes.

I didn't have much time. When it all came up, I didn't want to be near that tent. They'd hear and call Jim.

Lifting each paw carefully, laying it down softly, I didn't make a sound.

At the edge of the stream I circled in place. I'd seen insects do this when their guts had been squashed out and plastered to a spot.

The stuff still wouldn't come up. If I could have been assured at that moment that it would be painless and quick, I would have chosen to die.

Then it came up, a churning below, exploding up.

Usually vomit is a reassurance, I'm getting rid of what ails me. But on this night when I threw up there was no relief. I just kept sweating, then shivering, then burning again. My stomach did not settle. It kept trying to come up, the bag to follow its contents.

The final heaves brutalized me. When they were done, I had no strength left. Exhausted, like any common beast, I waited, head down, for a saving bit of strength to come back. Till that happened I was completely helpless, completely vulnerable.

Finally I had just enough strength to lift my head.

I was looking into the eyes of an animal.

He was an old lion, a male with a scruffy mane, some of it pulled out and worn away, moth-eaten in my frame of reference, quite shabby, surely over the hill.

His odor was heavy, it was ripe. You could see he'd been through a lot. An old male alone, Jim had taught me, has generally been driven out of the pride by younger rivals.

He snarled at me, still seemed anything but aggressive.

"Lions have nothing against humans at night," meant "Fear equals hate." This old fellow had no reason to fear me, so how could he hate me?

He'd obviously gorged. His belly hung like an old sack. When he took a step in my direction, his load swung from side to side.

This silly, squint-eyed old glutton was friendly, despite another snarl or two, and very curious. I guess he'd never seen an animal with so little hair. He kept looking at me, cocking his head to this side, then that. He had the kind of friendliness I've seen in very old dogs. When I swayed back and forth on all fours, he did too, playing the mirror game with me. Then he crouched on all fours like a kitten and watched me, his tail switching.

I knew I was helpless, but I didn't care. I believed he would not harm me. If he thought it necessary to harm me, that was all right too.

I was ready to pay for my past.

For a long time neither of us moved. The very end of his tail switched a few more times. I tried to remember whether Jim had said this was a friendly sign or hostile. Then the tail relaxed, disappeared from sight, and I knew.

I let him see, with my own body language, that I didn't feel well, shaking my head from side to side. I was careful not to make any sudden, frightening moves, for my own sake too. My head ached like a dying tooth.

I believe the old boy saw I was sick and helpless, perhaps even that I was offering myself for his mercy, petitioning his generosity.

His old face was an enigma, like prehistoric sculpted stone. He was a judge. Anyone can be who keeps looking at you and listening, yet shows no reaction.

"Why do you blame me?" I protested softly. "I got you jobs, didn't I? I kept your head above water. I kept you alive."

The old beast lifted his head in a proud gesture. Apparently he'd understood the spirit of my words, appreciated their intent. But he had no intention of thanking me.

The lion felt his superiority. Suddenly he looked vain and just a little pompous and more than a little patronizing and quite arrogant. He was equally foolish, equally absurd, equally lovable.

I spoke his name now, softly and in apology. "Sidney," I said. "Sidney, my old friend."

He didn't answer, of course, but he was listening.

I spoke his name again, now in the tone of confession.

Then it followed, I was telling the beast secrets I'd told no one else, not even myself.

I was confessing in a rush that I'd victimized him, not helped him, that I'd enjoyed his downfall. The pleasure I'd derived from helping him was the final evidence I needed for my superiority. Every good deed, every favor, every kindness I'd performed in his behalf was a punishment for his once having been superior to me. Every job, every understudy I'd sought for him, every recommendation, every twenty-dollar bill I'd ever slipped him were ways of asserting my superiority, of keeping him dependent and at my mercy.

That he'd had my mother, I'd never forgive him that.

I confessed all this to the lion.

He sat looking at me, patiently, making his judgments.

I hoped I was impressing him with my sincerity. I wanted him to trust me again. I wanted to be his friend for old times' sake.

Now I paused. I had a final confession, but it was hard for me to voice it because I really didn't quite understand it.

So I was silent.

The old animal lifted his head again and snarled at me. I thought it a gentle sound by then, an encouraging one. He was allowing me to go on.

Then something I didn't, still don't, understand happened.

I knew or felt or admitted that I was Sidney Schlossberg.

The lion had united us. We were one and the same.

I remembered in that instant certain dreams I've had where I changed my name to his, where I'd taken his talent, appropriated it, stolen it. I'd even had dreams where, along with the name and the gift, I'd seized the power and acclaim he used to have. I remembered those dreams, and in those dreams, finally, I'd become him.

I might as well confess it all. I've had dreams where I'd killed this man, then pulled out of his body all of him that I envied, the reasons I'd killed him.

And with him dead, I assumed his identity.

This is what I wanted to confess to the old lion and couldn't. It was this hatred, born of envy and self-scorn, that I wanted to admit and ask forgiveness for.

Here it is, plainer. For years I turned to the obit page of *The New York Times,* first thing every morning, looking for the name of my closest and oldest friend.

With him gone, I could be him.

The old lion cocked his head at me curiously. His look was steady.

He did not blink. He studied me, encouraged me, waited to see if I had anything more to say, gave me every chance to say it. He seemed to understand the difficulty I was having. His kindness and patience, God love him, made me frantic to express, somehow, that one final guilt.

But I never got it out, not that night.

Someone was calling from the camp. I could hear footsteps from the grove of fig trees above and behind me. There was the leaf-filtered light of a lantern.

Jim was looking for me. He'd found my tent empty.

I turned violently in place. "Let me alone," I shouted. "Go away. Don't come down here."

When I turned back, the lion had gone.

Then what I'd expected happened. I heard the camp being struck, and I woke in my bed.

The day before I'd been anxious that Jim not break off the safari, but now I couldn't have cared less. I'd finished with that place. I'd had that trip.

If Jim was surprised when he came in and said, "Guess we can start now," and I made no objection, he did not show it.

I dressed and walked out of the tent as if I'd agreed to the abrupt termination of the trip.

The boys had repacked the trailer, leaving niches for themselves in among the supplies and equipment. A bed had been made for me in the back of the Toyota. By the time we'd crossed the open country and hit the gravel road, I was asleep.

I still had the fever, but without the alternating cold spells. My head ached but did not throb. Jim took the bumps slowly. The motion must have been soothing. I slept through it all.

What woke me was that we'd stopped. I had no idea why, how long we'd been going, or how far.

Since I was lying on my back, the first thing I saw was a circus of birds overhead.

The kill was fifteen feet from where we'd stopped. Three cheetah, they were the mother and the two young we'd seen days before, Jim said, had consumed the rear quarters of a Thomson's gazelle. Satisfied, they were at play, totally indifferent to our presence. Even when they looked right at us they didn't see us.

"Can you sit?" Jim asked.

I did, with a hand up.

"Because this is as close to cheetah as you're ever going to get. It's the closest I've ever been."

It was an idyllic scene. The two young were playing kitten games while the mother, stretched on the ground, watched. They would pounce on each other, cuffing and slapping, then running, cutting tight corners, coming back to attack again. After a bit of this, they'd be still, staring into space as cats do. Suddenly, for no visible reason, they'd be up again, attacking their mother, practicing war on her. She'd strike back, repulsing them, but somehow also encouraging them to attack again. Through all this they never lost their mien of high seriousness, the King's Companion.

Even the boys were smiling with delight at the elegant cats.

"Cheetah are not big eaters," Jim said in a low voice. "They depend on their speed, so they don't load up their bellies like lion will. By the way, you were lucky last night. The boys told me they found the pug marks of a large lion around the edge of the stream, exactly where I found you."

Minutes before, in my half sleep, I'd concluded that I'd imagined my encounter with that old male.

I was too weak and hot to say anything to Jim more than, "I know. I was talking to him."

Not a flicker of reaction from my man.

Abruptly the mother cheetah stopped play and stood erect, her attention fixed. Her face, so deeply graven that no expression except an unwavering seriousness seemed possible, now showed a slight modification, a kind of regal amazement tinged with disfavor.

Jim nodded in the direction she was looking.

With his fellow lying on the ground, half-eaten, a little Tommy was trotting up to the cheetah, prancing, knees high in little steps, closer than he should have. He'd stop and look at the cat, his tail whisking nervously. Then, when she didn't come after him, he'd take another series of tiny steps toward her.

"What the hell is the little bastard doing?" I asked Jim.

"Watch."

"Frighten him off."

Jim didn't answer.

"He's going too close, isn't he?"

Jim looked scornful. "Yes, he is," he said.

I reached for the horn button, but Jim caught my hand.

"Don't do that," he said, his voice very unfriendly.

Now the little gazelle was hopping on all four feet, each hop taking him a tiny bit closer. As he did he shook his head and horns, challenging the cat to take after him.

The cheetah did not move. Her young were watching.

The Tommy bounded on all fours again, up off his feet, then down, straight up in the air, each foot equidistant from the ground, then down again, an inch or two closer with each hop, each inch doubling the danger.

"Jim!"

He didn't look around, but he was very much on guard against any move I might make. "Kindly mind your business," he said. "This is his."

It was then the cheetah bolted. The Tommy turned too late. The cat was almost on him when the Tommy swerved at right angles, then cut again, doubling back the other way. Scampering low over the ground, he stretched his body and his legs as far as they'd reach.

But the cheetah's legs were longer, so she kept gaining on him. Just as she seemed to have him, it was only a matter of another second, she stopped and walked away, stiff-legged, proud. She'd made a decision not to take the absurd little animal.

"Why did he do that?" I asked.

"It's a she, the cheetah's a mother," Jim said, "and if she were hungry she would have had him, easily."

"I meant the Tommy. Why did he challenge the cheetah that way? Why did he take that risk?"

"I don't know," Jim said. "You saw it. Why do you think?"

"I don't believe what I saw."

"Out of boredom maybe," Jim said.

"Did you see that little bastard hopping up and down on all fours that way? Wasn't he gallant, Jim?"

"You better lie down again. Oh, look at him now!"

The Tommy was prancing among his own, his foolish little tail twirling like a toy, his feet dancing those same tiny steps.

"Beautiful!" I said.

"They know just how close they can come," Jim said, "but that time he came too close."

"Why did he do that, Jim?"

"Better than waiting for it to come to you."

"It?"

"Those cheetah have probably been following that little herd for days, taking one of them whenever they were hungry. Perhaps this was like getting it over with, one way or another."

"It was worth the whole safari, Jim. It was beautiful."

"You got to do that once in a while, especially when you're feeling bad."

"Yes," I said, "yes." I fell back on the bed.

"Better than waiting for a lorry to run you down."

"I know what that little fellow was saying, Jim."

"Better be quiet and rest."

"It's like you doing sixty seconds. No, you're too fucking cool. It's like the friend you abandoned, Andrea, the first time she did it."

Jim didn't answer.

"Why did you turn against her?"

"Stop picking at me, will you please?"

"Those are the people, Jim. They are the people!"

"This is the last really rough part of the road," he said.

"That little Tommy was talking to me, Jim. They're all talking to me now."

"Lie down. We got another six hours to go."

"I'm O.K. Stop pretending to worry about me. Here's the thing. By defying it, you win a victory over it. It's the only victory you can win."

"But it doesn't work," Jim said.

"Nothing works, but it's the only thing that does for a while. Did you see how great that Tommy felt afterward, how big he felt? He was Muhammad Ali, the little bastard! It's worth risking your life for that!"

Then I was asleep.

Dreams, said the old Viennese male supremacist, are wishes trying to come true. For the duration of that long ride back to Nairobi I was in and out, not of a dream, for I did not sleep, but of a wish played out. I was the man I'd most wanted to be most of my adult life. The fever was a blessing. I could never have made it without that fever.

What a sense of power and pleasure I had through those hours! At last I was living as I'd always wished I could. I was Sidney Castleman at his summit.

Boston, the show a flop, the company of actors knew it was all over when the closing notice, which had been put up "provisionally" as soon as we moved into the theater for dress rehearsals, was not taken down before Thursday night's performance, an indication that our producers really did mean to close on Saturday.

But the star of the effort, I, Sidney Castleman, knew it opening night, halfway through the second act. I told my dresser and my understudy, who was always hanging around my dressing room with that hero-worshiping gape. "Boys," I said—it was a hospital play— "we're working on a stiff."

Unfortunately, this bon mot got around. When our playwright heard it, his feelings, already shredded by the cruel notices and the bewildered public reception, were crushed. He wasn't to be seen at the final curtain.

What rankled me wasn't only that a promising playwright was being profoundly discouraged and possibly alienated for good from the theater but that the actors, whose natural leader I was, would slink away from the engagement like a dog who'd shit on the living-room rug. After all, they'd done their best. They should leave the show and Boston proudly. I could not stomach the shame I saw on the faces around me that Thursday night.

There was another reason why our playwright, whom we'd nick-named the Pink Porpoise—he was terribly plump for a revolutionary intellectual—was very low. He'd been rejected in love by our leading lady, Peggy. What the enamored young man did not know was that she was, for the time, my consort. I'd hooked up with her only to make her road trip more enjoyable and give her a little more confidence in the love scenes. Anything for the good of the show!

The Pink Porpoise was a hard tryer, and when he was not re-sponded to by Peggy, his reaction was suicidal. I'd known from the first time I'd observed him watching us rehearse that he was going to want to mount her. I warned Peggy not to lead him on. But have you ever seen a young actress, just coming into her good looks and her first big chance, who could resist leading a promising playwright on "just a little"? Even if she was otherwise occupied, as Peggy was by me.

I also knew from sudden darknesses in our playwright's manner and certain internal evidences in his script that the man had suicidal tendencies.

So when we learned that our show had only three more perfor-mances to live, I resolved to save that promising playwright for the theater and my actors from shame.

I believed in the idea that was already old-fashioned, the leading man is the godhead of a production, responsible for all.

The party I threw was not really a week long. It started on Thursday night after the show, and it went on without a break until after the show on Saturday. It was a good party and a necessary party, but not the only one of its kind in the annals of the profession, as some of my young actors boasted. They just hadn't been around very long.

I was living in privilege, not at the Ritz, the preferred hotel where even the sheets had sheets and room service was performed by members of aristocratic Boston families, but at the Touraine. It was Olympian to be Sidney Castleman in those days, and the Hotel Touraine was at my disposal. That old place, now torn down, naturally, had a largeness of spirit. Anything went. All was forgiven. The evening sins were sent to the laundry every morning. All night through you could hear secret movements up and down the stairs, doors opening, doors closing, locked, unlocked. The telephone operators knew all and knew me well enough so they'd tell me, each dawn, the news of the night. In an emergency they'd been known to help a famous guest make intimate arrangements, knowing as they did who was in the hotel and who needed companionship.

Certainly "Mr. Sidney's" every need had to be taken care of. I could get anything I wanted any time, day or night, at the old Touraine. The entire staff served under my flag. The bellboys were my Mercuries.

I had the Presidential Suite. I don't know why it was called that. I can't imagine any president staying there. It would have stained his reputation beyond redemption. My suite, for instance, had four entrances-exits, facilitating a variety of moves under stress. There were also two kitchen-spas. It was a perfect place for a party.

The first thing that made it a memorable party was that I invited the critics. I didn't tell them the whole cast was going to be there. When they arrived, they found themselves facing a jury of their victims. They finally had to answer for their ignorance and their spite. I chose various members of the cast, each as I thought suitable, to read the notices out loud to resounding applause from the cast members. The parts dealing with the "grotesque overacting" in my own performance—I was already being faulted for this—I had read twice.

As for my chill-hearted, piss-pumping understudy, the only one in the cast to get good notices for that lousy five-minute bit I suggested be put in for him, I made that prim little bastard apologize to the entire cast for being out of step with their efforts.

Well, most of the critics got into the spirit of the thing, drinking and demeaning their profession, as what sensible person wouldn't. Only one seemed resentful. I, Sidney Castleman, champion of intellectual liberty, encouraged the man to express his mind. I knew full well what would happen. We were all too happy to let that pass. The orderlies from the last-act operation scene, well-oiled by now, took off this Aristotle's robes, threw them out of the sixth-story window and the naked man into the Touraine's corridors. This critic was as well hated in Boston as I was loved in the Touraine, so he had a tough time getting anyone, bellboy or maid, to help him. He must have reached home all right because he wrote his follow-up piece. It was characterized by caution. He didn't dare complain or bring charges against us. He knew that would make him the town joke.

The next thing that made it a great party—oh, you were great in the soul when you were Sidney Castleman in those years!—was that it found the sweet core of victory in the rotten fruit of defeat. The last performances of that play, instead of being disasters from which disillusioned and disheartened actors slinked away, were celebrations of the human spirit. Or the fact that we were still alive and well, that we had survived.

Riding in the jolly Toyota I was laughing in my sleep.

How trivial the failure of a single play seemed to us all that night in Boston! At first only I, Sidney Castleman, saw it in perspective, but by the end of that celebration, they all knew that so passing an episode must not ever be allowed to sour a life, or even a minute.

I had everyone flying so high that we carried our playwright with us, which was the first purpose of the party, remember? I was not going to have the symbol of our collective effort humbled. There was only one unanticipated problem. Because of this man's inverted psychology, at the peak of his exuberance, when he felt most loved, when he was so happy he couldn't stand it, what did he do but try to throw himself out of my front window, six stories over Tremont Street?

Now this plump soul weighed what you'd expect a man to weigh who wakes up at three o'clock in the morning muttering, "I've got to have some," and means ice cream. He was all pouter pigeon meat, slipped down a bit. When he went for the window, his charge had momentum difficult to block.

But I, Sidney Castleman, brought him down. People who saw my tackle said too bad it hadn't taken place in Yankee Stadium as thousands cheered. That tackle, long to be remembered, was so strong it almost carried my candle-flesh playwright out the window in the blessed company of the greatest actor of his day, a fulfillment the playwright, at that moment, would apparently have welcomed, because he kept scrambling for the open window's ledge, indeed had to be held down by the entire company.

This done, he reversed, became miserable, apologetic, and most unheroic. He began to whimper and cry for his leading lady, my girl Peg.

His grief was so profound and self-destructive, I had to step in. I whispered promises that he'd have her, and I meant to fuck, the very next night. Please, I said, be patient, leave it to me.

This quieted him immediately. A hopeful light made his eyes glow. He sat down, pulled a small pad out of his pocket, and began to make some notes.

When I gave that promise, I must confess, I had no idea how I might carry it out.

I began by the obvious, talking to Peggy. I told her I could not understand, since she had after all led him on, why she now objected so vehemently. The plump scribbler was physically repulsive, she said. I knew for a fact, I told her, that she had entertained less palatable flesh when it suited her purpose. None of this shook her. Finally I tried my last best tactic. I told her if she didn't help me now, I would not see her when we got back to the Big City.

This brought her to her senses. She got on the phone to her roommate in New York, a girl named Hilda, and asked her to come to Boston immediately. Hilda, apparently, was finding New York a sexual desert. She badly needed to get laid. So she agreed immediately. The friendly faggot who lived on the same floor would drive her up. "She'll be here in the morning," Peggy chirped as she hung up.

Of course this wasn't what the Pink Porpoise wanted, but it was at least something to work from. I began to exercise my mind.

The party swelled into the dawn. By the time Hilda arrived I had my plan.

She turned out to be a warm-hearted girl, one quickly affected by the eloquence of a Sidney Castleman. I poured it on, every word golden syrup. I had only one anxiety, that her first glimpse of the playwright's corpus might send her back to New York, lickety-split, in the car of her faithful faggot.

To get her through that trial, I decided to first show her the playwright from a distance, meantime telling her stories about his potency, already famous in theatrical circles, I said, its sublimation the true source of his protean gifts.

Finally she agreed. She wavered a little, on and off all afternoon, but I never left her side. I was taking no chances with her cooperation. The only thing that worried me was that she was showing signs of attachment to me.

Every tree I shook dropped its fruit in those halcyon days.

It took me most of Friday afternoon, a snow job without letup, one in which I persevered through the time I was making up, then leap-

frogged into the first intermission, then the second. I had my dresser
and my understudy guarding her while I was on stage, keeping her
occupied with conversation and carefully spaced drinks while I
played the play.

Thinking about it blew my fuse as we bumped back to Nairobi.

It was without a doubt the greatest performance our fated play
would ever have, which isn't saying much of course. That Friday
night our audience sensed a unique event of the spirit. At the final
curtain it stood up and cheered.

I don't know what made them cheer. Perhaps it was that bit of
perverse kindness which exists in every human spirit and comes with
sympathy to a mangled victim.

My understudy, that mechanical rabbit, said that the real reason
the performance was great—he admitted that—was that I was un-
concentrated. Get that? "When you don't try too hard," he said, "is
when you're good." Well fuck you, Br'er Rabbit.

Actually that closet Jesuit had evidence of why I was so relaxed.
He came into my dressing room between acts two and three and
found me adjusting my makeup while Peggy's friend, Hilda, was in
the one position women's liberation finds the most demeaning. I'd
decided it was necessary for my purpose. So I was pretty damned
relaxed for act three.

Yes, that whole Friday night's performance was devoted to my
leading lady's friend, Hilda, keeping her willing and available for the
ordeal ahead. It would take a full-hearted effort, I could see by that
time, to turn her from me to our suffering playwright. Finally I had to
accommodate her, which I did the instant I came in from the final
curtain call, locked the door and did her. But before I granted her that
favor, I made her promise on her father's grave that she'd follow my
every least instruction for the rest of that night, no matter how
unusual she might find what I'd ask.

She must devote herself—"Swear!"—to making our Pink Porpoise
forget his artistic disaster. She must grow garlands of triumph in the
rubble of his catastrophe. I actually said something like that. Hilda,
I'd discovered, was affected by purple.

She was as good as her word, a fine woman, that Hilda, once she
was brought to see the light.

How I could turn people on and off in those days! What a guide I
was for the souls of others in their journey through this dark vale!

What I did, in the company of my minions, was to lead true dear
Hilda to a room at the end of my warren of rooms. I always took an

extra bedroom in those years in case I had two visitors at the same time. There we ensconced the temporarily exhausted young woman, suggesting that she take a restorative nap, from which she would be wakened by a kiss. A drink of her favorite, Southern Comfort, sealed the understanding.

Then we sought our playwright, found him asleep in the last row of the dark, empty theater. The previous night's celebration had cost this man. Before we took him to Hilda we must find a way of restoring his energy, a shower would help, and raising his confidence to its greatest tumescence. Otherwise he might have another defeat as damaging to his tattered ego as the failure of his play.

While he was cleaning up, I, Sidney Castleman, got an actor from another show playing Boston, asked him to pretend he wrote profiles for a leading New York daily's Sunday supplement and had come all the way to Boston to interview our genius. We arranged this encounter. "She's waiting for you impatiently," we told the Pink Porpoise, "but she will understand why this is necessary. Be sure to mention her performance."

Tête-à-tête across a table in the Touraine bar, our conscript interviewer told the P.P. that he'd seen the audience rise to its feet that night, heard their ovation, considered it his duty to make sure the whole world had the privilege of seeing his play. At a table close by we watched the spirits and energies of our man rise. Ego first, cock will follow, an old rule and a good one.

Our interviewer told our genius, for a climax, that the tide of time would refloat his play off the cruel rocks of the Boston critics' spite. I gave him that line.

From our sideline we kept sending in drinks, keeping ourselves up at the same time. Every time our boy looked the least uncertain, we'd give him the full mouth of teeth and remind him by certain obscene gestures what he had to look forward to.

Oh, it was earth-shaking to be Sidney Castleman in those days!

The interview done, we informed our man, now bursting his skin with desire, that his dream was about to come true. In the dark corridor of the Touraine's sixth floor, we indicated the door to the room where his love waited, ardent if awake, supple if asleep. Just before he started for her, we laid down certain conditions, call them restrictions. He must not, we informed him, put on the lights, any light. His lady, after all, was married. Furthermore, he would have to surrender his glasses. I took them off the bridge of his nose and rubbed the place where they'd rested. Finally he must not talk throughout their romantic interlude in consideration of her profound and abiding shyness. He must communicate with her in only one way, the tactile. She would entertain him to the limits of his desire that night, but after he was done he must never speak of his happiness or ask for another meeting. Her husband, I made clear, was given to violent physical outbursts. So he must be careful never to hint by look, by gesture, by innuendo that anything had taken place between them. What she was doing, she was doing for only one reason, to thank him for giving her that great role in his play and as a token of her hope that he might someday write her another.

He passionately agreed to each and every condition. He had to be a true artist to be as naïve as he was. Furthermore, he complied with the conditions faithfully. Love, as well as the loss of his glasses, had made him blind.

Outside I blessed their union, dedicated the mass they were performing to St. Jude, the Saint of the Impossible.

When he came out of the darkened bedroom, the company at the other end of the hall cheered. It had been eighteen minutes by our watches. Apparently that was all he was capable of for the time being. Perhaps the liquor had dulled his point. But on his face I saw my reward, the glow of triumph, all confidence restored. Here was a completely rehabilitated man, full of that particular verve the critics had tried to crush forever.

"This has been the happiest moment of my life," he whispered to me. "So far! Thank you, dear Mr. Castleman. You have made it all worthwhile."

I returned his glasses.

Now we really opened that night's festivities. I had caused a piano to be moved—what people would do at my bidding in those days! —into my suite. That rational rabbit, my understudy, had told me, of course, that it couldn't be done, it was against the regulations of the hotel. "Regulations, since they are made by man, are broken by man," I said. The damned prig also warned me that the playwright would immediately recognize the redoubtable Hilda if she came into the party.

"With all that liquor in him?" I cried as I struck him over his tucked-under haunches with my gold-headed cane.

Oh, the delight of being Sidney Castleman, in those days! Everything was sheer, spontaneous pleasure, something that my understudy, that toy cop, would never know. He calculates every move, that miserable man.

So starting about three that morning, following the happy descent from heaven of our great-hearted author, the full company joined in singing all the good old ones, "Green Grow the Lilacs" and "Manhattan" and "Give My Regards to Broadway" and "Going Down the Road Feeling Bad" and "Show Me the Way to Go Home." All that Mazola!

Even my understudy joined in.

Hearing our voices in song, great-hearted Hilda came out of her room, beloved by all, our Saint of Charity. Damned if she didn't show that along with her more spiritual virtues, she had the best singing voice of us all.

Despite the dire predictions of my understudy, that tight-ass prude, our great-souled playwright did not recognize Hilda. In fact under our ever-wondering eyes they proceeded to become true friends and fast. He was so charged with newfound confidence from having fucked her before, so inflated in his ego from the love pouring down on him from everybody in the room—he was lying on the sofa, Hilda crouched on the floor at his side—that in short order he seduced twice-seduced Hilda, and they departed the party, this time using my other bedroom. There, as he later told me, he had her again, though he thought it was only for the first time, which was better for his ego so I let it lay. Hilda told me later he'd paid her a true compliment, told her she was a much better lay than her friend Peggy.

Oh, the joy of being Sidney Castleman! It spread on those around him, it reached everywhere, liberated everyone, a true miracle. Those were happy days and now they are gone. Oh, Sidney, oh, Schlossberg! Bring them back!

No one else in the party took a break. Everyone kept going. A poker game developed in one room, a strip poker party among the younger folks in another. The bedroom, now known as Hilda's Rest, was the scene of much social fucking and the civilized exchange of partners. Some lifelong friendships started that night and, if rumors are to be believed, two fine children were conceived in Hilda's Rest.

When our playwright came back from his second bedroom scene, he told me he'd forgotten all about Peg. She was rather inhibited, he said, but Hilda! He stood before the entire company with his arm around Heavenly Hilda's waist and made the announcement. No, you fool, not that, not that they were to be married on the morrow, but that he had been possessed, while he was in Hilda's arms, by an idea for a great new play. He would get working on it immediately, he promised us. "Thanks to you all, but especially to you, Sidney. You saved my life."

Hilda was equally proud and grateful for her own reasons.

The revived genius considered this an announcement of general interest. I, Sidney, said it was magnificent news, and that we'd all long remember that night when the new play was born. Actually, it was another flop, more miserable than the first, but who knew that then, and if they had, who would have cared?

It was the hour for dreams.

So it went through the second night.

The next day, I'd agreed to attend a lunch in my honor at Big Crimson, just to break the monotony for the boys and keep their hands out of their pants for a couple of hours. I called them and declared I'd go only if I could bring my friends. The entire cast showed up—over the objections of guess who? "It isn't fair, Sidney!" Imagine! Fair! The Harvard boys showed their class, splitting their Salisbury steaks and chipping in for the blown-up booze bill.

Oh, the largess I scattered everywhere in those days. I made everyone around me generous-hearted!

Except? Who do you think?

Before we left the hallowed ivy, I called a pep rally of my people. I commanded that no one take so much as a cat's nap till the party was over. This was it, the hard part. They were to go through the two performances as they were, in style, the last two experiences they'd have together, their last two contributions to this work of art. "Let's keep going. Let's not blow it now." Everybody cheered.

Except who would you say, offhand?

No one sneaked off to take a nap.

Except? You guessed it.

That rabbit!

Drinks were served between shows, a gesture of the playwright to show us his everlasting gratitude. He invited everyone to his room where he and Hilda received the company in bed. When the hors d'oeuvre were trucked on in, I, Sidney, forbade them to all except the happy lovers, who filled their naked skins with pigs in blankets and pimento cheese spreads. My command, "Don't eat. It will make you sleepy," was observed by all.

Except? Right. He was in his room, again, so missed the occasion, the tassled cap of our triumph.

I understand he also sneaked a hamburger.

Despite all this, that Saturday night's performance was the worst performance, not of that week, but of the history of the theater, pure garble, back to forward, scenes transposed, desperate improvisations to cover lapses in memory and play for time. Fortunately the author was in the arms of his ever-loving. He wasn't there to hear the audience hiss and the leading man, I, the great Sidney Castleman, keeping my face straight at all times, always "in it," always "up," hiss back. I put them in their place!

And what Actors Equity company deputy would you guess, if you had to guess, had the temerity to come into dressing room number one and scold his leading man? I cursed the day I'd bedded his mother.

No, even then I was gracious, even under that kind of provocation I was patient with my frozen-hearted understudy.

I only hit him once.

Much less than he deserved, wasn't it?

That was the end of the party, that blow struck between acts two and three marked the formal close of our celebration. Everybody knew it immediately.

I had my dresser commission a taxi to stand by at the stage door. I entered that vehicle in full costume, without taking off my makeup. On the New York sleeper I engaged an upper and a lower, since there was no bedroom or compartment available. And so to a deeply deserved sleep! What is more exhausting than triumph?

And who do you think lingered in Boston through that night to make a futile pass at the real Peggy? The next week in New York, when Peggy met me for the first of a series of "one-last-time" rendezvous, we had some good laughs over what that scared little poopoo tried to do with his trembling little do-do.

But did I put him down for that? Sidney Castleman is never small.

What I said to my understudy over the phone when I finally found time to talk to him was rather beautiful. "As you can see, my boy, the trick is not to survive, but to survive undiminished. And we did, did we not? We did not accept other people's evaluations of ourselves or our work. We did not tuck our tails between our legs and run. Those actors! It was the greatest week of their lives! They will never forget that week with Sidney Castleman and his friends in Boston, Mass."

And now, entering the outskirts of Nairobi, I had to admit it, after apologizing for causing him to hit me, I had to admit that I too would never forget that week with Sidney Castleman in Boston, Mass.

By which time I'd accepted that I was not the person I'd once most wished to be. I was a fellow with a fever and a touch of diarrhea and a number of other problems, riding in the company of two little black tribesmen and one normal-looking but terribly fucked-up Wasp, and so arriving in Nairobi City.

What a letdown! To be me again.

Still, as I found out the next morning, something of what came to be known within me as the *Spirit of Boston* did survive.

"Oh, you're awake," Jim said, pulling up the hand brake, "just in time. You know you were singing in your sleep?"

"Ah, but I was not asleep."

"That's a very good sign indeed. I mean your singing."

" 'Show Me the Way to Go Home'?"

"I believe that was one of them. You're going to be O.K. in the morning."

I didn't even see them bring in my luggage.

When I woke next morning I was well, not better, well, raring to go. I had an appetite and a hard on. I wanted the first plane home, called the airline, booked for the midafternoon.

At breakfast in bed, I had a visitor, Bennett Wells, the general manager of the safari outfit, a young man with pink cheeks who presented me a bill scribed in old-fashioned calligraphy, flourishes and all. "I trust you'll find this in order," he said.

"It's very pretty."

He reached me my folder of traveler's checks, which he'd guarded while I was away, and a pen. "If you do and so wish—" he said.

"My fever has left me exceptionally vulnerable to bills done in longhand," I waved my hand in a grand gesture, what Sidney might have said and done.

"Yes, yes, delighted you find it acceptable. By the way, Jim and I looked it up, just curious, don't you know? *D-e-n-g-u-e,* is that right, dengue fever?"

"That's the bugger." I signed in sweeps, trying my best to match his calligraphy.

"There is such a fever, but it does not recur."

"Mine did. I want to tip the boys. How about one of these?"

"No. The book was quite clear on that point. Dengue does not recur. Oh, twenty dollars. More than generous, more than generous."

"Not twenty, twenty apiece. We Americans, you know. Now, Jim. Will he accept a tip? So then, do tell me, what did I have?"

"Haven't the foggiest. Jim? I imagine he would, very gratefully."

"What does Jim say I had? He saw it. Fifty O.K.?"

"More than generous."

Sidney would certainly have given Jim a hundred. "A hundred," I said.

"My God, more than generous, yes, yes. Jim? What he said? 'Psychosomatic.' That's Jim for you!"

"If my fever was psychosomatic—here—I'd hate to have the actual thing."

"Thank you. Well, you know a little about Jim now, he can be quite a pill. Great in the Bush, but once he gets off safari he is quite impossible."

"I'd hoped to see him before I left. We never got to say goodbye."

"Probably just as well, don't you know."

What would Sidney have done? I'll tell you what Sidney would have done. He would have taken the man to dinner. Dinner, hell, he'd have thrown a goddamn party. How long do we live?

"I couldn't possibly leave without saying goodbye to Jim."

"Actually he did drop that he hoped to see you too, very much, but I rather discouraged it."

"What the hell did you do that for?"

"He's very black this morning, not himself, his mood, very scratchy!"

"Why?"

"One's never quite sure. He says you didn't have a very good time, and he blames himself but—"

"It's I who didn't give Jim a very happy experience."

"On the contrary, he enjoyed you enormously, said he'd never met anyone quite like you."

"You're aware that remark is open to more than one interpretation?"

"Oh, yes, yes. Well, I'll see to it that he's sober. The first day or two he's back, Jim, the city, our civilization, and so forth, it hits him pretty hard, and he drinks and becomes belligerent, talks about—well, this is the best of it—leaving the firm, going to Rhodesia, Australia, America."

I got on the phone, canceled the reservation I'd made, booked another on a plane that left at the easy hour of 2:40 A.M.

I knew I'd never see Jim again. I couldn't leave him that way, locked in his hell. In the spirit of Boston, I had to give him a last word of thanks, not one hundred cold dollars.

I spent the day shopping, bought Ellie a pair of turquoise earrings to startle her red hair and Little Arthur a lionskin wallet and belt like Jim's.

He came for me in a vintage Cadillac, a long black '62, the kind of car undertakers use. He'd been drinking and was definitely not himself.

Marge was crouched in the back seat, dressed in purple. Her eyes glowed malevolently. They weren't talking. I couldn't understand them as a couple. Obviously he resented her. Still here he was with her again.

Jim suggested the Indian restaurant. "Round things out," he said. There he chose the last back table. He had a sore on his lower lip that hadn't been there the day before. He kept pulling at it with his upper teeth.

I summoned the waiter and ordered drinks. "This is my party," I said, "and it's going to be a happy one. So why don't you two make up?"

Marge was sitting at an angle to the table, her legs crossed like a man's, ankle over knee, an attitude which seemed chosen to affront Jim. She displayed a pair of very long, very sharp heels, the kind Betty Grable used to wear.

"Marge," I joshed, "what's with those spikes?"

"She's looking for a short man to intimidate," Jim said.

"And what's eating you tonight?" I asked Jim.

"I can't take this city anymore," he said, "or anyone in it. I make the mistake of coming back here. Then I can't wait to get back into the Bush. Can we have a drink?"

"They're coming," I said. "Well, you'll be back in the Bush when?"

"I have to stay here ten days."

"Who you taking out?"

"Twenty-four of your tribe. Students. Longhairs, no doubt. Bisexed, I imagine."

He pulled the lionskin wallet out of his back pocket and found my check. "Thank you very much," he said, putting it on the table next to my knife and spoon. "I don't take tips from friends."

"It was meant as a token of appreciation," I said.

"That is a phrase used when letting servants go."

The waiter came with the drinks. Before he'd set them down, Jim ordered another round. Then he noticed I hadn't touched the check. "Will you please put that in your pocket?" he said.

"Bennett seemed to think that you'd accept—"

"Never mind what Bennett thought. Put your money away." He looked at me till I did. "I'm leaving Bennett's company," he said.

"What happened?"

"I'm leaving Kenya."

"Where you going?"

"I have a plan. I'll tell you later."

Marge made a mocking sound.

"Bennett told me this morning that you thought I didn't enjoy our trip," I said.

"You didn't."

"And that you blame yourself."

"I've reconsidered that," Jim said. "I don't believe I could have done anything more for you than I did."

"You're right. You did everything for me anyone could."

"I don't think you have a talent for enjoying things."

"Perhaps enjoy is not the right word, but I want to tell you our trip was a turning point in my life."

This seemed to intrigue him. "How?"

"I don't know exactly. But I feel so much more—I don't know."

"You had something on your mind through the whole safari," he said. "What was it?"

"I told you."

"Oh, I don't believe that. The man you described is not worth anyone's bother. Imagine how long he'd last if you dropped him into the Bush without a weapon or food."

"Do you judge people that way?"

"It's a damned good way."

"All people? Men and women?"

"Men and women," Marge said, mostly to herself. "And you, too."

The waiter came by with the second round. Jim took his off the tray, ordered a third round. I shook my head at the waiter, but Jim made a sign for him to ignore my refusal.

"When you go back to the States," Jim said, "put a pistol behind your friend's ear. It would be a kindness."

I reached across and shook his thick-muscled forearm gently. "Jim," I said, "we're all freaks and cripples and cowards and fools. We all need understanding. Be kind, Jim, be tolerant of those not like you."

He turned his head away.

"I'm sorry," I said. "I know that must have sounded terribly patronizing."

"It certainly did," he said.

"That's what's happened to me on this trip. What I've seen and the fever and certain things I've never let myself remember before, I've been softened—weakened, you'd call it."

Jim turned to me. "What makes you think I don't like all kinds of people?"

"Because you don't," Marge said.

For an instant I thought Jim would hit her. Then he bit his lower lip, finished his drink, looked for the waiter.

"You like yourself," Marge said.

"Don't we all?" I said.

They were silent behind their fortifications. Then, without turning his head, Jim said to her, "That man is looking up your skirt."

"Goddamn if I'll take this," I said. "Now come on, what's the matter? Marge? Jim, what's the matter with her tonight?"

"She's depressed," he said.

"No kidding. What about?"

"She had an offer of marriage. Oh, not from me. From a very decent—"

"What's wrong with that?"

Now Marge turned on me. "Do you think I'm that hard up? Don't you think I can get laid any time I want?"

Jim laughed. "I'm sure you can," he said.

"I'm going to eat somewhere else," I said, getting up.

"Marge!" Jim cracked out. "Go home. Now."

She looked at him a long time with her wounded eyes. Then she snatched at her purse and stood.

"Why do you treat me that way?" She was standing in front of Jim, breaking apart. "What have I ever done to you?"

"Oh, well, then sit down," Jim said.

"Fuck you, you sadist."

As she reached the street door, she passed a man coming in whom it took me a moment to recognize. He looked around, spotted us, then walked slowly down the center aisle of the place. When he came to the table next to ours, he sat. It was the Indian, Mr. Gargi. He nodded at Jim and me, then carefully composed himself in a chair, his ankles crossed, his palms on his thighs.

Jim had not seen the man. As Marge left, he'd dropped his head, ashamed and full of regret.

"Why do I do that to her?" he said, leaning toward me.

"Because every time you're with her, you blame her that you're not with someone else."

Aware of the man at the table next to ours, I didn't say the name.

"But I didn't ask her to follow me around. She's just a neurotic."

"So are you, Jim."

"I go mad in this city."

"So do they all. Have pity."

"I must ask you not to patronize me again," he said, his eyes like agates. "We're no longer on safari. I am no longer your employee. What do you know of what I've been through with Andrea? What I've taken from Andrea?"

The second time he said the name—perhaps my eyes shifted—he spun around in his chair and said, "Mr. Gargi, would you do me the courtesy of not listening to our conversation?"

"I'm not, sir," the Indian said.

"You chose to sit as close to us as you could in order to listen to every word we say, and I resent it."

"I've come to have a few words with you."

"We had a few words the other day. I haven't the time or the inclination to go into that matter with you again."

Jim turned back to me, rigid as steel.

"I didn't think you saw him come in," I whispered.

"I recognized his body's odor," Jim said audibly.

"Why don't you talk to him, Jim? I'd like to invite him to our table."

"Be very careful," Jim said. "I really hate that man. I can control it in the Bush, but here— You see, that's what I mean. You are full of false sentiment. Have you any idea what he does?"

"You told me, leather goods, shoes, skins."

"That's his father, though this one helps with the skins. He buys from poachers. He's listening? Good. I happen to know that you deal with poachers, Mr. Gargi," he said, not turning his head.

"That is a false accusation, sir."

"Where do you think all those skins come from?" Jim said to him. Then he continued to me in full voice. "But that's only his sideline. Gargi and his Heinie partner run the G-R Minibus Service. You saw them all over the Serengeti, those zebra-striped VWs. Remember? Full of sausage-fat Germans. He and this man in Frankfurt get all the Deutsche mark tourist trade here."

"Now I remember."

"Every time there's a kill, half a dozen of those ugly boxes swoop down and surround the poor beasts with krauts sticking their shaved heads through retractable tops and obese fraus shooting Leicas out of every window. The bloody lions can't even fornicate in peace."

He'd raised his voice. Everyone in the restaurant could hear him.

" 'Siehst Du wie often zat lion does it, Heinrich?' 'Already I count zweiundzwanzig, Bertha!' 'So, so!' 'Ja, ja!' It's people like this man listening behind me who are killing this place and driving me out. The animals can't live in peace so they disappear, die off. No one who could stop it cares. The African politicians are paid off. Pretty soon there won't be any animals or any parks, they'll have bloody well finished off the place. So don't ask me to talk to him. Besides, I want to talk to you."

Having delivered his diatribe, he leaned forward and spoke in confidence.

"I'm not myself today, just as you weren't yourself in the Bush. But I want you to believe me when I say that, despite everything, I like you. Because of you, in a curious way, our safari was a turning point in my life too."

He hesitated, worrying his lip.

"Will you forgive me for what I'm about to say, in advance?" he said.

"Of course I will."

"We'll see. Observing you as I did, I placed a new evaluation on myself. May I be absolutely candid?"

I nodded.

"I think I'm a better man than you. You are not nearly as capable as I am or as strong or as resourceful or finally as intelligent. Do you mind my saying that?"

"No."

"You're lying of course. You have no courage either. Forgive me, but these judgments are too serious to be trifled with. Again I must use you for contrast. If you can do well in the States, why can't I?"

"I see."

"That is what I want."

"I don't understand."

"You see there's no future for me here. That is one reason I dread marriage or any kind of permanent connection. At the same time, I want it. It's what my father and mother had before me and my grandparents on both sides before them, farms, substantial, permanent locations, and families. There is no reason why I shouldn't have a place and a family and a future, is there?"

"No reason."

"So I've made a decision. I admire your country, at least the reality under the pretense. Perhaps I admire it more than you do."

"Well, sure," I said, "I'll give you my address and when you get there—"

"I want you to help me get there."

He reached into his pocket and produced some government print.

"You may consider what I'm going to ask dishonest," he said, "but I assure you it's done every day of the year."

"What is?"

"This is your government's application form for a work permit. It is granted only when aliens have an offer of employment in the States."

"You don't have, do you?"

"I want you to say I do."

"From me?"

"Yes."

"What would you do there? We don't have safaris."

"Don't patronize me," Jim said. "I know your country very well, I have read many books, I read *Time* magazine every week."

"Jim, what makes you think you'd be happier there?"

"Because I—" He wrenched away. "Never mind," he said. "Forget it."

He folded the form, not looking at me now, and put it back in his pocket. Then he finished his drink and looked for the waiter. "I didn't expect you to help me," he said.

"I didn't say I wouldn't, but I don't employ people."

"I made a mistake."

"I work as an employee of various producers."

"No need to explain."

"So you see there is nothing I can honestly say that I—"

"Please don't feel obliged to—"

"Well, you seem upset."

"Not at all."

He was looking around for the waiter, his face clenched as a fist. The anger inside him was trying to shake loose, but he was still able to control it.

"Waiter!" he called, half rising from his seat. "Waiter! Here!" There was a thick husk over his voice.

"The waiter is coming," I said.

"What makes me think I'd be happy there? Because I was born to be. I've seen your big ones here. I've taken them out. I didn't have to give them the lessons I gave you."

"What lessons?"

"Get 'em off their feet and they're helpless. Grab 'em by the muzzle and hold on till they suffocate. Eat 'em while they're still kicking. Everything that horrified you, they knew by instinct. None of that flood of Christian mush you spill every time you open your mouth—"

"Don't talk to me that way, Jim. I don't like it."

"You asked for it. Why will I be happy there? Up the strong! They survive for a reason. Down with the weak. Don't protect them, eliminate them. Up the two-party system. Winners and losers! Democracy? Bloody nonsense. An elite of muscle. Your lions are your industrialists. They don't look it. That's their cunning. They have tooth, claw, and clout. They know the place in the neck to go for. They learned it with their mother's milk."

"Don't go by those people, Jim."

He looked away and said, "Let's talk about something impersonal."

The waiter put down two drinks, caught Jim's eye ordering more, left.

I looked at Mr. Gargi. The Indian's heavy brown eyes were lowered, but I could see that he was listening to us.

"Why do you keep looking at him?" Jim asked. Then, as if to himself, he added, "Same species."

"What did you say?"

"I apologize. You are somewhat better. Actually I hold nothing against you despite the fact that you've spent the better part of a week patronizing me and insulting me and shaming me in front of my boys. Don't you think I've been very patient with you?"

"Yes, I do. Very."

"What do you think their impression of you was?"

"The boys? I have no idea."

"They see everything, you know. Did you notice that neither of them said a pleasant goodbye to you yesterday?"

"I was out on my feet when we got back to the hotel."

"Just as well. As for me, despite the fact that you've refused to help me, I will hold my true feelings in check. After all, we live by our reticences, you and I, don't we?"

"Oh, for chrissake, Jim, say anything you want to. Who gives a shit?"

He smiled at me. "I wouldn't be you for anything," he said.

He finished his drink.

"Does that offend you?"

"No."

"A man who leaves his wife unprotected in the situation you described then melts his heart over a miserable wildebeest calf!"

"Jim, I can't pretend to have employment for you when I don't."

"Waiter!" he called.

"I realize how disappointed you must feel."

"Not at all. Waiter!"

"And angry."

"Waiter! Here! I'm not angry."

"Of course you are. You're furious."

"I'm not. There'd be no point to that, so I am not. Goddamn it where is that—?"

It was then that he began to go, shaking like a motor out of phase, his face clenching and flushing with his last efforts to deny what he was feeling.

Behind him, Mr. Gargi discreetly cleared his throat.

Jim wheeled in place, the feet on his chair screeching on the tile floor.

"Goddamn it, Gargi," he said, "didn't I tell you to stop listening to us?"

Mr. Gargi winced and drew back into a posture of defense. "I'm truly not," he pleaded pathetically. "But if you like I will—"

"You promised that before," Jim shouted, "but here you still are listening to every goddamn word—"

Mr. Gargi got up in panic.

"I'll go to another table," he said.

"Go to another restaurant."

"Please. I came here to talk to you."

"You're not going to."

Jim, now in an uncontrollable fury, began to move toward the miserable Indian. I tried to take his arm, but he pulled it free. I got up and stood between them.

"Jim," I begged. "Please, Jim, please."

He was raving over my shoulder. "I don't want to talk to you, Mr. Gargi. That matter is concluded. Now, get out of my sight! Go on! Go!"

Gargi fled.

I pulled Jim down. He sat trembling, stunned by the force of his rage.

Gently I pulled him around to make him listen. "Jim," I whispered, "Jim."

When he turned his face to me, there were tears in his eyes.

Mr. Gargi was standing at the other end of the room, waiting still.

"I couldn't sleep last night," Jim said. "Having that man's child! Look at him. I don't know why I'm living. My father, Ronnie, he's a cold man. My mother is dead. My stepmother resents me coming into her house, though she has excellent manners and thinks I can't see what she feels. This country, as soon as old man Jomo dies, it's not going to tolerate us whites. We'd be clever indeed not to be here the next day. I've got to go somewhere. Where?"

I felt ashamed that I'd refused him help.

"Jim," I pleaded. "Listen to me."

"I'm trying."

"When I get back to the States, I'll look around and see if there isn't—"

"Oh! Will you?"

"See if I can't find some real offer of employment—"

"Oh, will you?"

"No matter how temporary."

"Just let me get in there once."

"I'll do my best."

The waiter was standing over us.

"Now don't have another drink, Jim."

"All right." He waved the waiter off.

"Did you really mean that?" he said to me. "Will you do it?"

"I promise. I want to."

"Christ, that's funny."

"What's funny?"

"You'll have another—what's that man's name, the sponge?"

"Schlossberg."

"You'll have another Mr. Schlossberg on your hands. But I thank you. I will never ask you another thing."

"Now you do me a favor," I said. "Go to that miserable, frightened Indian. Maybe you can't help him but give him some sympathy. Imagine how he feels, Jim, and pity him. He's in terrible pain. Please, Jim."

"O.K.," he said. "If you want me to, I will."

He stood on his feet, rigid as a drill master. In his voice of command he called out, "Mr. Gargi! You will proceed to the corner table, the one behind the telephone compartment. In a moment or two I will come to you and hear what you have to say. You look so worried," Jim laughed. "What did she do? Kill herself? Leave you for a large male baboon?"

He turned to me, smiling now. "Wait for me here," he said.

"I will."

"Promise?"

"I will be here when you're through."

Jim turned and watched Gargi walk to the table he'd indicated. This maneuver performed to his satisfaction, he finished his drink, still standing.

"Order me a Scotch," he called out to Gargi. Then he turned to me. "Did I do O.K.?" he asked.

"You were magnificent," I said. "Thanks."

"I thank you. Of course, it's the only decent thing to do. Not for him, for her."

"There's one other thing you should do. Talk to Andrea herself. Tell her what you told me. She may very well understand the way you feel, and when she does it will make things easier for you. And for her."

"Christ, you're a bloody fucking saint!"

"Will you do that?"

"Yes. Yes, I will. I don't think Andrea could possibly respect him, do you? How could anyone respect a person that weak, constantly whining and complaining? I know her. It must drive her mad."

He reached for his drink, but the glass was empty.

"Waiter," he called, "we'll order dinner now."

"I'm really not hungry," I said. "I'm not going to eat."

"Oh, yes, you are, you must. You promised me a party. Let me order for you. Waiter! Ah, yes, here. We want a curry of lamb, and we want it mild, not hot." He turned to me. "These bloody Indians got into the habit of covering their meat with hot curry because they had no refrigeration at home and their meat was often in distressing condition. But this place is all right. I guarantee it. The curry will warm your belly and make you brave so your wife will be glad she's with you tomorrow night."

Suddenly he threw his arms around my neck and embraced me fiercely and lovingly. He was fantastically strong. Then he looked at the Indian sitting at the corner table, ankles crossed, palms on thighs, composed and waiting.

"I'm going to talk to that man only because of you," Jim said. "He's going to whine and complain but I will conceal my impatience, for her sake. I really like her, you know. I have no time for any women, but if I did it would be her. I mean if she were normal and in control of herself, which she is most certainly not, the bitch!"

He straightened up. "Here I go." He looked toward the Indian. "Offal," he said, audibly. Then he leaned over me and said, "I want to tell you something. I really do admire Andrea. She has more courage than anyone I've ever known. She is worth a thousand sane people."

"Those are the people, Jim."

"At one time I thought she was my only hope. I told her that. You see I did lead her on. I made her believe that someday—"

"That you loved her."

"No. I loathe that word. You Americans have spoiled that word. I admire her. That I can truly say, and that is enough."

But his face did not lie. If he had ever loved anyone, if he ever could, it was Andrea.

"Yes," he said, in correspondence with my thoughts, "she is my weakness."

He walked over to the table where the Indian was waiting for him. Halfway he looked back with a smile and said, "Don't forget what you promised."

He had the twisted smile of a doubting boy.

They had what seemed to be a civilized and reasonable conversation, even a pleasant one. They seemed to be in agreement, and I thought Jim was actually glad to be talking to the man.

Then the Indian told Jim something that I could see affected him deeply because he dropped his head and let it hang like that of a condemned man. There was a silence for a few seconds. Neither talked. Then Mr. Gargi drew a small pistol out of his pocket and shot Jim in the forehead.

For a second or two I could see Jim fighting it. Then he collapsed. That was the end. He slid off his chair and fell to the floor, rolled on his back, and stretched out dead.

The Indian stared into space.

No one in the restaurant dared move. Mr. Gargi still held the pistol.

On Jim's face was the trace of his smile.

When Jim was quite still, Mr. Gargi gently laid his weapon on the table in front of him. Then he crossed his ankles and rested his hands on his thighs, again composing himself to wait.

Now people rushed to the body. There was nothing to be done.

Mr. Gargi was quite calm through what followed. When the police arrived, he went with them as if he'd sent for them himself.

The plane out of Johannesburg was nine hours late, so I saw the morning paper. It told of Andrea's suicide and the shooting of Jim. Motive was not mentioned. Mr. Gargi was being questioned, the paper said.

What a Film Director Needs to Know*

This is the traditional instant for me to thank all of you who have helped mount this retrospective. I think you did a damned good job. Together we may have finally begun to move this university, and, by influence, those like it, toward a serious and devoted study of films as the art of this day. I hope and–judging by the number of you here present–have begun to believe that this retrospective and the appearance of a distinguished French critic on your campus will be the first of a series of similar events.

A reporter from your campus paper, the *Argus,* asked me why I'd given my papers to this university. I gave a superficial answer. I said Wesleyan is close to where I live, so my things would be available to me after an hour's drive. I added that the authorities here had been generous, eager, and accommodating. All true.

But the real reason was that for years I've been thinking it was about time our institutions of learning became involved in film as the subject of formal courses of study both for themselves as pieces of art and for what they say as witnesses to their day. I saw an opportunity here to progress this cause.

Tonight I urge you who direct the program of this university to now place the Movie on the same basis of regard, esteem, and concern as–for instance–the novel.

We simply can no longer think of movies in the way we used to years ago, as a pastime between supper and bed. What your faculty has particularly contributed here was to make these two weeks of study with Michel Ciment part of the curriculum. Credit toward graduation was given, a first step in the right direction.

* A speech delivered to the students at Wesleyan University, Middletown, Connecticut, on September 29, 1973

I have been examining the excellent book * you have assembled with this showing of my work—I was going to say life's work, but that would not be totally accurate. It should be noted that at the Yale Drama School and elsewhere I had a valuable time as a backstage technician. I was a stage carpenter, and I lit shows. Then there was a tedious time as a radio actor, playing hoodlums for bread. I had a particularly educational four years as a stage manager, helping and watching directors and learning a great deal. And, in between, I had a lively career as a stage actor in some good plays. All these activities were very valuable to me.

In time, I was fortunate enough to have directed the works of the best dramatists of a couple of the decades which have now become history. I was privileged to serve Williams, Miller, Bill Inge, Archie MacLeish, Sam Behrman, and Bob Anderson and put some of their plays on the stage. I thought of my role with these men as that of a craftsman who tried to realize as well as he could the author's intentions in the author's vocabulary and within his range, style, and purpose.

I have not thought of my film work that way.

Some of you may have heard of the *auteur* theory. That concept is partly a critic's plaything, something for them to spat over and use to fill a column. But it has its point, and that point is simply that the director is the true author of the film. The director *tells* the film, using a vocabulary the lesser part of which is an arrangement of words.

A screenplay's worth has to be measured less by its language than by its architecture and how that dramatizes the theme. A screenplay, we directors soon enough learn, is not a piece of writing as much as it is a construction. We learn to feel for the skeleton under the skin of words.

Meyerhold, the great Russian stage director, said that words were the decoration on the skirts of action. He was talking about Theatre but I've always thought his observations applied more aptly to film.

It occurred to me when I was considering what to say here that since you all don't see directors—it's unique for Wesleyan to have a filmmaker standing where I am after a showing of his work, while you have novelists, historians, poets, and writers of various kinds of studies living among you—that it might be fun if I were to try to list for you and for my own sport what a film director needs to know as well as what personal characteristics and attributes he might advantageously possess.

How must he educate himself?

Of what skills is his craft made?

What kind of a man must he be?

Of course I'm talking about a book-length subject. Stay easy, I'm not

* *Working With Kazan,* an illustrated filmography combined with statements from playwrights, actors, editors, producers, and others was published by the Wesleyan University Press.

going to read a book to you tonight. I will merely try to list the fields of knowledge necessary to him, and later those personal qualities he might happily possess, give them to you as one might chapter headings, section leads, first sentences of paragraphs, without elaboration.

Here we go.

Literature. Of course. All periods, all languages, all forms. Naturally a film director is better equipped if he's well read. Jack Ford who introduced himself with the words, "I make Westerns" was an extremely well and widely read man.

The literature of the Theatre. For one thing, so the film director will appreciate the difference from film. He should also study the classic theatre literature for construction, for exposition of theme, for the means of characterization, for dramatic poetry, for the elements of unity, especially that unity created by pointing to climax, and then for climax as the essential and final embodiment of the theme.

The craft of screen dramaturgy. Every director, even in those rare instances when he doesn't work with a writer or two—Fellini works with a squadron—must take responsibility for the screenplay. He has not only to guide rewriting but to eliminate what's unnecessary, cover faults, appreciate non-verbal possibilities, ensure correct structure, have a sense of screen time, how much will elapse, in what places, for what purposes. Robert Frost's *Tell Everything a Little Faster* applies to all expositional parts. In the climaxes, time is unrealistically extended, "stretched," usually by close-ups

The film director knows that beneath the surface of his screenplay there is a subtext, a calendar of intentions and feelings and inner events. What appears to be happening, he soon learns, is rarely what is happening. This subtext is one of the film director's most valuable tools. It is what he directs. You will rarely see a veteran director holding a script as he works—or even looking at it. Beginners, yes.

Most directors' goal today is to write their own scripts. But that is our oldest tradition. Chaplin would hear that Griffith Park had been flooded by a heavy rainfall. Packing his crew, his stand-by actors, and his equipment in a few cars, he would rush there, making up the story of the two reel comedy en route, the details on the spot.

The director of films should know comedy as well as drama. Jack Ford used to call most parts "comics." He meant, I suppose, a way of looking at people without false sentiment, through an objectivity that deflated false heroics and undercut self-favoring and finally revealed a saving humor in the most tense moments. The Human Comedy, another Frenchman called it. The fact that Billy Wilder is always amusing doesn't make his films less serious.

Quite simply the screen director must know either by training or by instinct how to feed a joke and how to score with it, how to anticipate and protect laughs. He might well study Chaplin and the other great two reel comedy-makers for what are called sight gags, non-verbal laughs, amusement derived from "business," stunts and moves, and simply from funny faces and odd bodies. This vulgar foundation—the banana peel and the custard pie—are basic to our craft and part of its health. Wyler and Stevens began by making two reel comedies and I seem to remember Capra did, too.

American film directors would do well to know our vaudeville traditions. Just as Fellini adored the clowns, music hall performers, and the circuses of his country and paid them homage again and again in his work, our filmmaker would do well to study magic. I believe some of the wonderful cuts in *Citizen Kane* came from the fact that Welles was a practicing magician and so understood the drama of sudden unexpected appearances and the startling change. Think too, of Bergman, how often he uses magicians and sleight of hand.

The director should know opera, its effects and its absurdities, a subject in which Bernard Bertolucci is schooled. He should know the American musical stage and its tradition, but even more important, the great American musical films. He must not look down on these; we love them for very good reasons.

Our man should know acrobatics, the art of juggling and tumbling, the techniques of the wry comic song. The techniques of the Commedia delle Arte are used, it seems to me, in a film called *O Lucky Man!* Lindsay Anderson's master, Bertolt Brecht, adored the Berlin satirical cabaret of his time and adapted its techniques.

Let's move faster because it's endless. Painting and sculpture, their history, their revolutions and counter-revolutions. The painters of the Italian Renaissance used their mistresses as models for the Madonna, so who can blame a film director for using his girl friend in a leading role— unless she does a bad job.

Many painters have worked in the Theatre. Bakst, Picasso, Aronson, and Matisse come to mind. More will. Here, we are still with Disney.

Which brings us to Dance. In my opinion it's a considerable asset if the director's knowledge here is not only theoretical but practical and personal. Dance is an essential part of a screen director's education. It's a great advantage for him if he can "move." It will help him not only to move actors but move the camera. The film director, ideally, should be able as a choreographer, quite literally so. I don't mean the tango in Bertolucci's last or the high school gym dance in *American Graffiti* as much as I do the battle scenes in D. W. Griffith's *Birth of a Nation,* which are pure choreography and very beautiful. Look at Ford's cavalry

charges that way. Or Jim Cagney's dance of death on the long steps in
The Roaring Twenties.

The film director must know music, classic, so called—too much of an
umbrella word, that! Let us say of all periods. And as with sculpture and
painting, he must know what social situations and currents the music
came out of.

Of course he must be particularly *into* the music of his own day, acid
rock, latin rock, blues and jazz, pop, Tin Pan Alley, barber-shop, corn,
country, Chicago, New Orleans, Nashville.

The film director should know the history of stage scenery, its
development from background to environment and so to the settings
inside which films are played out. Notice I stress *inside which* as opposed
to *in front of.* The construction of scenery for film-making was
traditionally the work of architects. The film director must study from
life, from newspaper clippings, and from his own photographs, dramatic
environments and particularly how they affect behavior.

I recommend to every young director that he start his own collection
of clippings and photographs and, if he's able, his own sketches.

The film director must know costuming, its history through all
periods, its techniques, and what it can be as expression. Again, life is a
prime source. We learn to study, as we enter each place, each room, how
the people there have chosen to present themselves. "How he comes on,"
we say.

Costuming in films is so expressive a means that it is inevitably the
basic choice of the director. Visconti is brilliant here. So is Bergman in a
more modest vein. The best way to study this again is to notice how
people dress as an expression of what they wish to gain from any
occasion, what their intention is. Study your husband, study your wife,
how their attire is an expression of each day's mood and hope, their good
days, their days of low confidence, their time of stress and how it shows
in clothing.

Lighting. Of course. The various natural effects, the cross light of
morning, the heavy flat top light of midday—avoid it except for an
effect—the magic hour, so called by cameramen, dusk. How do they
affect mood? Obvious. We know it in life. How do they affect behavior?
Study that. Five o'clock is a low time, let's have a drink! Directors choose
the time of day for certain scenes with these expressive values in mind.
The master here is Jack Ford who used to plan his shots within a
sequence to best use certain natural effects that he could not create but
could very advantageously wait for.

Colors? Their psychological effect. So obvious I will not expand.
Favorite colors. Faded colors. The living grays. In *Baby Doll* you saw a

master cameraman—Boris Kaufman—making great use of white on white, to help describe the washed out Southern whites.

And, of course, there are the instruments which catch all and should dramatize all; the tools the director speaks through, the *camera* and the *tape recorder*. The film director obviously must know the Camera and its lenses, which lens creates which effect, which one lies, which one tells the cruel truth. Which filters bring out the clouds. The director must know the various speeds at which the camera can roll and especially the effects of small variations in speed. He must also know the various camera mountings, the cranes and the dollies and the possible moves he can make, the configurations in space through which he can pass this instrument. He must know the zoom well enough so he won't use it—or almost never.

He should be intimately acquainted with the tape recorder. Andy Warhol carries one everywhere he goes. Practice "bugging" yourself and your friends. Notice how often speech overlaps.

The film director must understand the weather, how it's made and where, how it moves, its warning signs, its crises, the kinds of clouds and what they mean. Remember the clouds in *Shane*. He must know weather as dramatic expression, be on the alert to capitalize on changes in weather as one of his means. He must study how heat and cold, rain and snow, a soft breeze, a driving wind affect people and whether it's true that there are more expressions of group rage during a long hot summer and why.

The film director should know the City, ancient and modern, but particularly his city, the one he loves like DeSica loves Naples, Fellini Rimini, Bergman his island, Ray Calcutta, Renoir the French countryside, Clair the city of Paris. *His* city, its features, its operation, its substructure, its scenes behind the scenes, its functionaries, its police, fire-fighters, garbage collectors, post office workers, commuters and what they ride, its cathedrals, and its whore houses.

The film director must know the country—no, that's too general a term. He must know the mountains and the plains, the deserts of our great Southwest, the heavy oily-bottom-soil of the Delta, the hills of New England. He must know the water off Marblehead and Old Orchard Beach, too cold for lingering, and the water of the Florida Keys which invites dawdling. Again these are means of expression that he has, and among them he must make his choices. He must know how a breeze from a fan can animate a dead-looking set by stirring a curtain.

He must know the sea, first-hand, chance a shipwreck so he'll appreciate its power. He must know under the surface of the sea; it may occur to him, if he does, to play a scene there. He must have crossed our rivers and know the strength of their currents. He must have swum in our lakes and caught fish in our streams. You think I'm exaggerating. Why did old man Flaherty and his Mrs. spend at least a year in an environment before they exposed a foot of negative? While you're young, you aspiring directors, hitch-hike our country!

And topography, the various trees, flowers, ground cover, grasses. And the sub-surface, shale, sand, gravel, New England ledge, six feet of old river bottom. What kind of man works each and how does it affect him?

Animals too. How they resemble human beings. How to direct a chicken to enter a room on cue. I had that problem once, and I'm ashamed to tell you how I did it. What a cat might mean to a love scene. The symbolism of the horse. The family life of the lion, how tender! The patience of a cow.

Of course the film director should know acting, its history and its techniques. The more he knows about acting, the more at ease he will be with actors. At one period of his growth, he should force himself on stage or before the camera so he knows this experientially, too. Some directors, and very famous ones, still fear actors instead of embracing them as comrades in a task. But, by contrast, there is the great Jean Renoir—see him in *Rules of the Game.* And his follower and lover, Truffaut in *The Wild Child,* now in *Day for Night.*

The director must know how to stimulate, even inspire the actor. Needless to say he must also know how to make an actor seem NOT to act. How to put him or her at ease, bring them to that state of relaxation where their creative faculties are released.

The film director must understand the instrument known as the *voice.* He must also know *speech.* And that they are not the same, as different as resonance and phrasing. He should also know the various regional accents of his country and what they tell about character.

All in all he must know enough in all these areas so his actors trust him completely. This is often achieved by giving the impression that any task he asks of them, he can perform, perhaps even better than they can. This may not be true, but it's not a bad impression to create.

The film director, of course, must be up on the psychology of behavior, "normal" and abnormal. He must know that they are linked, that one is often the extension or intensification of the other and that under certain stresses which the director will create within a scene as it's acted out, one kind of behavior can be seen becoming the other. And that is drama.

The film director must be prepared by knowledge and training to handle neurotics. Why? Because most actors are. Perhaps all. What makes it doubly interesting is that the film director often is. Stanley Kubrick won't get on a plane—well, maybe that isn't so neurotic. But we are all delicately balanced—isn't that a nice way to put it? Answer this: how many interesting people have you met who are not—a little?

Of course we work with the psychology of the audience. We know it differs from that of its individual members. In cutting films great comedy directors like Hawks and Preston Sturges allow for the group reactions they expect from the audience, they play on these. Hitchcock has made this his art.

The film director must be learned in the erotic arts. The best way is through personal experience. But there is a history here, an artistic technique. Pornography is not looked down upon. The film director will admit to a natural interest in how other people do it. Boredom, cruelty, banality are the only sins. Our man, for instance, might study the Chinese erotic prints and those scenes on Greek vases of the Golden Age which museum curators hide.

Of course the film director must be an authority, even an expert on the various attitudes of lovemaking, the postures and intertwinings of the parts of the body, the expressive parts and those generally considered less expressive. He may well have, like Bunuel with feet, special fetishes. He is not concerned to hide these, rather he will probably express his inclinations with relish.

The director, here, may come to believe that suggestion is more erotic than show. Then study how to go about it.

Then there is war. Its weapons, its techniques, its machinery, its tactics, its history—oh my—

Where is the time to learn all this?

Do not think, as you were brought up to think, that education starts at six and stops at twenty-one, that we learn only from teachers, books, and classes. For us that is the least of it. The life of a film director is a totality, and he learns as he lives. Everything is pertinent, there is nothing irrelevant or trivial. *O Lucky Man,* to have such a profession! Every experience leaves its residue of knowledge behind. Every book we read applies to us. Everything we see and hear, if we like it, we steal it. Nothing is irrelevant. It all belongs to us.

So history becomes a living subject, full of dramatic characters, not a bore about treaties and battles. Religion is fascinating as a kind of poetry expressing fear and loneliness and hope. The film director reads *The Golden Bough* because sympathetic magic and superstition interest him, these beliefs of the ancients and the savages parallel those of his own time's people. He studies ritual because ritual as a source of stage and screen *mise en scène* is an increasingly important source.

Economics a bore? Not to us. Consider the demoralization of people in a labor pool, the panic in currency, the reliance of a nation on imports and the leverage this gives the country supplying the needed imports. All these affect or can affect the characters and milieus with which our film is concerned. Consider the facts behind the drama of *On the Waterfront.* Wonder how we could have shown more of them.

The film director doesn't just eat. He studies food. He knows the meals of all nations and how they're served, how consumed, what the variations of taste are, the effect of the food, food as a soporific, food as an aphrodisiac, as a means of expression of character. Remember the scene in *Tom Jones? La Grande Bouffe?*

And, of course, the film director tries to keep up with the flow of life around him, the contemporary issues, who's pressuring who, who's winning, who's losing, how pressure shows in the politician's body and face and gestures. Inevitably, the director will be a visitor at night court. And he will not duck jury duty. He studies advertising and goes to "product meetings" and spies on those who make the ads that influence people. He watches talk shows and marvels how Jackie Susann peddles it. He keeps up on the moves, as near as he can read them, of the secret underground societies. And skyjacking, what's the solution? He talks to pilots. It's a perfect drama—that situation—no exit.

Travel. Yes. As much as he can. Let's not get into that.

Sports? The best directed shows on TV today are the professional football games. Why? Study them. You are shown not only the game from far and middle distance and close-up, you are shown the bench, the way the two coaches sweat it out, the rejected sub, Craig Morton, waiting for Staubach to be hurt and Woodall, does he really like Namath? Johnson, Snead? Watch the spectators, too. Think how you might direct certain scenes playing with a ball, or swimming or sailing—even though that is nowhere indicated in the script. Or watch a ball game like Hepburn and Tracy in George Stevens' film, *Woman of the Year!*

I've undoubtedly left out a great number of things and what I've left out is significant, no doubt, and describes some of my own shortcomings.

Oh! Of course, I've left out the most important thing. The subject the film director must know most about, know best of all, see in the greatest detail and in the most pitiless light with the greatest appreciation of the ambivalences at play is—what?

Right. Himself.

There is something of himself, after all, in every character he properly creates. He understands people truly through understanding himself truly.

The silent confessions he makes to himself are the greatest source of wisdom he has. And of tolerance for others. And of love, even that. There is the admission of hatred to awareness and its relief through understanding and a kind of resolution in brotherhood.

What kind of a person must a film director train himself to be?

What qualities does he need? Here are a few. Those of—

A white hunter leading a safari into dangerous and unknown country.

A construction gang foreman, who knows his physical problems and their solutions and is ready, therefore, to insist on these solutions.

A psychoanalyst who keeps a patient functioning despite intolerable tensions and stresses, both professional and personal.

A hypnotist who works with the unconscious to achieve his ends.

A poet, a poet of the camera, able both to capture the decisive moment of Cartier Bresson or to wait all day like Paul Strand for a single shot which he makes with a bulky camera fixed on a tripod.

An outfielder for his legs. The director stands much of the day, dares not get tired, so he has strong legs. Think back and remember how the old time directors dramatized themselves. By puttees, right?

The cunning of a trader in an Bagdad bazaar.

The firmness of an animal trainer. Obvious. Tigers!

A great host. At a sign from him fine food and heart-warming drink appear.

The kindness of an old-fashioned mother who forgives all.

The authority and sternness of her husband, the father who forgives nothing, expects obedience without question, brooks no nonsense.

These alternately.

The illusiveness of a jewel thief—no explanation, take my word for this one.

The blarney of a PR man, especially useful when the director is out in a strange and hostile location as I have many times been.

A very thick skin.

A very sensitive soul.

Simultaneously.

The patience, the persistence, the fortitude of a saint, the appreciation of pain, a taste for self-sacrifice, everything for the cause.

Cheeriness, jokes, playfulness, alternating with sternness, unwavering firmness. Pure doggedness.

An unwavering refusal to take less than he thinks right out of a scene, a performer, a co-worker, a member of his staff, himself.

Direction, finally, is the exertion of your will over other people— disguise it, gentle it, but that is the hard fact.

Above all—COURAGE. Courage, said Winston Churchill, is the greatest virtue; it makes all the others possible.

One final thing. The ability to say, "I am wrong," or "I was wrong." Not as easy as it sounds. But in many situations, these three words, honestly spoken, will save the day. They are the words, very often, that the actors struggling to give the director what he wants, most need to hear from him. Those words, "I was wrong, let's try it another way," the ability to say them can be a life-saver.

The director must accept the blame for everything. If the script stinks, he should have worked harder with the writers or himself before shooting. If the actor fails, the director failed him! Or made a mistake in choosing him. If the camera work is uninspired, whose idea was it to engage that cameraman? Or choose those set-ups? Even a costume—after all the director passed on it. The settings. The music, even the goddamn ads, why didn't he yell louder if he didn't like them? The director was there, wasn't he? Yes, he was there! He's always there!

That's why he gets all that money, to stand there, on that mound, unprotected, letting everybody shoot at him and deflecting the mortal fire from all the others who work with him.

The other people who work on a film can hide.

They have the director to hide behind.

And people deny the *auteur* theory!

After listening to me so patiently you have a perfect right now to ask, "Oh, come on, aren't you exaggerating to make some kind of point?"

Of course I'm exaggerating and it is to make a point.

But only a little, exaggerating.

The fact is that a director, from the moment a phone call gets him out of bed in the morning ("Rain today. What scene do you want to shoot?") until he escapes into the dark at the end of shooting to face, alone, the next day's problems, is called upon to answer an unrelenting string of questions, to make decision after decision in one after another of the fields I've listed. That's what a director is, the man with the answers.

Watch Truffaut playing Truffaut in *Day For Night,* watch him as he patiently, carefully, sometimes thoughtfully, other times very quickly, answers questions. You will see better than I can tell you how these answers keep his film going. Truffaut has caught our life on the set perfectly.

Do things get easier and simpler as you get older and have accumulated some or all of this savvy?

Not at all. The opposite. The more a director knows, the more he's aware how many different ways there are to do every film, every scene.

And the more he has to face that final awful limitation, not of knowledge but of character. Which is what? The final limitation and the most terrible one is the limitation of his own talent. You find, for instance, that you truly do have the faults of your virtues. And that limitation you can't do much about. Even if you have the time.

One last postscript. The director, that miserable son of a bitch, as often as not these days, has to get out and promote the dollars and the pounds, scrounge for the liras, francs, and marks, hock his family's home, his wife's jewels, and his own future so he can make his film. This process of raising the wherewithall inevitably takes ten to a hundred times longer than making the film itself. But the director does it because he has to—who else will? Who else loves the film that much?

So, my friends, you've seen how much you have to know and what kind of a bastard you have to be, how hard you have to train yourself and in how many different ways. All of which I did. I've never stopped trying to educate myself and to improve myself.

So now pin me to the wall—this is your last chance. Ask me how with all that knowledge and all that wisdom, all that training and all those capabilities, including the strong legs of a major league outfielder, how did I manage to mess up some of the films I've directed so badly?

Ah, but that's the charm of it!

Reverence Is Not
an Artistic Emotion*

I stand before you only after considerable hesitation. To be plain about it, I am not qualified to speak on my topic. I have never put a fifth-century classic on film. Nor have I produced one of our three great tragic masters on the stage. There have to be men among us, Cacoyamnis for one, who would have been better choices.

Then what am I doing here in Athens? Those of you who know me know that excessive modesty is not one of my faults. You will believe me when I say that I have come here to learn. I hope to make a film based on one of the great tragedies, and I am here as part of the process of forming my ideas for the production—from our conversations, from the plays and performances I will see, and, above all, from the ancient sites of the action, which I will visit, and the remains of that period in art relics, which I will study.

I am so unqualified to speak on my topic that this thought occurred to me: perhaps I was chosen precisely because of my ignorance in the hope that, uninhibited by actual experience, I might say something that would not have occurred to a more knowledgeable director.

I have directed contemporary plays that were paid the respect given classics and perhaps these experiences might have some use. I did the original production of *A Streetcar Named Desire* on the New York stage, and a couple of years later, when the play had been sold to a film producer, Tennessee Williams urged me to make the movie. I really did not want to—it is like marrying the same woman twice—but finally I did.

I engaged a screen writer, and we spent five months trying to make the play more cinematic by moving the action out of the single room where the events of the stage play happen. For instance, we decided to

* A speech delivered in Athens, Greece, on July 5, 1976

introduce the heroine, Blanche DuBois, not upon her arrival in New Orleans but at that earlier moment when she is being run out of her home town because she is believed to be corrupting young boys. Typical movie material, that scene. So we thought.

The screen writer and I worked hard, and, when we were done, I congratulated him. "We've really made a film scenario out of this stage play!" I said. To make sure I had done right, I put the text away for a few weeks so that I would have complete objectivity when I read it again.

A month later, returning from a vacation, I locked the door and read our script. Something about it disturbed me. I saw that the compression of the stage play's action, confining Blanche and the man who was going to destroy her in one small apartment, was part of the reason the play worked. But I decided I could do that as well on the screen—and finally did. What really put me off was the uneasy feeling that I had violated a classic. To make a long story short, I threw away our scenario and went back to the Williams original. I photographed the stageplay and that was the film.

A few years later, I had a related experience with Arthur Miller. He asked me to make a film of *Death of a Salesman,* the first production of which I had also directed. Drawing from my experience on the Williams play, I told Miller, in a rather painful interview, that I did not want the job, that I revered his play but for that very reason I did not think it should be made into a film.

So Miller got hold of a film director who revered his play even more than I did, and therefore clung to the original so tightly that he produced—what? A pale copy of the original.

These two experiences stayed in my mind. In the case of Williams, I did not add anything of worth to his play when I put it on the screen; I believe my film inferior to my stage production. And I can not get rid of the feeling that if I had had the courage to persist in looking for another way of telling the same story, if I had not been so bound down by reverence for the original, I might have done something for the film and for the author, perhaps something original. I also wish now that I had gone ahead boldly and made my own film of the Miller play.

As I say, these two experiences stayed in my memory, and what I concluded from them is that if we are going to be faithful, it is better to be totally so and leave the stage classics on the stage.

Films are another language, they have a different vocabulary. What works well on a stage will very often not work on film.

Films can be poetic, of course, but it is a different kind of poetry, nearly always visual.

I also concluded this: that reverence is not an artistic emotion!

Now—what is more revered that the *Oresteia* of Aeschylus?

That is my problem. I would like to make a new film of that ancient tragedy.

A famous and successful stage play is like an ocean-going vessel. As it makes its journeys, year by year, it accumulates barnacles along its hull. These solutions of another time are called clichés, the calluses of culture, and, from time to time, they have to be scraped off.

There is no final solution in art, no ultimate form. Art is like a stream fed by a spring. The spring dries up at the end of a summer, the stream stops flowing and becomes stagnant. We wait for another spring and a fresh flow.

It is important above all for me to put aside the traditions of the stage productions I've seen, particularly the good ones, and find a new cinematic way to convey the emotion and the message of Aeschylus, to try to see his play for the first time again—as film.

If a work of art is alive, it will have, inevitably, a new meaning for each generation. It will certainly not have the same meaning. Usually it will fit into the contemporary context by challenging the past, express the new by rejecting the old.

No live art can look backward.

So here is the question. Setting out to make a film of one of the classics, if we don't look back at the stage productions we have seen, especially the successful ones, where do we look?

How does a film director set out to prepare a film from a play?

I am not talking about technical aspects. After a certain amount of experience, these tasks become comparatively simple.

How does the film director prepare himself artistically? Where does he look?

Of course, first of all, within himself, to resolve for himself what the play means and why he is attracted to it. That is a personal matter and I won't go into it.

Then he goes back to the original sources.

Which? Whose?

As much as possible the same ones Aeschylus used.

The director travels. When he walks out onto the citadel of Mycenae, he will get some idea of how the people who inhabited that place lived, where they slept, how they ate, what cold weather must have meant to them, what a view of their world these rulers had and what a difference there was between where the Kings were buried and where Clytemnestra and Aegisthus threw the body of Agamemnon to disgrace it.

At night, in his hotel room, the director reads from that most august source book, the *Iliad.*

Now please don't think me unfriendly if I am candid.

I have always been struck by the contrast between what I have seen on the stage of productions of the ancient plays and the images roused in my mind when I read the *Iliad*.

Listen again for a moment to the last lines of that book. Notice the flow of visual images, one on top another.

"When, on the next day, Dawn showed her rosy fingers through the mist, the people gathered around the pyre of Hector. First they quenched the flames with wine wherever the fire still burned. Then his brothers and his comrades gathered his white bones, with hot tears rolling down their cheeks. They placed the bones in a golden casket, wrapt it in soft purple cloth. This they laid in a hollow space and built it over with large stones. Quickly they piled a barrow, with men on the lookout all around in case the Greeks should attack before their time. This work done, they returned to the city and the whole assemblage had a famous feast in the palace of Priam their King. That was the funeral of Hector!"

How concrete those images. Plain! Hard! No psychology! Facts.

You have noticed that what makes that sceme vivid is a series of pictures for the eye, photographs described, pure cinema, everything in color, everything tangible. You can see, feel, taste, smell, measure, touch, the whole event on that dusty plain over which Hector's body had been dragged. It is, in effect, a film scenario.

Can we match that kind of writing, I ask myself, on film?

Only there, perhaps.

One has the same impression from looking at the vases. What a world of savagery and heroism is there—but always presented with complete objectivity. The sarcophagi, by contrast, seem romanticized, even sentimental. So do the so-called Elgin Marbles. They are beautiful, yes, those marbles reliefs, but romantic, like official art.

In the *Iliad*, on the vases, no one knows he is heroic. Only that he is human.

The quintessential problem, it seems to me, for making a film of the *Oresteia*, is the chorus of Furies. The chorus of old men in the *Agamemnon* is well conceived and quite manageable. They fit into the action and are always clear as to what they feel, say, and do. The chorus of Trojan slave women in *The Libation Bearers*, those who attend Electra, are more difficult, but once we are clear that they are slave women and have been for many years, once we have puzzled out their ambivalent relationship to Agamemnon and why they participate in the action of rousing his sleeping spirit, then they are excellent and viable dramatic figures.

But the Furies—there is the problem.

I must again risk offending friends and say that I have never been stirred to fear or belief by any representation of these figures on a stage. Perhaps they are impossible.

In the United States, I saw a production that a master director, Tyrone Guthrie, made in which many of the elements were excellent, but the Furies ridiculous.

Has anyone solved this problem? Not that I have seen. Usually they have been young women, most often dancers, wearing masks or not, and given over to standard gyro-gymnastics, the twists and grimaces of children's fright games—except that they would not frighten children, not those of our day. In a word, the Furies were always presented as grotesques.

I have been reading widely on the Furies, what they meant and what they represented. This is not the place to go into all that, but in a sentence I would say that they are in the *Oresteia* to protect their tradition, the oldest tradition of their time and society, one they value above all else on earth. In this sense, they are idealists, devotees of a kind of earth-religion. They are not fools or frights or ghosts or what we used to call, when I was a child, boogies. Instead they seem to be figures with their own kind of dignity, however eccentrically expressed, devoted totally to a cause, awesome, yes, frightening in their intensity, ruthless when confronted, deadly when they are defending what they value most.

Don't we admire that kind of person, that kind of commitment in life?

Aeschylus obviously did because he gave them, at the end of his trilogy, seats in the *Arios Pagos,* the highest court overlooking his city, where they will sit forever, watchdogs over what they behold.

As I read what scholars of cultural history have written about the Furies, it struck me that they are not grotesque, not at all, and should not be so presented. They are frightening only because they believe so strongly in what they stand for.

Perhaps, I thought, recalling the French women I had seen photographed in 1945, those who had hounded the bed-mate-collaborators of the German occupation trooops, shaved their heads, and driven them out of town, perhaps where I can find the images I need for the Furies is in my own experience, in my memories.

A couple of years ago, I made a trip into the Peloponnesus with Alexis Minotis. I was anxious to see *Mani,* which I'd read about, so we drove south past Areopolis and down into that rocky finger of land.

There, in the village women who had resigned their lives to the *Mavro,* in those stern-faced women who seemed to be the spiritual centers of each village, I saw something of what I was looking for. In their faces with their mouths drawn down, I saw the moral attitude that does not allow their tradition to be questioned. I found the hardiness and the toughness of spirit that only comes from unequivocal convictions. How formidable they would be if crossed, how ferocious when necessary. I knew, looking at them, that their role was to protect their way of life and that they *would,* no matter what and to the end.

There, certainly, was one source of what I was looking for.

I had the same kind of reaction, half awe, half fear, to some old women, impoverished but not humbled, that I saw coming out of caves in a rocky hillside in Mexico. I do not know who they were, but I have not forgotten their faces.

I have been in Northern Kenya, on the Somaliland border, and there I saw the so-called Hidden Tribes, half African, half oriental, whose women looked this white man straight in the eye, fearlessly, even scornfully. Here too, I saw something that was not to be trifled with, that frightened me at the same time that I respected it.

On another trip to the Peloponnesus, I came across a clutch of gypsies, women all, crouched at the side of a road. As we drew up in our car, I saw that what they had gathered around was a body, and the body was that of a young boy. He had been struck, run over, and killed by a speeding truck.

His tribeswomen were gathered around his body, releasing their grief and pain at the top of their voices. It was not a rehearsed or practised sound, it was not a sound that civilized women make. At first I could think of nothing but the *mirologhia* Dora Stratou has done us the service of gathering. But these cries were even more primitive and more uncontained. I realized that these exact cries had never been sounded before and would never be, in precisely that way, sounded again.

I could not think of these women as grotesque—though visually and aurally they were extremely exaggerated to civilized eyes and ears.

Civilized? Perhaps they, in the direct and uninhibited way they expressed their grief and anger at the fate that had struck down their boy, perhaps they were the truly civilized ones and I, who was astonished at their intensity, the uncivilized one.

You have heard of the new psychological therapy called the Primal Scream? The sounds those women released were precisely those the therapists in Primal Scream clinics work for months to evoke from their patients.

No, I couldn't say those women were grotesques.

The grotesque is the stereotype, the cliché of the Furies.

Orestes would be called grotesque, a twisted man. Clytemnestra who kills her husband *is* grotesque—though she has her reasons. Agamemnon, who killed his daughter—he *is* grotesque even in the *Iliad*. Electra is a blessed monster, even though we sympathize with her pain. Aegisthus is a castrated grotesque, Calchas a figure out of an Hieronymus Bosch fantasy. But the Furies?

They might even be called the idealists of the play. The puritans!

Aeschylus named his play after them.

That was the surprising discovery my research brought me to.

How often, in the great works, when we study them we find an element that surprises us. What on first view seems exaggerated, larger than life, turns out to be the simple truth.

Why did Beethoven's third symphony shock so many of the people who heard it for the first time? The third symphony! So simple, so lucid now! Chekhov's *Seagull,* at its opening, was a popular failure. People did not understand that kind of dramaturgy and resented it. It seems to be life itself now. Joyce doesn't outrage us anymore. It is Dublin.

What is required to make a film of one of the great fifth-century classics is an act of courage—above all to forget the past productions on the stage, particularly the good ones. Let them remain, fully honored, in the warehouses, along with the old wigs and costumes.

What we need to do, if we propose to make such a film, is cleanse ourselves of crippling reverences, leave traditions behind for the moment and finally, through returning to original sources and living materials to life itself, rediscover for ourselves the author's theme and story.

I do not say that mine is the correct way to view this particular classic. I do not believe in absolutes. There are many ways, and they all have value—*when they are personal.* The only approaches that do not have value are the imitations of other men's visions, other directors' productions.

Why do I say courage? Not because traditionalists might be offended. We have become accustomed to that.

The courage I speak of is to conquer the trepidation, the uncertainty within ourselves. That is the difficult thing.

Finally we all find that our most painful limitation is the one in our own talent. Our final obstacle is within ourselves.

Is not the ultimate respect we can pay to our ancestors this: to say to them, "You are still alive because I, living so many centuries later, feel the same way you did! Your experience is mine!"

Then we will feel the ultimate exhilaration. Time will collapse.

For art is certainly one of the last remaining areas of true adventure. And in the end it will be the last.